T0062892

THE QUEEN OF

THE QUEEN OF

Kittur

A HISTORICAL NOVEL

BASAVARAJ NAIKAR

PARTRIDGE

Print information available on the last page.

To order additional copies of this book, contact
Partridge India
000 800 10062 62
orders.india@partridgepublishing.com

www.partridgepublishing.com/india

Basavaraj Naikar (b.1949), M.A., Ph.D., D.Litt (California), Professor Emeritus and former Professor and Chairman, Department of English, Karnatak University, Dharwad (India), is a bilingual writer in Kannada and English. He has published several reviews and research articles in national and international journals. He reviews Indian literary works for *World Literature Today* (Oklahoma, USA) regularly. He has translated many works from Kannada into English and *vice versa*. His specializations in teaching and research include Shakespeare Studies, Indian English Literature, Indian Literature in English Translation, American, Anglo-Indian, Commonwealth Literature, Translation: Theory and Practice. He is the recipient of Gulbarga University Award for translation, Olive Reddick Award from A.S.R.C. Hyderabad for research, Gemini Academy Award from Panipat and Vasudeva Bhupalam Award from the Kannada Sahitya Parishat, Bengaluru and Kuvempu Bhasha Bharati Book Award and Life-Time Achievement Award from the Government of Karnataka.

He is a Fellow of the United Writers of India, New Delhi. His *The Thief of Nagarahalli and Other Stories* was short listed for the Commonwealth Fiction Prize for the Best First Book from Eurasia in 2000. His second collection of stories, *The Rebellious Rani of Belavadi and Other Stories* and first historical-political novel, *The Sun behind the Cloud* dealing with the colonial encounter between Bhaskararao Bhave of Naragund Kingdom and the East India Company, has been published recently. His third novel, *Light in the House* depicts the life and message of Sharif Saheb of Shishunala, a popular philosopher and apostle of communal harmony between Hindus and Muslims. His *Rayanna, the Patriot and Other Novellas* deal with the lives and struggles of Raja Mallasarja, Saint Kanakadasa, Architect Jakkanacharya and Rayanna, the Guerilla Warrior, who fought against the British East India Company. His latest novel, *Bird in the Sky* is a hagiographical novel delineating the life of the super-saint of Hubballi, Sri Siddharudha Bharati, his miraculous powers and his quest for spiritual salvation.

His Kannada publications include *Paduvana Nadina Premavira, Huchchuhole, Kollada Neralu, Jogibhavi* (staged, broadcast, telecast and prescribed as a text for B.A. Degree), *Nigudha Saudha, Govardhanram, Asangata, Kannada Asangata Natakagalu, Samrachanavada, Beowulf, Gilgamesh Mahakavya, Vatsalya, Bharatiya English Sahitya Charitre, Siddhanta Mattu Prayoga, Swatantryada Kanasugara, Kempu Kanigilu Mattitara Natakagalu, Androsina Kanye Mattu Phormio* and *Kitturina Virarani.*

His critical works in English include *Sarvajna: The Poet Omniscient of Karnataka, Critical Articles on Nirad C. Chaudhuri, Musings of Sarvajna, Sparrows, Shakespeare's Last Plays: A Study in Epic Affirmation, The Folk Theatre of North Karnataka, Sandalwood, Kanakadasa: An Ardent Devotee of Lord Adikeshava, Indian Response to Shakespeare, Indian English Literature (10 vols,) Critical Response to Indian English Literature, Perspectives on Commonwealth Literature, Indian Literature in English Translation, Literary Vision, A Dreamer of Freedom, Glimpses of Indian Literature in English Translation, The Dramatic Imagination,*

Dramatic Vision, Representation of History in Indian/ English Drama,Perspectives on Fall of Kalyana and *A Harbinger of Harmony.*

His English translations from Kannada include *Sangya Balya: A Tale of Love and Betrayal, Fall of Kalyana, The Holy Water, The Vacanas of Sarvajna, The Frolic Play of the Lord, Bhagavallila* and *Sri Krisna Parijata.*

Dedicated to

Dr. V.G.Marihal

Who was proud of Rani Chennamma

beyond measure

Preface

I was deeply impressed by the heroic life of Rani Chennamma right from my High School days. When I happened to browse through a book entitled *The Female Heroism* written by a foreigner, I eagerly searched for a reference to Rani Chennamma in it, but was utterly disappointed not to find any reference to her in it. The reason was obvious. The author of the book, who was a foreigner, could not lay his hands on any material on the life of the heroic Rani in English. There are quite a few books on the heroic Rani in Kannada both serious and popular, in which the source material on Rani Chennamma and the kingdom of Kittur is available, but it is not presented in a systematic, chronological, comprehensive and exact manner. While the serious books offer only partial information, the popular ones including the folk songs, tend to give a romantic, exaggerated and sometimes even wrong picture. I, therefore, thought of writing a historical novel on the heroic Rani, Chennamma in a systematic way.

When the idea was lingering in my mind, I happened to read an excellent historical novel, *A Soldier of India* by an Australian writer, Tom Gibson, I was deeply impressed by the way in which he combined historical scholarship with creativity. He has depicted the heroic and passionate life of Rani Laxmibai of Jhansi very realistically, which is backed up by thorough historical knowledge. But as a foreigner, he has written it from an outsider's point of view. I was inspired to write a similar historical novel about the patriotic and heroic Rani Chennamma, who, in spite of being a woman, fought against the East India Company heroically and lost her kingdom. For her, the autonomy of the kingdom, honour and freedom were more important than anything else. Therefore, credit should go to her for fighting against the East India Company thirty-three years earlier than Rani Laxmibai of Jhansi, who fought with the same East India Company in 1857.

In writing the present novel, *The Queen of Kittur*, I have drawn the raw material from the historical sources like monographs, letters, and official records of the East India Company, folk songs and even oral information that were available to me. Reconstructing the historical picture of the kingdom of Kittur was not an easy task for me, because the information about the historical facts and cultural details was available only in fragments, chaotic and non-chronological manner. Hence assembling the facts, arranging the chaotic information in an orderly, chronological way and presenting it in the fictional manner required a lot of time, patience and imagination.

When I launched upon the task of writing this novel, I was encouraged by Dr. V.G. Marihal, who helped me wholeheartedly by going through the manuscript regularly when it was in progress and by offering valuable suggestions for correction of facts. As his ancestors were closely connected with the court of Kittur kingdom, he was very proud of Rani Chennamma's dynamism, heroism, patriotism and political wisdom. He insisted on my publishing the novel at the earliest thereby giving international publicity that the Rani deserved. But I could not expedite the publication of the novel due to some gaps in it, which I wanted to fill in. I had to wait until I could complete the novel satisfactorily. But alas, Dr. V.G.Marihal is no more to see it in print. But I believe that the publication of the novel will satisfy his soul in Heaven.

Sivaranjani Nilaya
Basavaraj Naikar
Kotur Plots, Malapur Road
bsnaikar@yahoo.com
Dharwad 580 008
(Karnataka, INDIA)
M: 09591472345

Acknowledgements

I have drawn the relevant information from various sources, which are too many to be enumerated here. But I have mentioned only a select few, which are major sources like the following:

1. William Wilson Hunter, *The Thackerays in India and Some Calcutta Graves,* Originally published in 1897 from London and republished by Forgotten Books, 2013.
2. Ursula Low, *Fifty Years with John Company (From the Letters of General Sir John Low of Clatto, Fife: 1822-1858),* John Murray, London, 1936.
3. M.V. Krishna Rao & G.S.Halappa. Eds. *History of Freedom Movement in Karnataka, Vol. I.* Bangalore: Government of Karnataka. 1962.
4. Sridhar Telkar. *Kittur Chennamma Rani.* Bailahongala: KRCIM. 1957.
5. Bhaveppa Moogi, Ed. *Pharasi Kagadapatragalu,* Bailahongala: KRCIM, 1948.

6. Bhaveppa Moogi, Ed. *Kittura Kalaga*, Bailahongala: Rudragowda Prakashana, 1959.
7. Chennakka Pawate, *Kitturu Kathana*, Dharwad: Chennaganga Prakashana, 2002.
8. Halappa. G.S. *Bharata Swatantyada Bellichukki*. Dharwad: Karnataka Sahitya Sahakari Sangha, 1962.
9. Ishwar M. Sankal, *Sri Madivaleshwara Sivayogi, Garag*. Garag: Sri Cennabasavaswami Publication. 1977.
10. Rayanagowda Tallur, Ed. *Kittura Bandaya*. Bailahongala: KRCIM, 1924.
11. "The Kittur Insurrection in 1824" published in *The Asiatic Journal and Monthly Miscellany, Vol.I. Third Series*, May-October 1843.
12. Sridhar G.Hiremath, *Lion of Lahore & Tigress of Kittur*, Bailhongal: Shravani Publications, 2014.

I am thankful to Dr. T.R.Rajasekharaiah, whose English translation of Magundi Basava's ballad I have used in the novel.

Raja Mallasarja, who, true to his name, was like a fighting tiger, sat on his throne in a dignified style, resting his chin lightly on his left palm. His turban glittered in the yellowish light of torches lit in the court hall. His Diwan, Sardar Gurusiddhappa sat on the royal seat to the right side of and a little below the Raja's throne. The various scholars and poets of the court like Vengi Chennabasappa, Magundi Basava, Rudragowda and Amriteswara sat on their seats.

The folk artists, who had been invited by the royal orders, stood ready to begin their performance. Two main singers with white turbans on their heads held two small drums called *dundume*. They were flanked by the members of the chorus. The Raja beckoned to the Diwan with a wave of his right hand; the Diwan in return ordered the chorus leaders, "Gentlemen, you may start now." The leaders beat their drums half a dozen times and produced the rhythmic sound. The entire court hall fell into total silence. The artists raised their voices slowly and started singing their song:

> Listen to my song
> O gentlemen
> Listen to my song,
> *Dundume*

> Listen to my song carefully
> O gentlemen
> Listen to my song.
> Mallendra, the devotee
> Of the blue- necked Siva

Was born on the earth
Due to His grace.
Mallendra therefore
Shines like Devendra,
Dundume Dundume.

Mallendra is blessed
By the snake-decked Siva
And His Holiness Madivalaswami.
He lives in the capital City of Kittur.
That is beautiful in all
The fifty-one countries,
Dundume Dundume.

Raja Mallasarja was nodding his head in appreciation and beating the rhythm with his right fingers upon the hand-rest of the picturesque throne. As the tempo of the song increased, the entire audience seemed to enter into an ecstatic world thereby forgetting the mundane world. Their spirits seemed to be soaring high in the musical heaven to the accompaniment of the rattle and thumping of drums and the chime of tiny cymbals. It was only when the song came to an end that they were jolted into an awareness of the real world. The artists reverentially bowed to the Raja by touching the floor with their right hands. Soon the audience was clapping in appreciation of the artistic service rendered by the folk-singers.

Raja Mallasarja beamed with a smile of satisfaction. He said, "Bravo! Gentlemen, you are no ordinary singers but high priests of folk music. My kingdom is indeed lucky to have such great artists in it. I am very proud of you all."

The artists bowed to the King once again. They were filled with a sense of satisfaction at the royal appreciation of their art.

Raja Mallasarja turned towards Diwan Gurusiddhappa and ordered, "Diwan Sir, please arrange for the appropriate payment of cash and gifts to these artists."

"Yes, Sarkar. That shall be done instantly," said Gurusiddhappa in a reverential tone.

He, then, beckoned to the maidservants who stood behind the curtained door. Two maidservants clad in white uniforms brought two silver platters with a small purse of coins and two shawls with silk linings. The Diwan took the purse of golden coins from the platter and handed it over to the chorus leader. He then honored the two artists by spreading the shawls across their shoulders. The audience clapped once again in appreciation.

* * *

Raja Mallasarja was a very devout person and patronized all the religious institutions like temples, monasteries and mosques. Kallumath Monastery was known as Savira Samsthan Math as it had under its control a thousand monasteries scattered all over the kingdom.

One day His Holiness Sri Prabhuswami sat discussing the spiritual matters with the junior Madivalaswami in the Kallumath monastery. At that time Raja Mallasarja entered the monastery and bowed down to His Holiness reverentially and stood there.

His Holiness Prabhuswami said to the junior swami, "My dear boy, Madivala, this is the Raja of our kingdom, who is like a father and protector to all the citizens. It is our duty to treat him respectfully. Please get a wooden seat for him from inside."

Then the junior Madivalaswami said, "Baba, how can I refute your words? Is Almighty God not the Master and Father of the world? Is Almighty God not the master of you, our Raja and me? Can we reach the final goal of life if we depend upon the worldly father instead of depending upon the spiritual father?"

He went inside and fetched a wooden seat for the Raja.

Raja Mallasarja was dumbstruck with wonder at the high philosophical words coming from the mouth of a junior swami.

He exclaimed, "Your Holiness, what a beautiful idea! As you said, only he, who thinks of God, will be eternal. The rest of us are merely ephemeral beings. My being a Raja is the result of my *punya* of the previous birth as well as of the penance of holy gurus like you. Though you are still a boy, your philosophical thought is very high. You are indeed a great guru. I am really very happy about it. I shall give you whatever you desire. I shall execute whatever you order me to."

Then the junior Madivalaswami asked him, "Your Majesty, can you give me whatever I ask for?"

"Your Holiness, please order me. I shall give it definitely."

"Your Majesty, when the entire world is the gift of God, why are you so proud of giving it?"

Raja Mallasarja was deeply touched by the junior swami's words. He soon recovered his composure and said,

"Your Holiness, your elevated philosophy of life is indeed the result of your penance in the previous birth. Kindly forgive me for my ignorance. I shall give you whatever is gifted by God to me. I am only a medium. Kindly ask for it."

"Your Majesty, in that case, you please arrange for the regular *dasoha* in the monastery so that nobody can go without food in your ideal kingdom. Be a patron and donate the required amount of gold coins to me so that I may use it for feeding the poor people regularly every day."

"All right, Your Holiness. I shall do as ordered by you," said Raja Mallasarja.

Within a few moments he got the gold coins from the royal treasury and poured them reverentially into the palms of junior Madivalaswami. He felt the satisfaction of having done a permanent charitable act and returned to his palace happily. From that day onwards the regular *dasoha* was arranged in the monastery under the patronage of Raja Mallasarja. All the poor people, who visited the monastery, were fed there amply and freely.

* * *

Raja Mallasarja was a great connoisseur of the things of beauty in life. He used to wear fine clothes and therefore his wardrobe included elegant robes made in different parts of the country. He was also fond of beautiful plants, trees and flowers. That is why he had developed a botanical garden in Devarasigihalli. That garden contained a large variety of medicinal plants, umbrageous trees, and colourful and fragrant flowers.

Raja Mallasarja used to celebrate the Ganapati puja, Dasara and Dipavali festivals and the worship of Goddess Kariyamma regularly with great pomp. He would arrange religious discourses on *Basava Purana* and *Durdundeswara Purana* by Virasaiva scholars, in the month of Sravana every year. Similarly he would invite the subjects of 360 villages of fourteen Karyats of the kingdom to attend the religious discourses. After the discourses were completed on the last day of Sravana, Raja Mallasarja would arrange the programme of *Purana* scholars to be mounted on elephants and taken in a procession around the capital. Dasara happened to be the grand festival celebrated in Kittur, every year. On that day Raja Mallasarja would distribute alms and land grants to deserving individuals. For example, he granted Chitradurga village to a swamiji. Another year, he granted Sirahatti village to Sivamurti Laxmiswami. Yet another year, he granted Bidarkal village to Sri Madivalaswami of Garag.

* * *

One day Raja Mallasarja Desai sent for Diwan Gurusiddhappa. Diwan Gurusiddayya Charantimath hailed from Shapur village in Belgaum area and had been a loyal officer in the court of Kittur. He was popularly known as Gurusiddhappa. The Diwan bowed himself into the court-hall and stood askance before the Raja. Raja Mallasarja asked him, "Be seated, Diwan sir. I am worried about the incessant battles between Tippu Sultan and the Peshwas. Practically there has been no peace in the Deccan region. On the other hand, the Company sarkar has been growing more and more powerful. We'll have no future unless we do something for survival. We'll be swallowed by the demon called *Ingrezi* government. We cannot be easy victims to the British demon. That's why I have been planning to organize a band of Desais, Chieftains and Kings of the Deccan including the Raja of Kolhapur. We have to do this secretly, without giving any clue to the British fellows. Once we are united, we can fight the foreign enemies successfully. What's your opinion about this?"

Gurusiddhappa responded instantly, "Yes, Sarkar, we must do it at the earliest. It is high time for us to do so. Somebody has to take the lead for this venture."

Raja Mallasarja said, "I knew you would definitely approve of it. Gurusiddhappa, we cannot keep quiet at this time. I shall start this work from tomorrow itself. Several Desais and princes have sent messages to me about their assurance to join the struggle. Tomorrow we shall start our journey. I shall meet the Desai of Kakati and consult him about the organization. He is said to be a very powerful man in that part of the country. Please arrange for the tour tomorrow."

"Yes, Sarkar. I shall get the best horses for that purpose. I shall send word to the ostler right now," said the Diwan and bowed himself out.

* * *

In the early days Raja Mallasarja had ordered his soldiers to kill Bommappa Desai and eleven other members of the royal family of Belavadi kingdom. Hence the soldiers had made all the twelve people of Belavadi stand in a row and severed their heads one by one. This event had saddened Rani Rudramma because those people of Belavadi happened to her distant relatives. She had, therefore, quarreled with Raja Mallasarja and gone away to be her parental home at Tallur and stayed there for a short while. But she had returned to Kittur to stay with her husband only after she gradually forgot the sad event and grew reconciled to the harsh reality of life.

* * *

Early in the morning Raja Mallasarja was awakened by Rani Rudramma, who had already had her bath and performed the *istalinga* worship. The smoke of incense burning before the family idols was spiralling up slowly and radiating a sweet fragrance everywhere. Raja Mallasarja busied himself with morning ablutions. As he dressed himself in the silk dhoti and the royal apparel after returning from the *puja* room, Rani Rudramma instructed her maidservant to keep his breakfast ready on a plate resting on a tripod and was waiting for him.

Raja Mallasarja squatted on the picturesque seat and began to eat the sweet balls, steaming *rotis*, brinjal curry and green grams. Rani Rudramma was watching him silently. When he was through with his breakfast, she asked him,

"Sarkar, don't strain yourself too much in your tour. Please have sufficient rest at night time."

He stared at his wife for a moment. He went near her, caressed her cheeks and said, "Don't you worry, dear. I shall be careful."

Then Mallasarja walked to his chamber to change his dress. He put on his silk turban with golden embroidery and a tassel of pearls. He carefully arranged the fantail on top of it and then the pleats. He buckled a long sword on this left side and a dagger on his right. Then he secured the metal shield and a gun on his back. He slipped into his creaking shoes pointed upward with a flourish. He walked with royal dignity and style towards the ostler, who was eagerly waiting for him outside the palace. The ostler bowed to the king.

Raja Mallasarja mounted the white stallion and settled himself properly on the saddle. Diwan Gurusiddhappa and other Sardars of his retinue also jumped on to their horses and waited for their Raja to lead them. As Mallasarja spurred his horse, it began to move slowly, *clip, clop, clip, clop.* The other horses followed it, raising clouds of dust behind them. As they rode on, the trees and hills faded behind them. They climbed the hills and descended into the valleys and crossed the rivers. When the sun reached the zenith of the sky, they felt a bit tired and hungry. They, therefore, rested under the shade of trees near a large tank and had their lunch of sweet balls, *rotis*, rice and curds. Then they rested on the mattresses for an hour and had a brief nap.

Crows were occasionally cawing in the trees. When they woke up, they washed their faces in the water of the tank. Then they mounted their horsebacks and resumed their journey. As the sun was descending on the western horizon, their journey became more and more pleasant. The trees, bushes and grass looked mellower than earlier, in the golden rays of the evening sun. The cuckoos cooed and the sparrows twittered.

Diwan Gurusiddhappa said, "See, Sarkar, we have yet to travel six hours in order to reach Kakati."

"Is that so, Gurusiddhappa? You know it better than I do. I am coming on this route for the first time. Now that it is getting dark, we shall rest here near the temple," Raja Mallasarja said.

Gurusiddhappa jumped off the back of the horse and so did the others. The servants spread the mattresses and served the dinner to everybody. Then they prepared the beds for the royal personages. As they were extremely tired, they slept like logs in the pleasant breeze of the night.

The next morning they resumed their journey after breakfast. After about six hours' journey they came near Kakati.

Gurusiddhappa identified the locality and told Raja Mallasarja who said, "In that case we shall camp here tonight. We shall send word to Dhulappagowda Desai of Kakati tomorrow."

Then they dismounted their horses and relaxed upon the lush and green grass while the servants busied themselves in pitching four tents for the night camp. A few other servants collected twigs and dry faggots for fuel and cooked their lunch. They had their lunch and relaxed until the evening and chatted until the dinner was ready. They discussed the fertility of the land and the customs of the people belonging to the surrounding villages. After dinner, they entered their respective tents and slept off the fatigue of their journey.

* * *

Kakati was a small princely state near Belgaum.The progenitor of her (Chennamma's) family was Marimama Gowda, who migrated from Bijapur to Kakati (or Kagati), which was given to him as an inam by the Adil Shahis in recognition of his loyalty and heroism in capturing a cruel bandit who was a menace to the public as well as to the ruling Patwardhans. Kannagowda, the uncle of Chennamma was the 12th man in succession and came to limelight by around 1775. The jagir comprised of twenty-nine fertile villages in and around Belgaum. Dhulappagowda Desai and Padmavati lived there in peace and prosperity. When a baby girl was born to the couple theywere overjoyed by the event and named her as Chennamma.. The astrologers of the court studied the time of the birth of the baby; cast her horoscope and forecast that she would grow into a dynamic and celebrated lady. As the couple had no male progeny, they wanted to bring up their daughter as if she were a son.

As Chennamma grew up, her parents appointed a couple of able teachers to teach her Kannada, Marathi, Urdu and Persian. As she was a precocious girl, she made fast progress in her studies. She could read a number of books in all the four languages. She studied the *Basava Purana,* the *Ramayana* and the *Mahabharata*. She took keen interest in Sivayoga and contemporary history. She was also trained in music.

Her uncle, Kannagowda, and other coaches trained her in martial arts, like horse riding, fencing, swimming and spear throwing. She was a good hunter and enjoyed putting on male attire.

* * *

At the break of dawn, Raja Mallasarja woke up and completed his morning ablutions. He and his Diwan Gurusiddhappa had their breakfast prepared by the servants.

Then Raja Mallasarja called one of his messengers and ordered him, "Go to Kakati and inform the Desai that we are going to meet him for some confidential work. We shall set out for Kakati after you come back from him."

The messenger bowed himself away from there. He went to the tree, where his horse was tethered. He tidied up the saddle and the crupper, and stroked the horse's flanks affectionately. He then un-tethered it and jumped on to the saddle. The horse neighed a few times and started moving slowly spurred by the rider.

Raja Mallasarja looked around and felt thrilled by the verdant beauty of trees, creepers, bushes and hills.

"Ah!" he exclaimed, "see, Gurusiddhappa, how beautiful the wood appear in the golden rays of the morning sun."

Gurusiddhappa said in return, "Yes, Sarkar, it is indeed very beautiful. Two eyes are not enough to observe this beauty."

Raja Mallasarja sat watching the forest minutely as if he was studying it. Then he burst out, "This is an ideal spot for hunting wild beasts. My hands are itching for this game. Besides, we have nothing to do until the messenger returns from Kakati."

"Yes Sarkar, you may have some entertainment today," said Gurusiddhappa.

A few villagers, who were clad in soiled dhotis and turbans came and stood near the tents. Curious to know who these strangers were, they went near the tents and asked the royal servants in whispers who the royal personage was. The servants told them that it was Raja Mallasarja Desai of Kittur. The villagers appeared to be happy and whispered among themselves. Then they made bold to walk forth in a body and stood before Raja Mallasarja. They greeted him by joining their palms and said humbly,

"Sarkar, our land is indeed blessed by your presence. We are really very lucky. But we have a difficulty, which we cannot overcome by ourselves. We request you to help us out of it."

Raja Mallasarja looked at the villagers affectionately and said, "Gentlemen, let me know what your difficulty is. I shall definitely help you out of it, if I can."

Now the villagers were encouraged by the affectionate talk of the Raja.

"Sarkar, we have been terrified by a tiger which moves about here in the wood. It has killed two human beings. Only last week it swallowed a child playing outside the hut. So far nobody has been able to kill it. We live in constant dread of it. We do not know when we would enter into its jaws. Sarkar, you have come here as a god. We implore you to save us from its claws."

Raja Mallasarja understood the import of their words and felt deep pity for them. He said to them, "Gentlemen, I understand your problem. Don't you worry about it henceforth. I shall not leave this camp until I kill that tiger, however deadly it might be."

The villagers were overwhelmed with a sense of gratitude and bowed down to the Raja once again.

Raja Mallasarja urged them, "Leave the problem to me. Now you may go about your routine work." The villagers went away with cheerful hearts.

Raja Mallasarja asked his men to get ready for hunting. Half a dozen soldiers armed themselves with their bows and quivers packed with arrows and with guns. Raja Mallasarja took his gun and said to his Diwan, "Gurusiddhappa, you please take rest here in the tent until we return from our hunt in the wood."

Gurusiddhappa said, "All right, Sarkar. Let it be as you wish."

Raja Mallasarja and his soldiers mounted their horses and rode towards that part of the hill where the ferocious tiger was said to be moving about. They dismounted from their horses and tethered them to the trees. The wood was crowded with tall trees and wild undergrowth. Occasionally sparrows spattered and other birds twittered. The sun was slowly rising to the zenith of the sky. The soldiers scattered themselves and sat on the branches of different trees at strategic spots with their guns ready to shoot the ferocious animal. Raja Mallasarja had selected an important spot near which there was a stream in which the water was flowing with a gentle murmur.

Raja Mallasarja intuitively knew that the tiger would definitely come there to quench its thirst, about midday. He had instructed his soldiers to affect the bleating of sheep in order to arouse the curiosity of the tiger.

They waited patiently for nearly two hours as if their whole body was ears. The silence in the wood was occasionally punctuated by the warbling and cooing of birds. As the sun ascended in the eastern sky, the heat began to mount in the atmosphere. Raja Mallasarja and his soldiers grew more alert and waited for the fierce animal. His soldiers were bleating at regular intervals to entice the tiger.

After a little while, there seemed to be a little stir in the bushes at a short distance. Raja Mallasarja cocked his ears and turned in the direction from where the sound came. He concentrated his attention on that direction and heard the sound of dry leaves being crunched at a slow rhythm. Raja Mallasarja was sure that the tiger had started moving about. He charged his bow and sat in a ready position. As he heard the crunch of dry leaves and saw the stripes of yellow and black between the bushes, he instantly shot off the arrow, which bolted speedily with a whir in the air. As the arrow pierced the flank of the tiger, the Raja heard a piteous and thunderous roar. He waited for a little more time to see if it stirred any longer. But no sound was heard. He guessed that the tiger must have died. He climbed down from the tree and walked towards the spot, where the ferocious animal must have lain. He waited behind a bush and peeped beside it and lo! He saw the tiger lying stretched out.

Now he walked towards it with a greater confidence. The tiger lay motionless, but he was surprised to find two arrows stuck deeply into its body. He could not guess as to who must have hit the second arrow.

As he stood there staring at the dead tiger with blood oozing out, he was distracted by the tinkle of bangles and a melodious voice saying, "The tiger belongs to me because it was I who shot it first."

Raja Mallasarja was further surprised by the confident tone with which some young lady was talking to him for the first time in his life. As he turned in that direction, he saw an extraordinarily pretty young lady coming towards him. He sized her from top to bottom. His eyes were riveted on the wealth of her beauty. Her complexion, moonlike face, buxom breasts, handsome hips, tapering thighs beneath the silk sari trussed behind her, and creeping arms arrested his attention. His heart began to throb wildly and his entire being began to vibrate like a needle in the presence of a magnet. He remembered who he was and how he should behave himself.

He took a deep breath and asked the beautiful young lady, "Young lady, who are you? What's your name? How do you claim that you have killed the tiger?"

The young lady kept her arm on her waist and stood in a stylish manner saying,

"Yes, sir, it was I who shot the tiger first. You must have shot him after I did. The tiger, therefore, belongs to me."

As Mallasarja stared at her he lost his heart to her. Love did not allow him to argue with her any longer.

"All right, young lady, I agree that it is you who have killed the tiger. You could have taken it home, but before doing so please tell me who you are and what your name is!"

The young lady grew a bit shy. She bent her head a little and scratched the earth with her toes. Then she replied, "I am Chennamma, daughter of Dhulappagowda

Desai of Kakati. I come occasionally into the wood for hunting."

Raja Mallasarja broke into a gentle smile and said, "What a happy coincidence! Young lady, I have come here only to meet your father. I have sent a messenger to your father to ask him if we could meet him tomorrow."

Chennamma was observing his royal dignity and grace very carefully. She fell in love with his handsome personality. Her heart began to throb wildly as she grew aware of her own inner emotions. Then she asked him gently, "Dear sir, may I know who you are so that I can tell my father about you."

Raja Mallasarja told her, "Young lady, please tell your father that Raja Mallasarja Desai of Kittur wants to see him tomorrow."

The name of the king gave her a pleasant shock; for she had heard so much about his patriotism, love of arts and culture. Then she seemed to shrink a little out of a sense of embarrassment. She kept aside her bow said to him with joined palms.

"Sarkar, kindly excuse me for behaving so rudely. I did not know who you were. Kindly forgive me."

Raja Mallasarja relaxed into a gentle smile and said, "Don't worry about it, young lady. You did not do so deliberately. But please tell me how you'll take your tiger home?"

Chennamma said, I shall go home and send the servants to bring it home."

Raja Mallasarja said, "Don't you take that much of trouble, madam. I shall ask my soldiers to carry the tiger to your residence. Will it be all right?"

"I shall be grateful to you, Sarkar for this kind favour," said Chennamma rather shyly.

As Raja Mallasarja clapped twice, the servants who had stood at a reverential distance walked towards him and waited for his order. He said, "Gentlemen, this is the daughter of the Desai of Kakati. You escort her home safely along with this dead tiger."

The soldiers, therefore, collected a few twigs of trees and bound them into a frame on which they placed the dead beast and secured it tightly with some rope. Four soldiers carried the frame on their shoulders and followed Chennamma. Raja Mallasarja stood there until the young lady was out of sight. He then returned to his tent along with the remaining soldiers. The golden tint of the setting sun gave a peculiar glow to the landscape everywhere. The *koels* began to coo plaintively from the trees.

The next morning Raja Mallasarja's messenger returned with another from the Desai of Kakati, who greeted and said,

Sarkar, our Sardar Desai has extended a very hearty welcome to you. He has been eagerly waiting for you."

Raja Mallasarja put on his gem-studded turban with a fantail and mounted his horse. His Diwan and the other soldiers mounted their horses and followed their master. The morning sun was very pleasant. The greenery covered with the golden tint of the morning sun looked heavenly to Raja Mallasarja, who had a poetic heart. They rode along the fields, crossed a couple of brooks and finally reached the gate of Kakati, where the guard welcomed them with a call of his trumpet.

When they reached the mansion of Dhulappagowda Desai, they were received with boundless cordiality. They were all conducted to the dining hall and served with a course of food consisting of six flavors like sweet balls, *rotis*, curds, vegetables etc. All of them enjoyed the delicious food especially because of their journey, which had intensified their hunger. They were all satisfied with the rich food and ate their *pan* and betel and other condiments with real gusto.

After the breakfast, they were conducted to other chambers where they could relax. Raja Mallasarja and Diwan Gurusiddhappa relaxed in the large cushion chairs whereas the other soldiers rested in the other chambers.

Sardar Desai was beaming with a smile and said, "We are indeed very lucky to have you amidst us today. This is a pleasant surprise for us all. May I know the purpose of your visit here?"

Raja Mallasarja cleared his throat and said, "Desai sir, I have come here to discuss a very important problem with you. I hope you will cooperate with us."

Sardar Desai replied, "You need not have any doubt at all about our cooperation, but let me kindly know what exactly the problem is".

"You see, sir," continued Raja Mallasarja, "the people of Company sarkar have been trying to swallow our states like a cobra swallowing the poor frogs. If we remain idle now, there is no doubt they will conquer all of us and reduce us to slaves or nonentities. It is high time for us to be united and fight against the common enemy, I mean the foreigners like the British, the French and the Portuguese. You have to extend your full cooperation with us by sparing your army whenever we need it. Likewise I have been requesting the other Rajas and Desais for their sympathy and cooperation."

Now Dhulappagowda Desai realized the gravity of the situation and wished to contribute his mite for the mighty cause of fighting against the *vilayati* people.

He promised Raja Mallasarja, "What you have been doing is a great adventure indeed. I give you my word of honour that I shall offer all the possible help that I can. You may rely upon me for horses, soldiers or food grains. I shall keep all of them ready for you."

"That's all I want. In fact, I want your sympathy more than anything else. We can defeat the *Ingrezi* people only by consolidating our forces," said Raja Mallasarja.

Dhulappagowda Desai added, "We are also trying to mobilize the opinions of our neighboring chiefs like Desais and Gowdas to do our best to drive out the *Ingrezi* people..."

He then changed the topic and referred to the private problems. "Dear Sir, yesterday I was told by my daughter that you had gone hunting in the wood. How did you feel about it?"

Raja Mallasarja relaxed with a smile and said, "Yes, yes, I went to the wood as a hunter but returned as the hunted."

Dhulappagowda Desai was a little puzzled by the answer. "I'm afraid I do not understand what you mean by that. Can you tell me a bit more clearly?"

Raja Mallasarja did not say anything. Instead, he looked meaningfully at his Diwan Gurusiddhappa, who said jovially,

"Sir yesterday our Sarkar had gone into the wood for the tiger-hunt. He at last shot a tiger but found that your daughter had also shot it simultaneously. He admired the extraordinary courage of your daughter. That very moment he made up his mind to marry her. I, on my behalf, request you to give your consent to this alliance."

Dhulappagowda Desai's face began to beam with happiness. He heaved a sigh of pleasure and said, "What a pleasant surprise, I say? I never knew that my daughter had such courage."

Raja Mallasarja felt more and more confident by listening to Dhulappagowda Desai's dialogues and further beckoned to his Diwan who took the cue from his master and explained, "Your daughter will lack nothing in her husband's home. Mother Nilamma will take care of her like an elder sister. What do you say sir? You may consult the members of your family and tell us."

Dhulappagowda Desai said, "The proposal is all right for me, but let me consult my Desaini and daughter also for a minute."

Then Diwan Gurusiddhappa remembered something and said, "I had forgotten to tell you one more thing. Please wait."

Dhulappagowda Desai sat back in his chair expecting more information from him.

Gurusiddhappa explained further, "You may be puzzled by our request for your daughter as a second wife. You see, sir, our Sarkar has his first wife, but unfortunately she has not borne any issue so far. Our Sarkar must have a son for the throne of the kingdom of Kittur. That's why we are contemplating a second marriage for the Sarkar."

Now Dhulappagowda Desai of Kakati understood the contingency and felt a new confidence about the alliance.

"All right, you have explained to me everything. I shall consult the womenfolk," said the Desai and went into the interior part of his mansion.

The Desaini, young Chennamma and other women folk were sitting in the large interior hall.

The Desai walked to them and said to the Desaini, "See darling, Raja Mallasarja wants to marry our daughter. What's your opinion?"

The Desaini, who covered her head with the hem of her sari, said rather apologetically, "That Raja has already a wife at home. Our daughter will have to be a second wife to him. Can our daughter be happy in that atmosphere there, sir?"

Dhulappagowda Desai felt a bit discouraged by the wifely answer. But yet he turned to Chennamma and asked, "My dear daughter, do you like to marry him or not? I am not going to force you. Don't be shy."

But Chennamma replied shyly, "I shall do as mother says."

The Desaini expressed her doubt, "I thought that a second wife for a king or anybody would create legal problems for the children of both the wives. I hesitate to give my daughter only on this count."

The Desai tried to understand the problem from his wife's point of view. He also thought about it and said,

"Don't worry about that at all. There'll be no such problems for our daughter simply because the first wife has no issues. Our daughter will be not only the wife of a ruler but also the mother of a would-be ruler. After all

Mallasarja is a Raja. And a Raja can marry any number of wives only because he can afford to do so. In my opinion, we cannot think of a better husband for our daughter."

Then the Desaini consulted the other elderly women relatives and thought about the pros and cons of the alliance. All the elderly women gave a positive answer about it.

The Desaini then told her husband, "I had my own doubts about the proposal and expressed them frankly before you. Now that everybody assures me that my daughter will be happy there in Kittur, I have no objection."

The Desai felt very happy to know that his wife was convinced beyond a doubt about the desirability of the alliance.

He then formally asked Chennamma, "My dear daughter, what's your opinion now? Are you willing to marry him or not?"

Chennamma bent her face a little. She was scratching the carpet with her toes.

Everybody was eagerly waiting for her answer. Then she said, "Yes" mildly. Everybody heaved a sigh of joy and relief. The Desai felt very happy about the willingness of the women folk who had given their consent for the marriage of Chennamma. He hurried back to the hall where the guests were waiting for him.

Diwan Gurusiddhappa was eager to know the reaction of the Desai of Kakati and, therefore, asked, "What's the common opinion of your family about the alliance?"

Then the Desai cleared his throat and said, "See, Sardar Gurusiddhappa, I consulted all the elders of my family. They have all approved of this alliance. You may

consult your priests and tell us your convenient time and
muhurta so that we can arrange the marriage here only in
Kakati in front of our house."

Diwan Gurusiddhappa was very happy to have a
positive answer from the Desai family of Kakati and
said, "We are indeed very happy about your approval.
We shall let you know the convenient date of marriage
after returning to Kittur."

Raja Mallasarja felt very happy about the whole
episode. All of them had a grand feast at night and rested.
There was great excitement in the house of the Desai at
Kakati. Raja Mallasarja and Chennamma spent the whole
night in dreaming of each other. The next morning Raja
Mallasarja returned to Kittur with his companions.

After a few weeks, the wedding between Raja
Mallasarja and Chennamma took place at Kakati with
great pomp. The entire village was decorated with the
festoons of mango leaves and flowers of different shapes
and colours. The village was overcrowded with Desais,
Gowdas and other chieftains of the neighboring princely
states. The natives of Kakati did not have to kindle their
ovens for a week's time as they were all invited for the
seven-day wedding feast by the Desai. The entire village
was resounding with the music of drums, pipes and
shahnais. Every evening folk songs and folk plays were
arranged in the marriage pandal.

On the penultimate day, the engagement ceremony
was performed according to Lingayat rituals. The women
folk smeared the body of Chennamma with turmeric
paste. Similarly they smeared the wrists and cheeks of
Raja Mallasarja with turmeric paste. Then the elders of

both the Desais exchanged betel leaves and betel nuts symbolically solemnizing the alliance. On the last day the bride and the groom were bathed with warm water and then led to the marriage pandal where they were made to sit on the black woolen blanket decorated with the tracery of rice-grains. The priest was officiating and guiding the ritual of wedding. He was chanting the Sanskrit and Kannada *mantras* rhythmically and melodiously. Finally he asked the bridegroom to secure the sacramental *tali* around Chennamma's neck. The priest raised his voice and chanted *Sumuhurte savadhana* in the highest pitch. The relatives, friends and admirers who had gathered there sprinkled the holy *aksata* grains on the young couple and blessed them. The *shahnai* and drums were played in their high pitch and quickest tempo.

The Desai of Kakati and his Desaini shed tears of joy at the wedding of their beloved daughter Chennamma who looked like Goddess Rati herself in her bridal dress. Raja Mallasarja looked like Lord Kama himself in the human shape. Then all the kith and kin waved the *arati* in front of the newly wedded couple and blessed them. After the ritual of *arati* all the invitees were conducted to the large banquet hall and fed with an extra-ordinary variety of delicacies. After the grand feast, the guests ate the betel leaves and slivers of betel and blessed the hosts inwardly and went home with a sense of great satisfaction. The wedding was so grand that the natives of Kakati and Kittur did not forget it for many years.

Chennamma, who had become the second wife of Raja Mallasarja, was now to return to Kittur along with her parents according to the Virasaiva convention. One of Chennamma's friends teased her by snapping her knuckles upon her temples.

She said to her, "Now that you have become a Rani, you might forget us your poor friends."

Another teased her, "Rani Sarkar, how did you like your Raja? You must be dreaming only about him now, mustn't you?"

But Chennamma would reply to them, "How can I forget you, my bosom friends? Of course, I love my Raja, as he is very bold and smart. That doesn't mean that I would forget you. You must visit me after every Ugadi festival. Similarly I shall come and meet you all during every Naga Panchami." Then the friends would stop teasing her.

When the day for the first departure to her husband's home came, everybody in the Desai's house at Kakati grew rather unhappy at having to part from the young Chennamma. That morning the parents and friends of Chennamma adorned her with gold necklaces, armlets, anklets, bangles and wreaths of jasmines and *champaks*. As she sat on the woolen blanket decorated with a drawing of rice-grains, the womenfolk including the young and the old waved *arati* lamps around her face and dotted her forehead with sacramental vermilion dot one by one. When everybody had her turn of *arati* waving, a group of young ladies sang a benedictory song wishing her well at her husband's home, the chorus of feminine voices was very mellifluous and touching:

> The Banyan tree has no blossoms,
> Borrowing money has no end,

The Hawthorne tree has no shade,
Daughter, the parental home is not permanent.

Revere your parents- in- law,
The neighboring people around,
And the king, who rules over the kingdom,
My daughter, this is how
You should live in your in-laws' house.

Daughter, be like a goddess of wealth to
    neighbours,
Discriminate not between the members of the
    family,
Wreck not the big and beautiful family, O my
    daughter.

People will respect and invite you as a sister
If you lead a good life.
If you lead an irrational life,
You will surely be an enemy of your parents.

"This is not my daughter, but yours
Hence treat her with affection."
With this request will I hand over
My daughter to you, O Mother-in-Law.

Chennamma sat in the chariot with her parents.
The chariot was decorated with wreaths and festoons of
colourful and fragrant flowers like roses and jasmines.
The relatives sat in the other chariots. As the charioteer
whipped the horses, they started pulling it rather gently.

The chariots were led and followed by a number of soldiers on horseback. They traveled the entire day and the entire night. The rosy sun was rising slowly in the east and spreading the golden tint everywhere, when they reached Kittur.

They were welcomed with the sweet notes of *shahnai* and beats of *karadi majalu.* As the chariot stood near the palace gate, the womenfolk of Raja Mallasarja's palace welcomed them with sweet smiles.

Chennamma climbed down the chariot and so did the others. She was conducted through the main gate and then towards the main door of the palace. She stood near the silver plated threshold on which a silver can with rice-grains was kept. Five *sumangales* of Mallasarja's household stood inside the door and waived *arati* lamps around her and applied the vermillion dot on her forehead, by turns.

An elderly lady said, "My darling daughter in law, you please fill our house like this can filled with rice-grains. You push this can with your right foot and enter the house."

Accordingly Chennamma lifted the folds of her sari a bit and pushed the can with her right foot thereby scattering the rice-grains inside the door and entered the husband's home. There was a lot of jubilation in the palace. Rudramma, the senior wife of Raja Mallasarja clasped Chennamma affectionately and led her towards her lord. Raja Mallasarja was feeling excited and blushed behind his moustaches. Chennamma knelt shyly and saluted her lord by touching her forehead to his feet.

He touched her head and blessed her, "May Lord Gurusiddha's grace be upon you!" He then held her arms and helped her to stand up. Chennamma stole a glance at her lord and beamed with pride and excitement. She was then led to the kitchen, where all the kinswomen of Kakati were fed with sweet delicacies.

In the evening, the new kinsmen from Kakati sat in the big hall exchanging information and chatting until they were reminded by the cooks that dinner was ready. The entire hall was flooded with the sweet aroma of delicacies like *holige*, ghee, vegetables, fried chips and *bhajis*. The men folk and women folk washed their hands, faces and legs and smeared their foreheads with triple marks of *vibhuti*. Men and women sat in separate rows on wooden seats before their plates kept on tripods. The priest inaugurated the banquet by reciting the holy tag *Hara Hara Mahadev* in a high pitch. Then they started tasting the extra-ordinary variety of delicacies and joking in between.

A couple of hours had gone by after the banquet. Now the time for *Sobhana* was fast approaching. Raja Mallasarja was eagerly waiting in the room decorated with wreaths and festoons of flowers and consecrated for the ritual of consummation. Oil-lamps were burning in all the corners of the room. Chennamma was led by an elderly matron to the hall. She carried a tray with two golden bowls with sweet and hot milk in them. As she entered the room, the matron closed the door and secured it from outside.

The bed was decorated with jasmines the sweet smell of which intensified their attraction for each other.

Chennamma sat shyly by the side of her lord and offered him the golden bowl of milk, which he took gently and sipped it slowly and held the other bowl to her mouth for her to drink. Then she kept the empty bowls on a stool near the bed.

Mallasarja held her hands in his and said, "My darling, how many days I had to wait for this moment! You have already filled my heart and mind. Now you have filled my home also."

Chennamma, whose heart was beating fast, said in a tremulous voice, "So also did I wait, my lord. I am indeed lucky to have you as the lord of my heart."

Then Mallasarja drew her gently to his side and clasped her tightly. As he entered the world of ecstasy he forgot the mundane world around him.

*   *   *

Chennamma was absorbed into Raja Mallasarja's household so affectionately that she did not miss her parents there at all. As she was extraordinarily fair and beautiful, Raja Mallasarja was deeply attached to her and used to call her Chennagowri affectionately. Everyday she would learn some detail or the other about the history of Kittur dynasty and their heroism. There were many things about her husband she did not know.

One afternoon, Rani Chennamma was playing chess with Rudramma, the senior wife of Raja Mallasarja. Rani Rudramma appreciated Rani Chennamma's intelligence in playing the game.

"You are so clever, my dear Chenna, that you are a worthy partner of our Raja."

Rani Chennamma felt a bit shy and said rather apologetically, "I am not an expert in this game, sister. I have yet to master this art. You must train me up in this art."

"Don't you worry, Chenna," said Rudramma, "the Raja of your heart will train you up. His love for you is boundless, you know."

Rani Chennamma blushed, but asked further, "Sister, I am longing to know some details of my Raja's past life. I have heard from hearsay that he suffered a lot in the past. Would you mind telling me some details of it?"

"Oh, that is a big story," said Rani Rudramma, "You will be simply thrilled to know the story of our Raja."

She leant against the silk pillow and began to narrate the history of Kittur rulers. Rani Chennamma also leant her face on her left palm and began to listen to it with rapt attention.

Rani Rudramma began the story leisurely, "Hiremallasetty and Chikkamallasetty were the two brave warriors serving with the Adil Shahis in the sixteenth century. They had settled down in the Sagar Desha(the present Shahapur taluka of Gulbarga District) The Adil Shais were pleased with the honesty, integrity, courage, bravery and the successful military campaigns of the two brothers and consequently granted them the Sardeshmukhi of six villages, namely Rayara Hubballi, Sampagaon, Itagi, Hunasikatti, Kadaravalli and Hirebagewadi. Almost all these villages were located in the southern part of the Malaprabha River. Besides, the elder brother, Hiremallashetty was conferred with the title of *Shamsher Jung Bahadur*. On getting the coveted Sardeshmukhi of the prestigious town of Hubballi, they migrated from Sagar Desha in 1585 and settled down at Sampagaon near Belgaum and established their traditional business of trading and money-lending. They persuaded their kith and kin to come and settle in and around. In course of time they cleared the Hongal forest into a habitable place, which was later known as Bailahongala (which means cleared forest).The fortified town of Kittur was built by Allappagowda Desai. One may be surprised to notice that it looks like a replica of the city of Basava- Kalyana. The Kittur kingdom was founded in 1585 by the benign blessings of the Swamiji of Kallumath Monastery, the first pontiff, who had come from Ulavi and who had brought to Kittur a copy of the manuscript of *Mitaksara*, a legislative text written by Vijnaneswara.   T h   e flag of Kittur known as Nandi Dwaja was a symbol of Basaveswara's philosophy as well as the main occupation of agriculture on which the masses of Kittur Kingdom depended.The *Gadada Maradi* was built on the line of *Dasara Dibba* or the *Maha Navami Dibba* of Hampi, the capital city of Vijayanagara Empire.

Our Raja Mallasarja happens to be the adopted son of Virappa Desai of Kittur throne. He hails from a relative's family of a nearby village called Bogur. He was only seventeen year old when he occupied the throne of Kittur kingdom. Before Kittur had its present name, it was called Gijaganagudu i.e. a nest of bottle-birds. Since the capital was shifted from Sampagaon to the present place, it was called Kittur, i.e. a shifted city. Hardly had three years elapsed after he assumed charge of the kingdom when he had to fight with Tippu Sultan's assistant Badrul Zamal

Khan, who tried to capture our fort at Desanur. You may not believe the fact that I also participated in that. Defeated by Raja Mallasarja, Badrul Zamal Khan went back crestfallen. But the vindictive Tippu Sultan came back again with Badrul Zamal Khan and defeated us and took our Raja as a captive. They kept him in prison at Kapaladurga near Periyapattana and fed him with only millet flour mixed with ash. Do you know his age then? He was hardly twenty. He spent nearly three years there and his health was deeply upset. And I was leading a hellish life here at Kittur. But anyway, after the lapse of those three years, Raja Mallasarja cleverly escaped from the prison and went to Coimbatore, which was under the British rule then. He disguised himself as an ordinary person and travelled from place to place, suffering in various ways. At last he reached Babaleswara in the Bijapur region, which was under the Mughals. As he was seen by my relatives there, he was given shelter by them. It is through them that he learnt the development of the kingdom of Kittur. As soon as our people here at Kittur came to hear the news of Raja Mallasarja's presence at Babaleswara, they went there and brought him here. They arranged a grand reception to him and celebrated his homecoming. Then he took the reigns of administration in his hands once again."

Tears trickled in the eyes of Rani Chennamma as she listened to the tale of her lord's suffering, and that too at such a young age. At the same time she felt proud of being his wife. "I must be worthy of the lord of my heart," decided she inwardly.

Then a maidservant came and told them, "It is time for the evening *puja* now." Rani Rudramma and Rani Chennamma got up and went towards the *puja* hall.

* * *

The fort of Kittur was very impressive. The construction of the fort, which had started in 1676 by Raja Allappagowda, was completed after 40 years in 1716 by Chikkamallappa Desai. The fort, circular in plan, consisted of double walls separated by moats on the outer sides, with semicircular bastions on the exterior of the outer wall. Originally the main gateway was on the east, approached by the causeway across the outer moat known as *Ane Honda* or Elephant Pond, which was used for bathing the elephants.

The entrances through the walls were deliberately not aligned, evidently in the interest of security. After passing by the winding path through the walls, one was led to the front side of the imposing main entrance of the palace located near the northern area of the inner fort wall. To the south of the palace inside the fort were the horse stables and residential buildings. To the southwest was the heavily built watchtower called *Bahadurgad.* The main gateway to the palace was provided with a series of guardrooms for soldiers and horsemen. The most impressive feature of the palace was the front porch, which was relieved by a series of tall structural stone pillars with a heavy stone base.

The entire palace was a masterpiece of planning. It had three storeys. The circumference of the palace measured 3,564 feet. The main porch was very imposing and measured 100 feet long and 30 feet wide. The relative positions of the sitting-cum-guest rooms, the assembly hall, the dining hall, the storerooms, the bathrooms had been so well arranged that every part could be approached without passing through the other parts. Every room was provided with two entrances, each leading to a different room, and all these providing examples of meticulous planning. The most impressive interior part of the palace was the assembly hall, which was not too large and which was meant for confidential meetings with sardars and high officials. The Hall was provided with back-rests in the adjoining walls. The dining hall could accommodate 1,000 people for dinner at one time. There were barracks, stables for horses, elephants and camels. In front of the fort people could sit and wait for their turn to have an audience with the ruler.

In the front portion of the palace, to the left side was a special room for a unique purpose. In the middle of the walls of this room was an obliquely fixed iron pipe of about one and half feet in diameter open to the sky and meant for viewing the Pole Star. In front of the pipe was a platform to sit and view the Pole Star. Perhaps such an architectural arrangement was not to be found in any other palace of the country.

More ingenious than all these was the excellent water supply system from one common source to the whole palace. In the center of the open back verandah there was a well. Water receiving bowls made of stone and water tankers on the sides and at two corners had also been kept. Adjoining the inside pack wall of the palace, water was poured from the well into these bowls from where it was carried to all the water tanks and to the well behind the kitchen by concealed copper and china pipes. Stone wash troughs had been provided at the right places in different parts of the dining hall, kitchen and other rooms.

Another interesting feature of the palace was the excellent garden provided with cisterns and fountain jets. The bricks used for the floor in the garden were of very high quality and of different shapes and sizes. The walls were only six inches thick, but incredibly strong.

The whole palace was of ashlar masonry built with hematite quart, rubble and dressed stone and strong slaked lime mortar. The pillars were also constructed with circular discs, greenish stones, placed one on another, using the same mortar as binding material. The windows and niches in the walls were so arranged as to provide sufficient light and air to the side-walls and rooms. The ashlar masonry and arched niches indicated the combination of the Muslim and the Maratha architectural styles.

On the front porch of the palace the Nandi Dwaja fluttered beautifully from the flag post. The flag had the picture of a white bull sitting in front of Iswara. In the left corner of the flag was the sun and in the right corner was the moon. The pictures of the bull and Iswara symbolized the Virasaiva faith of the rulers of Kittur kingdom. The white bull was the mount of Lord Siva of the Hindu mythology. In the real world the bull symbolized agriculture, which is the foundation of all culture.

* * *

In 1802, Raja Mallasarja saw a lot of political turbulence around his kingdom. He used to hear the news of countless clashes between the British people and the local kings and Desais.

One day Diwan Gurusiddhappa asked Raja Mallasarja, "Sarkar, the Peshwas have been quite cordial with the British since they signed the Srirangapattana Agreement in 1792. Now we have heard reports that General Wellesley is going from Srirangapattana to Pune to reinstate Bajirao Peshwa. Several estate holders along the route have been assisting Lord Wellesley with soldiers and other equipment. Should we also contribute our mite to their services just to have their goodwill?

"Raja Mallasarja thought deeply for a moment and said, "Yes, Diwan Sir, we must extend whatever little help we are capable of, to the British. It is, after all, a question of survival for us. Please see what we can spare for their help."

Diwan Gurusiddhappa said, "All right, *Sarkar* I shall send word to our Commander and enquire about other things that we can spare." He bowed to Raja Mallasarja and took his leave.

A couple of days went by. Raja Mallasarja was seated in his Durbar Hall when Diwan Gurusiddhappa bowed himself into the hall and said, "*Sarkar*, our messengers have brought news that Lord Wellesley has come near our border along with his troop. He is on his way to Pune."

Then Raja Mallasarja said, "In that case we shall go and meet him there tomorrow."

The next day Diwan Gurusiddhappa and other important members of the court followed Raja Mallasarja to the camp where General Wellesley stayed. The following morning Raja Mallasarja sent word to Lord Wellesley.

After an hour a servant came and told Raja Mallasarja, "His Excellency has permitted you to see him."

Raja Mallasarja, Diwan Gurusiddhappa and his military Commander were conducted by the servant into Lord Wellesley's chamber. Raja Mallasarja did not know enough English to converse with the British officer directly. He had, therefore, taken with him a gentleman called Rachappa, who was a bilingual translator or *dubhasi,* who could help both the parties understand each other by his two-way translation of their dialogues.

Lord Wellesley said, "We are very glad to meet you, Raja Mallasarja. Please be seated. By the way, what brings you here?"

All of them sat on their seats. Then Raja Mallasarja said in Kannada, which was translated by Rachappa into English. "We have come here just to pay our respects, Your Excellency."

Then Lord Wellesley said something in English, which was translated by the *dubhasi* into Kannada: "That's very kind of you, Raja Mallasarja of Kittur. Thank you very much."

Then Mallasarja said, "Your Excellency, we would like to offer you a little help from our side, if you don't mind."

Lord Wellesley closed his eyes for a few seconds and thought about their needs and requirements. He opened his eyes and said, "All right. We are badly in need of a building to store some of our boats and other things and also to house a hospital. We need some space for housing our soldiers etc."

Raja Mallasarja understood the needs of the British officer and thought for a while. Then he answered, "In that case, we shall give you the fort at Sangolli where you may keep your ammunition. We shall also appoint a few soldiers to guard it. My military power is very limited. Nonetheless we shall spare a hundred horses and a hundred foot soldiers."

Lord Wellesley was very pleased by the courteous gesture shown by the Raja of Kittur. His face relaxed in a smile and he said, "We are very happy to have the voluntary help and cooperation you have so kindly offered."

Meanwhile a servant brought some tiffin and tea into the chamber. "Please have some refreshment," said Lord Wellesley.

But Raja Mallasarja replied, "Kindly excuse us, Your Excellency. We thank you profusely for this hospitality. But the discipline of our Lingayat religion does not allow us to have our breakfast until we have had our bath and *puja*. Kindly don't misunderstand us."

"Oh, is that so? I'll not force you at all, if it is against your religion," said Lord Wellesley.

He beckoned to the servant, who took back the tray of tiffin, tea-kettles and cups. A few minutes passed in silence.

Then Lord Wellesley said, "You are under the Peshwa dominion, aren't you?"

Raja Mallasarja replied immediately, "Yes, Your Excellency. We are quite independent, but we have been giving an annuity of Rs. 60,000 every year to the Peshwas.

But we would like to have our autonomy as usual. Your Excellency must help us."

Lord Wellesley understood the subtle problem and said, "Don't you worry Raja Mallasarja, we'll see that you enjoy the autonomy of a tributary prince in future. We shall speak to Bajirao about this when we meet him next."

"Thank you very much, Your Excellency. Now kindly allow us to take leave of you," said Raja Mallasarja.

"Thank you, Raja Mallasarja," said Lord Wellesley.

Then Raja Mallasarja, Diwan Gurusiddhappa and his companions stood up and walked out of the Governor-General's chamber. The same afternoon they returned to Kittur.

The very next day the Commander sent a hundred horses and a hundred native soldiers to Lord Wellesley's camp where they were received with thanks by the officer in charge. Raja Mallasarja and his officers were very happy to remember that they had earned the goodwill of the British authorities in the country.

*   *   *

In 1804, Bajirao Peshwa felt rather uneasy when some brahmins of Kittur explained to him about the growing popularity of Raja Mallasarja. These brahmins had gone all the way from Kittur to Pune to slander the Raja of Kittur.

"*Sarkar*, said one of the brahmins, "the Raja of Kittur has been growing more and more arrogant these days. He has been mobilizing opinion of the neighboring Chiefs, Kings and Desais. One day he might even think of rebelling against you. It is better to nip him in the bud."

"Yes, yes, Sarkar," said another brahmin, "What my friend says is true. The Raja of Kittur is very diplomatic also. He has been maintaining very good relationship with the British authorities as well. Who knows one day he might betray you, I mean, us to the *firangis* and weaken our strength."

Bajirao Peshwa listened to the words of the brahmins of Kittur patiently and seemed to agree with their opinion as they belonged to his own community. He thought there must be some truth in what they said.

He said, "There is an element of truth in what you say. I have heard a lot about the king of Kittur. He seems to be very popular and dynamic."

"We only tried to alert you, Sarkar. Please don't mistake us as slanderers. Because of our community feeling, we took the liberty of supplying intelligence to you," said the senior brahmin.

"Don't you worry, friends. We are indeed very thankful to you for alerting us at the right time," said Bajirao Peshwa and sent them back with handful of gold coins and other gifts.

Bajirao Peshwa knew in the heart of his heart that Raja Mallasarja was a very bold but well-mannered king in the south. Yet he grew alert about the possibility of some danger from Raja Mallasarja in the near or distant future. He began to imagine that Raja Mallasarja might be a potential future enemy. He called his Diwan and other officers and consulted them about Mallasarja. After the secret meeting and mutual consultation, he decided to write a letter to Lord Wellesley to dethrone Raja Mallasarja by canceling the autonomy of the kingdom of Kittur.

Accordingly he dictated a letter to his clerk and handed it over to a messenger. The messenger kept the letter safe in his cloth bag and rode his horse towards Calcutta and relayed the letter to the next messenger going to Calcutta. Finally the letter was delivered to Lord Wellesley. Bajirao Peshwa and his courtiers waited eagerly for the reply from the Governor-General of India.

Nearly a weak elapsed. At last a messenger returned from Calcutta and handed over a letter to the Diwan of Bajirao Peshwa and withdrew from the court-hall.

Bajirao said to the Diwan, "See, how prompt is the Governor-General in replying to our letter. Let's see how he plans to dethrone the Desai of Kittur. Please open the sealed letter and have it read out."

The Diwan took out the letter and saw that the letter was written in English. A translator who understood both English and Marathi read out the contents of the letter. After hastening through the epistolary formalities, the *dubhasi* came to read out the main portion of the letter:

> "… I beg leave to deprecate a contest with him (the Raja of Kittur), excepting in case of very evident necessity in which the whole force of the Government can be employed. Like Wynad, Coorg, Ballum, Bendur and Soonda, Kittur is situated in, and immediately to, the eastward of the range of Western Ghats. It is, equally with them, difficult for troops; it is inhabited by a similar race of people and the operations of war in it would possibly be attended with the same losses and disasters… The country is situated on

a defenseless point of the Company's frontier. The fort of Haliyal has no garrison because I have been obliged to draw the troop from there to complete the corps at Goa; and the possession of that fort would give the Raja of Kittur a secure communication and entrance into Canara and Bidnur, both provinces entirely defenseless; and the former, upon the resources of which Bombay, Poona and the army, depend entirely for subsistence... These facts, however well-founded, are not known and point out clearly the necessity of avoiding to attempt to dispossess the Raja of Kittur of his country till adequate means can be found to insure the object and to guard against the Desai of annoying us which he has in his power."

When the translator explained the contents of the letter in Marathi, Bajirao and his Diwan grew pale with disappointment and looked at each other helplessly.

Then Bajirao consoled himself by saying, "Let's teach him a lesson at the proper time and keep him under our thumb. Now let us keep quiet for some time." The Diwan also added to it, "Let us wait for the right time. Until then we cannot do anything."

Then they dispersed.

* * *

It was in the year 1809 when Bajirao Peshwa realized the essential goodness of Raja Mallasarja. He was forced to revise his opinion about Mallasarja because of Lord

Wellesley's good opinion about him. He, therefore, sent word to Raja Mallasarja for an agreement. Raja Mallasarja accordingly went to Pune along with his Diwan, commander and other important officers.

The meeting was held in a big a hall. The officers of Kittur and those of Bajirao were working out the details of revenue, land and property. Raja Mallasarja saw the rough draft of the agreement.

At last the Diwan of Bajirao Peshwa stood up and read out the agreement: "In accordance with the agreement between His Highness Bajirao Peshwa of Pune and Raja Mallasarja of Kittur, the latter is allowed to enjoy the freedom and full autonomy for his kingdom on condition that he would pay to the former an amount of one lakh seventy thousand rupees every year. He should be loyal to the Peshwa."

Then the Diwan of Kittur stood up and read out the answer part of the agreement: "Raja Mallasarja of Kittur has agreed to pay an amount of one lakh seventy thousand rupees every year to His Highness Bajirao Peshwa of Pune for the enjoyment of full autonomy of Kittur kingdom."

Then both Bajirao and Mallasarja signed the documents and exchanged them. The respective secretaries took the agreement papers and kept them in sturdy boxes safely.

In the evening all the courtiers gathered in the court hall. His Highness Bajirao sat on the golden throne. The court musicians with turbans on their heads sang a devotional song to the accompaniment of *mridanga*, *shahnai* and *sarangi*. When the singing was over, everybody clapped in appreciation. Then the Diwan of Peshwa Kingdom stood up and announced, "Gentlemen, we have gathered here to honour Raja Mallasarja of Kittur. Bajirao Sarkar and his courtiers remember with gratitude the help and co-operation extended to us by Raja Mallasarja in defeating Tippu Sultan of Srirangapattana in 1781. He showed extra-ordinary cleverness in escaping from the prison of Kapaladurga. Besides he is a very able administrator of his kingdom. In recognition of his valour, cleverness and ability Bajirao Sarkar is pleased to confer the title of 'Pratap Rao' on Raja Mallasarja. He handed over the scroll to His Highness Bajirao who held it up for the audience to see. The citation was written in Modi script. Raja Mallasarja walked up to the throne and received the scroll of honour from His Highness Bajirao. Then His Highness presented a sword to Raja Mallasarja. The entire audience clapped in appreciation.

* * *

Raja Mallasarja returned to Kittur with his officers. Rani Rudramma and Rani Chennamma received him with great pride and admiration. They waved *arati* around his face and dotted his forehead with vermillion mark. That evening they arranged a special *puja* in the palace temple. They invited a few *jangamas* and offered them a special feast. The *jangamas* were satisfied with the special feast and treatment, and blessed the royal household and wished great prosperity for Raja Mallasarja.

The next morning, Raja Mallasarja sent for Diwan Gurusiddhappa, who came forthwith and saluted him formally.

"What's the royal order, Sarkar?" asked Gurusiddhappa.

"Diwan Sir, I am thinking of commemorating the title 'Pratap Rao' conferred upon me. I would like to have a fort erected at Nandagad. We can name it as Pratapagad Fort. What's your opinion?"

"It is a very good idea, Sarkar. Anyway we need a fort there at Nandagad, which is our international trade centre. We entertain the merchants from Arabia and Europe via Goa. This centre should be protected against looting by vandals and robbers. We need a garrison against Eurasia through the Western Ghats. This is a very good proposal. Shall I make arrangements for the construction?" asked Diwan Gurusiddhappa.

"Please do it tomorrow itself. But before that call in a few expert engineers to prepare a plan and see that the fort should be as strong as beautiful."

"Sarkar, I shall arrange for every thing tomorrow itself."

The Diwan look his leave and returned home.

*   *   *

Around 1810 Raja Mallasarja had reached the height of popularity not only in his own kingdom but also in the neighbouring ones. He was a great patron of all kinds of arts, literature and scholarship. Every evening he used to attend the musical concerts, dances or poetry recitation.

One evening when the audience had gathered in the Durbar Hall, a court poet, Amriteswara was to read his newly composed poem.

Raja Mallasarja sat on his throne with his usual grace and dignity. The two maid-servants, who stood on both sides, were leisurely fanning him with peacock-feather fans. Rani Rudramma and Rani Chennamma sat on their seats in the enclosure covered with a thin muslin curtain. The audience was eager to listen to the poet's recitation of a new poem.

Diwan Gurusiddhappa, who sat a little below the King, stood up and started the function with a wave of his right hand. Then Amriteswara clad in a white dhoti, and a shirt with a beautiful turban on his head stepped up to the throne and bowed down to the Raja with joined palms. Then he shuffled back to the seat and sat on it.

He said in a stylized fashion, "Victory to Raja Mallasarja," and opened the bundle of manuscript leaves. He said in an elevated tone, "Brothers and sisters, I have composed this narrative poem glorifying the greatness of our beloved Raja Mallasarja. That is the reason why I have entitled it as *Mallendra Manasollasa Mallatarangini.* I have composed it in medieval Kannada. I have done only a squirrel's service to the glorification of our beloved master. Now please listen to me carefully and patiently."

He, then, began to recite his poem in a sing-song *gamaka* style. As his recitation progressed, a pin drop silence fell upon the audience, who felt as if they were transported to the heavenly world. The other court poets and artists like Kolli Rangacharya, Vengi Chennabasappa, Kasiraja, Vararudrakavi, Nilakantharya, Magundi Basava, Sivalingasastry and Rudragowda, who understood the stylistic features, the beauty of imagery and the mellifluent language better than the other members of the audience, were nodding their heads and waving their hands with a flourish in appreciation of his recital of poetry. Occasionally Diwan Gurusiddhappa would look

at Raja Mallasarja's face and notice that he was beaming
with satisfaction. Rani Rudramma and Rani Chennamma,
who were rapt in listening to the poetry, were swelling
and beaming with pride and satisfaction .The souls of all
the listeners appeared to be cloyed with the ambrosial
sweetness of Amriteswara's poetry.

It went on and on for nearly two hours. Finally
Amriteswara concluded his recitation with a prayer
beginning with 'victory to Raja Mallasarja.' The Raja,
the Diwan, the officers and other members of the audience
clapped loudly in appreciation of the poet's talent.

Raja Mallasarja slowly returned to the mundane world
from that of poetic ecstasy. He relaxed with a smile and
said, "Our dear poet-laureate Amriteswara, today you have
filled my heart with great satisfaction. You have described
every important event of my life and my kingdom. I am
really proud of having such an extra-ordinary poet in my
court. You have made me immortal in your poem."

In answer to Raja Mallasarja's appreciation,
Amriteswara said, "*Sarkar,* today is indeed the crown
and glory of my poetic career, because my hard work
of several years has borne fruit today. There is nothing
greater for me than your heart-felt appreciation."

He bowed down to the Raja once again reverentially
joining his palms.

Then Raja Mallasarja said to Gurusiddhappa, "Diwan,
Sir, please arrange for special gifts to our poet-laureate."

The Diwan beckoned to the servants. Within a few
moments a maid-servant walked gracefully towards
the Diwan and handed over the tray with gold coins
and ornaments. Diwan Gurusiddhappa took the tray to

Raja Mallasarja, who touched it with his hands. Then the maid-servant took the tray from the Raja and held it before Gurusiddhappa who took up the gold necklace and garlanded Amriteswara and slipped a gold bracelet around his right wrist. Then he took the silver plate with betel leaves, coconut and a purse of gold coins and handed it over to Amriteswara. Tears of happiness were trickling down the cheeks of the poet. He bowed once again to Raja Mallasarja and shuffled back to his seat.

* * *

The junior Madivalaswami happened to be five years younger than Prince Sivalingarudrasarja. Both of them were classmates studying under the tutelage of Vengi Channabasavasastri and Kolli Rangacharya. Madivalaswami made rapid progress in his studies and precociously become an expert in the *Vedanta*. That was the reason why he had become a darling of H.H. Prabhuswami and Raja Mallasarja. Prince Sivabasavasarja liked him for his sharp intelligence, but Prince Sivalingarudrasarja disliked him because of jealousy. Madivalaswami also developed miraculous powers at a very young age. Even Sri Chidambara Diksita of Gurlahosur, who was about forty years senior to him, was attracted by his occult powers. H.H.Prabhuswami ordained Madivalaswami according to Virasaiva custom when the latter was hardly eight-years-old.

Boy Madivalaswami never used to go to the palace along with H.H.Prabhuswami on account of Bapusaheb's (alias Sivalingarudrasarja) jealousy. But one day he volunteered to accompany him, who was going to the palace. His Holiness Prabhuswami felt very happy about it and took the boy with him. When both of them reached the palace, the doors were opened to H.H.Prabhuswami but closed to Madivalaswami. Hence Madivalaswami had to wait outside the palace. The holy man went ahead into the palace thinking that Madivala was following him.

He washed his hands, face and feet in the palace and sat on the seat. Raja Mallasarja offered worship to his holy feet with great pomp and received the holy water from him. Then he suddenly remembered Madivalaswami and asked the people around him to fetch the holy boy. But there was no proper response. He was exasperated beyond measure by this event.

He got up from the seat and burst out, "What an insult is this, Majesty? In fact, the boy was not willing to come here as he was fed up with Bapusaheb's machination against him. But he was persuaded to come here by your Ranis. This is the reception given to him. Some evil must be awaiting your brainless Bapusaheb. When you don't want the disciple, why then do you want the guru? I must be going away now. Never shall I step into your palace."

Deeply irritated and upset, he walked away from there briskly and reached the main-gate of the fort. He crossed the gate and saw the boy waiting for his guru there itself. Madivalaswami understood the cause of his guru's anger and tried to console him.

"Reverend Sir, I could not enter the fort because Bapusaheb ordered the main gate to be closed when he saw me. He is also one of the actors in the Cosmic Drama." In fact it is not Bapusahab's duty to have the gates closed... But this act indicates the future of the kingdom. The *punya* of Kittur kingdom must be coming to an end. The closing of the main gate of the fort might be symbolic of that. As Lord Krisna says in the *Bhagavd Gita* all these people are already destroyed or going to be destroyed shortly. We have to remain as witnesses to all these events." H.H.Prabhuswami's anger was lessened by the prophetic words of the precocious disciple Madivalaswami. Then both of them walked slowly towards the monastery.

* * *

Raja Mallasarja felt deeply sad about the unfortunate event. From that day the regular worship of the guru's holy feet was automatically stopped in the palace. Raja Mallasarja called a confidential meeting of Rani Chennamma, relatives, the Diwan and other officers. Everybody looked serious. They gathered and sat in silence.

The Raja with a serious look on his face said, "My dear ladies and gentlemen, I had not thought that the matter would become so serious. It is very unfortunate that the holy worship of the royal guru has been stopped so unexpectedly. Firstly, our reverend guru's anger culminated in a curse on us. Secondly, we insulted the junior pontiff, Madivalaswami. Thirdly, Rani Chennamma's vow of receiving grace and *prasada* from the guru every day has been terminated abruptly. Fourthly, our whole kingdom is put to shame on account of Bapusaheb's mischief. And fifthly... fifthly....," Raja Mallasarja could not continue his talk and remained confusedly silent.

Everybody who had gathered there was frightened by Raja Mallasarja's ominous silence. All of them deliberated and finally decided to seek shelter at the guru's feet.

Raja Mallasarja, therefore, went to the monastery with all his family and retinue. Having sought the prior permission of His Holiness Prabhuswami, they entered the central hall of the Kallumath Monastery and bowed down to his feet individually.

Raja Mallasarja stood in a humble posture and requested the Pontiff, "Your Holiness, our young son Bapusaheb is an ignoramus who knows not the values of life. He has committed the sin in his crass ignorance. Because of his foolishness, we have all been suffering. Your Holiness, we bow down to your feet and request you to forgive us and grace the palace with your regular visits and worships. We cannot afford to live without the Guru's grace."

Raja Mallasarja bowed down to His Holiness's feet and stood waiting for the latter's response.

His Holiness thought about the predicament of the royal family and commiserated with them inwardly. But he said, "My dear Raja, I cannot take back the word that I have uttered once. It is not becoming of the guru or his word if I did so. But at the same time I wish that your religious rituals should take place regularly in the palace. Please suggest some alternative plan if there is any. I also shall think about such a plan."

Everybody thought about the problem for a long time but could not get a solution to it. His Holiness sat silently with his eyes closed for a while. There was an embarrassing silence. Finally he opened his eyes and offered a suggestion.

"My dear Raja, you may arrange for the construction of an underground passage from our monastery to your palace. We shall send the holy *tirtha* and *prasada* to the palace every day through the passage. Please tell me if you have a better plan. Otherwise you have no choice except this."

Raja Mallasarja now could not dare contradict or disobey His Holiness Prabhuswami. He said, "All right, Your Holiness, I shall instantly arrange for the construction of an underground passage as ordered by Your Holiness. May your blessings be on the palace for ever!"

He bowed down to the holy feet of the Pontiff. Others followed suit. Then all of them returned to the palace with a sense of satisfaction.

In course of time Raja Mallasarja got the underground passage from the monastery to the palace constructed. From then onwards the members of the royal family began to get the holy *tirtha* and *prasada* from His Holiness Prabhuswami every day and felt a sense of relief. But they were unfortunate to have missed the opportunity of receiving His Holiness at their palace. Both Raja Mallasarja and Rani Chennamma worried about it secretly and thought it to be a bad omen perhaps indicating the future degeneration of the Kingdom.

*   *   *

Bajirao Peshwa had arranged a sojourn to the southern part of India. He had come with all his entourage of infantry and cavalry. After visiting the places of his choice he felt like having the *darsan* of Lord Kartikeya, the famous deity situated at Sandur. He, therefore, ascended the high hill along the narrow serpentine path and reached the relatively level ground on the elevated spot where the temple of Lord Kartikeya stood. The brass crown of the temple glittered in the sunlight. He was followed by a limited number of officers and soldiers.

As soon as the priests of the temple heard about the arrival of Bajirao Peshwa, they grew very busy and alert, and began to attend to their duty with a greater attention.

Then Bajirao washed his hands, face and feet in the water available at the fount outside the temple, entered the compound, walked up to the *sanctum sanctorum* and saw the beautiful idol of Lord Kartikeswara carved in bluish-black stone. The smooth curves of the limbs of the idol gave him an impression that it was made of black butter as it were. The deity was perching on his beautiful vehicle, the peacock. There was an inexplicable serenity on his face.

Bajirao joined his palms in reverence to the deity and mentally prayed to Him. He then asked the priest to offer a special *puja* to Lord Kartikeya on his behalf. Accordingly the priest arranged for a special service to the deity. The deity was washed clean once again and decked with vermillion dots, marks of *vibhuti,* and several flowers and garlands. A big bowl of incense was burned and the whole temple was filled with the aromatic smell of the wafting smoke of incense. The priest tinkled and clangoured different kinds of bells, broke open eleven coconuts and offered the consecrated food to the deity. Bajirao once again saluted the deity with joined palms.

Later he arranged for a special feeding of all the brahmins gathered there and gave away gifts of silver and gold to them munificently. He donated one lakh *varahas* for replacing the brass crown by a golden crown on the spire of the temple. He had a sense of fulfillment after having the *darsan* of Lord Kartikeswara.

Then he descended the hill slowly, joined his large army and resumed his northward journey. He travelled nearly five hundred miles by crossing the undulating land with rocky hills and green valleys. He passed through Gudur, Kampli, Hosapete, Bagilukote and Gurlahosur. He used to send for his subordinate chiefs and Desais, who would rush to meet him to pay homage and lavish gifts on him.

When he reached Bailahongala, he remembered Raja Mallasarja. He camped there and sent out his spies to collect intelligence about him. Accordingly the spies went around in the region, mingled with people and enquired about Raja Mallasarja and his administration. Then they returned to Bajirao and told him privately that Raja Mallasarja was a very popular king whose subjects enjoyed the peace and richness of their country and therefore, sang about his glory and magnanimity.

When Bajirao heard this secret information, he felt pangs of jealousy towards Mallasarja Desai who would not be dethroned easily.

Allappagowda Desai of Shegunashi was feeling very restless and angry with Raja Mallasarja, who had refused to adopt the former's son for the kingdom of Kittur. He wanted to take revenge against Raja Mallasarja at the appropriate time. Now when he heard the news that

Bajirao Peshwa had camped near his place, he thought it a golden opportunity to exploit the situation and vanquish Mallasarja Desai.

That day Bajirao had finished his breakfast and was relaxing in his tent at Bailahongala. Allappagowda Desai went to Bailahongala and sent word to Bajirao about his desire to have an interview with him.

The guard went into the tent, informed Bajirao about it and came out and said, "You may meet the *Sarkar* inside the tent, Sir."

Allappagowda entered the tent and saluted Bajirao with joined palms and sat in the chair directed by the Peshwa lord.

"Sarkar, perhaps you don't know me personally. I am Allappagowda and hail from a village called Shegunashi. I came here just to pay my homage to you, Sarkar."

Bajirao Peshwa said, "I am very glad to meet you, Allappagowda. By the way, how is Mallasarja Desai faring in this area?"

Allappagowda, who was waiting for such an excellent opportunity, assumed a posture of mock humility, lowered his tone to a very confidential whisper and said,

"What to say about Mallasarja Desai, my lord! He has been growing more and more popular and powerful day by day. If he grows so powerful, that too so fast then, I am afraid, one day he might defy your lordship also, Sarkar."

Bajirao Peshwa listened to his words patiently and counter-questioned him,

"Do you really mean what you say or is it just a guess work?"

Allappagowda felt disconcerted by the direct question. Yet he composed himself and replied hypocritically, "No, Sarkar, I am stating the facts very plainly. I have no ulterior motives in giving you this piece of information, because I am a very honest man."

"I am very thankful to you for this information, which perfectly agrees with the intelligence that I have received from my spies," said Bajirao.

"I have only done my humble duty, Sarkar, and nothing else. I am a very honest man," said Allappagowda.

"We are very thankful to you, Allappagowda, for this information. Please keep us informed about these things. We will reward you amply for the service. Today itself I shall send a messenger to Mallasarja Desai to come and meet me here," said Bajirao thankfully. "All right, Sarkar, I shall return to Shegunashi," said Allappagowda and greeted Bajirao once again before taking his leave.

Bajirao's jealousy of Mallasarja Desai was aggravated by Allappagowda's malicious interpretation of Mallasarja's popularity. Being prejudiced against Mallasarja without sufficient evidence, he decided to trouble Raja Mallasarja systematically, thereby forestalling even the distant possibility of rebellion against himself. Raja Mallasarja remained blissfully ignorant of all these conspiracies against him, and immersed himself in the betterment activities in his kingdom.

* * *

Saidansab of Amatur, who wore a goatee and a fez cap, walked up to the Diwan's home and requested the guards, who stood with swords slung on their left sides, to admit him into the Diwan's chamber. One of the guards went in and came back within a few minutes. He beckoned to Saidansab to enter the chamber.

Saidansab stepped into the chamber and bowed down to Diwan Gurusiddhappa, "*Salam* Sarkar."

"Oh Saidansab, how are you? What brings you here?"

Saidansab clasped his fingers in front of him reverentially and said, "Sarkar, I have been trying to renovate the mosque in our Kittur. I request you to recommend my case to Raja Sarkar and help me get some grant from him."

Diwan Gurusiddhappa listened to him patiently and knit his brows a little. Then he said,

"Look here, Saidansab, I cannot force Raja Sarkar in this matter. But I shall definitely bring it to his notice and let you know what he says."

"Kindly help me Sarkar," said Saidansab and bowed down to the Diwan once again went out the chamber.

Next day when the Durbar met in the evening, Diwan Gurusiddhappa brought Saidansab's request to the notice of Raja Mallasarja. But Karbhari Mallappasetty and Venkatarao opposed it vehemently. Though Raja Mallasarja was faourably disposed to Saidansab, he had to keep quiet because of the strong opposition from his own officers.

Two days went by. Again Saidansab went to Diwan Gurusiddhappa and bowed down to him and asked him,

"What happened to my request, Sarkar?"

Diwan Gurusiddhappa said in a drawn-out tone, "See, Saidansab, I brought your request to Raja Sarkar's notice, but he is preoccupied with other matters of the kingdom now. Therefore, I did not press him much. You may try some other time."

Saidansab grew pale and did not know what to do. He said,

"All right, Sarkar, I shall try once again." He saluted the Diwan and took his leave. Later Diwan Gurusiddhappa brought the matter to the notice of Rani Chennamma.

Saidansab could not sleep at all that night. For, he was bent upon renovating the mosque, which was dilapidating day by day. In the early morning when he heard the muezzin's call, he got up and went to the mosque for prayer. While returning from the early Morning Prayer, a new idea flashed across his mind.

"Why not meet Rani Chennamma who is like a mother?" thought he.

He returned home and had his breakfast of *roti* and boiled eggs. Then he donned a clean dhoti, shirt and fez cap. He combed his goatee properly and walked up to the gynaeceum, where Rani Chennamma used to reside. He told the guard about his desire to meet the revered Rani. The guard went in and came out within a couple of minutes. He beckoned to Saidansab to go in. Saidansab walked in gently and saw Rani Chennamma reclining against the pillow. She welcomed him with affectionate smile. The triple mark of *vibhuti* on her forehead with a vermilion dot in the middle looked very beautiful against her fair complexion. Saidansab felt for a moment as if he was in the presence of Goddess Lakshmi, he greeted her reverentially.

"Come on, Saidansab. How are you? Is everything all right?" asked Rani Chennamma.

"Everything is all right, Rani Sarkar," he said and scratched the back of his head.

"What brings you here? Is there anything you want?" she asked.

"Rani Sarkar, I have come to beg you for a small favour."

"Is that so? Let me know what it is," she with dignified ease.

"Rani Sarkar, I want to repair the mosque, which is crumbling down day by day. I wanted some help for that from the Sarkar."

"Did you approach Diwan Gurusiddhappa or Mallappasetty in this regard?" asked Rani Chennamma. "Yes, Rani Sarkar, but some how they are not showing any interest in it. Therefore I was rather disappointed. At last I thought of approaching you," said Saidansab reverentially.

Rani Chennamma sent for Karbhari Mallappasetty, Venkatarao and Diwan Gurusiddhappa. When all of them entered her chamber and took their seats, Rani Chennamma asked Mallappasetty,

"See, our Saidansab says that their mosque had crumbled down completely. There are many Mussalmans living in our kingdom. Do they not need a mosque for their daily prayers? Have you not granted money from the royal treasury for the construction of Hindu temples? Mussalmans are also the subjects of our kingdom. Our unwillingness to help them will be tantamount to grave injustice."

Mallappasetty reacted to her words very strongly,

"Rani Sarkar, I think that helping the Mussalmans will be like helping the enemies. Mussalmans have always been the enemies of Hindus. Don't you remember how much our Hindus have been tortured by them in the past? Though they have been living in our country for so many centuries, they have never shown any love for Hindus, but always nourished hatred and animosity towards us. Rani Sarkar, you have not seen how much Tippu Sultan tortured us in the past, before your arrival here."

Venkatarao continued, "Rani Sarkar, Mussalmans are a great threat to our country. Helping them will be as futile as feeding a snake with milk."

Rani Chennamma listened to their argument quite patiently. Then she said very seriously,

"What you say may be true politically. But the present case is not a political one. Saidansab happens to be a subject of our kingdom. He is asking for some help for the renovation of the mosque. He is not asking for any personal favour. We cannot generalize from a few isolated cases and hate the entire community of Mussalmans."

Mallappasetty said, "Rani Sarkar, whatever you may say, it is simply not agreeable to us."

Then Venkatarao reacted wildly, "Rani Sarkar, you may grant any amount to Saidansab because the treasury is yours. Why should we serve in the court if you take arbitrary decisions like this?"

Listening to their words of opposition, Saidansab began to shed tears. Diwan Gurusiddhappa heaved a deep sigh rather helplessly.

Rani Chennamma was silent for a few seconds and then assured, "Don't you worry Saidansab. God is one and the same, although He is worshipped in temples, *basadis* or mosques with different names. I shall help you rebuild your mosque. I shall give you ten thousand rupees from my privy purse. You start the work immediately."

Mallappasetty and Venkatarao were surprised beyond measure by Rani Chennamma's decision. Since they had no right to talk about her personal purse, they took their leave from there after saluting her. But yet they were happy to know that their plan had been successful as they stuck to their views.

Diwan Gurusiddhappa felt quite satisfied by the Rani's decision. Saidansab was so thrilled that his eyes were bedewed with tears.

Rani Chennamma said, "Wait for a little while," and went into her inner chamber. Then she came back with a cloth purse jingling with gold coins. She gave it to Saidansab.

"You start the work tomorrow itself. Come to me again if you need more," said she.

Saidansab felt a lump in his throat and stammered, "You are like a mother to all of us." He bowed to her once again and walked out of her chamber with the purse bulging with coins.

*   *   *

Raja Mallasarja sat on his throne in the Durbar Hall along with his Diwan and other officers. The maid-servants were fanning him with peacock-feathered fans.

He said to them, "Gentlemen, Bajirao Peshwa visited the Temple of Lord Kartikeya at Sandur hill recently and is on his way back home. He has sent word through his messenger that I should go and meet him. But somehow, I don't feel like going there. I learn through my spies that a few Desais of the surrounding princely states including our arch enemy, Allappagowda Desai of Shegunashi have carried tales to Bajirao Peshwa against us."

Mallappasetty stood up and said, "Sarkar, in that case, you must go and meet Bajirao Peshwa to clear the misunderstanding."

Raja Mallasarja asked, "What happens if I don't see him at all?"

"No, Sarkar," said Venkatarao, "it doesn't look nice for you to ignore Bajirao Peshwa especially when he has sent for you."

"Sarkar," said Sivabasappa, "You must remove the poison from the mind of Bajirao Peshwa injected by Allappagowda and others."

"What's your opinion, Diwan Sir?" asked Raja Mallasarja.

Gurusiddhappa stood up and suggested, "Sarkar, what I feel is that you should wait until Bajirao Peshwa reaches Pune and then you may go and meet him at Pune itself."

"But," said Mallappasetty, "that will not be appropriate. It is better to go and meet him here at the camp itself rather than go all the way to Pune to do so."

Sivabasappa also stood up and said, "Sarkar, there is nothing wrong in meeting Bajirao at his camp."

"I am also of the same opinion, Sarkar," said Venkatarao.

Raja Mallasarja listened to their opinions patiently and finally said, "If all of you feel that I should meet Bajirao Peshwa at the camp, I'll do so."

* * *

Raja Mallasarja entered the Queen's quarters with a pale face. Rani Chennamma welcomed him with a cheerful smile. Mallasarja clasped her and planted a few kisses upon her cheeks. She then led him to the bed and sat beside him.

She stared at him for a moment and asked him, "Why are you looking so pale today, my lord? Is their any problem?"

Mallasarja smiled wanly and said, "My darling, a king's life is not a bed of roses."

"I know that," she said, "but what exactly is the matter?"

He grew a bit serious and said, "Darling, Bajirao Peshwa has come and camped near Bailahongala and sent word to me to see him. Left to myself I have no desire to see him. But the members of our court have opined that I must go and see him. They say that I must meet him and clarify certain doubts in his mind, which is poisoned by other Desais of neighboring states, especially by my arch enemy Allappagowda of Shegunashi."

She listened to him attentively and said, "My lord, why do you worry for this? We shall all accompany you. The entire family can go with you."

"No, dear Chenna," he said,, "first of all, Bajirao Peshwa is an arrogant king who has been growing more and more jealous of me. He may not relish my going to meet him with all the pomp and glory. I think, it is better for me to go there with a limited entourage."

"Should I also not come with you, my lord?" she asked.

"You better stay back, my darling," he said. "Don't you remember that Saidansab has been renovating the mosque mainly because of your encouragement? Besides, mother Nilamma would feel lonely if you come along with me."

Chennamma grew pale and realized her responsibility. "In that case, I'll not go with you, my lord, but you should return at the earliest."

"All right, darling. How can I stay away from you for long?" he said and clasped her in his arms once again.

The next day he set out on his journey towards Edur with a limited entourage in order to pay his homage to Bajirao Peshwa. Rani Chennamma arranged special *pujas* in all the temples of Kittur in order to wish him good luck in his journey.

*　*　*

A week elapsed since Raja Mallasarja had left for Edur. But no news about him was received by anybody. The courtiers and the laity grew more and more anxious about their king. Diwan Gurusiddhappa was tired of answering queries from the public.

"I am as ignorant about Sarkar's whereabouts as you are," he would reply to the civilians of Kittur. Rani Rudramma grew very anxious and gave up her food. When the womenfolk of the royal household pressed her for food, she would reply, "No, I'll not have any food or water until I see the face of my lord."

The maid-servants could not dare force her any further.

Rani Chennamma was also deeply disturbed and could not sleep properly at night. She sent for Diwan Gurusiddhappa. He rushed to the palace and entered her chamber and greeted her with joined palms.

"Why did Rani Sarkar send for me?" asked he.

"Diwan Sir, our sarkar left Kittur last week, but so far we have received no news about him," she said.

"I am also deeply worried about it, Rani Sarkar," he replied.

"The elder queen has given up her food and water. I also cannot console her, as I am myself deeply worried about my lord. I have been seeing very bad dreams nowadays," she said.

"I understand your anxiety," said Gurusiddhappa, "I am no less anxious. If you permit me, I shall make a trip to Edur myself and find out the truth."

"Diwan sir, you'll attain a lot of *punya* if you do that. We shall be very grateful to you for this courtesy," she said.

"Don't worry, Rani Sarkar. I shall leave for Edur tomorrow itself and return with Raja sarkar," assured Gurusiddhappa.

He bowed down to her once again and took his leave.

The next morning Diwan Gurusiddhappa left for Edur along with a few soldiers. They whipped their horses so fiercely that the animals began to race and cover vast distances within minimum time. While he was on his way, he learnt from some travellers that Allappagowda of Shegunashi had died of goitre on the way back to his village.

Rani Rudramma and Rani Chennamma were languishing in Kittur and were longing for the news of Raja Mallasarja. Four days went by like this in mere anticipation. On the fifth day a messenger returned from Pune and handed over a letter to Rani Chennamma and walked out of the chamber. As she pored her eyes upon the letter she felt as if she was struck by lightning. She could not speak as she felt a lump in her throat. Her eyes brimmed with tears. She covered her mouth with the hem of her sari and began to sob. But soon her practical sense awakened. She wiped her eyes and sent for the women folk of the household, Prince Sivalingarudrasarja and the members of the court. When all of them rushed to her chamber, she handed over the letter to Mallappasetty who took it up and read it aloud:

"Unto the royal presence of Rani Sarkar are due the salutations of Gurusiddhappa. I would like to bring the following things to the notice of Rani Sarkar. When I left Kittur and reached Edur, I discovered to my surprise that Raja Mallasarja had left Edur for Pune following Bajirao Peshwa, who had left a message for him to do so. In order to confirm everything I continued my journey to Pune. When finally I reached there, I was shocked out of my wits to know that Raja Mallasarja had been arrested and kept in prison in Mudholkar Wada as a result of the enemies' slander against him. I felt very sad. Therefore I desperately sought audience with Bajirao and explained every thing to him. After having all his doubts cleared Bajirao

Peshwa confessed his mistake and agreed to release Raja Mallasarja Sarkar on condition that we agreed to sign a treaty with him. According to that, the Peshwas would keep their army in Kittur for our protection and we must bear all the expenses of its maintenance. These terms were so humiliating for us that I did not agree for that. At last, I agreed to the condition that we should pay 1,75,000/- rupees as revenue to the Peshwa. This I did only to release our Mallasarja Sarkar from prison.

"When I asked our Sarkar why Bajirao Peshwa had treated him so badly he gave me several details one of which was very insignificant from our Sarkar's point of view, but taken very seriously by Bajirao Peshwa. It is briefly like this: Once Bajirao Peshwa had called a meeting of all the subordinate princes in his *Shanivara Wada* for breakfast. The invitation was, of course, extended to Raja Mallasarja also. But Mallasarja Sarkar, who is a staunch Virasaiva, refused to partake of breakfast offered by Bajirao Peshwa who happened to be a *bhavi* according to Virasaiva point of view. When this opinion was conveyed to Bajirao Peshwa, his brahmanical ego was deeply hurt and he, therefore, wished to take revenge upon our Mallasarja Sarkar by humiliating him personally and financially. It was only when I explained the matter in a pleasing manner that Bajirao softened up and agreed to release him on condition that we would pay an annual tribute of

1,75,000 rupees. The other details I shall convey in person.

"Kindly note that Mallasarja Sarkar's health was already bad enough when we left Pune. We requested him to lie down in the palanquin provided by the Peshwa and brought him towards the south slowly so that he should not feel any strain. As we came near Edur, Mallasarja Sarkar called me and expressed his desire of having the *darsan* of the famous family deity. I, therefore, arranged everything according to his wish, by sending a few messengers in advance to the Temple of Lord Virabhadra. When we reached Edur, all the arrangements were made for the *puja* to Lord Virabhadra in spite of his physical weakness. Several *jangamas* were fed and offered gifts by him. Then we continued our journey and now we are camping at Arabhavi. I take the liberty of suggesting to Rani Sarkar that all the members of the royal family and the court should go over to Arabhavi and receive him. Mallasarja Sarkar is not keeping good health, but yet there is no cause for any concern. I pray to the Almighty God to bestow good health upon Mallasarja Sarkar.

Yours obediently
Sardar Gurusiddhappa

As Mallappasetty finished reading the letter all the members of the family and the court realized the gravity of the situation. Their faces grew dim and eyes wet with tears.

Rani Chennamma said to Mallappasetty, "Gentlemen, we shall start for Duradundi today itself. Please make all the arrangements."

"All right, Rani Sarkar," said Mallappasetty and went around issuing orders to his subordinates.

Within a couple of hours Rani Rudramma, Rani Chennamma, Prince Sivalingarudrasarja and the members of the court were all ready for the trip. Whereas the two Ranis sat in the palanquins the others rode the horses, of course, accompanied by a sizable number of soldiers.

They reached Arabhavi and rushed to the camp where Raja Mallasarja was resting. Rani Rudramma and Rani Chennamma were shocked to see their king to be very weak and emaciated. They broke into tears and clasped his feet. All the other members were also shedding tears silently. Prince Sivalingarudrasarja sat beside the ailing king with a lachrymose face.

Raja Mallasarja wore in a wan smile and with a wave of his hands tried to console them, "Don't be sad. It's a natural law that whoever is born must die someday or the other. I know you are all equally able to protect our Kittur kingdom. Gurusiddhappa, you are an able and experienced Diwan. Our Prince Sivalingarudrasarja is still young, though very able. You appoint him as my heir and guide him along the right path. Prince Sivalinga, you must treat your mothers with respect and see that they lack nothing in life."

Everybody was silently shedding tears and nobody had the capacity or mood to talk.

Then they took Raja Mallasarja in a palanquin to Belavadi and rendered a special *puja* to Lord Virabhadra there and arranged a feast for *jangamas.* Then they returned to Kittur. As they approached the palace the sound of cannon fires was heard.

Raja Mallasarja who had grown very weak asked Prince Sivalingarudrasarja, "What's this sound?"

He replied, "Father, the people of Kittur are celebrating your homecoming. Thirty four cannons are fired in memory of your regime of thirty-four years."

The entire population of Kittur had gathered around the palace to have a glimpse of their beloved king.

* * *

That night Raja Mallasarja took rest. On the next morning he was not feeling better at all. But, however, after his bath he went with his entire family to Chowkimath Monastery and rendered a special *puja* to the family deity, Lord Gurusiddha. He fed several jangamas and distributed a hundred and one cows to them. He had a sense of spiritual fulfillment, although he was worried about the future of Kittur. He returned home with his family in the palanquins. In the afternoon his condition was not satisfactory.

In the evening, Raja Mallasarja's health grew more and more critical. His voice grew weaker and his eyesight became more and more dim.

Rani Rudramma sat near his feet. She burst into tears and said, "How shall we live in this palace without you, my lord!"

Rani Chennamma also sobbed and said, "Don't leave us in the lurch, lord!" Raja Mallasarja said in a faint voice, "Don't you worry, my dear. Lord Gurusiddha will be there to protect you after my departure from this world. Be bold and help Prince Sivalingurudrasarja in controlling the kingdom."

The two Ranis were not in a position to talk back to him, as tears were trickling down their cheeks continuously.

By that time Diwan Gurusiddhappa and a few other important courtiers came there and saluted the ailing Raja reverentially. Raja Mallasarja beckoned to Diwan Gurusiddhappa and Prince Sivalingarudrasarja to his side. The two Ranis stood up and made way for them.

Then the Raja held the two hands of the prince and put them into those of the Diwan and said, "Gurusiddhappa, I have given charge of the prince to you. You should enthrone him and guide him like a father."

Tears began to gush out of Gurusiddhappa's eyes. He felt a big lump in his throat. But yet he managed to say between sobs, "Sarkar, I shall do my duty with utmost sincerity. You need have no worry at all."

He stood there shedding tears silently.

The court physician checked the pulse beat of Raja Mallasarja every now and then, and grew more and more worried. The courtiers, who gathered around the Raja, saw the face of the physician and understood what would come about soon.

The men, women and children sat outside the palace on the parapets, under the trees and on the lawn waiting for the news from inside the palace about their beloved Raja.

On Sunday evening, Raja Mallasarja entered into an unconscious state and began to jerk his limbs spasmodically. The royal priest came to the spot and began to chant the *pancaksari mantra*. The Ranis and the counters sat through the entire night watching their beloved Raja on the royal bed dying gradually. Finally when the sun rose in the east, Raja Mallasarja breathed his last and his hand fell suddenly to the right side.

The royal priest declared to the gathering, "Raja Mallasarja Sarkar has finally merged into the Absolute Linga."

Rani Rudramma and Rani Chennamma lifted their voices and cried so piteously that it rent the hearts of all the courtiers.

They fell upon the cadaver of Raja Mallasarja and wailed and lamented, "How could you leave us in mid water, my lord?" wailed Rani Rudramma.

"Why should God Almighty not take our life also?" wailed Rani Chennamma.

The women folk of the palace joined the Ranis in the funeral chorus of crying. The citizens of Kittur heard the news. They stopped their cooking or eating and all other daily activities and rushed to the palace crying and wailing. Fifty cannons were fired from the top of the palace by way of respect for the departed Raja Mallasarja.

As per the directions of the royal priest, the servants lifted the body of the Raja and washed it with cold water and covered it with the best garments. They, then, carried it to the court hall where they fixed the body in a sitting i.e. lotus posture. The royal priest decorated it with marks of *vibhuti* and flowers. He also placed the golden crest on the head of the late Raja and sprinkled some scent on it. He performed a puja to the body of the Raja by burning the incense. Rani Rudramma and Rani Chennamma waved *arati* to the dead lord by turns and sat on either side. The other womenfolk of the royal household waved *arati* to their beloved master and sat huddled together on one side of the hall.

Rani Chennamma, who could not control herself, wailed and cried in a singsong manner. She said between sobs, "Oh my Raja, you were like the veritable lord Parameswara. Like him, you have two wives, but unlike him you have three sons. Oh my Raja, like Lord Parameswara, who was the master of fourteen worlds, you were a master of fourteen *karyats.* Why have you left us forlorn in this world? Why have you not taken us also with you?"

The other womenfolk, who heard this heartrending wail of Rani Chennamma, began to wail louder still and mourned his death by describing his best qualities in a very touching and poetic manner. One could easily trace the history of Raja Mallasarja's life and achievements through the elaborate descriptions offered through the female mourning.

The whole palace had assumed a very grave atmosphere. Gradually the courtiers entered the Durbar Hall and began to heap flowers and garlands on the body of their beloved Raja as a token of their last homage to him. Then the citizens of Kittur started crowding into the hall to have the last vision of their lord. Sepulchral gravity reigned supreme everywhere. The Desai of Wantamuri took an active part in supervising the funeral rites of Raja Mallasarja.

The Sardars, the Gowdas and the Desais, who learnt about the death of the Raja of Kittur, rushed on horsebacks and in bullock carts to Kittur with their choruses of *bhajans* and instrumentalists. They heaped flowers and garlands on their beloved lord and burned heaps of incense. The members of *bhajan*-choruses belonging to different parts of the kingdom sang sad songs one after another. Most of them dealt with the theme of ephemerality of the mortal life and the inevitability of going to Lord Siva's abode. The philosophical songs seemed to agree with the sorrowful mood of the listeners and helped them achieve some kind of emotional relief. Some groups concentrated on the heroic feats of Raja Mallasarja and his magnificence. Outside the palace the funeral drummers and trumpeters were playing upon their instruments with exquisite skill and attracting the attention of the nearby villages.

The body of Raja Mallasarja was propped on a hearse in a lotus posture. The hearse had a seven-tiered structure decorated everywhere with silver dolls, flowers and garlands. It was mounted on a chariot and taken in procession through the lanes of Kittur, with the entire military accompaniment. The drummers, pipers and trumpeters were playing upon their instruments with real pride and respect for their departed lord. All the citizens, who stood near the windows and on the balconies and roofs, saluted the late Raja with joined palms and cried loudly.

The funeral procession at last reached the precincts of Kallumath Monastery. The gravediggers had already finished their job. The body of Raja Mallasarja was slowly lifted down and kept near the grave facing east. Then the final *puja* was rendered to the body of the Raja by the royal priest, who broke open eleven coconuts and burned incense. He spattered the four walls of the grave with musk, *vibhuti* and vermillion powder. At last he took the golden crest from the head of the late Raja Mallasarja and placed it on that of Prince Sivalingarudrasarja, which symbolically suggested the transfer of power of the kingdom from the father to his successor. Rani Rudramma and Rani Chennamma offered their tearful salutation to their lord by touching his feet with their foreheads by turns. There was a sudden outburst of wailing and screaming from the womenfolk. The priest slid the body of Raja Mallasarja into a shroud of white cotton cloth sewn in the form of a big bag and lifted it down into the grave. Prince Sivalingarudrasarja, Rani Rudramma and Rani Chennamma took fistfuls of mud and threw it into the grave. Then the other relatives, courtiers, Sardars, Gowdas and Desais sprinkled fistfuls of mud into the grave. Finally the gravediggers filled the grave with mud and arranged the heap of mud into a shapely mound. Then the royal priest offered the final *puja* to the mound of grave and distributed gold coins and silver bowls and plates to innumerable *jangamas* and labourers, who had attended to the funeral programme. Then the entire gathering walked back silently.

Before leaving the graveyard, the womenfolk of the royal family removed the sacramental *talis,* ear rings, nose rings of Rani Rudramma and Rani Chennamma, and broke their bangles and wiped away the vermillion-dots from their foreheads as they had now become the widows of Raja Mallasarja. The faces of the two widows without the five symbols of wifehood looked very grave and bare. The womenfolk who saw their faces felt great sympathy for their plight of widowhood. Their sorrow was beyond words. Sepulchral silence reigned supreme everywhere.

* * *

The atmosphere at Kittur was very grave and bleak. For a couple of days the courtiers and the citizens of Kittur sat in their houses mourning the death of their beloved king. The business in the market slackened. The farmers forgot to cultivate their lands for several days.

Rani Rudramma was deeply steeped in sorrow. She would to dash her head against the floor of the chamber and decided to die. The blood oozing out of her forehead was frozen. She could not recover from her shock.

"I would not live without my lord. What meaning has my life without him?" she would exclaim between her sobs.

It was a great task for Rani Chennamma to console the elder queen. "If you yourself cry like this, who should console the countless children of Kittur?" she asked.

"No my Chenna, I cannot live without my lord. Let me join him in Heaven." replied Rani Rudramma.

Rani Chennamma clasped her, wiped her tears from her eyes and said, "You cannot forget your responsibility. You should see that there would be no chaos in the kingdom. Please think of arranging the enthronement of the Prince."

Rani Rudramma continued to shed tears. Rani Chennamma tried to suppress her own sorrow in order to enhearten Rani Rudramma.

* * *

The next day Sardar Gurusiddhappa went to meet the bereaved Ranis. As soon as the two Ranis saw him, they burst into tears. Sardar Gurusiddhappa also broke into tears contagiously. All the three were crying and sobbing without being able to talk with one another. After the excess of sorrow was spent, they grew relatively calm and began to mumble.

Sardar Gurusiddhappa said in a mellow voice, "Rani Sarkar, Raja Mallasarja left us all, according to God's will. Please tell me who can ever stay here on earth permanently? Everybody will have to wait for his turn, that's all."

Rani Rudramma burst into tears again. "Why should I live on this earth without my lord? Tell me, Diwan Sir, why should I?"

Sardar Gurusiddhappa wiped the tears off his eyes with the hem of his turban. "Rani Sarkar, I understand the agony in your heart. But how long can we afford to sit mourning like this? Kindly think of the Prince and try to live for his sake."

Rani Rudramma was simply unable to reply to this.

Rani Chennamma wiped her tears with the hem of her sari and said, "Gurusiddhappa, kindly think of the enthronement of the Prince at the earliest. Otherwise there'll be danger for the kingdom."

Sardar Gurusiddhappa said, "We shall arrange it just the day after tomorrow. If you two Rani Sarkars continue to cry like this, the Prince will be discouraged. At least for his sake you have to conceal your sorrow."

Diwan Gurusiddhappa bowed to them with joined palms and took his leave.

* * *

The next day messengers were sent out to all the eight hundred villages to announce the date of enthronement of Prince Sivalingarudrasarja. Similarly the town criers were sent into the lanes of Kittur to announce the news of coronation.

They went into the western part of the city and stood near a corner. One of them sounded his drum and announced in a raised voice, "Listen to me, O gentlemen, listen. It is decided to have the coronation of Prince Sivalingarudrasarja tomorrow in the palace of Kittur. The entire public is requested by the court of Kittur to attend the same."

Then the other man of the group sounded a big drum *dhum, dhum*. The men, women and children cocked their ears and listened to the royal announcement. The town criers then went into the southern, the eastern and the northern part of the city and repeated the royal news. Soon the citizens of Kittur were able to recover from the mourning mood caused by Raja Mallasarja's sad demise. The sepulchral atmosphere was slowly transformed into one of jubilation.

The palace, roads and lanes were decorated with festoons of mango leaves; various kinds of flowers, plantain leaves and colourful cloths. The people painted their houses with lime, red-mud and greenish cow dung. Colourful parlors of bamboo and cloth were erected in the squares. The rich people took upon themselves the responsibility of feeding the guests who would be coming from the surrounding eight hundred villages to attend the coronation ceremony.

That day Prince Sivalingarudrasarja got up early in the morning and had his 'holy bath'. All the courtiers and citizens of Kittur flocked to the Durbar Hall. The prince, who was clad in the best silk dhoti, royal gown and decked with gold rings, chains studded with precious glittering gems and stones, entered the hall. He knelt down and saluted his mother Rani Chennamma. His Holiness Prabhuswami of Kallumath Monastery, Sardar Gurusiddhappa and others had gathered there to bless the young prince. All the Sardars, Desais and Gowdas of eight hundred villages were seated on their respective seats. The womenfolk were seated on one side of the Durbar Hall to watch the coronation ceremony.

Prince Sivalingarudrasarja knelt on the silk cushion in the centre of the Durbar Hall. Sardar Gurusiddhappa placed the golden crown on the head of Prince Sivalingarudrasarja. As His Holiness beckoned, Sardar Gurusiddhappa stepped up to the Prince and ceremonially presented the ancestral sword to him.

Then His Holiness said, "Child, please take the oath in the name of Lord Gurusiddha, as recited by the Diwan.

Accordingly the Prince repeated the oath as uttered by the Diwan."

"I, Sivalingarudrasarja, who am crowned as the Raja of Kittur kingdom, swear by Lord Gurusiddha that I shall serve as the servant of my subjects; that I believe in the ideal that honour is greater than my life and that I shall be ever ready to serve and die for my kingdom."

Then Sardar Gurusiddhappa raised his voice and uttered the slogan "Victory to Raja Sivalingarudrasarja!" Then the whole assembly repeated it twice. There was great excitement in the Durbar Hall.

Raja Sivalingarudrasarja stood up, turned towards His Holiness and bowed down to him reverentially. His Holiness raised his palms in a gesture of blessing and uttered the benedictory words, *"Shubhamastu. Shubhamastu.* Everything happens as per God's will. Be a worthy king of Kittur kingdom and raise its honour and glory to the skies."

Then Raja Sivalingarudrasarja slowly turned towards the throne, bowed down to it and ascended it ceremonially. All the courtiers sprinkled the petals of roses and other flowers on the newly enthroned Raja, who looked like a veritable god on earth. The teenager Rani Viravva looked at the beaming face of her husband and felt proud of him.

Although Sivalingarudrasarja was junior to Sivabasavasarja, he was the son of the senior Rani, Rudramma. People had started gossiping about Rani Chennamma's intention of enthroning her own son Sivabasavasarja. Rani Chennamma had, therefore, decided to put an end to the gossip by keeping her promise to her late husband. She had arranged the ritual of *Bhairava*

Kankana for her own son, Sivabasavasarja immediately after the enthronement of Prince Sivalingarudrasarja. Accordingly Sivabasavasarja stood near the throne facing the audience. Diwan Gurusiddhappa gently moved towards him and secured the yellow string called *Bhairava Kankana* on the right wrist of Sivabasavasarja. His Holiness blessed the young Prince.

Then Prince Sivabasavasarja recited the oath of *Bhairava Kankana* as uttered by Diwan Gurusiddhappa, "I shall not long for any kind of power or privileges. I shall be the bodyguard of my younger brother, Raja Sivalingarudrasarja. I am ever ready to lay down my life whenever there is danger for our kingdom."

All the courtiers witnessed the ritual solemnly and secretly admired Rani Chennamma's large-heartedness. Rani Rudramma was overwhelmed by a sense of gratitude to the junior Rani. Rani Chennamma felt a sense of satisfaction in having fulfilled her promise.

The instrumentalists began to play on their *shahnais* and drums to mark the auspicious occasion. The women of the royal family waved *arati* lamps to the Prince by turns. Rani Rudramma and Rani Chennamma did not wave the *arati* to the prince as being widows they were forbidden by their culture from doing so. But they were watching the coronation of the young prince with a sense of satisfaction.

Diwan Gurusiddhappa stood up and shouted at the top of his voice, "Victory to Raja Sivalingarudrasarja! Victory to Raja Sivalingarudrasarja!"

The entire Durbar Hall echoed with the repetition of the hortative slogan by the gathering of courtiers,

Sardars, Desais and Gowdas. Then the important persons of the Kittur kingdom went to the throne, greeted Raja Sivalingarudrasarja and offered him gifts of gold, silver, ornaments with gems, diamonds, pearls, topazes and silver and gold coins.

As part of the coronation ceremony, there followed a variety of entertainment programmes, like wrestling matches, swordplay, spear fighting, folk songs and dances. The bards of the palace recited the glorious history of the Kittur dynasty in a singsong style at the top of their voices. After the programme was over, all these skilled artists and soldiers were amply rewarded with gold and cash.

In the evening Raja Sivalingarudrasarja sat on his horse and went in a procession around the city. The entire entourage followed him. At every square he would stop to receive the public honour. The married women would pour pitchers of water on the ground before him and wave *arati* lamps to him. The musicians would be playing on their *shahnais* and drums. The *lavani* singers would sing the glory of the kingdom of Kittur. The wealthy people tossed silver coins in jubilation, which were picked up by poor people and children. The procession thus went through the important lanes of Kittur and returned to the palace.

After the grand dinner at night, the folk-artists staged a folk-play in the royal theatre, which went on throughout the night. While Raja Sivalingarudrasarja sat witnessing the play, Rani Rudramma, Rani Chennamma and Sardar Gurusiddhappa sat in the inner chamber at midnight discussing the future of Kittur kingdom.

*   *   *

His Holiness Prabhuswami of Kallumath Monastery
expired a month after the demise of Raja Mallasarja.
Consequently the junior Madivalaswami was deeply
saddened for several days. But gradually he grew
reconciled to the death of his guru.

As Raja Sivalingarudrasarja was jealous of
Madivalaswami, who was five years junior to him in age,
he wanted to drive him out of the Kallumath Monastery.
He, therefore, thought of a clever plan. Pretending to be
very polite, he requested Madivalaswami to go to the
distant city of Kashi and bring the holy *tirtha* from the
River Ganga. He arranged to send Basalingappa Jakati
to accompany the junior swami to the city of Kashi.
Although Madivalaswami understood the ulterior motive
of Raja Sivalingarudrasarja, he did not express his feelings
openly but agreed to oblige him. Within a couple of days
he set out on his journey to the city of Kashi along with
Basalingappa.

Meanwhile Raja Sivalingarudrasarja invited Sri
Gurusiddhaswami from Gandigawada village and
appointed him as the Chief Pontiff of Kallumath
Monastery.

After a couple of months Madivalaswami returned
from the city of Kashi to Kittur and was rather surprised
to learn about the appointment of Sri Gurusiddhaswami
as the Chief Pontiff of Kallumath Monastery by the Raja.
Being a renunciant, he wanted to say goodbye to Raja
Sivalingarudrasarja. As he went to the fort, the Raja ordered
the main gate of the fort to be closed. Madivalaswami
called the gatekeepers repeatedly to open the gate, but the

gate was not opened. Hence Madivalaswami walked away from the fort. Then in a moment of intense renunciation, he removed all his saffron robes except the loincloth and became a naked sadhu. He left the city of Kittur for good and started wandering about the country.

* * *

After the demise of Raja Mallasarja, the administration of Kittur underwent a good deal of change. Although Raja Sivalingarudrasarja was a good man, he was too young to understand the subtlety and complexity of human nature. In the morning hours, he would attend the tuition class conducted by Chennabasappa Vengi, who had been specially invited from Hanagal. The scholar used to instruct the young Raja in Nayyayika school of logical philosophy in particular and other scriptures in general. Similarly the Raja acquired the knowledge of Virasaiva philosophy through the able guidance of the expert Chief Monk of Kallumath Monastery.

Every day Venkatarao and Mallappasetty would meet the young Raja Sivalingarudrasarja and try to impress him about their own knowledge of administration. The young Raja could not see through their wiles.

One day Venkatarao went to Mallappasetty's house. After the exchange of amicabilities, Ventatarao said, "See sir, I do not know when that old fellow will retire from service. He'll never agree with what we say."

"You are right, Venkatarao. But what can we do about it at all? asked Mallappasetty.

"We must influence the young lord in such a way," said Venkatarao, "that old Gurusiddhappa should be neglected by the royal household."

"Yes Venkatarao, you are right. We must do that, but a bit slowly, because he enjoys the confidence of all the courtiers."

"But let us do our best," said Venkatarao.

They, then, began to peel the bananas brought by the maid-servant and eat them slowly.

* * *

The atmosphere in the palace began to change slowly. Sardar Gurusiddhappa, who had heard about these changes felt rather disconcerted.

A servant went and told him, "Diwan sir, nowadays the *jangamas* and other priests are not getting enough alms from the palace. The royal grandmother Nilamma seems to control everything."

"What a contrast!" exclaimed Sardar Gurusiddhappa inwardly. "Raja Mallasarja was so liberal in the distribution of alms and busy with charitable activities, but nowadays things seem to have gone to the other extreme."

"I just wanted to bring it to your kind attention. The rest is left to you. Sir," said the servant and went away after bowing down to the Diwan.

Gurusiddhappa grew a bit worried and began to pace up and down in the outer hall of his house. He was immersed in thought. He was jerked out of his thoughtful mood when he heard the footsteps of somebody enter the hall.

As he turned his eyes towards the door, a soldier bowed himself and saluted him. "What brings you here my dear fellow?" asked Diwan Gurusiddhappa.

"Diwan Sir, we soldiers have not been getting enough grains from the palace these days. We are all hard pressed for it. I, therefore, thought of bringing this common grievance to your notice so that you might do something about it", explained the soldier.

"Don't worry, young man. I shall look into the matter," assured Gurusiddhappa. The soldier then saluted the Diwan ceremonially and strode away.

* * *

Diwan Gurusiddhappa observed the slow changes, which had been taking place in the palace of Kittur. Day by day Raja Sivalingarudrasarja grew more and more intimate with Venkatarao and Treasurer Mallappasetty. It was against Gurusiddhappa's nature to force himself upon anybody.

One day he completed his *puja,* donned his silk turban and walked to the inner chamber of Rani Chennamma. With the marks of *vibhuti* on his forehead, he looked like a veritable saint. He was, of course, accompanied by his two soldiers. Rani Chennamma had just finished her *puja* and was about to have her breakfast.

"*Namaskar,* Rani Sarkar," said Diwan Gurusiddhappa with joined palms.

"What a pleasant surprise, Diwan sir? I was about to have my breakfast. It's good that you have arrived at the right time," said Rani Chennamma.

She turned to the maid-servant and beckoned to her. Within a few seconds, a maid-servant clad in a white sari and blouse, brought two plates of *paradi payasa,* two bowls of milk and kept them on the round tables.

"Please have it Sir," said Rani Chennamma.

Sardar Gurusiddhappa did not wish to insult the revered Rani by refusing to partake of the breakfast. He lifted morsels of the *payasa* with his right fingers and thrust it into his mouth. He enjoyed it as it was very delicious. Then he quaffed the hot sugared milk from the silver bowl. The Rani also finished her breakfast. Then the young maid-servant brought the silver box of *tambula* and kept it before the Diwan. Sardar Gurusiddhappa took up two betel leaves and removed their stubs. He applied a bit of quicklime paste on the leaves and folded them into a small ball. He popped a few slivers of betel into his mouth and stuffed it with the folded roll of leaves. Then he popped a few pieces of cloves and cardamoms into his mouth. He began to eat the aromatic *tambula* with a crunching sound. The whole thing was so aromatic that he enjoyed eating every bit of it.

Rani Chennamma also munched her betel and leaves in the like manner. Then she asked him, "What's the matter, Diwan sir? Is everything all right?"

"Rani Sarkar, I have come to consult you on an important thing," said Sardar Gurusiddhappa.

"What is it, please tell me without any hesitation," said the Rani.

Sardar Gurusiddhappa cleared his throat and said rather hesitantly, "Rani Sarkar, of late I have been thinking of taking retirement from the royal service… because of… my old age."

The Rani was shocked out of her wits. She contorted her face and asked, "What do you mean, Sardar Gurusiddhappa? We are already feeling so insecure in the absence of Raja Mallasarja. Our kingdom will go to ruins if elderly people like you take retirement. Besides, who is there to guide the young prince Sivalingarudrasarja?"

"Rani Sarkar, there are so many other people in Kittur," he said, "for example, there are people like Mallappasetty and Venkatarao, who can guide the young lord. He has also great faith in them."

"No Sir," said Rani Chennamma, "I have studied them very closely. They are not reliable. Our young Raja has no experience yet. That is the reason why he has trusted them."

"Rani Sarkar, the kingdom of Kittur can take care of itself without an old fellow like me. The young Raja will have no problem when you are there to guide him," he said humbly

"No Sir," said Rani Chennamma concernedly, "What can I, a woman do without a confidant like you? Our old Nilamma spends most of her time in the *puja* room in meditation. Then the entire burden of the household and the kingdom falls on my shoulders. Don't make me helpless by retiring from service. I request you to be my major supporter," said the Rani with joined palms.

Tears began to trickle from her eyes in spite of her strong will. When Sardar Gurusiddhappa saw those tears in the eyes of Rani Chennamma, his eyes were also bedewed with tears. A few moments went by in silence.

He realized the gravity of the situation and the importance of his service for the kingdom.

He recovered his ability to speak and managed to say, "All right…Rani Sarkar… I shall not retire now… as per… your wish."

Rani Chennamma wiped her tears with the hem of her sari and said, "I don't want a mere promise, Sardar sir, please touch the sword of Raja Mallasarja and swear that you'll never retire until your death."

He walked gently to the wall where the sword of Raja Mallasarja was hung. He touched it and swore, "I swear by the sword of our beloved Raja Mallasarja that I shall not retire from the royal service until my death."

It was only after the swearing that he could perceive some calmness on the face of Rani Chennamma.

*   *   *

Raja Sivalingarudrasarja had heard rumours that the relationship between the British and the Peshwas was growing less and less happy. He remained rather nonchalant about them as he thought it was no concern of his. It was the year 1818, when he was relaxing with his philosophical studies, listening to poetry and watching folk-drama.

One day Diwan Guruisiddhappa went to the Durbar Hall and bowed to Raja Sivalingarudrasarja. The Raja welcomed him with a cheerful smile and asked him, "What is the matter, Diwan sir? You look a bit serious today."

Diwan Gurusiddhappa said gravely, "Sarkar, today we have received a letter from Bajirao Peshwa."

Raja Sivalingarudrasarja's face grew suddenly serious. He asked, "What are the contents of the letter, Diwan sir?" and sat upright on his throne.

The Diwan said, "Sarkar, Bajirao Peshwa of Pune has said that they have to fight with the British in Belgaum and therefore have requested us to render whatever help we can, - be it soldiers, horses, arms or food grains."

For the first time after assuming charge of the kingdom, Raja Sivalingarudrasarja felt the gravity of administration.

Diwan Gurusiddhappa continued, "Sarkar, this is not the full story. We have also received a letter from His Excellency Elphinstone, the Governor, asking for help with men and materials in the case of a fight with the Peshwas."

Raja Sivalingarudrasarja was really floundered by the two contradictory letters and did not know what to do. He heaved a deep sigh of anxiety and said, "We cannot rest in peace any time in our life. Nor can we take sides so easily. What's your opinion about it, Diwan Sir?"

Diwan Gurusiddhappa scratched the back of his head behind the turban and said, "Sarkar, I require some time to think over the matter. This is not to be solved so easily nor is it a matter of joke."

"All right, Diwan Sir, please think about it. You call a meeting of all our courtiers and officers tomorrow so that we can have some deliberation about the problem."

Diwan Gurusiddhappa said, "Yes, Sarkar, I will," and bowed himself out of the Durbar Hall.

In the evening Rani Chennamma sent for Sivalingarudrasarja. The Raja went and sat in front of his mother. She broached the matter to him, "My dear son, I would like to know how you think about this contingency. Do you like to extend help to the Peshwas or to the British?"

"*Avva*, I think we should not help the Peshwas because they are our bitterest enemies. Don't you remember how the Patwardhan of Nippani had kept our Virappa Desai under *nuzarbund* until his death and Bajirao Peshwa kept our father Raja Mallasarja under arrest until his last moment? These Peshwas will not let us free even if we help them now."

She appreciated the political awareness of the young Raja from his point of view. She thought for a few seconds and said, "My dear son, you think of only the immediate. But you do not know the things in the long run. The British fellows are the common enemies of Peshwas and us. We are sure to suffer if the Peshwas are defeated by the British."

"But if we help the Peshwas," said Sivalingarudrasarja, "we cannot be totally free from them either. They continue their high-handed approach towards us."

"No son, if we please the Peshwas by helping them this time, we may be able to live on par with them."

"But I don't want to take an independent decision, *Avva*. I shall consult the members of the court and do as per their common opinion."

"Anyway," said Rani Chennamma, "be careful in taking any decision, my son. Think of the pros and cons of the situation, before you take any course of action."

"Yes, *Avva*," said Sivalingarudrasarja and walked out of her chamber.

* * *

In the evening the court met in the Durbar Hall. All the courtiers had occupied their respective seats. Raja Sivalingarudrasarja reclined on his throne.

He addressed the gathering, "Gentlemen, we have gathered here to discuss whether we should help the Peshwas or the British. All of you should come out with your frank opinions about the problem."

Then Sardar Gurusiddhappa stood up and bowed to the Raja. He said, "Sarkar, I personally feel that we must help the Peshwas, so that we can earn their good will and be independent of them."

As Sardar Gurusiddhappa sat down in his chair, Treasurer Mallappasetty stood up and greeted the Raja and addressed the gathering, "Sarkar, I beg to differ from Diwan Gurusiddhappa. I feel that we should help the British and not the Peshwas. As you all know, the Peshwas are unreliable. Don't we remember how they deceptively imprisoned our beloved Raja Mallasarja? We all suspect that they must have poisoned him when he was in their custody at Pune. It's no use feeding the snake with milk, because it won't leave you unbitten. Please tell me whether I am right or not."

Mallappasetty sat on his seat. Venkatarao, then, stood up and bowed to the Raja and said, "What Mallappasetty has suggested is quite agreeable to most of us."

Then the other courtiers expressed their opinion in favour of the British. Sardar Gurusiddhappa was rather unhappy to know that the opinion of the majority ran counter to his.

Finally Raja Sivalingarudrasarja sat erect and announced, "We are at last convinced by the majority opinion of the cabinet. We, therefore decide to send our soldiers and *saranjam* to Belgaum where the Brigadier-General Munro will be waiting."

Though Sardar Gurusiddhappa grew pale because he could not persuade the courtiers to support his point of view, he had to discharge his duty as a Diwan. He, therefore, said dutifully, "Yes, Sarkar, I shall arrange everything according to your order."

* * *

The soldiers of Kittur rode with their *saranjam* to Belgaum and joined the British army under the leadership of Brigadier-General T. Munro. The soldiers of Kittur were surprised at the sight of howitzers, the battering train, two iron 18 pounders, and four brass 12 pounders and other ammunition erected at different angles facing the fort of Belgaum which was under the Peshwa control. The battle started and continued for nearly twenty days. The soldiers of Kittur contributed their mite to the British army. At last the Peshwas were defeated by the British. The *Bhagava Zenda* (the Peshwa banner) was lowered and the Union Jack was hoisted on the fort of Belgaum.

Brigadier-General T. Munro was very happy with the Raja of Kittur for the timely help and thanked him and sent a message to that effect to the Raja. In this war with the Peshwas, Kittur army lost one of its very important leaders and that happened to be young Sivabasavasarja, the natural son of Rani Chennamma. The soldiers of Kittur rendered an appropriate kind of royal funeral to the soldier Sivabasavasarja, who had died a heroic death on the battle field and attained the glory of a true soldier.

When the army of Kittur was sent back to Kittur by Munro, the soldiers returned to their kingdom with mixed feelings. They were happy to have helped the British army to defeat the Peshwas and very sad to have lost their precious soldier Sivabasavasarja, the darling son of Rani Chennamma. Rani Chennamma, Rani Janakibai, Rani Rudramma and the other members of the royal family mourned the death of Prince Sivabasavasarja for a few days. Rani Janakibai was the most disconsolate among them. Rani Chennamma was the most aggrieved member of the family as she had lost her only son in the battle with the Peshwas. She felt deep sympathy for her widowed daughter-in-law Rani Janakibai and tried to console her in different ways. But she had the satisfaction that her son lived up to the ideal of *Bhairava Kankana* by laying down his life for the kingdom.

Brigadier-General Munro moved with his army towards Bijapur. But before that he sent an official message to Raja Sivalingarudrasarja to keep the fort of Belgaum for themselves as a reward for their help in the war with the Peshwas. Raja Sivalingarudrasarja, his courtiers and the dignitaries of Kittur were very happy to have vanquished the Peshwas at Belgaum and earned the goodwill of the British government. They thought that their future would be bright.

In the fourth Maratha war, it was the British rulers, who achieved victory over the Peshwas. Consequently they annexed the Peshwa kingdom to the East India Company. They arrested the Peshwa king Bajirao II, and kept him as a prisoner in Biruru village of Brahmavarta area. They fixed his yearly pension at Rs. 800,000 per annum. As a result all the native chiefs, who were under the Peshwa control, came under the control of the British.

* * *

One day, Raja Sivalingarudrasarja was relaxing in his chamber when a servant came and said, "Sarkar, a messenger has come from the British Commissioner. Diwan Gurusiddhappa and others are waiting for you in the Durbar Hall."

Raja Sivalingarudrasarja put on his gold threaded *pagdi* and walked to the Durbar Hall. All the courtiers stood up to show their respect for him. They sat down after the Raja sat on his throne.

"What's the matter, Diwan sir?" asked the Raja. Diwan Gurusiddhappa stood up and said, "Sarkar, today we have received a letter from the Commissioner, Munro. It says that he was happy to have had our cooperation in the battle against the Peshwas. He has thanked us all profusely."

Raja Sivalingarudrasarja beamed with pleasure as he listened to the letter. So also did the other courtiers who had gathered in the Durbar Hall.

"But the most important part of the letter," said Diwan Gurusiddhappa, "is as follows. Thomas Munro has said that since the Peshwas have been vanquished by the British, he has now invited the Raja of Kittur to enter into a new agreement with the British. The meeting is called at Belgaum on the next Tuesday."

The face of the Raja grew a little pale as he listened to the latter part of the letter. For a moment there was a pin drop silence in the Durbar Hall.

It was again Raja Sivalingarudrasarja who broke the silence, "Now, gentleman, let me know what you feel about this."

Diwan Gurusiddhappa stood up once again and said, "Sarkar, I suggest that we need not attend this meeting called by Munro, Since the Peshwas have lost their power, we are no longer subordinate to any one now. We are an independent kingdom now. Mr. Munro should let us live by ourselves peacefully. I have offered my views. It is left to you, Sarkar, to take the final decision."

Diwan Gurusiddhappa sat on his seat.

Raja Sivalingarudrasarja sat erect on his throne and said, "Our Diwan has given a very good suggestion. Is it agreeable to all of you?"

Venkatarao stood up and said, "Sarkar, I beg to differ from the Diwan. I feel that we are not independent now. Formerly we were paying our annuity to Bajirao Peshwa. Now when he is vanquished by the Company sarkar, our loyalty and allegiance are automatically transferred to the latter. We have therefore, to enter into a fresh treaty with the Company sarkar. Otherwise we will be swallowed by them within no time."

As Venkatarao sat down, Mallappasetty stood up and said, "Sarkar, I agree with what Venkatarao has said. We have no choice now except change the masters. As we all know the *firangis* are far more powerful than any of the native kings put together. I, therefore, personally feel that we should not incur the wrath of the *firangis*. On the contrary, we should enter into a new agreement with them and be friendly with them."

Mallappasetty sat down after expressing his opinion. The other courtiers also offered their opinion about the contingency.

At last Raja Sivalingarudrasarja announced, "Gentlemen, after listening to the consensus of our courtiers, we have decided to send our envoys to Thomas Munro and sign a new treaty. We have realized that there is no way out." Then the courtiers dispersed from the Durbar Hall. Sardar Gurusiddhappa heaved a sigh and went out of the Hall with a heavy heart.

*   *   *

Mallappasetty and Venkatarao rode their horses with a few officers to Belgaum as envoys of Raja Sivalingarudrasarja. After their breakfast in the bungalow, they entered the hall, where Thomas Munro was waiting for them. They were greeted by the British officer and asked to take their seat.

"Welcome, gentlemen, welcome. Where is your Raja Sivalingarudrasarja?" he asked.

Mallappasetty replied, "Our Raja could not come to the meeting as he was not keeping good health. He, has, therefore, deputed the two of us to attend the meeting."

"Very good, gentlemen. Please have your tea, before we start our deliberations."

A waiter brought a tray of teacups and biscuits and served them to all the members in the meeting hall. Mallappasetty and Venkatarao crunched the biscuits and sipped the tea leisurely. Then the waiter removed the tray and cleared the table. The British officers who sat on the opposite side of the table were busy poring into the big files. Then Thomas Munro, who sat on the presidential chair, announced the new terms and conditions of the agreement and called upon Mallappasetty and Venkatarao to sign the documents.

Mallapasetty and Venkatarao were alternately excited and depressed by the items, but could not dare disagree with any of them. Finally they dipped the pens into the inkbottles and scribbled their signature by turns and stamped the royal insignia of Kittur upon it. They felt so helpless by the trap laid down by the British Government.

They got up and greeted Thomas Munro who ordered them, "Gentlemen, you have signed all the documents, but the main *Sannad* will have to be signed by Raja Sivalingarudrasarja. We will send our officers with you in the evening when you start for Kittur and you get the *Sannad* signed by your Raja and send it back tomorrow so that I may endorse it with my own signature and send a copy of it back to your Raja. All right?"

Both Mallappasetty and Venkatarao felt so foolish that they said, mechanically, "All right, Sarkar, all right," bowed to Thomas Munro and walked out of the hall with all the documents and returned to the bungalow where their companions were waiting for them. They then had their lunch and a brief siesta in the bungalow. In the evening they mounted their horses and rode back to Kittur late at night. They were accompanied by two officers of Munro's office.

* * *

Raja Sivalingarudrasarja woke up in the morning and was very eager to know the terms and conditions of the new agreement with the Company government. He hurried through his morning ablutions and *puja.* Having had his breakfast, he walked up to the Durbar Hall where Mallappasetty and Venkatarao were waiting to hand over the documents to him. Diwan Gurusiddhappa had also come there on time.

As the Raja entered the Durbar Hall, all of them stood up as a mark of respect for him and sat down when he relaxed on his throne. The Raja then, said, "Gentlemen, what are the new terms and conditions of our agreement with the Company sarkar?"

Mallappasetty stood up and said in a loud voice, "Sarkar, first of all Thomas Munro was extremely happy with your kind self for the cooperation that you have shown to the Company sarkar in fighting with the Peshwas. He has expressed his thanks profusely to you."

Raja Sivalingarudrasarja was beaming with pleasure as he listened to this piece of news. Then Mallappasetty continued, "Munro Saheb has laid down the following conditions in the new agreement. I shall read out the contents"

After slurring over the documentary formalities, Mallappasetty came to the main points and read them out as follows:

> We have no objection to your retention of the land that you have acquired from the Peshwas. We shall honour your *status quo.* As a token of our thanks to you for your cooperation with us in our

fight with the Peshwas, we shall exempt you from the payment of one year's annuity out of two years' which you owed to the Peshwa. We recognize you as a tributary prince and offer you an annual gift worth Rs. 3950. An annual *pesheesh* of *shapoor* rupees one lakh seventy-five thousand will be taken from you and the Samsthan continued to your children and their children ("*Putrapoutra*": from generation to generation)." This *Sannad* is signed by Thomas Munro.

Raja Sivalingarudrasarja was nodding his head in appreciation, whereas Diwan Gurusiddhappa sat in his chair with a grim face.

Mallappasetty continued, "Another important item of the agreement is that we can do away with 473 cavalry, 1000 infantry kept by the Peshwas at Khanapur taluka and Rs. 25000/- Instead of that, we have to give up the Khanapur taluka to the Company sarkar for their use."

Raja Sivalingarudrasarja was overjoyed to learn the new terms of the agreement. He sat up erectly and said, "Dear Mallappasetty and Venkatarao, I am very happy to note that you have carried out the business of this treaty very smoothly without in any way causing displeasure to the Company sarkar. I am very thankful to you for the royal service."

Mallappasetty and Venkatarao were elated by the Raja's expression of gratitude and saluted him in return. They were swollen with new pride and conceit. Diwan Gurusiddhappa's face grew pale with disappointment and anger. As the courtiers dispersed, he bowed to the Raja rather peremptorily and walked away with a heavy heart.

* * *

In the evening Diwan Gurusiddhappa entered the Rani's chamber and sat on the seat after greeting her.

Rani Chennamma was looking fresh as a lotus after the siesta. She sat upright on her cushioned seat and asked, "What happened in the new treaty with the Company sarkar, Diwan Sir?"

Gurusiddhappa looked rather disappointed and said grimly, "Rani Sarkar, the new treaty has not made me happy, though the young Raja is very happy about it."

Rani Chennamma's face lost its fresh glow and grew red with confusion. "What are the main points of the treaty?" she asked.

Gurusiddhappa adjusted his turban with his hands and said, "The most important items of the treaty are that we have to pay the annuity of Rs. 1,75,000 to the Company sarkar and give up Khanapur taluka to them."

The Rani's face turned red with anger. She raised her voice and said, "What's this? We have not won our freedom at all. We have only exchanged our masters. Can we not live independently? Why should we give up Khanapur to the British? I would not have agreed for such terms and conditions if I could attend such a meeting."

Gurusiddhappa swallowed the saliva thereby wetting his parched mouth and said grimly, "What could I do, Rani Sarkar! Of late Raja Sivalingarudrasarja has developed great faith in Mallappasetty and Venkatarao. He deputed them for the meeting and this is the inevitable result."

There was silence for a few seconds. Then Rani Chennamma said in a low pitch, "Diwan sir, you know that our Sivalingarudrasarja is still young and inexperienced. He takes all that is white as milk. Those fellows, I mean Mallappasetty and Venkatarao cannot be relied upon for anything."

"I know that Rani Sarkar," said Gurusiddhappa, "I have already appointed spies to keep an eye upon them, because I suspect them. They are so unscrupulous that they can take advantage of the young Raja's faith in them."

"Not only that," said Rani Chennamma, "I can persuade the Raja even to dismiss them from royal service."

"Please, don't do that, Rani Sarkar. We shall watch and even wait and see how things take their shape. I shall do my best to prevent those snaky fellows from harming the young Raja."

Rani Chennamma inhaled deeply and said, "In that case, we shall wait for a while. But Diwan sir, please keep a strict watch over their movements. I shall also try to convince the young Raja about their nature."

"Yes, Rani Sarkar, I shall do as per your wish," said Gurusiddhappa. He bowed down to her and walked away from her chamber briskly.

Rani Rudramma was very unhappy about her son's helping the British against the Peshwas. She was deeply hurt by his disobedience to her advice. She thought that the honour and glory of Kittur kingdom would diminish due to his immature political behaviour. She took it to heart and decided to spend the rest of her life in spiritual pursuit. She, therefore, moved to the palace at Sangolli and immersed herself in the worship and meditation of God. In course of time she breathed her last in the same palace. Her funeral was conducted according to royal protocol and honour. She was buried on the bank of River Malaprabha. Later an impressive grave was built there.

*   *   *

Rani Viravva, the daughter of the Desai of Shivagutti, was only a minor girl of eleven years when she was married to Raja Sivalingarudrasarja. As she had not matured yet, her husband could not have a normal marital life with her. He, therefore, began to take more and more interest in the cook, Mahantavva. He did not have his food served to him by either Rani Viravva or Rani Chennamma, but by the cook, Mahantavva. This behaviour of his hurt the feelings of Rani Viravva and Rani Chennamma.

Mahantavva was a very beautiful married woman of Gejji family of Nesaragi. She had quarreled with her husband and left him for good. Then she had come to Kittur and joined service as a cook in the palace. As she was a very wily and clever woman, she attracted the amorous attention of Raja Sivalingarudrasarja by her charms and charisma. She grew very intimate with the shrivelled old Nilamma, who, under her influence, began to interfere in all the affairs of the household. She was also in league with the *karbharis* like Mallappasetty and Venkatarao, and the chief security officer of the fort, Sivabasappa, and took active part in their conspiracy. Because of her cleverness, she became a very important person in the palace in spite of her low position. Consequently she began to be cross even with Rani Chennamma, who was deeply hurt by her arrogant behaviour. It was also rumoured that she had even tried to poison Prince Sivabasavasarja, Rani Chennamma and Raja Sivalingarudrasarja on different occasions. But when her evil attempts were aborted by the other maidservants in the palace, Raja Sivalingarudrasarja realized his folly, dismissed her from service and drove her out of the palace. Then the people of Kittur laughed at the young Raja's immature nature and inconsistent behaviour.

*   *   *

St. John Thackeray was born in 1791 in England and arrived in India in 1809 as he was sent out by the East India College, which grew into Haileybury. He had three brothers out of whom two (William Thackeray and Webb Thackeray) had served in India in various capacities and the youngest one, Charles Thackeray served in Calcutta. John Thackeray spent his first three years in the Board of Revenue and in the diplomatic or 'Political' Department of the government. He completed five more years of training in District work and in 1818 was chosen to help bring into order the territories just won from the Marathas. It seemed, indeed, to be the common lot of the Thackerays to introduce the British administration into newly annexed provinces.

*   *   *

Walter Elliot, born in 1803 at Roxburgshire, and educated at Haileybury College along with the eminent persons like Adam Smith and Thomas Malthus, joined the

East India Company at Madras in the Madras Presidency as a 'writer.' He showed his special proficiency in learning the South Indian languages. When a separate district of Dharwad was carved out of the Southern Maratha Country, Mountstuart Elphinstone, the Governor of Bombay Province desired to staff at least one or two Englishmen, who knew Kannada (or Canarese as it was called then) to the Collector's Office at Dharwad. Walter Elliot, who was also related to Elphinstone, was very much suited to the job. He was, therefore, transferred to Dharwad in 1823 as an Assistant to the Collector and Political Agent Mr. J. M. Thackeray (the uncle of W.M.Thackeray, the future novelist of the Victorian England). By now Walter Elliot was making remarkable progress in his learning of South Indian languages and Epigraphy thereby paving the way for subsequent scholars like Sir Fleet. Hence he was known as the pioneer of the Karnataka Epigraphy and also known for his multi-faceted scholarship. He was an archeologist, epigraphist, ornithologist, Orientalist, Ethnologist, an authority in revenue matters, an administrator, besides a hunter and a sportsman. Above all he was the best friend of Charles Darwin, to whom he had supplied the skins of various domestic birds from India and Burma.

*   *   *

Once the people of the surrounding villages complained against the menace of wild animals in the forests of Balagunda, Huliyakattala and Handuru, and requested Raja Sivalingarudrasarja to kill them by hunting. The Raja felt pity for the subjects and thought it to be his duty to help the people of his kingdom. He, therefore, rode to the nearby forest alone to hunt the wild animals.

For about half a day he roamed the forest and killed a few wolves and panthers and felt satisfied. But because of the continuous movement he felt very thirsty. By that time he happened to see Thackeray, who also had come there for hunting. Both of them exchanged amicabilities. They walked to the rest house, which was built in the middle of the forest and sat there on the stone seats.

Raja Sivalingarudrasarja said, "Thackeray saheb, today I have killed a few wild animals. I am therefore feeling very thirsty."

Thackeray felt that this was the most opportune time to exercise his evil plan. He assumed a very confidential tone and said, "Don't you worry Raja, I have brought some medicine with me which will remove your thirst and pacify you."

"Is that so, saheb? Then I shall be happy to take that medicine," said Raja Sivalingarudrasarja. Then Thackeray opened his kit, brought out a vessel of milk. He opened the lid, dropped a couple of poisonous pills and shook it properly. The gullible Raja watched everything innocently. Then Thackeray handed over the vessel of milk to the Raja, who took it and quaffed it at one go. Thackeray sat watching him curiously. Raja Sivalingarudrasarja blinked a few times. There was no servant or companion around him to take care of him. As a few minutes went by, the Raja began to lose control over his limbs. He felt a gradual blackout of consciousness and finally sagged to the floor.

Thackeray felt happy to see his plan being executed very successfully. He stood up, closed the door of the rest house and locked it. He was happy to know that none of the Raja's people had noticed what he had done to the king. He untethered his horse, mounted it and rode back to Dharwad with a sense of satisfaction.

That night Rani Viravva, Rani Chennamma and Rani Janakibai waited for Raja Sivalingarudrasarja's return to the palace late in the night and felt anxious. As they slept uneasily, they saw ominous dreams.

The next morning all of them hurried to the forest along with courtiers and royal servants. As they went near the rest house, they saw the main door locked and felt surprised and worried. But some of the curious royal servants went around the rest house and peeped through the ventilators and saw their Raja lying there on the floor. They, therefore, hastened to the main door, broke the lock open with stones and opened the door. Alas! They found their Raja in a semi-conscious condition. He had lost the power of speech.

Rani Viravva, Rani Chennamma and Rani Janakibai began to wail piteously. The courtiers and servants grew sad, but nobody could guess what exactly had happened. They were so much overwhelmed with sorrow that they did not have any evidence to guess what might have happened to their king. They immediately arranged to bring the semi-conscious Raja to the palace in a palanquin.

As soon as they reached the palace, all the courtiers and dignitaries of the kingdom gathered. They laid the Raja on the royal bed. The royal physician hurried to the spot, examined the Raja's pulse and grew pale in his face. The people understood the meaning of his pale face.

Rani Chennamma sat on the bed and kept the head of Raja Sivalingarudrasarja on her thigh and shed tears. Rani Viravva sat at the Raja's feet and wailed loudly. All the courtiers and officers stood sobbing and crying piteously. The court physician advised the members of the royal family to take special care of the Raja. He was unable to diagnose the disease of the Raja. Hence they kept the Raja under meticulous medical care.

*   *   *

Once he recovered from his illness, Raja Sivalingarudrasarja began to spend more and more time in the company of Mallappasetty, as he liked the latter for his diplomatic behaviour. Mallappasetty would sit for hours together with the young Raja and discuss with him matters of the kingdom and administration. Many times he would accompany the young Raja for hunting or visiting the interior places of the kingdom.

One evening Sivalingarudrasarja went into Rani Chennamma's chamber and bowed to her.

After the usual amicabilities, he broached the important idea to his aunt, "*Avva*, I have come to consult you for an important thing."

"What's that Baba?" asked Rani Chennamma. "Diwan Gurusiddhappa is now very old and cannot stand the rigors of administration. I would like to retire him from the royal service and appoint Mallappasetty as the Diwan, because the latter is quite able and diplomatic."

Rani Chennamma grew rather grim and said, "No son, you should not take such a rash decision. Diwan Gurusiddhappa is very a loyal and experienced officer.

You cannot trust Mallappasetty and Venkatarao, though they are very sweet-tongued."

Raja Sivalingarudrasarja understood his stepmother's mind and did not dare oppose her. She continued further, "Even if you appoint Mallappasetty, I am sure he will not enjoy the public confidence in Kittur. On the contrary they may even rebel against him. You are too young to understand their subtleties and tactics."

The young Raja was disarmed by her answer. "In that case," said he, "let it be as you wish."

He bowed down to Rani Chennamma and went out of her chamber.

*   *   *

A couple of months elapsed in the routine life of Kittur. Rani Chennamma was busy with her supervision of the royal household.

One day a servant came and told Rani Chennamma, "Rani Sarkar, the young Raja Sarkar has developed high fever and is lying on his bed."

"In that case," said Rani Chennamma, "you go and fetch the court physician Bhaurao immediately."

"Yes, Rani Sarkar," said the servant and bowed himself out. Rani Chennamma grew a bit serious.

"It must be ordinary fever," said she to herself, but yet she felt rather restless. She rushed to the chamber where the young Raja lay on the high cushioned bed. She sat near him and felt his forehead, which was burning with high fever.

"Get me a piece of cloth," she said to a white-clad maid - servant. When the latter brought a patch of cloth,

Rani Chennamma soaked it in the cold water and placed it on the young Raja's forehead.

"Let it be there until the physician comes here," she said as she sat near her son on the bed.

Physician Bhaurao walked in with his bag of *ayurveda* medicines. The women made way for him. He sat on a low stool near the bed and felt the pulse of the young Raja. He, then, opened the lids of the Raja's eyes. Then he asked the Raja to open his mouth and show his tongue.

"It's only fever and nothing else," murmured the physician to himself.

He opened the decorated bag of medicine and took out a bit of herbal powder and mixed it water in a small bowl and gently poured it into the Raja's mouth.

"Let him sleep well. Nobody should disturb him," he said to the members of the royal family, took up his bag of medicine and walked away.

Nearly ten days went by, but there was no improvement at all. On the contrary it worsened.

The court physician also grew puzzled and said, "I have exhausted all of my medical knowledge but fail to identify the disease. Lord Gurusiddha alone should save him!"

He sat there with a pale face. All the courtiers were deeply worried about the unexpected deterioration of the young Raja's health.

But yet Diwan Gurusiddhappa tried to enhearten the young Raja, "Sarkar, you will get better soon. Don't worry."

All the members of the family had gathered there and were eagerly waiting for the response of the ailing Raja.

Rani Chennamma and Rani Viravva sat by the side of the patient, shedding tears. The courtiers sat at the opposite side with lachrymose faces.

Raja Sivalingarudrasarja said in a weak voice, "Diwan sir, I have a feeling that I won't survive this strange disease. There are certain things in life, which are far beyond anybody's control. We have got to simply accept them. What about the kingdom after my departure?"

Diwan Gurusiddhappa said thoughtfully, "There's no way other than adopting some boy, Sarkar."

*   *   *

The next morning Thackeray, the Collector of Dharwad visited Kittur out of courtesy and met Raja Sivalingarudrasarja and enquired after his health. Thackeray who was a friend of the Kittur royal family right from Raja Mallasarja's days used to go for hunting in the nearby forests with them. Now he had come to Kittur casually to see the young Raja.

When Thackeray entered the room where the young Raja lay on his bed, the courtiers made way for the guest and offered him a seat near the patient's bed.

"Hallo, Raja Sivalingarudrasarja, how are you?" enquired Thackeray.

The young Raja replied in a weak voice, "I am down with some unmentionable fever, Saheb."

"Did you consult your physician?" asked Mr. Thackeray.

Then the Diwan said, "Our royal physician has examined him and given him some *ayurvedic* medicines. But he has not been able to identify the exact disease."

"The young Raja looks very weak. If your physician is not able to diagnose the disease properly, I shall send our doctor tomorrow," said Mr. Thackeray.

"We'll be very thankful to you for such a favour, Saheb." replied Diwan Gurusiddhappa.

"Don't worry, Diwan sir. We'll do our best to help you."

Then the servants came and offered some fruits and milk to Mr. Thackeray, who ate them slowly by peeling the skin of the bananas with style and sipped the milk leisurely.

After the amicable conversation was over Thackeray stood up, shook hands with the young Raja by saying "Please get well, soon," and took his leave from there. The members of the royal family and the courtiers were hopeful that the British doctor might be able to cure their young Raja with their European medicines.

The next morning the British physician sent by Thackeray reached Kittur and rode towards the palace where the young Raja Sivalingarudrasarja was ailing with the peculiar disease. The royal physician of Kittur was also there. All the other important courtiers were present there. They welcomed the British doctor, who had brought his modern items like a stethoscope and other tubes etc. He sat on a stool and examined the pulse of the young Raja. He made him open his mouth and show his tongue. Then he made him open his eyes and examined his eyelids. He felt the lungs and chest of the patient and asked cross-questions about how long he was suffering like this, what were his food habits and other day-to-day activities. The dignitaries were eager to listen to the British doctor's opinion. The doctor gave a few tablets to be given to the patient immediately and walked out of the Raja's chamber and sat in the next chamber of the palace talking with the officers.

Diwan Gurusiddhappa could not control his curiosity and, therefore, asked him, "Doctor Saheb, could you please tell us as to what disease our Raja Sarkar is suffering from?"

The doctor thought for a while and replied, "See, Diwan sir, looking to the symptoms, I can say that your Raja has been suffering from tuberculosis for the past few years."

They were simply shocked out of their wits to hear that their Raja was suffering from such a deadly disease.

Diwan Gurusiddhappa asked further, "Doctor Saheb, can you not cure him of this disease?"

The British doctor replied, "You see, I can give medicine for the temporary relief, that's all. I don't think I can cure him of it completely as I suspect that it has reached an advanced stage now. It is a bit too late to control it now."

All the courtiers and relatives of Raja Sivalingarudrasarja felt so helpless. But none the less they treated the British doctor hospitably and sent him back with due respect.

After the departure of the British doctor, the relatives of Raja Sivalingarudrasarja and the courtiers grew more worried about the health of the young Raja and the future of Kittur kingdom. They could not take the matter lightly at all. Everybody was thinking of some plan or the other to get over the problem.

After a couple of days, the courtiers gathered in the Durbar Hall to discuss the future of Kittur kingdom. Rani Chennamma presided over the function.

Diwan Gurusiddhappa said, "Gentlemen, you all know that the health of Raja Sivalingarudrasarja is deteriorating day by day and therefore we must do something for the heir-ship of the Raja. Though the young Raja married thrice, the last wife being Rani Viravva, he could not unfortunately have any issues. Now the matter is open for discussion before you."

After a general whisper and murmur for a couple of minutes, Mallappasetty stood up and said, "Diwan Gurusiddhappa had suggested in the last meeting that some boy has to be adopted for the heir-ship of our kingdom. But before that could be done, I have a suggestion to make."

Rani Chennamma said, "Come on, tell me your suggestion."

Then Mallappasetty said, "Rani Sarkar, in case you wish to adopt somebody, you have to take the permission of Collector Thackeray from Dharwad."

The Rani's blood was up when she heard this suggestion. She grew terribly angry like a wounded tigress. She raised her voice and burst out, "Who's that fellow called Thackeray? What business has he to interfere with our family affairs?"

Mallappasetty sensed the Rani's anger, but tried to argue a bit legally, "Rani Sarkar, don't you remember that we have changed our allegiance from the Peshwas to the Company sarkar? It naturally follows from this that we have to seek their permission before going ahead with adoption."

Rani Chennamma's anger mounted. She burst out, "That simply can't be, Mallappasetty. The people of Kittur will never accept the authority of the British. We are free to manage our kingdom the way we like. Our treaty with Munro says that."

Mallappasetty said a bit seriously, "Rani Sarkar, it is not advisable for us to antagonize the Company sarkar. We'll be simply wiped out like bugs."

"Let them taste the power of Kittur once. Would they have won the fort of Khanapur from the Peshwas, if we had not extended our help and cooperation?" shouted Rani Chennamma.

"It's only because of our concern for Kittur that we helped the British, Rani Sarkar." clarified Mallappasetty.

"We know how much concern you have for Kittur. You need not tell me all that," shouted the Rani.

Mallappasetty felt nettled. He, therefore, said, "Rani Sarkar, you should not interfere with the administrative matter of the kingdom."

Anger surged up the spine of the Rani, who burst out, "Hold your tongue, Mallappasetty. Do you know with whom you are talking? Know your limits before talking with me."

"In that case," said Mallappasetty, "you do whatever you like. I'll not bother about these things any more," and with suppressed anger he walked away from there.

*   *   *

The next day Raja Sivalingarudrasarja sent for his confidants. Konnur Mallappasetty, Kannur Virappasetty and Subhedar Mallappasetty came and joined Sardar Gurusiddhappa in the royal bedroom. As it was a confidential meeting nobody was allowed into it. The guards kept a strict watch at the entrance.

Raja Sivalingarudrasarja propped himself up against a pillow and said in a weak voice, "See, gentlemen, I have a feeling that I won't survive this deadly disease. It is inevitable for me to adopt some boy from among our close relatives. You please go to your villages and bring a few suitable young boys so that I can select and adopt one of them for the throne of Kittur."

Subhedar Mallappa said, "Sarkar, I am ready to go wherever you order me to and try my best."

"So shall I do," said Sardar Gurusiddhappa.

"In that case," Raja Sivalingarudrasarja said, "Subhedar Mallappasetty, you go to the villages of Murgod taluka and bring some suitable boys from there."

"Yes, Sarkar, as you wish,"

Subhedar Mallappasetty said and left the palace.

Then Raja Sivalingarudrasarja turned to Sardar Gurusiddhappa and ordered, "Sardar sir, you go to the villages of Shahpur taluka and bring some eligible boys."

"As you wish Sarkar," said Sardar Gurusiddhappa and took his leave.

* * *

The same evening Subhedar Mallappasetty and Sardar Gurusiddhappa left Kittur and rode to the villages. Raja Sivalingarudrasarja waited eagerly for their return.

A few days went by. Then both of them returned from their respective areas.

Subhedar Mallappasetty was the first man to see the Raja in his bedchamber. After greeting him, he said, "Sarkar, I searched in many families of our relatives in the villages of Muragod taluka, but could not find the boys of suitable age and ability. Most of them are already far advanced in age. I, therefore, returned alone."

"Don't be disappointed, Subhedar Sir. Let's us see whom Sardar Gurusiddhappa brings," consoled the Raja.

After a couple of hours Sardar Gurusiddhappa entered the bedroom and greeted the Raja and said, "Sarkar, I made a hectic search for suitable boys in the village of Sindholi, Marikatti, Khodanpur and Mastamaradi in Shahpur taluka and discovered eight boys, who are eligible for adoption according to me."

He then called in the eight boys and asked them to greet the Raja and be seated in the chairs. The boys walked towards the Raja, made their obeisance to him and returned to their seats by turn.

Raja Sivalingarudrasarja was watching all the eight boys very keenly. Before making the final selection of the boy, the Raja wanted to test their intelligence and aptitude. He, therefore, asked Diwan Gurusiddhappa to take the boys now to the Guest House and treat them properly and suggested that a subtle kind of test be conducted the next morning. Diwan Gurusiddhappa accordingly took them away to the royal Guest House near the main palace.

The next morning the servants arranged a few things in a big hall near the Durbar Hall. They kept several stools at different places along the four walls and kept different kinds of objects like dolls, carts, bulls, idols of deities, drums and swords on the stools. The preparation for the test was ready.

After breakfast, Diwan Gurusiddhappa fetched the eight boys to the palace. Raja Sivalingarudrasarja also doddered to the hall just to watch the test.

He addressed all the eight boys, "Dear boys, now each one of you go into the big hall and see the beautiful things kept on the stools there and finally select one object of your choice and come out. You can take home whatever object you select."

The boys were really overjoyed. Diwan Gurusiddhappa so far did not know the exact nature of the test. But after the young Raja explained it to him, the latter really admired the Raja for his subtle process of testing.

The boys went into the hall one by one and observed a variety of beautiful objects exhibited there. It was quite a task for them to select their favorite objects because of the variety of objects present there. Each boy took quite some time to observe the pretty things.

Raja Sivalingarudrasarja and Diwan Gurusiddhappa sat near the hall watching the behaviour of the boys. Thus all the eight boys went into the hall and brought back the objects of their choice after a long deliberation. One boy selected a drum for playing, another boy brought a statue of a bull, a third boy brought a statue of a divine car, etc. One among them brought a sword with him by holding it in a very stylish fashion.

Raja Sivalingarudrasarja was observing everything very keenly. Then he ordered Diwan Gurusiddhappa to take all the boys back to the Guest House. Accordingly the

Diwan walked back to the Guest House with all the eight boys and arranged for their lunch. He then went back to his residence for lunch and did not know exactly which boy would be selected by the Raja for adoption.

In the evening Diwan Gurusiddhappa went to the palace as usual to meet Raja Sivalinguradarasarja. He greeted him with joined palms and sat in his chair.

"Which boy did you select, sarkar?" asked the Diwan.

The Raja sat upright against the pillow and counter questioned, "What's the name of the boy who selected the sword in the test, sir?"

"Oh, that is Master Sivalingappa, son of Balappagowda of Mastamaradi," said the Diwan.

"I am really impressed by that boy, I would like to adopt him as my heir. We shall solemnize the adoption ceremony when I feel I am at the end of my life," Raja Sivalingarudrasarja said.

"Sarkar, shall I retain the boy here or send him back?" asked Diwan Gurusiddhappa.

"You may send back the boy. But meanwhile send a formal letter to Sri Balappagowda of Mastamaradi intimating him about our intention of adopting his son. But please see that all this arrangement is kept confidential for sometime."

"Yes, Sarkar, everything shall be as you desire," said Gurusiddhappa. He beckoned to the white-clad servant and ordered him, "Get the scribe immediately."

The servant walked out hurriedly. The scribe came to the chamber within a few minutes and saluted. Sardar Gurusiddhappa dictated the letter in Marathi after consulting Raja Sivalingarudrasarja. The scribe dipped the quill into the black ink and began to write slowly on the rough paper. After completing it, he read out the contents so that Raja Sivalingarudrasarja might hear it. After the epistolary formalities, he came to the main part:

> I have no children of my own. We have decided to get your son Master Sivalingappa here and adopt him as our son and heir to our throne of Kittur. My health is deteriorating. We shall solemnize the adoption ceremony at the earliest convenient time. Until then this matter should be kept strictly confidential.

Then he read out the formal epistolary conclusion.

"Is there anything that should be added, sir?" asked the scribe to Sardar Gurusiddhappa.

"Nothing else. Please seal the letter," said the Diwan.

He beckoned to a servant and asked him to call in a soldier. When the soldier came in and saluted, Gurusiddhappa told him, "You take this boy and this sealed letter to Mastamaradi and hand them over to Sri Balappagowda Patil. And ask him to keep everything confidential."

The soldier took up the letter, kept it in his bag, saluted the authorities and went out of the chamber. He first sat the boy on horseback and then mounted it himself and rode towards Mastamaradi.

Then Gurusiddhappa dictated another letter to Mr. Thackeray, the Collector of Dharwad and Political Agent of South India as per the wish of Raja Sivalingarudrasarja.

The scribe completed the writing and read it out. After skipping the epistolary formalities, he read:

> Being extremely ill and reduced I feel desirous to appoint an heir to the Samsthan and have to this end appointed and confirmed by seal, Mallasarja (the original name of which adopted son was Sivalingappa of Mastamaradi) as the Sir-Desai, Sir-Deshpande and Nadagowda of Hubballi, the Sir-Desai and Sir-Deshpande of Azumnagar suruff, Khanapur suruff, Chandgad suruff, Supa etc., etc., to the Samsthan.
>
> It rests with you therefore in your goodness to continue him the Samsthan, which has been enjoyed by my ancestors and myself by your liberality.

Raja Sivalingarudrasarja said to Diwan Gurusiddhappa, "Diwan sir, I shall put my signature on this letter, but let it be with you only. You may send it to Thackeray when the occasion demands it."

"So be it Sarkar," Gurusiddhappa said. He then beckoned to the scribe to go away from there.

After a few days Raja Sivalingarudrasarja, who was feeling a little better now, called a confidential meeting of his well-wishers and officers in his private chamber.

He led the boy Sivalingappa by hand and told the gathering, "I think this boy is a suitable successor to me in all respects. I, therefore, desire that he should succeed me and I beseech your consent and approval."

All the well-wishers unanimously said, "Sarkar, we agree with your decision. There's no disagreement at all."

Raja Sivalingarudrasarja was quite happy to have the approval of his kith and kin and courtiers.

He said to Sardar Gurusiddhappa, "Diwan Sir, let the boy stay here in the palace along with his father. You may please acquaint him with all the administrative matters. We shall perform the adoption ceremony at a later date. But please get the documents of adoption ready and fix a tentative date for the adoption ceremony."

"As Sarkar wishes," said Gurusiddhappa.

After a couple of days, Diwan Gurusiddhappa took the scribe to the private chamber of the Raja and dictated the citation of the adoption deed and read it out for Raja Sivalingarudrasarja to hear it.

The Raja approved the wordings and other details. "When shall we fix the date for adoption, sarkar?" asked Gurusiddhappa.

The Raja replied, "Diwan Sir, now that I am feeling a little better, I think there is no hurry for the adoption ceremony. We shall conduct it after a few days at our convenience."

"All right, sarkar, as you please," Diwan Gurusiddhappa said. He preserved the document in a sturdy box and locked it safely. Thus a few weeks went by in a normal fashion. Everybody busied himself in the day-to-day life and did not have any tension about the future of Kittur kingdom.

But in the early days of September 1824, Raja Sivalingarudrasarja fell ill once again. The court physician and other guest physicians tried their best to cure him of his consumptive disease, but alas, they could not succeed in it. The Raja's health deteriorated conspicuously day by day.

On September 11, 1824, Raja Sivalingarudrasarja felt that his end was very near. The entire morning he brooded over the fate of Kittur. About 2 o'clock in the afternoon he sent for his Sardars and courtiers just to have an exchange of views. As the news of his illness circulated everywhere, the courtiers and the dignitaries rushed to the palace to have the last *darsan* of their ruler. But Raja Sivalingarudrasarja was so weak that he was not able to sit up and talk properly with them. Beckoning with his eyes and hands was his only response to the questions of the relatives and officers. People were sure that their beloved Raja would not live long. The citizens of Kittur were rushing into the palace to pay the last homage to the dying Raja. They wondered at the effect of the merciless time on the human beings in general. They contrasted in their imagination the cadaverous figure of Raja Sivalingarudrasarja with his healthy figure in the past and exclaimed helplessly. They returned from the palace with lachrymose faces. The crowd began to dwindle after midnight. It was only the close relatives and top-ranking authorities, who sat around Raja Sivalingarudrasarja.

There was sepulchral silence everywhere because death had cast its shadow. In the early morning, about 4 o'clock, the head of Raja Sivalingarudrasarja sagged to the left side of the pillow. The soul of the Raja left his body, and merged with the Absolute Linga.

Rani Chennamma, who saw the death of the Raja, fell upon his chest with a heart-rending cry, "How did you leave us all, my darling son?"

Suddenly all the relatives and the courtiers rushed to the bed and had their last vision of the Raja. Rani Viravva was crying at the highest pitch of her voice, whereas the other womenfolk were wailing, crying and sobbing. In spite of the rosy dawn, the kingdom of Kittur seemed to enter into a thick darkness.

The body of Sivalingarudrasarja was bathed in cold water, decorated with silk robes, pearls and jewels. It was kept in the *Divankhana* for public display. The natives of Kittur kept on rushing into the hall for mourning their beloved king.

The relatives of the late Raja Sivalingarudrasarja could not have the luxury of mourning his death freely. They had to worry about the adoption ceremony, which had been kept pending. Rani Chennamma therefore sent for all the officers of the kingdom and ordered them to arrange for the adoption of Master Sivalingappa immediately.

She asked Sardar Gurusiddhappa, "Diwan sir, you know what the wish of Raja Sivalingarudrasarja was. We have no time now for postponing it anymore."

Diwan Gurusiddhappa busied himself with all the formalities of the adoption ceremony. Soon all the people gathered in the Durbar Hall for the adoption ceremony. Rani Chennamma, Rani Viravva and other womenfolk of the palace gathered on one side of the hall whereas the men folk sat on the other side of the hall. The public of Kittur was not invited for this closed-door ceremony.

Only the close relatives and officers were invited for the function.

Master Sivalingappa was anointed with sandal oil and made to sit on a wooden seat in the bathroom. Half a dozen young men and women poured perfumed water upon the boy's head and offered him a holy bath. Then they led him to the Durbar Hall where he was adorned with the royal insignia of Kittur kingdom. Diwan Gurusiddhappa announced,

"Brothers and sisters, as per the wish of the late Raja Sivalingarudrasarja, we have adopted the Master Sivalingappa and renamed him as Sawai Mallasarja II. He has been invested with the sovereign power over Kittur as the legal successor."

Then five *muttaides* offered *arati* to the new ruler of Kittur. Rani Chennamma was witnessing everything with mixed feelings. The entire responsibility of Kittur had fallen upon her shoulders. Rani Viravva could not forget her late husband, who had been interned the very previous night. She was not in a mood to enjoy the sight of the adoption ceremony although it was done according to her husband's wish. The drummers and pipers were playing upon their drums and *shahnais* to mark the ceremony of adoption. The real father of the boy, Balappagowda Patil, was witnessing the adoption ceremony with pride and patriotism and secretly wondered at the strange turns of luck for his son, who had become the ruler of the kingdom of Kittur. The relatives of the late Raja Sivalingarudrasarja and the courtiers heaved a sigh of relief at the completion of the formality of the adoption ceremony.

The next day Rani Chennamma called a meeting of all the courtiers in a separate hall. All the dignitaries like Mallappasetty, Kannur Mallappa, Sardar Gurusiddhappa, Himmat Singh, Nursing Rao and Guruputra Virappa were all there. Rani Chennamma sat on her cushioned seat and addressed the confidential gathering,

"Gentlemen, you all know that dark clouds have gathered upon the kingdom of Kittur. Sawai Mallasarja is still a slip of a boy. I, therefore, have to act as his guardian and virtually manage everything. But a mere woman that I am, I cannot go ahead without your help and cooperation. I, therefore, appeal to you to forget your individual differences and get united for the welfare of the kingdom. I would like to know if you are willing to offer me whole-hearted support."

Then Kannur Mallappa stood up, greeted the Rani, touched his sword and said, "Rani Sarkar, I swear by my sword that I shall extend all the possible help and support for the cause of the kingdom."

Then the other dignitaries followed suit and declared their whole-hearted support to the Rani and the kingdom. Rani Chennamma felt enheartened by the avowed support of the courtiers and thanked them all cordially. Then they all moved back to the Durbar Hall, where Sawai Mallasarja was seated on the throne.

Rani Chennamma called Sardar Mallappasetty and asked him, "Dear Mallappasetty, please do me a favour. You take this letter to Dharwad and hand it over to Thackeray. This letter was written by Raja Sivalingarudrasarja a few days back."

Mallappasetty received the letter from the Rani and said, "It shall be done as per your wish, Rani Sarkar."

Then he disappeared from there. The Rani heaved a sigh of relief temporarily as she got the letter dispatched to Thackeray. Sardar Mallappasetty and Kannur Mallappa mounted their horses and rode towards Dharwad. Sardar Mallappasetty had kept the letter safely in his cloth-bag. After covering the distance of a few miles, he noticed the beauty of the landscape and suddenly remembered that they were going past Tegur hills, which was used by the natives as well as British officers for hunting and other entertainments. Mallappasetty knew that Thackeray used to go there every often to spend his time in the company of his mistress known for her extraordinary beauty and liveliness. He knew how Thackeray had got an excellent mansion built for his mistress there at Tegur hills.

He explained his plan to Kannur Mallappasetty and asked him, "Shall we take a chance and see if Thackeray Saheb is anywhere near here? He must have come here for hunting and meeting his mistress."

Kannur Mallappa laughed at Sardar Mallappasetty and said, "Is it wise to disturb him at such a time?"

"Don't worry about that. He is not so very officious in his behaviour. Let's just take a chance," said Sardar Mallappasetty.

"All right, friend, do as you wish. But I shall remain at a safe distance." said Kannur Mallappa.

Then both of them rode along the upward side of the hill and saw a few figures in the distant spot. There was some indication that people had come there for hunting. As they rode near, Sardar Mallappasetty saw that his guess was correct. He saw Thackeray with his gun and his few assistants near him. They must have finished their hunting and were taking rest under the shade of a mango tree.

Sardar Mallappasetty went ahead whereas Kannur Mallappa remained behind deliberately. Mallappasetty stopped his horse and tethered it to a nearby tree and greeted Thackeray with joined palms.

"Hallo Mr. Mallappasetty, how are you? How is your Raja? How is his health?"

"Saheb, our Raja is on his deathbed. He has sent this letter for your kind consideration."

Mallappasetty took out the letter and handed it over to Thackeray.

"I was going to Dharwad to deliver this letter to you in the office. But I happened to see you here on the way," said Sardar Mallappasetty rather apologetically.

"Don't you worry about the formalities," said Thackeray and ripped open the letter and pored his eyes over the contents. He noticed that the letter was dated 10th September 1824, but was handed over to him on the 12th September 1824.

"All right, Mallappasetty, I shall read the letter carefully after I reach my office at Dharwad. By the way, how is the condition of Raja Sivalingarudrasarja?' asked Thackeray.

"His condition is very critical, Saheb. He may die anytime," replied Mallappasetty.

"Is that so? Then I am very sorry for him," said Thackeray.

"Then may I take your leave, Saheb?" asked Mallappasetty.

"All right, you may leave now. I have noted the contents," said Thackeray.

Sardar Mallappasetty mounted his horse and joined Kannur Mallappa, who was waiting for him at a distance. Now that there was no necessity of going all the way to Dharwad, they returned to Kittur quickly.

* * *

After spending the night in the arms of his mistress at Tegur bungalow, Thackeray returned to Dharwad in the early morning to attend to his duty in the Collector's Office. He went to the office and read the letter once again and thought of some plan. He then sounded the bell.

When the soldier walked in, he ordered him, "Please rush to the Civil Hospital and bring Dr. Bell immediately."

"Yes sir," said the soldier, saluted him and disappeared from there.

After half an hour Dr. Bell walked in with a 'good morning sir,' and stood before Thackeray. "Hope you are all right sir," said Dr. Bell.

"I am all right, Dr. Bell. There's an urgent case you have to attend. Please rush to Kittur and examine Raja Sivalingarudrasarja, who is said to be on his deathbed. Let me have your report about his health. The matter is very crucial," said Collector Thackeray.

Dr. Bell understood the gravity of the situation. "All right sir, I shall start the journey right now."

He rode back to the Civil Hospital, collected his medical kit, sat in the *sarot* with his attendant. "Take me to Kittur quickly," he ordered his driver.

The heat was mounting gradually. The driver whipped the horses, which began to trot with a slow clip-clop.

He crossed the undulating land with greenery everywhere. Though the hot sun was beating down mercilessly, the sultriness was frequently relieved by the cool breezes from the green trees and creepers. When he was two miles away from Kittur, he saw a native solider riding in the opposite direction. Dr. Bell thought of satisfying his curiosity. He beckoned to the soldier to stop. The soldier led his horse near Dr. Bell and stood askance.

"Gentleman, how is Raja Sivalingarudrasarja?" the soldier raised his hands and looking up towards the sky said, "Oh. Our Raja united with the Absolute Linga."

Then he rode away from there.

Dr. Bell thought, "What's the use of medicine for the dead king? Nevertheless, let me see the body in order to report to the Collector."

He continued his journey to Kittur. He rode to the Mahal, where people were flocking in and out. He enquired of a guard about Diwan Gurusiddhappa. The guard took him to the Diwan, who conducted the British doctor to the *Diwanakhana*, where the body of the late Raja Sivalingarudrasarja was seated with all the decoration and finery of silk, gold, silver and flowers. The crowd of people made way for the British doctor and looked at him with suspicion.

Dr. Bell moved slowly towards the decorated royal corpse. He instinctively crossed himself and said 'Amen' indistinctly. He sniffed at the air just to see if the dead body had started putrefying, but could not find it. The natives were crowding in to have their last *darsan* of the king and pay their last homage. He saw that all the authorities of Kittur were moving about hectically and making arrangements for the funeral ceremony. In front of the dead body sat a chorus of singers who were singing sad and philosophical *bhajans* to the accompaniment of drums and *ekdaris*. Men and women were crying in muffled voices.

Dr. Bell noticed that after the initial sight, nobody paid any heed to him. Even then he managed to call Diwan Gurusiddhappa aside and asked him, "When did Raja Sivalingarudrasarja adopt the son?"

"Just yesterday," replied Gurusiddhappa.

"How could he adopt anybody without taking the permission from the Collector?" asked Dr. Bell.

"Your Collector has no right to interfere with our administration," replied Diwan Gurusiddhappa.

Dr. Bell was rather embarrassed by the answer. But yet, he cleared his throat and asked him, "Our Collector Thackeray does not approve of this illegal adoption."

"Let him not approve of it. We don't need his approval. The citizens of Kittur have approved of it."

"Why did you not care for Mallappasetty's warning against the adoption?" asked Dr. Bell.

"The Diwan of Kittur has better responsibilities to discharge than answer your questions," Gurusiddhappa gave a cryptic answer and strode away from there briskly.

Mallappasetty, who was with Dr. Bell whispered into his ears, "This is the old gentleman, who is in league with

Rani Chennamma. Together they expedited the adoption ceremony. They did not bother about my suggestion."

"All right, I shall report it to the Collector," said Dr. Bell to Mallappasetty.

Both of them moved to a corner in the palace and discussed a few things in low pitch. After about half an hour Dr. Bell threaded his way out of the crowd. Nobody paid heed to him. He said goodbye to Mallappasetty and mounted his *sarot*. He was really impressed by the loyalty of the people of Kittur for their dead king. He returned to Dharwad and rested for a whole day until the physical fatigue of the tedious journey to and back from Kittur disappeared. The same day the funeral of the late Raja was conducted in Kittur according to Lingayat conventions, accompanied by cannon fire.

The next day, September 13, 1824, Dr. Bell composed his thoughts. He sat up tight in his hospital office and wrote down the report as follows:

From: G.H.Bell Esq.   13th September 1824
First Surgeon at Dharwad.

To

Thackeray Esq.
Political Agent at Dharwad.

Sir,

I have the honour to inform you that I went to Kittur as directed by you on the 12th instant to visit the Desai.

About two miles from Kittur, I was met by a man, who informed me that the Raja was dead. As, however, I thought desirable that I should be able to inform you of the state in which I might find the corpse, I proceeded to Kittur. On my arrival (at 3 o'clock p.m.) I requested that I might be shown the Raja's body. I found it laid out in state in open "Diwan Khana' and bedecked in all imaginable finery. I could not ascertain that there was any putrescent smell arising from the corpse, but I should think from its appearance from the time it must have taken to dress, remove and lay out in the manner in which I found it, that death must have taken place sometime before my arrival. The courtyard of the Mahal was crowded with natives and there seemed to be free admission to the inhabitants to view the corpse.

Dharwad   I have etc.
13th Sept. 1824.   Sd/- G.H.Bell
                                First Surgeon, Dharwad

*   *   *

In the Chowkimath Monastery a royal throne was placed. It was decked with a beautiful silk covered cushion. It was carved very beautifully and studded with gems and precious stones. His Holiness Gurusiddhesa, clad in his saffron robes, waited in his chamber for the arrival of the royal family. The entire compound of the monastery was filled with happy voices, tinkle of bangles and anklets, rustle of silk saris and new dhotis, and cries and laughter of children.

A messenger rode to the monastery and informed the officers that the royal family was on its way to the monastery. Then the pipers, drummers and cymbal-players and other accompanists walked away from the monastery to receive the royal personages. The *shahnai* piper was playing a tune in *Bhimapalasa Raga.* The drummer was rattling and thumping on his drum in a very stimulating manner. The cymbal-player would chime the metallic plaques and produce an exciting rhythm. They were all shaking their limbs according to the rhythm of the tune. The listeners were enthused so much by the tunes that they would also gesticulate the beats either with their fingers or with their feet.

As the horse-carriages containing the members of the royal family came near them, the musicians doubled the tempo of their tunes and resorted to *tara-saptak.* Everybody was enraptured by the happy harmony of mesmerizing sounds. As the Diwan beckoned to the musicians they turned back and began to march slowly towards the monastery, leading the royal personages in the carriages.

When they reached the main gate of the monastery, Rani Chennamma, her heir designate Master Sivalingappa, Diwan Gurusiddhappa and others alighted gently from the carriages and walked into the compound and climbed the stone-stairs. They entered the central hall of the monastery where the throne was placed temporarily and sat on the royal chairs meant for them.

The hall, which was filled to capacity, was echoing with the din of jubilant voices. The priest was ready with the ceremonial items like flowers, garlands, sandal paste, coconuts, joss sticks, etc. His Holiness Gurusiddhesa of Kallumath Monastery was seated on the tiger-skin seat. Other persons like Diwan Gurusiddhappa, Rudrappa and other courtiers were all present there. Amatur Balappa of Sadhunavar family, the bodyguard of Rani Chennamma stood behind her.

All the courtiers stood up for a moment and sat down after Rani Chennamma took her seat, turned to his Holiness of Kallumath and said, "We're waiting for your orders, Holiness."

H.H.Gurusiddhesa, who was clad in a saffron gown and bedecked with *rudraksi* and *vibhuti* said, "The time is auspicious now. The ritual may be started," and waved his right hand upward.

The young boy, Sawai Mallasarja II knelt on a silk cushion at the centre of the hall. Diwan Gurusiddhappa placed the golden crown on the young Prince's head. Then he ceremonially offered the ancestral sword to the young Raja, who held it in his hands in a dignified manner.

As the Diwan administered the oath the young Raja recited the oath very seriously, "I, Sawai Mallasarja II, who am enthroned as the Raja of Kittur kingdom today, swear by Lord Gurusiddha that I shall serve the subjects of my kingdom wholeheartedly. I believe in the ideal that the honour and glory of my kingdom are greater than my life. I am ever ready to sacrifice my life for the welfare of my kingdom."

His Holiness shuffled to him, raised his palms in a benedictory gesture and blessed him. Then Sawai Mallasarja II turned towards the beautifully carved throne, bowed down to it and ascended it ceremonially. He sat on it in a majestic manner. Then all the courtiers and relatives sprinkled the petals of beautiful and fragrant flowers on the young Raja. His forehead was adorned with the triple marks of *vibhuti* and his limbs with gold chains, bands and rings. The drummers and *shahnai* players began to play their tunes loudly.

The crowd cheered by shouting, "Victory to Sawai Mallasarja II," "Victory to Rani Chennamma," and "Victory to the kingdom of Kittur" consecutively.

Then the married women shuffled to the throne and offered *arati* service to the newly coroneted young Raja.

After the ceremony was over Rani Chennamma stood up and addressed the gathering,

"My dear brothers and sisters, I am grateful to you all for your love and sympathy towards your young Raja. As you all know, he is too young to understand the intricacies of administration. It is, therefore, my duty to guide him along the right path until he is able to manage everything by himself. This was exactly the wish of late Sivalingarudrasarja. I request you all to stand by me in stress and strain and help me protect our beloved kingdom."

The gravity of the request by the Rani was borne in upon everybody in the Hall. There was pin drop silence everywhere. The Rani went back to her chair and sat in it.

Rudrappa then got up and greeted the young Raja. He addressed the gathering,

"My dear brothers, you have just listened to the words of the Rani Sarkar and understood the spirit behind her speech. Let us all give our word of honour that we'll stand by her, come what may. I, for one, swear by Lord Gurusiddha that I will dedicate my entire life for the protection of Kittur from the enemies."

After the excited oath, he sat down in his chair. His spirited words seemed to enthuse the other men in the Hall. They also felt the urge to do so.

Then Rayanna, who had come from Sangolli, stood up and addressed, "As the Rani Sarkar has appealed to all of us, I would like to swear by Lord Gurusiddha that I shall devote my whole life for the protection of Kittur and fight for my land until my last breath."

He bowed down once again to the Rani and sat down in his chair.

Then Balappa also stood up and addressed the gathering, "Though I am very young, Rani Sarkar will forgive me for declaring my loyalty amidst all the elderly people gathered here that I shall dedicate myself entirely for the protection of our Kittur kingdom." He sat down after his brief but spirited speech.

Although the entire gathering was growing cheerful, Diwan Gurusiddhappa did not seem very enthusiastic. He was watching everything rather resignedly. Rani Chennamma, who noticed it, asked him,

"Why, Diwan Sir, why are you looking so gloomy today? What is the matter that's bothering you?"

Diwan Gurusiddhappa stood up rather slowly and said, "Rani Sarkar, you have rightly detected my mood. Yesterday Venkatarao came from Dharwad. I have a premonition that he may twist the facts and prejudice the mind of Mr. Thackeray. I am really worried about that." He sat down in his chair.

Then Rudrappa stood up and said, "Diwan sir, you need not worry about that snake called Mallappasetty. I shall be an eagle for that snake. You may go ahead with your own duties."

As he sat down, Rani Chennamma stood up and requested H.H.Gurusiddhesa, "Your Holiness, we are waiting for your kind guidance and blessings."

As she sat down in her chair, H.H.Gurusiddhesa cleared his throat, sat upright in his chair and addressed the gathering:

> "My dear little mother, brothers and sisters of Kittur, as you all know, the young Sivalingarudrasarja's demise has created great emptiness in our hearts. It has increased the burden of responsibility upon the Rani Sarkar. May the Almighty Gurusiddha give us all the courage to face the contingency! You should forget all your internal differences and get united for the protection of the honour of Kittur from the *firangis* and other enemies. May Lord Gurusiddha bless us all!"

The entire audience in the Hall felt elated and spell bound by the enheartening speech of the dynamic monk from the Monastery.

* * *

A large mansion was constructed at Tegur. The stone and timber building was very imposing from outside and very commodious inside. Thackeray had taken a special interest in the construction of this mansion, as he wanted to house his mistress, who was a dancer in the court of Kittur, and wished it to be very comfortable. Ever since he had met her, he had fallen for her extraordinary beauty. Unmarried as she was, she was also elated to be the mistress of a very high British officer like Thackeray, who could command such great respect from the officials and princes. That is why she had agreed to be his mistress. It was as per her wish that Thackeray had made all the arrangements for the construction of the large mansion so that he could spend many a happy hour in her sweet company.

* * *

That day an hour had gone by after dusk. Sairabanu donned her silk sari and blouse with silver threads in them. The intricate reddish pattern of *madarangi* painted on her palms and ankles looked very beautiful. She dyed her eyes with *kajal* and sprinkled the *screw-pine* perfume upon herself. She decked her hair bun with a bunch of jasmines, as she knew her paramour liked that smell very much. Her cook was already boiling the chickens in the kitchen as per her instructions. Sairabanu opened the silver box and began to chew betel nut, betel leaf and quicklime as usual. Her heart began to thump as the time of Thackeray's arrival approached. The plaintive notes of *koels* in the garden awakened and intensified her amorous feelings. She began to burn all over and felt impatient.

* * *

Lo! The sound of horse hooves in the distance began to grow slowly. Her heartbeat also increased proportionately. The sound of horse hooves grew louder and slower. The whine of the horse was heard outside the mansion. Then the sound of boots was heard. As there was a knock on the door, Sairabanu rushed to the door, opened it and welcomed him with a cheerful smile. Thackeray caressed her chin gently and stepped in. She went behind him and helped him doff his overcoat dripping with raindrops.

"Oh God, I am so busy these days that I cannot have time even to meet you. But the paradox is that I cannot spend even three days without seeing you," said Thackeray passionately.

"But what about me, Saheb? At least you'll forget me when you are in your office. But being idle at home all through the day, I keep on remembering you every moment," she said amorously.

* * *

"What can I do, dear? I would have kept you at my own home at Dharwad – but for political reasons."

Thackeray hung his hat on the peg and removed his boots and socks. He sat chatting with her for an hour or so. Sairabanu was never aware of the passing of time when she was in the sweet company of her paramour.

A white-clad maidservant brought two glasses of wine and kept them on the tray before them. Both Thackeray and Sairabanu began to sip their wine in between their talk. The liquor sent up waves of warmth in their veins.

They began to feel more comfortable now in spite of the
chill atmosphere outside. Another hour passed in chatting.
Then the maidservant brought the dinner consisting of
chicken *biriyani*, hot *rotis*, potato curry, slices of onion
and cucumber. The flavour of food was very appetizing
for Thackeray. They sat at the dinner table. Thackeray
ate his food with knives and forks, whereas Sairabanu ate
with her delicate fingers only. For in spite of Thackeray's
persuasion, Sairabanu was not able to handle the forks and
knives. Once or twice she had tried that but only to hurt
her mouth. From then on Thackeray had conceded to her
native habit of dining with fingers only. She would feed
him sumptuously with loving persuasion.

* * *

After the dinner Sairabanu prepared a big roll of betel
nut, betel leaf, quicklime, cloves, and cardamom with all
other sixteen spices and stuffed it into Thackeray's mouth.
Then she prepared a smaller one for herself and began to
chew it.

In the kitchen the servants and other members of her
family were having their dinner. Thackeray and Sairabanu
chatted about gold, silver, diamonds, clothes, etc. As the
night advanced, the members of the family and servants
retired to their respective rooms. The nocturnal silence
became more conspicuous. The twittering of birds and
the fluttering of their wings was heard from outside
occasionally.

"Don't go, dear Saheb. Why not stay here today also?"
asked Sairabanu in a beseeching voice. "No darling, I
have got to attend to several things in the office. Don't

worry. I shall come again after two days," said Thackeray gently. After giving her a parting kiss, he mounted his horse and began to ride towards Dharwad.

* * *

After three days Thackeray felt terrible itch and burning sensation in his privy parts. He, therefore, rushed to the Civil Hospital near the Fort at Dharwad for a medical check-up. The British doctor took him to the inner room and asked him to lie down on the high wooden table. Accordingly Thackeray lay down on the table and opened the fly buttons of his trousers. The doctor held his private parts and examined them closely with a magnifying glass and felt surprised and shocked by the ugly fact. Then he asked Thackeray to get up and go to the outer room. The doctor prescribed some tablets and some ointment for the affected parts and told him,

"Sir, you have contracted venereal disease. I have prescribed some tablets and ointment for you. Please take them regularly. By the way I would like to advise you to minimize your contact with women. Otherwise the consequences will be serious."

'All right, Doctor. I shall try my best to follow your advice," said Thackeray with a mischievous smile on his face.

Then Thackeray collected his tablets and pouch of ointment and rode back to his residence.

* * *

Political Agent Thackeray failed in his duty of expressing his condolences to the bereaved dowager Rani Chennamma, not because he was not aware of this etiquette, but his mind was totally preoccupied with the 'wealth' that was supposed to be hidden within the precincts of the Fort of Kittur. It was not an ordinary sum, but was estimated to be twenty-five lakhs worth gold and silver, besides priceless diamonds, rubies and jewels. It was more than five times of what Scindia had paid as his parting presentation to the Mughal Emperor Shah Alam II. He was thrilled by the dream of this fabulous wealth and was keen to add it to the coffers of the east India Company. He was confident that it would fetch him a handsome amount of prize money, an equal amount of share in the booty that follows and the recognition enough to spend his retirement peacefully back in England sitting in the House of Lords or that of Commons.He did not believe in the legality of the adoption case. His doubts had grown deeper as much because of Dr. Bell's oral report as by Mallappasetty's confidential opinion. He had also heard rumours about how the officers of Kittur kingdom had been embezzling money, gold and jewels from the treasury. He, therefore, thought of preventing the misuse of the royal wealth and maintaining law and order in the kingdom.

So one day he took an army of five hundred soldiers and went to Kittur. The natives of Kittur were taken aback by the unexpected arrival of the Company soldiers. So were the officers of the court.

Thackeray led the soldiers to the palace and sent for Diwan Gurusiddhappa and told him, "Your adoption of the boy is illegal and therefore it is not approved by our higher authorities. I shall refer the matter to the Commissioner Chaplin. Until I get his reply, I have to maintain law and order in Kittur, which belongs to the Company now."

Diwan Gurusiddhappa's anger knew no bounds. He burst out, "Who cares for whether you accept it or not. The citizens of Kittur have already approved of that."

"Mr. Gurusiddhappa, don't babble like a child. As there is no legal heir for Kittur, the kingdom belongs to the Company now according to the Doctrine of Lapse. If you argue further, everybody here will be under detention."

Diwan Gurusiddhappa was nonplussed. Mr. Thackeray asked Mallappasetty, "Show me where the treasury is."

Mallappasetty led him to the treasury room where the money, gold and jewels were kept in a number of boxes. Diwan Gurusiddhappa remained a silent observer there.

"Mr. Mallappasetty, tell me how much money is there in the treasury," asked Thackeray. "There isn't much money, sir. When Raja Mallasarja was imprisoned at Pune, lakhs of rupees were spent on his health," replied Mallappasetty.

Half a dozen Company soldiers stood guard to Thackeray. "No, I cannot believe that. Show me the accounts," thundered Thackeray.

"We've no accounts. Raja Sivalingarudrasarja kept his own accounts. Hence we don't know anything about it," replied Diwan Gurusiddhappa.

"I cannot believe this cock and bull story. Soldiers, open the locks of these chests."

Half a dozen Company soldiers knelt down and struggled with some master keys, but the locks did not obey the keys. The soldiers expressed their inability.

*   *   *

"In that case," said Thackeray, "you seal all of these chests with our new locks on top of the old ones."

The soldiers began to obey the orders dutifully. Thackeray was watching everything very attentively. When all the chests were sealed with additional locks, the treasury- room was also locked and sealed likewise.

Thackeray called Mallappasetty publicly and said, "From today I have appointed you and Mr.Venkatarao as the internal supervisors of the kingdom of Kittur. And Mr. Venkatarao will be your counterpart from our side. You must see that the treasury is guarded properly."

*   *   *

Mallappasetty joined his palms in greeting and said gratefully, "As you wish, Saheb. I shall take care of it."

Diwan Gurusiddhappa was terribly hurt and insulted by Thackeray's high-handed behaviour, but could not do anything because of Rani Chennamma and H.H.Gurusiddhesa, who had asked him to restrain himself.

The same day Collector Thackeray sat in a room of the Kittur palace and shot a letter to Chaplin explaining all the precautionary measures he had taken to annex Kittur to the Company government. The letter was as follows:

Sir,

One of the principal servants of the Kittur named Kannur Mallappasetty came to me about noon on the 12th instant to say that his master was dying and to deliver a letter of which I submit a copy, announcing the adoption of a son, the letter is dated the 10th September, and mentions that the adoption had then taken place.

Mallappasetty stated that when he left Kittur on the 12th instant the Desai was insensible, but that the ceremony of adoption was performed on the morning of that day and that a salute was afterwards fired in honour of the event.

Having heard many reports regarding the Desai's death, and having every reason to believe that no regular adoption had taken place I asked Mallappasetty whether it was not desirable that the Civil Surgeon should visit his master, and on his assenting I requested Mr. Bell to proceed to Kittur. That gentleman immediately did so but found the Chief had already expired, and from the appearance of the corpse, there is every reason to conclude that death had taken place before Mallappasetty left Kittur. Even, therefore, if the Desai had even applied for and obtained leave to adopt, there would have been the strongest grounds to doubt whether he had availed himself of the permission.

On my return from Kolhapur in May, the Desai requested that I would send medicine and pay him a visit to Kittur on my way to Dharwad. I complied with the request, and had a long conversation with him on the 18th May, but although he was dangerously ill and spoke very freely of his affairs he was entirely silent on the subject of adoption.

After Desai's death I reminded his head servant of the circumstances and asked him how he could reconcile his assertion as to the time of the adoption with the date of the letter announcing it. Mallappasetty did not attempt to explain the contradiction, and from all I have heard it as evident that although the deceased might have been much importunated by his interested servants, he never consented to the adoption even in his weakened moments, that he never intended to apply for permission to adopt, and that if the ceremony of adoption took place at all it was not performed until the Desai was either dead or quite insensible.

The child alluded to in the letter is a very distant collateral relation of the late Chief, and it does not appear that either he or any other of the Desai's relations has a right to succeed on the score of descent, to the newly elected Samsthan of Kittur. The boy in question is said to have been selected and introduced into the *gadi* for the purpose of adoption, but for the reasons already stated it seems evident that this was a manoeuver of the Desai's servants whose only object was to perpetuate their own influence. It is to be remarked that the Desai's signature in the outdated letter is scarcely legible, and that the characters are quite different from the usual handwriting, which was remarkably good and distinct.

The family of the deceased consists of his widow whose age is only 11 years, his stepmother and widow of his brother who is about 16. The rest of the relations are descended from collateral branches so remote that I have not yet been able to trace the common ancestor. Whatever therefore be the decision of the Government regarding the succession, if the estate be not resumed, a long minority must occur, and I trust you will approve of my having proceeded to Kittur in order to make local enquiries respecting the adoption, and to take measures for securing tranquillity and preventing abuse.

In the first place it seemed expedient to summon all the Sardars and heads of Departments, and after they had acknowledged their responsibility, to inform them, that as the adoption appeared illegal and as the Desai's widow was a minor, the subject of the succession would be referred to Government and that in the mean time it would be my care to preserve order, to protect the country, and to see that every man performed his duty according to *mamool*.

Hearing many different and no satisfactory account of the state of the Treasury, I consulted the principal members and servants of the family on this subject. They stated that the Desai was entirely his own cash-keeper, that he wrote his own accounts and trusted no one with his treasure, and as their information was extremely unsatisfactory, it appeared desirable that no time should be lost in examining the cash accounts and in sealing up the treasury so that the whole might remain in deposit, pending a reference on the subject.

I, therefore, requested Messrs. Stevenson and Frere, who came with me to accompany principal servants to the Treasury and to see the whole secured in their presence under the late Desai's seal as well as my own. This measure has been adopted and from what I have since heard, I am convinced that it has prevented much plunder. It did not appear necessary to count the treasury, and the locks of some of the chests did not obey the keys, but from the Maratta memoranda in the Desai's own hand, which were found in the boxes that were not opened, it is probable that the treasure contains about eight or nine lakhs of rupees.

Report says that there are hidden treasures and large amount that were hoarded in the time of former Desais, but the principal servants affirm that no credit is due to this report and that Mallasarja, the late Desai's father, when at Pune a few years ago, expended 25 lakhs of rupees.

With respect to the characters of the late Desai's servants, they are probably as respectable as those usually found in similar situations, but as they have not produced a single account that is satisfactory, as they have endeavored in some instances to deceive me and as the affairs of the estate would not be safe if left exclusively in their hands, I propose for the present to conduct the administration by means of two joint managers, one on the part of the Government and one on that of Desai's family. This arrangement will check abuses and preserve order without interfering in the usages of the country and the customary system of management.

A large balance of last year's *pesheesh* is still due, but this can be realized at any time from the cash in deposit.

With regard to the claims of the family, I have not yet succeeded in procuring a satisfactory account of the pedigree, but from all I can learn it appears that as he has left no sons or brothers, his widow is the only person who can be considered in any respect as his heir and in order that it may be decided whether the terms of *Sannad* extended to her, I submit a copy of the article, which relates to the succession.

I hope very soon to send you a genealogical account of the family. In the time of the deceased Desai's father about all the relations who had any pretensions to a share of the Estate, are said to have been put to death and the collateral branches that remain appear to be so remote that I doubt whether any of them could succeed, even had the

Samsthan of Kittur existed as an independent state during the time of the common ancestor.

Camp: Kittur   J.Thackeray.
14th Sept. 1824.

He put the letter in a cover, sealed it with wax and gave it to the Company courier and ordered him to hand it over to Mr. Chaplin, the Commissioner of the Deccan at Pune. The courier took the letter and kept it in his bag safely, jumped upon his horse and began to ride towards Pune instantly.

Then Mr. Thackeray returned to Dharwad along with his army. It was late night when he reached his residential quarters and rested with a sense of satisfaction.

*　*　*

That morning Rani Chennamma sent for Sardar Gurusiddhappa. He mounted his horse and rode towards the fort. As he climbed down, a servant led the horse and tethered it to a peg.

Sardar Gurusiddhappa walked in the corridors and entered the chamber and greeted, "*Namaskar*, Rani Sarkar."

"Please, come in, Diwan Sir," said Rani Chennamma rather mechanically. "I'm no longer a Diwan, Rani Sarkar. From yesterday I have ceased to be the Diwan. Thackeray Saheb has dismissed many of us including me and appointed Konnur Mallappasetty and Haveri Venkatarao as the joint managers of the kingdom."

Rani Chennamma was exasperated beyond measure. Her eyes grew fiery and she burst out, "What right has he to dismiss our servants? It's none of his business. Gurusiddhappa, you continue to be in your position as long as I am here."

Gurusiddhappa understood the Rani's anger and helplessness.

"We'll stand by you, Rani Sarkar in rain or sun. Please don't have any doubts about our loyalty," he answered. But I just wanted to inform you Sarkar what all that Thackeray Saheb has done. He has not only sealed all our treasure-chests but also made a detailed list of all the things and belongings of the household. He said that 'the treasury at Kittur is not safe as it is surrounded by the Desai's guards commanded by a thief'. He further said that our own guards might plunder the treasure. If our thirty guards are posted near the eastern gate inside the fort, Thackeray Saheb has posted his own thirty guards near the western gate inside the fort. Now both the groups of guards are there on duty."

Rani Chennamma's anger was surging beyond measure. "How could he remove any of you without consulting the members of our family?" she asked.

Sardar Gurusiddhappa said resignedly, "Thackeray Saheb has been behaving very high-handedly and arrogantly. There's nobody to check him."

"That's simply intolerable," said the Rani fumingly, "we must do something about it."

"I do not know what to do, Rani Sarkar," said Sardar Gurusiddhappa.

"What to do, Diwan Sir, we have got to rise to the occasion and show our mettle. There's no other way."

Sardar Gurusiddhappa bowed to the Rani and took his leave.

The same evening Rani Chennamma sent for Sardar Avaradi Virappa, who was the Commander of the army of Kittur. He went into the Rani's chamber and saluted.

"Please come in, Commander Sir," said the Rani.

Avaradi Virappa sat in his chair and said in a reverential tone, "May I know the reason why the Rani Sarkar sent for me?"

The Rani's face was unusually effulgent with the triple marks of *vibhuti* on her forehead. "Commander Sir, I just wanted to know what the total strength of our army is in all the villages belonging to our kingdom."

The Commander sat upright and said, "Sarkar, the total strength of our army has shot up to sixteen thousand. All the *rahuts* including the regular ones and the new recruits have been practising their art at scheduled time. In case there is any emergency, we'll give a bugle call here at Kittur, and that will be relayed up to the last village on the border of Kittur kingdom. And within two hours the entire army can be at our disposal here at Kittur. This is the arrangement that I have made so far. Kindly order me if there is anything else to be done."

The Rani seemed to be very happy about the arrangements. "Commander sir, I am very happy about all that you have done. Let everything be ready. We don't know when we'll have to wage the war," she said.

Then Avaradi Virappa bowed down to her and took his leave of her.

* * *

The next day all the courtiers gathered in the Durbar Hall of Kittur in response to the Rani's order. The Diwan and the other sardars sat in the conventional order in their seats. It was a close meeting. Rani Chennamma sat on her throne with her usual royal dignity. Two maidservants in white uniform were fanning the Rani with the peacock-feather fans. The Rani radiated the spirit of self-confidence, vibrancy and determination around her. The guards stood at the Main Gate to prevent the unauthorized entry of the officers and other gentlemen. The Rani looked like the veritable Goddess Parvati with her radiant face and the holy marks of *vibhuti* on her forehead.

"Gentlemen," she said in a clear and self-confident tone, "we have called this meeting to discuss what we have to do in future for the good of our kingdom. I would like to know your views on this matter."

Everybody cocked his ears and listened to the Rani.

Sardar Rudrappa stood up and asked, "Rani Sarkar, last month we had appealed to Governor Elphinstone. Your trusted assistant Marihal Rachappa was deputed to Pune to communicate the misdeeds of Thackeray to the Governor. We would like to know whether any reply has been received from him in this matter."

Then the Rani looked askance at the Diwan. Sardar Gurusiddhappa stood up and said, "As you all know, we not only wrote an appeal to Governor Elphinstone but even sent our *vakil* Rachappa personally to explain our difficulties with Mr. Thackeray. Our *vakil* accordingly went to Pune and represented the case to the Governor. But so far we have not received any reply from that end."

Diwan Gurusiddhappa sat down. The sardars looked at one another silently and waited for the Rani's response.

The Rani, who was leaning against the throne, sat upright and said, "Gentlemen, as you know, we have reached the end of our tether now. We have made all the preparations for the war, which we shall declare at an opportune time. We cannot tolerate this slavery any longer, as we have never been subjected to it in the past. We shall fight with the red-faced monkeys of Britain until the last drop of blood remains in us. We have already written to the Maharaja of Kolhapur, the Portuguese of Goa and the other princes in the Deccan. They may also lend their support to our patriotic cause. I want your wholehearted help and cooperation in this sacrifice. I would like to know what you think about it."

There was pin drop silence in the Durbar Hall. All the sardars were deeply touched by the Rani's impassioned appeal through which they could easily make out her confidence and determination.

Sardar Mallappa stood up and said, "Rani Sarkar, there is no second opinion or contradicting your views on the matter. We swear in the name of God that we will do our best to protect the honour of Kittur," and sat down.

Then the other sardars also stood up and declared their allegiance and promised their wholehearted support for the cause of Kittur. There was a lot of excitement among the courtiers who had taken a major decision. There were tears in the eyes of all of them. They wiped them with the edge of their silk scarves and pretended not to cry.

Sardar Virappa stood up and interrogated the Rani very gently, "Rani Sarkar, the civilians have been asking us again and again about the arrangements of *Navaratri* festival. How shall we answer them? When the palace treasury has been sealed by Thackeray, how is it possible to meet out the expenses on the festival? We have a tradition of celebrating *Dasara* every year. Our army with its elephants, camels, horses and bullocks has to march past in the city. For that purpose, we need all the gold ornaments and the *howdah* for the procession. The Kittur royal court has a tradition of giving alms to *jangamas* on that auspicious occasion. But we are penniless now as everything in the palace is sealed by the Political Agent Thackeray."

Every sardar was expecting an answer of helplessness from the Rani.

But the Rani surprised them all when she said, "Gentlemen, don't you have any anxiety now. We have done all that we could. We have also waited enough. Now I shall order the Commander to take a sizable chunk of the army to the treasury and break it open and distribute the money for all the arrangements regarding the *Navaratri* festival."

The sardars were not only surprised by the Rani's determination but also began to admire her inwardly.

Then suddenly Sardar Chennabasappa stood up and expressed his sense of apprehension, "Rani Sarkar, what if the British henchmen appointed by Thackeray go and report it to him? Who knows our own Mallappasetty may carry tales to Thackeray at Dharwad?"

Everybody in the hall thought about this possibility seriously. Then came the self-confident assurance from the Rani, "Don't you have any worry about anybody now. Let it be the British henchmen or Mallappasetty or anyone. We have to face the consequences. Nobody need have any apprehension. We have got to show our mettle at the right time."

Everybody in the hall was disarmed and silenced by the Rani's answer. They seemed to be injected with a new confidence and strength in their veins as it were. Then they dispersed with lightened hearts. The Durbar ended with a *mangalarati* by the palace priest.

* * *

The next morning the Commander marched with a sizable army towards the palace. The Company guards stood opposite the Kittur guards in front of the door of royal treasury hall. They also had guns in addition to swords and spears. They looked at the Kittur guards and grinned as usual. The Kittur guards saw their grin and twirled their moustaches in a challenging gesture.

The Commander was followed by his soldiers, one section of whom had swords; another section, spears; and the third section, guns. The Commander was accompanied by the blacksmiths, who held rods and mattocks in their hands. The entire army entered the corridors of the palace though the eastern gate. The Company soldiers seemed to hear the sound of footsteps in the distance but ignored it as they thought that the Rani herself was reduced to the level of a prisoner.

The Commander stopped the march of his soldiers near the northern gate of the palace and asked the blacksmiths to go ahead to the treasury hall and try to break open the locks.

"Don't you worry. You go ahead. Then we'll follow you within a few seconds."

In accordance with the order of the Commander, the five blacksmiths walked through the southern corridor. As they went near the treasury hall, the Company guards were taken aback and grew alert.

"You cannot open it until our authorities allow that," they said and barred the way of the blacksmiths by holding their guns at the ready. The twelve guards of Kittur stood there smiling under their moustaches. The Company henchmen seemed to be very confident about themselves. But when the Commander of Kittur marched in there followed by the relatively large army, the Company henchmen grew really nervous, understood the gravity of the situation and ran away from there leaving their guns, and clothes. The soldiers of Kittur did not try to kill the Company henchmen, as per the order of their Commander. The blacksmiths laughed at the sight of the Company henchmen running for life. One of the blacksmiths picked up a cap left by the Company henchmen and tossed it in the air. The cap went up reeling and fell back awkwardly. Everybody saw it and laughed.

"This is no time for joking. Come on, do your job," said the Commander in his stentorian voice.

The blacksmiths hitched their *dhotis* around their waists and stood ready. One of them took up a long rod and inserted it into the curving latch of the key and began to press it downward with all the force in his body. But the lock was so sturdy that it did not open. When he attempted it for the second time, the rod slipped down thereby making the blacksmith also fall down. The blacksmith fell on the floor with such a force that his buttocks began to pain severely. So he sat down there near the wall to ease his pain.

"Come on, you try it," said the Commander to the second blacksmith who picked up the rod and inserted it into the curve of the latch and began to yank it with short jerking movements. After a few repeated attempts, the lock appeared to be slackened but still could not be opened.

"Now, you go and try it with a hammer," said the Commander.

The third blacksmith lifted up the heavy iron hammer and struck on the front edge of the lock for nearly ten times. When he struck the eleventh time the lock was separated from its latch and fell down. There was a loud cheer among the soldiers of Kittur.

Now that the Company lock fixed there by Thackeray was broken, there was no problem for the Commander to open the other native locks for which they had the keys easily available. The main steel door of the treasury hall was opened finally. The Commander and a couple of confidant Sardars entered the hall and took stock of the chests of jewels, hard cash and gold ornaments. A servant was asked to sweep the floor of the treasury hall and arrange the chests in an order. Then the Commander ordered the hall to be locked again with new padlocks, kept a large number of native soldiers.

He went straight to the Rani's chamber and reported, "Rani Sarkar, we have taken charge of our treasury by breaking open the locks put by Thackeray. The Company soldiers have run away from the spot," and saluted. "I am very happy to hear the news," said the Rani and beamed with pleasure.

* * *

When the *Navaratri* Festival was only three days ahead, Diwan Gurusiddhappa ordered the royal soldiers to make arrangements for the yearly festival on a grand scale as usual. The soldiers and servants took out the idol of Goddess Rajeswari from the huge wooden box and cleaned it. Likewise they took out the other ornaments and brushed them bright. During the next two days, they painted the hall and erected a *mantap*, which they decorated with colourful silk cloth, pearls and mango leaves. They installed the idol of the Goddess in the *mantap*. The entire palace was echoing with the hustle and bustle of busy workers.

On the day of *Ghata Sthapana*, the royal priest started the ceremonial worship of the Goddess. Wick lamps were lit in and around the *Puja Mantap*. Bananas, guavas, limes, apples and coconuts were kept on big silver plates. All the courtiers had gathered in the *puja* hall for the holy ceremony.

When the Rani entered the hall, everybody stood up as a mark of respect for her and sat down after a while. The court bards chanted the fame of the royal family, its ancestry and valour of Rani Chennamma. The Rani's face looked bright with the marks of *vibhuti* on her forehead.

She sat down in her chair and asked the Diwan, "Is everything ready?"

Diwan Gurusiddhappa said gently, "Everything is ready, Sarkar. We are just waiting for His Holiness from Kallumath Monastery.

"All right," said the Rani and sat watching the decoration of the *mantap* and the idol of the Goddess.

Outside the hall musicians were playing upon *shahnai*, drums and cymbals, some familiar and melodious tune in *Sivaranjani Raga*. All the spectators in the *puja* hall were silently listening to the melodious notes with appreciation.

As the Swamiji entered the hall, everybody stood up for a while. His Holiness Gurusiddhesa walked gently towards the *Puja Mantap* with wooden clogs on his feet making a soft patting sound. Then he looked at Rani Chennamma with a serene smile of recognition.

"You may start the *puja* now." said His Holiness to the royal priest, who began to chant the *mantras.*

He applied the holy *vibhuti* on different parts of the idol of the Goddess. Then he dotted a little mark of sandal wood paste and vermilion on the forehead of the idol, kept roses and *bhel* leaves on the limbs of the Goddess and waved the incense burning on the silver thurible. The smoke of the incense was rising slowly in ever widening circles. The pleasant aroma gently flooded the nostrils of all the spectators gathered there. Then the priest held a coconut in his palms. His assistant placed a few crystals of camphor for *arati* on the coconut and lit it. Everybody in the hall stood up with folded palms. The *jangama*, clad in ochre robes, raised his voice and began to sing a benedictory prayer by St. Nijaguna Sivayogi:

The Light is shining,

The flawless Light Supreme
Is shining eternally.

The Light is beyond
The reach of speech and mind;
The Light that is indescribable,
Indeterminate, and immaculate,
Is shining eternally.

On the pillar of Siva-faith,
In the lamp of heart-lotus of discrimination
With the inexhaustible oil of righteous devotion,
On the wick of immaculate lustre,
The Light Divine is shining eternally.

The overcrowding moths of sensuality
Fly into it and die.
The darkness of demonic thought
Dissolves.
The great halo of righteous knowledge
Spreads everywhere.
The soot of *maya* covers it not.
The Peerless Light is shining eternally.

The Light that is an incarnation of 'Om.'
The Light that is undefiled by the triple
    attributes;
The Light that is beyond the human
    comprehension;
The Light that flickers not a bit;
The Light that is the crest-jewel of liberation,

The Light that is Sambhulinga Himself,
Is shining eternally.

After the prayer was over, the priest, who had held the coconut in his palms, lifted it and broke it against a round stone kept there and offered it ritually to the idol. Then the consecrated food consisting of sweets, holy rice and other delicacies were offered to the deity.

Now the Rani stepped forward and joined her palms reverentially to the patron-goddess of the kingdom. Then she turned towards His Holiness Gurusiddhesa, seated on his cushioned chair and bowed down and touched his feet with her forehead.

His Holiness blessed her with his words, "May Lord Gurusiddha bestow all the peace and plenty on you and your kingdom."

Then His Holiness offered the Rani a coconut, a few flowers, *vilya,* betel and *vibhuti* cake, which she collected in the hem of her sari and gently went back to her seat. Then the other courtiers walked towards the deity and then to His Holiness to offer their obeisance.

In the evening a portable deity of the goddess was carried in a picturesquely decorated *howdah* on the back of a royal elephant. In the front of the elephant were the *shahnai* players, who were playing upon their pipes to the accompaniment of various drums and trumpets like *kali, karni, ranahalige, karadi-majalu.* A group of singers were singing the religious *bhajans* with great rapture. Some young men, who wore silk turbans of red, green and yellow colours, were dancing ecstatically with picturesque gestures. The spectators encouraged the male dancers with exhortations and whistles. The dancers felt a new enthusiasm surge in them and begin to dance with double vigour spurred on by the grand rhythm of drums and cymbals.

Behind the *howdah* were the *muttaides,* who carried the *arati* plates on their palms. They were followed by another group of *muttaides,* who carried brass pots and copper pots filled with water and decorated with *vibhuti* marks on them. The entire situation used to provide a grand feast for the eyes and ears of the spectators.

The procession started from the palace and followed the main road of Kittur. It stopped at regular intervals when the women of the nearby houses poured one or two pots of water before the elephant carrying the idol of Goddess Rajeswari and waved their *aratis.* Meanwhile the male dancers continued their dancing and singing on a relay basis. The spectators cheered them by tossing dates and puffed rice in the air. After a stanza was over, they would resume the march. Likewise the *muttaides,* who carried *arati* plates on their palms, were singing the folk songs celebrating the glory of the Goddess. Behind them marched a large platoon of soldiers of infantry, cavalry and all types of *sardars, subhedars, shetsannadis, walikars* and *talavars,* who represented the entire structure of administrative system of the kingdom. All of them exhibited their pomp and glory by walking together united and seemed to enact their solidarity symbolically as it were. The holy procession thus moved on the royal road of Kittur, until finally it reached the Kallumath Monastery, where His Holiness Gurusiddhesa offered a brief service to the royal deity. After that the procession

returned to the palace from a different route to enable
the citizens to offer their obeisance by pouring water and
waving *aratis.* When the procession finally reached the
palace, it was past midnight.

* * *

Thackeray had decided to defeat the Rani of Kittur
and annex the kingdom to the Company government. He
thought inwardly that the kingdom of Kittur was a mere
straw before the mighty military power of the British. He
had received information from Kaladagi that the British
Company of the 5th Regiment of Native Infantry, 500
strong and about 100 strong Horse Brigade artillery were
moving to Belgaum. He felt very happy and wanted to
make use of this opportunity to overawe the natives of
Kittur. He even imagined the Rani dallying with him in
his sandal-wooded mansion at Dharwad after she was
thoroughly defeated. He chuckled for a moment and
smacked his lips. He pressed the bell-button. The uniform-
clad attendant appeared instantly before him. Thackeray
ordered, "Please ask the clerk to come immediately." The
attendant disappeared from there. After a few minutes the
clerk entered the office chamber with a wad of papers, a
pen and an inkpot. He came and sat down in the chair
dutifully ready to write. Thackeray said, "Take down,"
and began to dictate the following letter:

> I learn that your 5th Regiment of Native
> infantry and Horse Brigade are moving to
> Belgaum from Kaladagi. But may I request you
> to slightly alter your route and go to Belgaum

via Dharwad and Kittur so that we may be able to overawe the people of Kittur into submission? Expecting your immediate response.

Yours
J.Thackeray

The clerk read out the contents of the letter to Mr. Thackeray and carefully crossed the 't's and dotted the 'i's. Then Thackeray scribbled his signature below the letter. The clerk sealed the letter carefully and dispatched it to Kaladagi with a soldier.

*   *   *

On 18[h] October 1824 Rani Chennamma called a meeting of all the sardars and officers of the court. When all of them gathered in the court-hall, she surprised them by revealing the secret measures that Thackeray was taking to annex Kittur.

She gave an impassioned speech: "Dear brothers, Kittur is ours. We are masters of our own territory. The British say that the adoption is not valid because we did not take their permission. Where is it stipulated that we should take their permission for taking a son in adoption? Kittur had an agreement with Munro that we were their friends, i.e., tributary princes. The internal administration is ours. We are their friends. Adoption is our internal affair. The Political Agent, Mr. Thackeray, in his insolence of power, has said that we have lied regarding the adoption. He is prepared to believe the words of a mere servant of the Company, like Dr Bell, but is not prepared to believe us. These British people have come to our land on the pretext of carrying on trade and now they want to see that we quarrel amongst ourselves. They want to grab our land and rule over us. They want us to pay them huge sums of *nazrana.* They might have vanquished other rulers in this part of the country by their cunning and wicked manoeuvers. If the Peshwas have done some wrong to us, let us not forget that they are our own kith and kin. Someday they may realize their follies and join hands with us to drive away these foreigners from our sacred land. Are these British our kith and kin? Do they belong to our country? Thackeray and his sycophants are labouring under a great illusion that they can vanquish Kittur, a small princely state, in no time. They are certainly mistaken. They do not know that the people of Kittur love freedom more than life. Their wealth is not their money, gold or ornaments or land, but it is their 'self-respect.' This sacred land of Kittur has been sanctified by the blood of thousands of martyrs, who have fought for independence and held its banner of freedom flying high all these years. We are no doubt a small state. Our army compared to the British may be small in number. But our soldiers are not mercenaries. Patriotism, love of this sacred land and love of freedom, flow in their veins. Each one of us is equal to tens of their soldiers. We will tell Mr. Thackeray and Mr. Chaplin that we will not submit to them, whatever be the consequences. Kittur will fight to the last man on its soil. They would die rather than be slaves of the British."

The officers gathered in the Durbar Hall were inspired so much by Rani Chennamma's impassioned speech that they burst into slogans, 'Long live Kittur,' and 'Long live Rani Chennamma!'

Everyone was inspired by everyone else. The bugles were blown, the sound of which resounded in the ramparts of the fort of Kittur. The Rani felt a sense of satisfaction to know that her words had touched the chords of sympathetic hearts.

* * *

That evening Rani Chennamma was feeling very exultant after the meeting with all the sardars and courtiers was over. She had the satisfaction of having taken a firm decision to face Mr. Thackeray and the Company army, however big it might be. She had noticed that her courtiers and other leaders of Kittur were also inspired by the patriotic zeal. With their cooperation, she thought she could save the kingdom from the foreign enemies. She retired to her bedroom after her dinner. She lay on the bed thinking of the plight of Kittur, especially after the demise of Raja Mallasarja. She did not know when she fell into a sound sleep.

Rani Chennamma was wandering all alone on the ridge of a mountain. She looked everywhere but there was not a single human soul around. There was nothing but rocks and boulders wherever she ran her eyes. She was feeling utterly lonely and deserted. She went ahead rather mechanically. Lo suddenly she saw Raja Mallasarja riding his horse towards her. She felt a sudden surge of excitement and her heart began to flutter wildly. She stood watching Raja Mallasarja come nearer and nearer. He was smiling bewitchingly at her. She was gaping at him silently. He came near her and jumped off the horseback.

He walked to her, held her hands and said, "Darling, don't be disheartened. I'll be always there to help and protect you. You hold the sword and fight the enemies boldly. I shall be following you wherever you go.

When she looked around, the rocks disappeared. The entire palace looked like an endless garden with trees and creepers with all kinds of fruits and flowers. Raja Mallasarja clasped her tightly. The Rani's heart began to beat fast because of the joy of union with her lord.

Suddenly she was awakened by the clangour of bells in the distant monastery. Only then did she realize that the lord of her heart had come to meet her secretly in her dream. Being suddenly jerked into the world of harsh reality she remembered the enormity of the problems that she had to face. But yet she felt quite confident to face the difficulties as she was inspired by her late husband, who had appeared to her in a dream at the right time.

Rani Chennamma rose from the bed. Dawn was breaking gently in the east. She took her bath and robed herself in her usual sari and blouse made of *kinkaff.* She smeared her forehead and limbs with *vibhuti.* A maidservant clad in white uniform, hurriedly collected flowers, coconuts, *vibhuti* and incense in a cane basket.

The chariot was ready outside the residential quarters. Rani Chennamma put on her veil and mounted the chariot. She was accompanied by two maidservants. The horses of the chariot trotted rhythmically towards the monastery. The charioteer stopped the chariot near the gate of the monastery. The Rani dismounted from the chariot and entered the verandah of the monastery. The maidservants followed her silently. Then she climbed the stone stairs and walked into the chamber, where she saw His Holiness Gurusiddhesa seated in a lotus posture on the tiger-skin seat on a cushion.

He welcomed the Rani with a serene smile. Rani Chennamma knelt down and offered her salutation to His Holiness. Then she took up a coconut and a few flowers from the maidservant and offered them to His Holiness who took them in his palms, mumbled holy *mantras*, blew them gently with his breath and offered them back to the Rani.

"Your Holiness, I need your blessings. For I have decided to fight the British enemies. I can defeat them with the help of your blessings." His Holiness Gurusiddhesa was really touched by Rani Chennamma'a appeal and also felt proud of her.

He raised his palms in a benedictory gesture and wished her, "Dear daughter, may Lord Gurusiddha bring victory to you and your kingdom. Please go ahead with your plans without any hesitation."

Rani Chennamma felt as if a new energy was injected into her veins. She felt heartened. She bowed to His Holiness once again and walked towards the Chowkimath of Lord Gurusiddha a few yards away from the chamber. She offered a special service to the shrine. The aroma of incense filled her with a sense of holiness and calm. She received the consecrated *prasada* and *tirtha* and walked back to her chariot. The maidservants followed her silently. When the Rani and the servants mounted the chariot, the charioteer whipped the horses, which began to clip-clop steadily towards her residential quarters.

The Rani went to her chamber and dispatched a messenger to fetch Diwan Gurusiddhappa and other officers immediately. Within half an hour Gurusiddhappa and other officers gathered in the Durbar Hall of the palace and waited for her. She entered the Hall with her usual poise and dignity. All the officers stood up as a mark of respect for the queen, who was almost like a mother to them.

She sat on her seat and addressed them seriously, "My brothers and patriots of Kittur, I have called this meeting only to intimate to you the course of action we have to follow. I have decided to fight the British and try my best to defeat them. This I can do only with your help and cooperation. I know you will all support me because the kingdom of Kittur is basically yours and I am only the figurehead. We have the support of late Raja Mallasarja whose spirit hovers around the kingdom to inspire us. We have also the blessings of Lord Gurusiddha. I want you all to fight bravely in the war with the British and defeat them or else sacrifice your lives for the sake of your kingdom."

There was pin drop silence in the Durbar-Hall. As soon as the Rani's address was over, the officers whispered among themselves for a few minutes.

At last Diwan Gurusiddhappa stood up and said, "Rani Sarkar, I, on behalf of all the leaders of Kittur give my word of honour that there is no second opinion about the decision that you have taken. Your Highness is not merely a queen but a mother figure as well. Today we all swear that we will fight for our kingdom until the last drop of blood remains in our veins. Either a victory over the British or a heroic death on the battlefield will clinch the matter. Nothing shall deter us from our patriotic path."

Everyone in the Hall was enthused by the passionate speech made by Diwan Gurusiddhappa, and they concluded it with the slogans, "Victory to Rani Chennamma," and "Victory to the kingdom of Kittur." Everybody joined the chorus of slogans.

Rani Chennamma's face was beaming with a smile of satisfaction. After the din of slogans faded out, She sat upright and addressed the gathering, "My dear brothers, I am very thankful you for your loyalty and patriotism. Now that you have all agreed to abide by my decision, I have to chalk out a plan of action and division of work for different people. First, I would like to declare that Sardar Avaradi Virappa be appointed as Commander-in-Chief of our army. I request everybody to obey him in all the military matters like planning of attack and execution. Do you have any objection to this?"

The Rani waited for a few seconds for the response of the audience. "No objection," said the officers in a chorus.

"Now, all the *sardars, subhedars, killedars, dalavais* and *chaubaris* of Kittur should be properly instructed about their duties. Similarly all the *shetsannadis* of our villages should be asked to rush to the city of Kittur. We should also request King Rajaram of Kolhapur to send a contingent of his army to Kittur to help us against the British. We must start this work today itself in right earnestness."

Avaradi Virappa stood up facing Rani Chennamma. He joined his palms in salutation to her and said, "Rani Sarkar, you have placed a very heavy responsibility upon my shoulders by making me the Commander-in-Chief. I do not know whether I am capable of this great task. But, however, I shall pray to Lord Gurusiddha to give me the necessary courage and intelligence to face the situation. I shall swear by my sword that I have consecrated every drop of my blood to the cause of Kittur."

He touched his forehead to his sword in a gesture of reverential determination. Rani Chennamma was also moved by Avaradi Virappa's passionate patriotism.

She said to him, "I am very happy to know that you have accepted the responsibility and I am sure you will do your best for the kingdom of Kittur. Commander Sir, you have to carry out all the instructions given by me just now not only quickly but systematically also."

"Rest assured, Rani Sarkar, I should do everything to the best of your satisfaction."

The meeting was dissolved after a few minutes.

*   *   *

The same evening many messengers were dispatched by Commander Avaradi Virappa to all the villages of Kittur kingdom in order to convey Rani Chennamma's express orders. The messengers rode their horses in all the eight directions. The city of Kittur was surrounded by eight hundred villages. Any enemy, who wanted to attack the city of Kittur, had to face the *shetsannadis* of these villages before he could reach Kittur, which was situated at the centre of the kingdom.

As soon as these people received Rani Chennamma's message, they began to send their soldiers to Kittur with all the weapons they could collect. Besides, they posted sentries on their respective hills or hillocks in order to relay the news of the arrival of enemies through bugle calls during the day and through bonfire signal during the nighttime. All the able-bodied young men, who had been trained in the art of swordplay or of handling the country-guns, began to rush to Kittur on horsebacks. The entire population was bubbling with patriotic feeling and readiness for fighting for their motherland.

* * *

Thackeray set out to Kittur along with Captain Elliot, Captain Deighton, Captain Black and other officers. The 5th Regiment of Madras had moved from Kaladagi up to Dharwad and now proceeded towards Kittur according to Thackeray's wish. His intention was to overawe the citizens of Kittur by exhibiting the military wealth of the Company government. The carts carrying the artillery trundled along the zigzag path surrounded by greenery.

They were preceded by the cavalry. The hooves of horses were stamping the earth in rapid rhythms and raised huge clouds of dust behind them. Then the buggies and *sarots* followed them. In them sat the wives and children of the British soldiers and officers. The windows of these vehicles were covered with curtains in order to prevent the infiltration of dust and scorching sun into them. The whole procession moved along rather slowly. A few servants had already gone to Kittur and started pitching tents for the soldiers, their wives, children and cooks.

* * *

Commander Avaradi Virappa heard from his spies that the Company servants were erecting their tents two miles west of the city of Kittur. He was surprised by the suddenness of it all. Nonetheless he got over the feeling of surprise and dispatched a few more of his soldiers to the western outskirts of the city and to ascertain all the details about the enemies. After a couple of hours he had the full report about the tents. He instantly rushed on horseback to the palace and barged into the Rani's chamber.

"What brings you at this time of the day, Commander Sir?" asked Rani Chennamma.

"Rani Sarkar, just now I have confirmed the news that the Company soldiers have been erecting their tents two miles away from Kittur towards the western side. I have, therefore, come to inform you about it," said Commander Avaradi Virappa.

The Rani suddenly grew very serious and said, "Commander Sir, I think the time for action is fast approaching. Now we have no time even to worry. You please place sentries at all the vantage points and keep our army ready for action."

"I have made all those arrangements, Rani Sarkar," said Sardar Virappa.

Then he took his leave of the Rani and went to supervise the military preparations.

The sentries, posted at Gadadamaradi, were watching all the movements of the Company soldiers, who were busy pitching the tents. Every three hours or so, they used to send reports to the Commander-in-Chief through the regular messengers.

The blacksmiths of Kittur were all busy in their smithies manufacturing new weapons like spears, guns, swords and daggers and sharpening the old ones. The agriculturists stopped visiting their fields and began to collect food grains and fodder in their houses, which might be required during the emergency.

Almost all the young men of the kingdom of Kittur had volunteered to join the military service and were practising swordplay, horse riding, shooting and fighting in the enclosed yard near the palace. The old men took up the responsibility of transporting or supplying weapons and food from smithies and homes to the yard of military training. The old and young women began to clean the cereals and grind them in their hand-mills on a rotational basis.

* * *

A sentry stood on the top of the hill at Narendra, which was the last border picket of Kittur kingdom and nearest to Dharwad. It commanded a wide view of the surrounding landscape. The sentry, who had been a loyal servant of Rani Chennamma, was only too eager to clear the debt that he and his family owed to her dynasty from generations together. As he stood on the top of the hill of Narendra and strained his eyes to scan the landscape around, he descried in the distance in the direction of Dharwad, a slow movement as if of ants followed by tiny clouds of dust. He also heard a faint din of horses' hooves. Lo, here are the enemies of our revered Rani, thought he.

Instantly he lifted up his bugle and put it to his mouth. He turned in the direction of Kittur and sounded it with all the energy in him .He repeated the call seven times and waited for the response from the next hill. Soon the sentry on the next hill relayed the call to the next sentry on the next hill. The sentry posted at Narendra felt a sense of satisfaction at having done his duty to the Rani. He knew the message of imminent danger would be conveyed to her within such a short time.

*   *   *

The sentry, who stood on the hill of Gadadamaradi, received the phonic message from the nearest hill and answered it with the sounds of his bugle. A messenger rushed to the Commander-in-Chief and conveyed the news of the arrival of the army.

Commander Avaradi Virappa rushed instantly to the Rani's chamber and said, "Rani Sarkar, we have received the message that the Company army is marching towards Kittur."

Rani Chennamma replied with bold determination, "All right, Commander sir. Please keep our soldiers at the ready for any eventuality." Commander Virappa bowed to the Rani and took leave of her.

All the soldiers were impatiently waiting for the Rani's orders. They were practicing their art very meticulously. They had promised their parents, wives and children that they would either return home victorious in the battle or attain heroic death and asked them not to cry for them but instead to feel proud of them.

*   *   *

On 21 October 1824, Thackeray thought of cowing the people of Kittur into submission.

"This time," he said to himself, "I shall be able to silence them."

He got up with determination and completed his morning ablutions. He looked at the fort of Kittur with supreme confidence tinctured with contempt. As soon as he finished his breakfast of egg omelette, bread toast and tea, he sent for his political assistants Stevenson and Elliot, and waited eagerly for them. After a few minutes, Stevenson and Elliot entered his tent with a salute.

"Please come in and be seated, Mr. Stevenson and Mr. Elliot. Please have some tea."

A servant brought three cups of tea and placed them on the cane tray. All the three of them helped themselves and sipped the tea leisurely.

"Today you should go to the Kittur fort and take a bond from all the leaders as being answerable for the treasury. Otherwise we cannot control these native fellows," said Thackeray.

Stevenson and Elliot looked at Thackeray for a moment and said, "Yes, Sir, We shall do it."

Then they discussed a few details and took their leave of Mr. Thackeray.

Stevenson and Elliot mounted their horses and rode from their camps of Kemmanamaradi to the fort at Kittur. They were accompanied by a few bodyguards. As they reached the fort, they dismounted from their horses and walked into the visitors' chamber. They sent the Company soldiers to bring in the important leaders of Kittur.

After nearly half an hour's waiting, Diwan Gurusiddhappa, Sardar Mallappa and a few others were brought to them. All the leaders of Kittur looked very defiant and contemptuous of the officers. They sat silently adjusting their silk turbans. The silence was very embarrassing to the British officers. Stevenson and Elliot looked at each other.

Then Stevenson said to the leaders seated before them, "Gentlemen, our Collector Mr. Thackeray has ordered us to take an undertaking from you to the effect that you are all responsible for the treasury of Kittur. You have to sign on this bond paper here."

The leaders of Kittur were obviously angered by the proposal. A fire was seen in their eyes. They twirled their moustaches in anger. Diwan Gurusiddhappa said, "Sir, please tell your Collector Thackeray that we will not give any undertaking or sign any bond without our Rani's permission."

Elliot tried to persuade them, "You have to sign. Otherwise our Collector will take a serious note of it."

Even as he was speaking the sentence Diwan Gurusiddhappa and other leaders stood up and walked away from there without caring for Stevenson and Elliot. The political assistants felt embarrassed and did not know what to do. Then they returned to Thackeray's camp on Kemmanamaradi hillock and reported all that had transpired.

Stevenson said, "Sir, we conveyed your message to Mr. Gurusiddhappa and other leaders of Kittur. But they said they were not ready to sign any bond or agreement without the Rani's permission."

Thackeray was terribly exasperated by the report.

Then Elliot continued, "I felt Sir, that somehow they were in a defiant mood this time. They didn't even have the courtesy to sit there patiently before us. On the contrary they refused to comply with our orders and just walked away without caring for us. We did not know what to do next. So we returned to report the same to you."

Thackeray also felt nonplussed for a moment. He remained silent and pressed his lips tight and stared at the ceiling of the tent. Stevenson and Elliot sat there patiently waiting for Thackeray's further orders.

Then Thackeray said to them, "Gentlemen, please send in the Commander of the Horse Artillery immediately."

"All right, Sir, we shall," said Stevenson and both of them took leave of Thackeray.

The Commander of the Horse Artillery bowed himself into the tent and said "Good morning Sir."

Thackeray said, "Good morning to you, Sir. Please be seated."

"What's the matter, Sir?" asked the Commander.

Thackeray cleared his throat and said, "See, Mr. Commander Sir, the leaders of Kittur have become very arrogant of late. I have to teach them a lesson. Today you must rush into the fort with your hundred horsemen and capture all those leaders including Mr. Gurusiddhappa. I must have them before me by the evening."

"But how to identify the leaders, Sir?" asked the Commander.

"Don't you worry about that. I shall send a few persons, who will help you to identify them," said Thackeray.

"In that case, no problem, Sir. I shall proceed on the work instantly."

He stood up to attention, saluted Thackeray and walked out of the tent.

Within half an hour a hundred horsemen were ready with their guns and swords. They marched along the dusty road from the western side towards the fort. They were accompanied by several other soldiers and their wives and children, who had come from Kaladagi, and who had been asked by Thackeray to go via Dharwad and Kittur.

According to Thackeray's plan all those soldiers along with their wives and children and military paraphernalia were asked to accompany the Horse Artillery and parade their military strength so that the natives of Kittur would be sufficiently cowed and overawed. Hence all the soldiers and their wives and children sat in these carriages and moved along with the Horse Artillery. It was indeed a very impressive sight. Thackeray thought that the exhibition of the guest soldiers along with the regular Horse Artillery would definitely create a very enervating effect upon the minds of natives.

The British military officers and their wives and children were followed by the hundred horsemen, who were followed by thirty-six cannons, dragged by several oxen. The cannons trundled along the uneven path of mud and gravel.

The soldiers of Kittur were ready to fight the enemies. They stood at all the vantage points of the fort. Commander Virappa was waiting for the right moment to take action against the Company army. As the Company horsemen entered the fort, the natives of Kittur did not show any resistance. Then the Company officers and their wives and children entered the fort. The front gate of the fort was kept open. Then the thirty-six cannons trundled along slowly into the fort. The soldiers of Kittur were waiting patiently for all that. As per the orders of Thackeray, Captain Elliot and Stevenson were to lead the Horse Artillery and the other Company officers through the fort of Kittur to overawe them into silence and submission. The Company soldiers accordingly thought that the soldiers of Kittur were helplessly watching the whole scene. The Company soldiers swelled with pride to show off their military strength.

When all the thirty-six cannons entered the fort, Commander Avaradi Virappa sounded his bugle and beckoned to his troops from the height of the ramparts. Before the horsemen of the Company artillery had time to arrange their own position or angle of attack, lo, they were surrounded by the soldiers of Kittur, who began to pierce and hack them to death indiscriminately. The soldiers of Kittur, who were hiding in the ramparts and halls, poured like ants and fell on the Company soldiers. Meanwhile the other soldiers rushed to the gate, closed it and secured it tightly. Now the horsemen of the Company Artillery were taken aback by the overwhelming army of Kittur. In the fight that ensued, many horses were mortally wounded and fell dead. There was a chaotic din of shouts, yells, shrieks and moaning. The Commander of the Horse Artillery did not know how to face the soldiers of Kittur, but pursued the fight in a dogged manner. Many Company soldiers were wounded by the swords of Kittur soldiers and tumbled down to the earth with piteous cries

and yells. Blood spurted and trickled from the wounds
made by the swords of Kittur heroes. The fight went on
in a hectic manner. Meanwhile patriotic cheers were heard
from the soldiers of Kittur.

When the Company soldiers saw some of their own
men lying dead in the fight, they began to scatter and
run for their lives. Some of them ran back to the fort-gate
and to their distress found it closed and bolted securely.
Then they ran along the fort-wall and escaped through the
sally port. Thus within a couple of hours the Company
Horse Artillery of hundred soldiers were routed. The dead
bodies of a few Company soldiers lay on the ground for
hours together. Crows and eagles began to hover around
them with their cawing and screaming. The retreat of
Thackeray's Horse Artillery gave new confidence to
Commander Virappa, who went and reported the matter
to Rani Chennamma jubilantly.

Rani Chennamma learnt that a few of the Company
soldiers had sought shelter in the civilians' houses and that
some others were hiding in the tents near Kemmanamaradi.
Commander Virappa also reported that the soldiers of
Kittur had captured a few Company soldiers and their
wives and children and brought them to the palace. He
asked Rani Chennamma whether the prisoners could be
shown into the Durbar Hall. When the Rani's permission
was granted, the Company prisoners shuffled into the
Durbar Hall with pale faces. Rani Chennamma was rather
surprised to notice the fact that the prisoners included a
few women and twelve children also including two of
Thackeray.

She ordered Commander Virappa, "Commander Sir, send these men into the prison."

The Commander beckoned to his soldiers, who led the male prisoners out of the Durbar-hall into the prison-cells. Then there remained only the British women and children. As Rani Chennamma scanned their faces, her heart melted out of pity for them.

She asked Commander Virappa, "Commander Sir, who are the fellows, who have captured these innocent women and children?" Commander Virappa felt rather embarrassed and fumbled for words. "Rani Sarkar, our soldiers, I mean our soldiers wanted to..."

"Should they not have had some common sense? These innocent women and children are like our own sisters and children."

The British women and children, who could not understand the vernacular dialogues of the Rani and her officers, stood helplessly blinking at them. Terror-stricken as they were, their hearts were palpitating and pounding ceaselessly.

Rani Chennamma stood up and went near the children and fondled their cheeks and patted their shoulders.

"Dear little ones," said the Rani, "please don't have any fear. We'll not do you any harm. Please feel free and comfortable."

Although the British women and children could not follow the Kannada language spoken by Rani Chennamma, they sensed the spirit behind her words and began to feel less tense. They watched the immaculate white marks of *vibhuti* on her forehead and the serene beauty of her face. For them Rani Chennamma looked like a veritable Goddess of the Orient.

Then the Rani ordered Commander Virappa, "Commander Sir, let these women and children be led into the guest hall of the palace and given food, shelter and other comforts."

Commander Virappa beckoned to the maidservants, who led the women and children into the guest-hall of the palace. Then they were fed with all the local delicacies, which were meant for the royal guests of Kittur palace.

*   *   *

When the Company soldiers reported the news of the death of many and the escape of a few soldiers and officers in the tussle with the patriots of Kittur, Thackeray felt furious and humiliated simultaneously. He felt so restless that he began to walk up and down in his own tent. He did not know how to tackle the people of Kittur. Besides, his ego was deeply wounded. He hurried through his dinner and drank a full bottle of whiskey just to forget the feeling of humiliation and tension. The butler and the servants withdrew to their tents lest their presence should irritate their boss. Though he lay down on his bed, he could not sleep even for a few hours. He could hear the occasional barking of dogs and screeching of wolves in the night. He began to puff at his *cheroot* continuously.

Thackeray was awakened by the twittering of birds in the Benjamin trees. He got up with a firm determination. He completed morning ablutions. He had mentally chalked out the plan of action for the day. When he finished his breakfast of boiled eggs and bread and started to sip his tea, a turbaned messenger came from the palace of Kittur and conveyed Rani Chennamma's message.

"Saheb Sir," said the messenger, "our Rani Sarkar has sent word through me that your women and children are quite safe in the royal guest house and treated with all due care and affection; that you need not worry about their safety and that you may take them away any time you like."

On hearing the message from the Rani, Thackeray felt relieved about the Company women and children. The turbaned messenger took his leave from there after ceremonially saluting the District Commissioner. Thackeray said to his subordinate officer,

"This Rani seems to be a thorough gentle lady. I was really worried about our women and children, but now I am free from tension. She is really a courteous lady. I had not expected this kind of gesture from her."

"Indeed, she must be a very fine lady," said the subordinate officer. "I am really touched by the Rani's kind gesture. She seems to be misled by her officers. I would like to meet her and convince her personally so that we could avoid so much of loss and tension on both the sides."

The subordinate officer endorsed it by saying, "There is no harm in trying that."

"Yes, that's a good idea," said Thackeray, "tomorrow I shall have an interview with her and persuade her to enter into an agreement with the Company government thereby putting an end to all the hostility between the two parties."

He went on waiting for that opportune time.

* * *

The next day Thackeray finished his morning ablutions and set out to the fort of Kittur along with his retinue. As he reached the fort he sent a messenger with a written message to the Rani and waited patiently there under the portico.

Rani Chennamma was consulting her officers about the burning problems of the kingdom. The guard entered the assembly hall and intimated the arrival of the messenger to Diwan Gurusiddhappa, who went towards the Rani and informed her. When the Rani's permission was conveyed to the messenger he entered the hall and handed over the script of message to the Diwan and withdrew.

As the Diwan handed it over to the official *dubhasi,* the latter read it silently and translated it as follows: "Rani Sarkar," he said, "Thackeray Esquire has asked you to surrender the kingdom peacefully to the Company Government and be satisfied with an *inam* of eleven villages. Otherwise you'll have to face a number of problems in future."

As the Rani and other officers heard the message, they knit their brows and grew very irritated by the proposition.

The translator continued further, "Thackeray Saheb wants to be allowed to have a personal interview with you, Rani Sarkar, in order to convince you about this proposition."

There was pin drop silence in the assembly hall. Rani Chennamma suddenly burst into guffaws of laughter and said, "Look at the cheek of Mr. Thackeray. What does he think of himself, and of me too? Does he think that I am a beggar to be satisfied with an *inam* of eleven villages? It is simply impossible."

Diwan Gurusiddhappa gnashed his teeth with anger. So did the other officers, *desais* and *shetsannadis.*

Sardar Konnur Mallappa stood up and said, "Rani Sarkar, nowadays Thackeray's arrogance is growing limitless. We must break it as early as possible."

He was panting with anger and excitement. As he sat down, Lingappa, another courtier stood up and said, "Rani Sarkar, it is below the dignity of your Highness to have an interview with Thackeray. We have heard many tales about his debaucheries. We cannot even discuss those things here. Kindly forgive me for this opinion," and sat down.

Then a few other members expressed their views.

After a consensus was arrived at, Rani Chennamma ordered Sardar Gurusiddhappa, "Diwan sir, please send the message that we are not willing to accept Thackeray's terms and that we are not able to have an interview with him because of indisposition."

The scribe wrote down the message. Then they sent a messenger with the letter and asked him to hand it over to Thackeray.

* * *

Thackeray was eagerly waiting in his tent for a message. He was discussing various methods of achieving success for the Company government. His assistants were listening to him patiently. Then a native messenger entered the tent with a salute and handed over the script of the message and went away. Thackeray flicked open the letter and pored over the lines.

"What does the Rani say?" asked the Assistant.

"Oh, the Rani is a very tough lady. She has not agreed to our proposition about the *inam*. She does not want to meet me today because of her indisposition," said Thackeray.

"Then what's the way out?" asked the Assistant.

"She is actually trying my patience. But she seems to be a fine gentlewoman. Let me wait for one more day. Tomorrow she may be in a better position to meet me," said Thackeray.

*　*　*

That night Rani Chennamma called a secret meeting of all the Sardars including Diwan Gurusiddhappa in the hall of Chowkimath Monastery and discussed the pros and cons of the encounter with the Company government.

Sardar Gurusiddhappa stood up and said, "Rani Sarkar, Thackeray has already installed his army near the Kemmanamaradi. Then what's the use of meeting him, who has already made up his mind to fight with us?"

The same opinion was endorsed by the other Sardars.

"In that case," said Rani Chennamma, "please send word to Thackeray that we are not willing to meet him personally."

The Court *dubhasi* prepared the script of the message and kept it ready.

*　*　*

The next day Thackeray went in his palanquin to the fort of Kittur. He sat in the *kutcheri* and sent his messenger to Diwan Gurusiddhappa asking for an interview with Rani Chennamma. Within a short time he received the return message in which the Rani had declined to see him personally as it was against the code of royal family. On reading the message, Thackeray felt deeply humiliated and exasperated. His anger rose to his cheeks and made them red with fury.

"Look at the cheek of the ordinary Rani refusing to see me. I was actually planning to help her settle everything peacefully. But she doesn't seem to want it. It's a mere child's play for me to destroy her and her kingdom," thought he.

He saw many civilians going into and coming out of the palace. He beckoned to many officers of Kittur, but they walked away from there without caring for him or for any Company officers. Vengeance began to take shape in him. In a huff he returned to his tent on Kemmanamaradi and began to plan the course of action and method of attack. His secret plan of having an amour with the Rani had also been frustrated. He changed his uniform and slipped on his nightgown. He beckoned to his butler, who began to lay the table.

After relaxing for an hour or so Thackeray got up from the string-cot and put on his uniform. He lit his *cheroot* and began to puff at it. The rings of smoke started wafting in the air slowly. As he rang the call-bell, a soldier appeared before him with a ceremonial salute.

"Please send in three messengers."

The soldier disappeared after the salute. Thackeray was puffing at his *cheroot* leisurely and mentally working out the details of military action. Within twenty minutes appeared three soldiers and saluted him ceremonially.

"Please go into the court of Kittur and ask all the leaders including Sardar Gurusiddhappa to come and see me immediately," ordered Thackeray.

The soldiers saluted the Collector and departed from there. The butler brought in the tray and kept the teapot and went away. Thackeray helped himself and sipped his tea and lit another *cheroot*.

Captain Black dropped in with a smile. "O please come in. I was about to send for you," said Thackeray. The butler brought in another kettle of tea and kept in on the cane table.

"Please help yourself," said Thackeray. Captain Black poured some tea into the cup and sipped it. Then he took out a *cheroot*, lit it and puffed at it.

"How far have you succeeded in negotiating with the Rani?" asked Captain Black.

"Yes, yes," said Thackeray, "yesterday I also tried to meet and convince the Rani, but she refused to see me."

"The Rani seems to be a very tough lady. We must admire her mettle," said Captain Black.

"Of course, her uncompromising patriotism is okay, but you know, it runs counter to our interests," said Thackeray.

Another officer entered the tent and joined them. All the three of them sat discussing the details of military operation. Then the three messengers returned from the fort of Kittur and saluted Thackeray.

"Sir," said one of the messengers, "we met Sardar Gurusiddhappa and informed him to come and meet you, but he refused to do so."

Another messenger continued, "He complained that he has not been treated by you with courtesy and respect. That is the reason why he has declined to meet you."

"So did the other Sardars and courtiers," said the third messenger.

Thackeray's fury knew no bounds. His blood rose to his cheeks. Captain Black and the other officers were observing him very keenly. Thackeray started panting with anger.

He pounded the table before him with his fist and said, "I must teach these bloody fellows the lesson of their life. They simply have no idea with whom they are dealing."

Captain Black said, "These natives seem to be very defiant and lose their lives unnecessarily."

Thackeray then said, "I have waited too long and patiently too. It's high time for me to act now. Captain Black, you please station two mortar guns near the gate of the fort immediately."

"Yes Sir, I shall attend to it," said Captain Black and went out of the tent.

Within no time were the horses hitched to the mortar guns and goaded on by the soldiers. The two guns trundled along the gravel path one behind the other. The guns were so heavy that the horses were foaming at the mouths. As the horses pulled them slowly, raising cloudlets of dust behind them, the civilian women and children stood and stared at them with curiosity mixed with fear. As the soldiers approached the fort gate, they unhitched the

horses from the mortar guns and pushed the guns to two
vantage points and stationed them facing the gateway of
Kittur fort. By that time dusk was setting in slowly on
the earth.

Captain Black walked into the Commissioner's office
tent and told Thackeray that the mortar guns were parked
near the fort-gate. Now Thackeray wanted to lose no time
as he had already decided to act and wreak vengeance
upon the Rani and the courtiers of Kittur. He struck the
call-bell. A soldier appeared instantly and saluted.

"Please send in the messenger," ordered Thackeray.

The soldier disappeared and sent in the messenger.

"Go and tell the Rani's Diwan Mr. Gurusiddhappa that
the Rani must surrender the kingdom and accept all our
terms and conditions failing which serious consequences
would follow," ordered Thackeray.

The messenger saluted and walked away from there.
The butler brought in a bottle of whiskey and two clarets
and placed them on the cane tray. Thackeray and Black
poured the whiskey into their clarets and sipped it after
saying, 'cheers' to each other. The candle-light was
flickering on the tray.

* * *

That night Rani Chennamma called a secret meeting in
the hall of Chowkimath Monastery. It was strictly guarded
by the soldiers. The yellowish torches were flickering in
all the corners of the hall. All the courtiers had gathered
there to discuss the details of the forthcoming war. Diwan
Gurusiddhappa, Rayanna, Amatur Balappa, Habsi Ram,
Rudrappa, Aravalli Virappa, Kamma Imamsab, Jamadar

Babasaheb and others were eagerly waiting for the Rani's order.

As Rani Chennamma lifted her veil from her face and began to address the gathering, there descended a pin drop silence on the audience. "My dear brothers of Kittur, I have called this confidential meeting to discuss our aims and plans of the battle that's likely to start any moment. As you all know, Thackeray's army has already camped near Kemmanamaradi. He seems to have made up his mind to destroy our kingdom. But we have also taken a decision to fight against the Company government until the last drop of blood remains in our body. I request all of you to fight for your kingdom and to be ready for the victory in the war or lay down your lives. You should all do your duties as assigned to you. Our Sardar Avaradi Virappa will be the Commander-in-Chief of our army. All the sixteen thousand soldiers have gathered in our city already and willing to lay down their lives for the motherland. I once again appeal to all of you to be alert and attend to your duties conscientiously." Rani Chennamma finished her words.

Then the courtiers wished to respond to her passionate request. Sardar Gurusiddhappa stood up and said, "Rani Sarkar, you need have no worry at all. We have sworn in the name of Lord Gurusiddha that we'll not shy away from anything. We'll fight unto our last breath."

Then Rudrappa stood up and posed a question to Rani Chennamma, "Rani Sarkar, please appoint a few special bodyguards for you in the ensuing battle, because your life is more precious than anybody else's."

Rani Chennamma said, "No, you are wrong, Rudrappa. Everybody's life is equally precious. You need not worry about my life."

"Nonetheless, you must appoint a few more bodyguards," suggested Sardar Mallappa. Rani Chennamma then said, "Let Amatur Balappa and Habsi Rama be my bodyguards."

"Yes, Rani Sarkar, that is a very good selection," said Rudrappa appreciatively. Amatur Balappa stood up and said, "Rani Sarkar has brought me up like her own son. She is more than my own mother. I shall protect her until my last breath," and thumped his chest with his right palm to show his determination.

Then Avaradi Virappa stood up with his sword drawn in his right hand and swore, "There is nothing more sacred for me than to protect my mother Chennamma."

Everybody in the hall said 'bravo' to them.

Finally His Holiness Gurusiddhesa said in his serene voice, "May Lord Gurusiddha give all the necessary courage to fight for your motherland!"

Everybody came in a queue and offered his obeisance to him by touching his feet with his palms reverentially.

His Holiness blessed them, "Little Mother, be victorious in the war."

After the secret meeting was over, Rani Chennamma returned to her chamber. She joined her daughter-in-law Rani Viravva and had her dinner. She then fondled her adopted grandson Master Sivalingappa for a while and returned to her bedroom. She was totally preoccupied with the war with the Company that was likely to begin the next day.

As Rani Chennamma rode her horse along the mountain slope, she spotted somebody riding opposite her. Out of curiosity she stood her horse and began to stare at the approaching figure. Her heart began to flutter fast and she understood that the approaching figure was none other than that of Mallasarja, who was smiling at her affectionately.

"Oh, is it you the lord of my heart? How long was I searching for you" exclaimed Rani Chennamma.

"I was also searching for you, oh mistress of my heart," said Mallasarja.

Both of them dismounted from their horses and went near each other. Rani Chennamma went into his arms. He smothered her with kisses and held her tight against his chest.

"My lord, how should I, a mere woman, manage the entire kingdom without you? Tomorrow I have to fight the battle with the Company army led by Thackeray," she said. "Don't worry, my Queen. I shall be always around you to protect you in the battle with Thackeray. You don't budge even an inch. I shall be inspiring all our soldiers on the battlefield. You don't have to worry at all. Go ahead you must," said King Mallasarja.

Rani Chennamma felt enthused by his assurance. She stood there affectionately gazing at Mallasarja's lustrous face.

The Rani was suddenly awakened by the shrill cockcrow and twittering of birds. She got up and completed her morning ablutions and worship of *istalinga*. She touched her palms to the feet of His Holiness Gurusiddhesa of Kallumath Monastery, who had rushed to the Rani's *puja*-room early in the morning. She also remembered her husband, the late Raja Mallasarja and felt new energy rush through her veins. Then she went into the kitchen and had her breakfast of *roti*, brinjal curry and curds.

Before she could wash her fingers, a maidservant entered the kitchen and informed her that Commander Avaradi Virappa, Sangolli Rayanna and Amatur Balappa were already waiting for her in the hall. Rani Chennamma robed herself in a *kinkaff* sari and blouse. Then she trussed the sari around her legs and tucked it behind and fixed it with a gem-studded girdle called *vadyana*. Her forehead was already decked with the triple marks of holy ash. Her wrists were covered with broad-brimmed gold bangles. Her *istalinga* was tied in a cloth around her neck. She then put on her helmet and steel shirt. She fixed the sword to her girdle. She slipped her shoes on and walked into the hall where the Commander and other military officers were waiting for her.

They stood up and saluted her immediately. There was firm determination writ upon her face. She turned to Sardar Avaradi Virappa, "Commander Sir, have all over soldiers gathered?"

"Yes, Sarkar. All the sixteen thousand soldiers of Kittur kingdom are waiting on the fort-precincts for the royal order. Besides we have secured the Main-Gate of the fort and taken charge of the guns and the few Company soldiers, who were on sentry duty yesterday. Hope it is all right."

"Commander Sir," said Rani Chennamma, "You have done well. We are all ready for action now. Where's my stallion?"

"It is waiting outside the hall, Sarkar," said Sangolli Rayanna. "Balanna, you have to be around me," said the Rani.

"Don't bother, Queen- Mother. What else am I here for if not to protect you?" assured Amatur Balappa.

"Come on, let's go," said the Rani and walked out of the hall. She then stepped on the crupper and jumped on to the broad back of the stallion and held the reins. In her heroic posture, she looked like the veritable Goddess Chamundi ready to destroy the Demon Mahisasura.

She rode towards the wide playground where sixteen thousand soldiers stood in regular files and platoons. The cavalry stood before the infantry. The soldiers of Kittur were clad in white narrow pajamas and tunics. Their heads were covered with tightly wound coils of turbans. The soldiers were eager to start the fight with the Company. They, therefore, twirled their moustaches and stamped the ground with their feet impatiently. Rani Chennamma rode between the files of the soldiers and received their salute. She was accompanied by Diwan Gurusiddhappa and the bodyguard, Amatur Balappa of Sadhunavar family. As she rode through all the files of the infantry and the cavalry, new energy surged through the veins of soldiers. After receiving the military salute Rani Chennamma stood on an elevated earthen platform. Commander Virappa and the bodyguards stood behind her. Rani Chennamma drew the sword from its sheath and held it high in the air. The blade of the sword flashed in the light of the morning sun.

"My brothers and heroes of Kittur," said Rani Chennamma in an elevated voice, "today is the decisive day in the history of Kittur kingdom. It is left to you to bring victory and glory to your motherland. You must all teach an unforgettable lesson to Thackeray and his soldiers."

The sixteen thousand soldiers cocked their ears and listened to Rani Chennamma's exhorting words.

Finally she shouted, "Victory to Kittur!" and "Victory to our Motherland!"

The entire army repeated the slogans in a loud chorus that boomed and echoed in the surrounding hills.

Then Commander Virappa shouted, "Victory to Rani Chennamma!" and "Victory to Kittur!"

The army once again repeated the slogans in a still louder chorus, which echoed back from the corridors of the fort. The Rani, then, rode towards the Main Gate. She was preceded by Commander Virappa and followed by her bodyguards. Then the *dalavais* and *dalapatis* began to direct their platoons according to the scheduled plan and occupy the vantage points of attack.

* * *

On the same morning, i.e., 23 October 1824, the artillery officer of the Company army rode to the fort of Kittur to change their guards. When he went near the outer gate, he was rather surprised to see it closed tightly.

He approached the Kittur guards and requested, "Excuse me, why is the gate closed? We have to change our guards. Please open it."

"We have been ordered by our superiors," said the Kittur guards, "not to open the gate."

They looked defiant in their tone and grew more alert in their duty. Then the artillery officer sent an express message to Mr. Thackeray, who was still waiting in his tent near Kemmanamaradi. He rushed to the fort-gate in a palanquin and saw that it was closed and bolted firmly from inside. Initially he felt disconcerted. Still he controlled himself and sent a message to Diwan Gurusiddhappa that the gates must be opened and sentries allowed in changing guards for duty.

The messenger walked towards the sally port and conveyed the message to the Kittur messenger and waited for a reply. Several minutes went by, but there was no response at all. The messenger returned and reported the same to Mr. Thackeray. Growing impatient, Thackeray sent another messenger repeating the same message and waited restlessly.

The second messenger went to the sally port and conveyed the same to the Kittur officer and drew a blank. After a few minutes he returned and reported it to Thackeray, who began to grow more and more furious.

Captain Black was also there watching the whole situation. "Captain Black," said Thackeray, "please get the other two mortar-guns and have them parked here in front of the gate."

"Yes sir," said Captain Black and walked a little away from there and shouted his order to his soldiers.

The Company soldiers went back to where the two mortar-guns were parked. They hitched them to two horses each and moved them towards the fort. The wheels of the mortar-guns creaked and rattled along the uneven gravel path. As they reached the fort, they unhitched the horses from the guns and pushed the heavy guns towards the gate. They kept them with their muzzles facing the fort-gate as directed by Captain Black.

When Thackeray was waiting near the gate, one of his spies went near him and whispered into his ear, "Sir, we have received intelligence from reliable sources that already two hundred native soldiers have gathered near the temple gymnasium in the fort and also that more and more number of soldiers have been streaming into the fort from surrounding villages."

On hearing this piece of news Thackeray felt a little nervous for the first time in his life. Yet he consciously tried to recover from it. He thanked the spy and beckoned to Captain Black, who stood a few yards away from him.

When Captain Black walked to him, Thackeray said to him, "Captain Black, the situation appears to be quite serious. Please get the Horse Artillery and the Cavalry as early as possible."

Captain Black immediately rode back to the tent near the hillock called Kemmanamaradi, where the army had camped. As soon as he gave order, his bugle man sounded the bugle, and all the soldiers of cavalry and infantry became alert, put on their uniforms and gathered their guns. Within a very short time they formed their platoons and marched towards the fort of Kittur.

The heat of the tropical sun was mounting slowly. Their guns were all greased with the fat of cows. Captain Black, Lieutenant Deighton and Mr. Sewell led the different sections of the army.

As they reached the fort, Thackeray gave his orders, "Captain Black and Lieutenant Deighton, you stand on both sides of the gate with your mortar guns and soldiers."

"Yes sir," said Captain Black and Lieutenant Deighton and walked towards their respective spots.

Thackeray ordered, "Mr. Sewell, you be ready with the entire artillery and cavalry a few yards away from the main gate and be ready to attack if necessary".

"Yes Sir," said Mr. Sewell and began to shout order to his soldiers.

When all the soldiers and officers occupied their places, Mr. Thackeray supervised the whole thing with a sense of satisfaction. He then sent a messenger to Sardar Gurusiddhappa asking him to open the fort-gate immediately.

A few minutes elapsed in expectation. Then the messenger returned and informed Thackeray, "Sardar Gurusidddhappa says that they will not open the gate unless our army is moved away from the gate to a safe distance. Mr. Thackeray's fury knew no bounds.

"Look at the hauteur of these fellows!" exclaimed he to himself.

Captain Black, Lieutenant Deighton and Mr. Sewell were watching him curiously. Mr. Thackeray lost his patience and sent another message through the courier.

"Ask Mr. Gurusiddhappa," he said, "to open the gate within a *gharri*, otherwise the gate will be blown open."

The messenger went to the sally port and conveyed the message. Mr. Thackeray waited for some reply or the other. But nothing was communicated. Every soldier and officer was tense and curious to know what would follow. Mr. Thackeray was looking at the clock. The needle of the second was darting around quickly. Sixty seconds went by. Then two minutes. Then five minutes elapsed. There was no sign. Ten minutes passed. There was no communication from the fort of Kittur. Fifteen minutes passed. There was tense silence in the army except for the neighing of horses. Twenty minutes elapsed and there was no response.

When the twenty-fourth minute was over, some stirring was heard behind the gate. The clanking of unclasping the metal bars and chains was heard from behind the gate. Mr. Thackeray felt happy to hear the sounds and guessed that at last the Rani of Kittur had come round.

Lo! The gate was suddenly burst open but to Thackeray's dismay, several thousands of Kittur soldiers rushed out on horseback with their swords raised high. It was so unexpected that Mr. Thackeray did not know how to cope with the situation. Captain Black and Lieutenant Deighton on either side of the gate wanted to operate the mortar guns. But alas, they had no time to do all that. The gallant soldiers rushed around them and began to hack them to pieces. Commander Avaradi Virappa was directing his army very intelligently. Soon Captain Black and Lieutenant Deighton were hacked to death. The blood of the enemies was spilled.

. Thackeray was watching everything furiously as well as helplessly. The heroic soldiers of Kittur rushed forward into Mr. Sewell's section of soldiers and started to hack them to pieces. There was a din of confusion. The shouts and cheers of Kittur soldiers were interspersed with the wailing, screaming and moaning of the Company soldiers whose arms or legs or other limbs were hacked and mangled indiscriminately. The bugle man was blowing his bugle as per the order of the Commander-in-Chief.

When Thackeray, seated in the palanquin, carried by eight Company soldiers, looked up at the rampart of the Kittur fort, he saw Rani Chennamma riding her horse and directing the Kittur soldiers to shoot at the Company soldiers below. She held her sword high in the air and was giving orders to her soldiers. The bodyguards like Sangolli Rayanna and Amatur Balappa of Sadhunavar family were protecting her from the possible attack from the Company soldiers from below.

When Thackeray saw the Rani riding her stallion on the rampart of the fort, terrible anger surged within him.

Rani Chennamma was observing. Thackeray from the top. Amatur Balappa, who was an expert shooter, had held his gun aiming at Mr. Thackeray's chest. Mr. Thackeray wanted to shoot at the Rani and, therefore, took up a gun from his soldier.

Rani Chennamma saw all this and shouted her order to Amatur Balappa, "Balya, shoot him."

Amatur Balappa lost no time and triggered the gun, which burst with a bang. Within no time the bullet hit the chest of Mr. Thackeray, who fell down on the plank of the palanquin with a jerk. Blood began to ooze out of the hole in his chest. Rani Chennamma saw it and felt extremely happy.

She looked appreciatively at Amatur Balappa and said, "Well done, my dear Balya."

Amatur Balappa was extremely happy to be appreciated by Rani Chennamma, who was like a mother to him.

The Kittur soldiers were engrossed in hacking, striking and mangling the Company enemies. When the thick lipped Negroid Habsi Ram saw Thackeray being killed by the bullet, he rushed to the spot and killed the palanquin-bearers. Some of them left the palanquin there and ran for life. Fury rushed through Habsi Ram's veins. He jumped down from his horse. He lifted up his sharp and glittering sword and struck it with all the force in him at the throat of the late Thackeray. Blood spilled out of the gash and the head was severed from the trunk.

He took up the dripping head of Thackeray and pierced it upon the pointed edge of his sword. He held it high for everyone to notice and began to shout, "Thackeray is dead. Thackeray is dead."

He began to move about on the battlefield. When the still surviving Company soldiers heard the news about the death of their leader, they started running away from the battlefield, leaving their guns and arms there.

Soon the gallant soldiers of Kittur began to cheer and shout, "Victory to Kittur! Victory to Rani Chennamma!"

The sun was setting in the western horizon and darkness was creeping in everywhere. But the cheers of the Kittur soldiers were being echoed in the corridors of the fort. They captured nearly forty soldiers belonging to the Company native infantry and European artillery, and led them to the fort and locked them in the dark dungeons.

A few officers of Thackeray's group escaped from the battlefield. They were running for their lives in different lanes of Kittur. A.R.Stevenson, Elliot and Sirastedar, Srinivasarao were running in different directions. The civilians of Kittur were watching the enemies very curiously.

Elliot was running along the road in a lane. There was darkness everywhere, but yet he could make out the contours of things though dimly.

"Why are you running? Please come here Saheb," said somebody in the dark.

Elliot felt that there was somebody eager to help him. He approached the anonymous figure in the dark. He could now make out that it was a turbaned and dhoti-clad man.

"What do you want to say?" asked Elliot.

The turbaned man said in Kannada, "You may have your shelter here tonight. You can eat and sleep here," with appropriate gestures of eating and sleeping.

Elliot could understand the spirit behind the civilian's words though he could not grasp the full import of Kannada words. He followed him into a big house. He saw the oil-mill operated by a bullock in the front room of the house. He obviously understood that the house belonged to an oil supplier. The host offered Elliot hot water to bathe, food to eat and a secluded room to sleep in. Likewise Stevenson and Srinivasarao took shelter in some other civilians' houses and spent the night in tension.

All through the night they worried secretly about how to escape from Kittur at the opportune time.

That evening Rani Chennamma called a meeting of all the officers in the Durbar Hall. All the important officers, sardars and desais had gathered there. Everybody was in a jubilant mood. She addressed the gathering, "My heroic brothers of Kittur, I have called this meeting to discuss some common issues."

Everybody was curious to know the agenda of the meeting.

The Rani continued, "Diwan Gurusiddhappa will explain the details," and looked at him meaningfully.

Diwan Gurusiddhappa stood up and addressed the assembly, "Dear patriots and gallants of Kittur, you have shown unprecedented heroism in killing and chasing away the British soldiers. But we are very sorry to know that some of our own people have worked against us by carrying tales and secret information to Mr. Thackeray and his company. Diwan Kannur Mallappa, Kannur Virappa and Sardar Mallappasetty are the traitors who, in spite of eating the salt of Kittur, have betrayed us to the *firangis*. It is up to you now to decide what punishment is to be given to these traitors."

But another officer opined, "Before punishing these traitors, let us try them in the court of our palace and see if they have relented."

"Yes, yes, that is a good idea," agreed another officer.

Diwan Gurusiddhappa asked the Rani in at a low pitch, "Rani Sarkar, if you permit us, we shall get those criminals here within a few minutes."

Rani Chennamma assented to the common opinion of the courtiers and nodded her assent. The people, who had gathered in the Durbar Hall, began to murmur and whisper about the traitors, who were going to be brought there. But soon the din of noise in the Durbar Hall disappeared as the three traitors were led into it handcuffed by the soldiers. Kannur Mallappa, Kannur Virappa and Sardar Mallappa were all looking crestfallen. As they had no moral courage to face either the Rani or the other courtiers of Kittur, they walked ahead with bent faces. They were made to stand in front of Rani Chennamma. Everybody was looking daggers at the common traitors. Diwan Gurusiddhappa felt like sundering them into pieces. But still he controlled himself. There was pin drop silence in the Durbar Hall. Everybody was eagerly waiting for the proceedings of the meeting.

Now the Rani could not control herself and asked them, "Gentlemen, we thought you were our people and fed you and your families for generations together. So you cleared your debt in a very memorable way, haven't you?"

There was absolute silence in the Durbar Hall. The three traitors were standing silently with their bent faces.

The Rani continued, "Tell me gentlemen, what I had done to you to deserve this kind of treatment from you?"

Again there was no response from the prisoners. The silence was very embarrassing for one and all.

Diwan Gurusiddhappa thundered, "Open your dirty mouths and answer the Rani Sarkar, you scoundrels."

Then Sardar Mallappasetty, who was looking pale, lifted up his face and answered in a rather arrogant tone, "What crime have we committed?"

Now uncontrollable anger shot up in the Rani who burst out, "Do you want us to declare your crimes as if they are not known to you?"

Then Mallappasetty replied, "We have not committed any crime."

Again the courtiers and the Rani were irritated beyond measure by the arrogant answer of Mallappasetty.

"You have betrayed us to our enemies by ganging up with Thackeray and his government. Isn't it a crime?" burst out the Rani.

"No., we have not betrayed you or the kingdom. We only wanted to be friendly with Thackeray, simply because the Company rulers are a very big power in our Hindustan and we could not afford to be inimical to them," replied Mallappasetty.

"Does that mean you should forget your own people, kith and kin and play into the enemies' hands?" retorted the Rani.

"We acted according to our limited light," replied Mallappasetty. "Can you swear by God that you have not received handful of bribe from Thackeray's officers?"

Mallappasetty felt deeply embarrassed and kept quiet.

"Don't you have an iota of patriotism in you? Do you think your personal growth is more important than the welfare of the whole kingdom, which has nourished you for generations together?" asked the Rani.

Again there was silence. "Do you think your dead-and-gone Thackeray will come and save you all through your life?" burst out the Rani. But there was no reply from the three prisoners.

Diwan Gurusiddhappa thundered. "You are not human beings, but cobras. Though we fed you with milk, you have given us only poison. In fact you are even worse than snakes which bite us only on provocation, but you have bitten us without any rhyme or reason."

The prisoners remained speech-less.

"Send them back to the dark dungeon until we take some decision about them," ordered Rani Chennamma.

Then the soldiers led the prisoners back to the dungeon cells.

The meeting continued. The Rani presided over the function. Diwan Gurusiddhappa stood up and addressed the gathering, "Dear patriots of Kittur. You have all shown unprecedented heroism and gallantry in the war and helped us to teach an unforgettable lesson to the Company people. It is therefore our duty to honour all the Sardars and soldiers, who have done their patriotic duty sincerely. Our Rani Sarkar wishes to know your opinion about the same before taking her final decision."

Then one of the officers stood up and said, "Rani Sarkar, we have all struggled to fight for Kittur out of our patriotic zeal and respect to the royal family. We have done so without any selfish desire. We, therefore, refuse to offer any suggestions about rewards. It is up to the Rani Sarkar to offer some appropriate initiatives to the soldiers and the widows of those, who have lost their lives in the battle."

When the Rani heard these words of the officers she felt disarmed by their selfless service and true patriotism. There was murmuring and whispering among the officers, who had gathered there for a while.

Then the Rani sat upright on the throne and announced, "Dear brothers, you have left everything to my discretion. Then I shall not fail to return your debt. I have decided to arrange a *dasoha* for about a thousand *jangamas* in the Kallumath Monastery tomorrow and alms for all the poor people of our kingdom. We shall present cash prizes, gold and silver bracelets, armlets, swords and new garments to our beloved soldiers. Our Sardars, who have helped us in defeating the enemies, will be given additional land grants. Please tell me if you want anything more."

There was a great cheer and clapping in the gathering. Everybody shouted the slogans, "Victory to Kittur and victory to Rani Chennamma, the Mother-Goddess for all of us!" The officers left the hall with cheerful smiles and lightened hearts. Rani Chennamma enjoyed the sight of their happiness to her heart's content.

The next morning all the important Sardars and soldiers gathered in the Durbar Hall of Kittur palace and received appropriate rewards like new swords, gold bracelets, armlets and precious garments. They were all overjoyed to receive them from Rani Chennamma. Then a *dasoha* was arranged for a thousand *jangamas* in the Kallumath Monastery. The *jangamas* partook of the delicious meal and blessed the Rani and her kingdom in general. Thus there was an atmosphere of jubilation everywhere in the city.

In the evening, a meeting was called again in the Durbar Hall. Rani Chennamma presided over the function as usual. All the Sardars occupied the appropriate seats. As the Rani looked at Gurusiddhappa and suggested to start the proceedings of the Durbar, he stood up and addressed the gathering,

"Dear patriots and gallants of Kittur, you have shown unprecedented heroism in killing and chasing away the Company soldiers. But we are sorry to know that some of our own people have betrayed us very heinously. You have seen how shameless and unscrupulous they are. They carried tales and secret information against us to Thackeray and his Company. Diwan Kannur Mallappa, Kannur Virappa and Sardar Mallappasetty are the traitors, who, in spite of eating the salt of Kittur, betrayed us to the *firangis*. It is up to you now to decide what punishment to be given to these traitors."

The courtiers stood up one by one and expressed their opinions. One of them, said, "Rani Sarkar, these traitors should be hanged by the banyan tree."

Another stood up and said, "Rani Sarkar, in my opinion, these traitors should be drowned in the open well."

Then yet another courtier stood up and said, "Rani Sarkar, I feel that the traitors should be stoned to death."

Then the fourth courtier stood up and suggested, "In my opinion, the traitors should be trampled upon by elephants."

A few others also stood up and expressed their opinions.

Diwan Gurusiddhappa stood up and requested Rani Chennamma, "Rani Sarkar, you have listened to the diverse opinions of the courtiers. Now you kindly approve of one of these modes of punishment for the traitors."

Rani Chennamma said, "Diwan sir, one thing is clear from your opinions that these men, who have eaten our salt and yet betrayed us, deserve to be killed by some mode or another. But I do not want to select a particular mode of killing, because my opinion is not different from yours. Whatever mode is commonly decided by you is acceptable to me."

The members of the assembly whispered among themselves and finally conveyed their consensus to the Diwan.

Then Diwan Gurusiddhappa stood up and said, "Rani Sarkar, the assembly has at last decided that the traitors should be trampled to death by the royal elephants." He waited for the Rani's response.

She said, "Whatever decision the assembly has taken has my approval. You may go ahead with the same."

There was a sense of satisfaction on the faces of courtiers because they felt their opinion was upheld by the Rani. Then they dispersed.

The next morning the traitors were brought out of the dungeon to the open ground where the onlookers had gathered to witness the scene. They had both pity and hatred together for the traitors. All the three traitors, namely Kannur Mallappa, Kannur Virappa and Sardar Mallappasetty were bound in shackles. As the soldiers led them, their shackles clinked and clanked. The traitors had bent their faces low in shame. The three *mahouts,* who sat on the elephants, were goading them with their tridents. The elephants ambled ahead slowly but majestically. The soldiers were trying to stave off the crowd of men, women and children, who were rushing towards the spot, where the traitors stood. As the bugle man gave the first call, the soldiers forced the three traitors to lie down on the ground. They lay down on their bellies helplessly. They remembered their wives and children and their entire past life and wept.

Then the bugler sounded the bugle for the second time. The *mahouts* started goading their elephants, which trumpeted hoarsely, stepped ahead slowly and stood near the traitors lying before them. Three more soldiers came near the elephants and impelled them to trample on the lying traitors. But the elephants hesitated for a few moments, as they were not used to such behaviour in the past. Then the *mahouts* goaded them with their tridents when the elephants suddenly stepped upon the traitors with their front legs. And lo! The bones of the traitors cracked as they screamed piteously and in a heart-rending manner. Their skins were torn and the blood and bowels oozed out with a horrible smell.

The womenfolk, who were witnessing the scene, started to cry in muffled voices. A few women, who could not stand the sight, fainted and fell down. The other men and women covered their eyes with their palms in order to avoid the pathetic sight and walked away from there. When the crowd dispersed from there, the crushed bodies of traitors were left there only for eagles and jackals to feast upon.

"Look at the fate of those who betrayed their own kingdom to the red monkeys," said the old women to the other women who were returning home.

* * *

Now that the old scores were settled, the people of Kittur rushed to the palace to celebrate their unprecedented victory in the battle against the Company. Thousands of wick lamps were lit on the parapets of the palace and the fort. The people of Kittur were so happy that they lit the wick-lamps on their thresholds, in their God-niches and offered special service to their family deities and prepared the best delicacies for the feast.

There was great jubilation in the palace. Every courtier and officer was happy. Rani Chennamma was, of course, the happiest of all. Everybody had put on his or her best garments and was giggling or smiling happily. The palace corridors and parapets were lined with thousands of wick-lamps. It appeared as if the people of Kittur were celebrating a very grand *Dipavali.* The royal priests offered a special service to Goddess Durga under the supervision of His Holiness Gurusiddhesa of Kallumath Monastery.

Rani Chennamma, whose face was effulgent with ecstasy, offered her salutations to the Goddess and then to His Holiness Gurusiddhesa. Then all the courtiers and officers followed suit. The royal troupes of instrumentalists were playing upon *shahnais,* drums, cymbals and other native pipes with the greatest enthusiasm. All those who listened to the exciting tunes and rhythms began to dance in ecstasy.

After the special service was rendered to the family deity, Rani Chennamma sat on her throne in a dignified posture. The minor son Sivalingappa sat near her on a separate chair. His Holiness Gurusiddhesa sat on a separate chair. Diwan Gurusiddhappa, Sangolli Rayanna,

Amatur Balappa and other Sardars and *shetsannadis* sat in their respective places to watch the entertainment programmes, which were to follow.

There came the court dancer Chandrasani with jingling bells on her ankles. The instrumentalists sat on the cushiony carpet near the wings of the stage. Everybody in the audience began to look at the stage curiously. The fiddler began to rub his bow upon the strings of the instrument. The delicate and sweet notes of the fiddle captured the attention of the audience. Then the drum-player started to thud and thump upon his instrument and provided the time beat to the fiddle notes. The cymbal players also took their cue from their leaders and began to chime them rhythmically.

When all the notes of the instruments set about the regular rhythm, Chandrasani stood up in a ready position. She was dressed like a goddess. She was robed in a shining silk sari and blouse with golden sepia border. She had trussed the shining folds of her sari around her thighs and tucked them up behind her waist. Her slender waist was secured with a golden belt. The front portion of her sari was decked with a semi-circular hem of rose coloured cloth with beautiful pleats. Her forehead was dotted with a saffron mark and the parting of her hair was adorned with a beautiful aigrette of yellowish pearls. Her arms and wrists were decorated with golden arm-bands and wrist-bands respectively. Her ankles were encircled with anklet bells.

As the rhythm of instrumental music reached a moderate tempo, Chandrasani moved her legs up and down, right and left, back and forth rhythmically, thereby producing a matching pleasant jingle of bells. She gesticulated her hands and fingers in a symmetrical way and mimed Goddess Durga's destruction of demons with a trident and the joy of success. The audience, who knew the mythical story of the Goddess, was watching the whole scene with expectation and appreciation. Her braid of hair swung and tossed with a flourish like a snake.

After the first phase of miming was over, the tempo sped from slow to medium. The dancer grew more agile in her limbs and quick in her gesticulations. Her earrings, nose-studs, necklaces, bracelets and wristbands glittered speedily in the yellowish light of the torches around. The ears of the audience were attuned to the bewitching music providing the backdrop to the harmonious movements. Then the tempo increased from medium to quick. The dancer began to move about with fourfold speed. She swung her shapely hips and bounced her beautiful breasts; she bent her knees and flexed her fingers. She hopped, swirled and jigged. She smiled and ogled fascinatingly. The quick jingle of her anklet-bells created a musical trance for the audience who were enraptured into it and felt as if they were floating in the high sky.

The members of the audience were awakened from the aesthetic trance only when the cocks began to crow in the morning. The dancer concluded her dance and received a small purse of gold coins from the officers. Then the members walked out of the hall towards their respective homes with lightened hearts.

* * *

The Company officers, who had escaped from the battlefield at Kittur, were fleeing all through the night for their lives. Dr. Turnbull, Officer of the decimated Horse Artillery, reached Dharwad about 6 o'clock in the evening. There was a gloomy atmosphere all around the hills of Dharwad. He jumped down from his horse and rushed into the office where Musgrave Harris sat. "Hallo Dr. Turnbull, how do you do? You seem to be tired and down in spirits. What's the matter?"

Dr. Turnbull slumped in the chair and said in a morose voice, "How shall I tell you, Mr. Harris! Many of our soldiers are wounded and killed."

Musgrave Harris was simply shocked out of his wits. He knit his brows and contorted his face, "What! So many are dead? Hope you are not lying!"

Dr. Turnbull cleared his throat and said in a low pitch, "No, I am not lying. It is a hard fact."

"I cannot believe my own ears. Could you tell me a few more details, please?" asked Harris.

Then Turnbull narrated how Thackeray was hard pressed for soldiers and weapons and how he therefore sent him to Dharwad to convey the urgent message requesting for more troops from other headquarters. Musgrave Harris could not sit idle after hearing the disturbing news. He instantly called his clerk and dictated the letter. The clerk wrote down the fair copy of the letter as follows:

To
Lt Col W. Durand
Commander of the Army
Dharwad.

Sir,

I write to inform you that an engagement has taken place at Kittur, between the troops of the deceased Rajah and part of the Horse Artillery, sent by the Political Agent, Mr. Thackeray. A horseman, who has just arrived at this place, Dr. Turnbull, states that the Artillery are entirely cut up, several of the Europeans both civil and military -- either severally wounded or killed-- Mr. Thackeray has given information at Belgaum to Colonel Pearce, and I have thought proper to send this information to you, as Commanding Officer to act as you think proper.

Dharwad	Sd/-
October 23, 1824	Musgrave Harris
	Civil Service.

Musgrave Harris scribbled his signature at the right side of the bottom. He then asked his clerk to send it to Colonel Pearce instantly. The clerk folded the letter, kept it inside a cover and handed it over to the messenger who took it and rode towards the cantonment.

Musgrave Harris heaved a sigh of relief temporarily. Walker Fullerton sat with him in a rather disturbed mood. A servant brought a tray with a kettle of tea and a few cups. Harris, Fullerton and Dr. Turnbull helped themselves and began to sip their tea rather mechanically. The darkness was thickening outside gradually. The clock struck seven. The candles, which were already lit by the servants, began to burn more brightly because of the growing darkness outside. Dr. Turnbull was narrating to them how the Rani of Kittur and her native soldiers were in a defiant mood and ready to face the Company.

Suddenly a messenger rushed into the chamber and said, breathlessly, "Sir, our Thackeray is no more. He was killed by the soldiers of the Rani."

All the three officers felt as though the news was a bolt from the blue. "Hope you are not lying or confused!' exclaimed Musgrave Harris. "I have been sent here by Mr. Thackeray himself. Is it possible that he is no more?" asked Dr. Turnbull in an incredulous voice.

The messenger cleared his throat and said, in a low but firm tone. "I saw him die with my own eyes, sir. First he was shot and later his head was severed from his trunk by some native black soldier. I rushed here to convey the news."

They were all panic-stricken by this news. They felt not only sad but deeply insulted also. Mr. Walker Fullerton, the Assistant Collector of Dharwad, called his scribe and dictated the following letter:

Directions

Ride...................Ride

Any Officer whatever Belgaum

Speed, all speed

Sir or Sirs

For God's sake send a force immediately without delay to Kittur. The artillery is cut to pieces — Mr. Thackeray supposed to be killed,

Captain Black cut to pieces. Sewell expected
to die—Deighton killed, and Thackeray's two
Assistants Elliot and Stevenson not heard of...
For God's sake, send immediately. Our force is
no use whatever, as we only muster 100 strong.

Dharwad   Yours
8 o'clock at night 23rd.   Sd/-
                                    Walker Fullerton
                                    Assistant Collector

That night there was a great commotion among the
Company military and civil officers at Dharwad. They
grew restless and began to consult one another about
what steps to take further. Messengers were sent to and
fro between offices and residences. They started sending
messages to all the military stations asking for urgent
movement of troops. They went on doing this until late
into the night when they could not remain awake any
longer.

The next morning they woke up with anxiety and began
to make hectic consultations and enquiries. Lieutenant
Colonel Durand sent a messenger to the Commanding
Officer at Bellary to apprise him of Thackeray's death and
the rebellion at Kittur headed by the Rani, who was also
planning to attack Dharwad. The messenger collected the
letter and rode towards Bellary forthwith.

In the meanwhile, the Company soldiers brought the
dead bodies of Thackeray, Captain Black, Lieutenant
Sewell and Lieutenant Deighton to Dharwad and kept
them in the Commissioner's bungalow for display to the

Company public. The bodies were shrouded in white cloth and placed on the floor of the hall, where all the military officers and civil officers offered their salute and crossed themselves. The women and children were crying and sobbing rather silently in the corner.

After three hours the dead bodies were kept in separate coffins and taken in *sarots* to the European cemetery to the northeast of Dharwad city. All the other officers followed them on horseback. When they reached the cemetery, the gravediggers were giving finishing touch to the grave-pits. The priest performed the last rites. The whole gathering sang the prayer. Then the Company soldiers offered a military salute to the departed souls. The band set with their pipes and drums sang a mourning tune. The priest read a little portion of the *Bible*:

> Let us commend our brothers departed to God.
> The souls of the righteous are in the hand of God:
> And no torment will ever touch them.
> Let us pray.

> Almighty God, with whom do live the spirits of them that depart hence in the Lord, and with whom the souls of the faithful are in joy and felicity. We commend into thy hands the souls of these brothers; trusting that thou will bring them into sure consolation and rest. Grant. We beseech thee that at the day of Judgment these and all thy people departed out of this life, may with us, and we with them, fully receive thy promises, and be

made perfect, through the glorious resurrection of
thy son Jesus Christ our Lord, Amen.

Then the coffins were lowered into the pits. The
gravediggers began to fill them with mud with their
shovels. The Company officers dispersed to their
respective residences with heavy hearts.

* * *

When the Rani and her soldiers had achieved victory
in the war, all the people of Kittur celebrated it by making
a song and dance of it. That very night Rani Chennamma
took leave of her army and went to the Chowkimath
Monastery along with her assistants and Commander
of the army, Sardar Gurusiddhappa, Snagolli Rayanna,
Avaradi Virappa, Sardar Himmat Singh, Sri Narsing Rao
and others. The Rani's horse carriage was followed by all
these dignitaries on horseback through the lanes of Kittur.
Everywhere the civilians were lighting the lamps in front
of their houses and on the thresholds.

When they reached the precincts of the monastery,
Rani Chennamma got off the carriage and entered the
hall and then the *sanctum* and offered *bhel* leaves and
flowers to the deity, i.e., Lord Gurusiddha and offered her
salutations by reverentially joining her palms. The other
sardars and the Commander also followed suit. Then the
Rani gently walked into the other hall where His Holiness
Gurusiddhesa sat on his tiger-skin seat.

Rani Chennamma bowed down to His Holiness by
touching his feet with her forehead. His Holiness raised his

right palm in a benedictory gesture and wished her, "May Lord Gurusiddha shower all his blessings upon you!"

Then the other sardars also offered their salutations to His Holiness. After the reverential formalities were over, His Holiness beckoned to all the visitors to be seated. They all occupied their respective seats. Then Rani Chennamma said enthusiastically, "Your Holiness, today we have won victory over the Company army and taken many prisoners."

His Holiness felt cheerful to have heard the news of victory and said, "Daughter, you have brought great honour to the kingdom of Kittur. Your victory is ascribable to your righteousness in thought, speech and action. Lord Gurusiddha is behind all your actions," and raised his palms towards Heaven.

"My soul is filled with happiness today," continued His Holiness. There was silence of satisfaction for a couple of moments.

Then Rani Chennamma said, "At present we have achieved victory over the Company people, but we cannot sleep over it now. We have received intelligence that the Company officers have sent messengers to Belgaum to bring troops to Kittur. They may not sit idle now. They will muster all army at their command."

His Holiness cleared his throat and said, "I am very happy to know that you are well aware of your responsibilities. Daughter, you please remember the fact that you have wounded the snake, i.e., the Company sarkar and not killed it. You know that the wounded snake will be all the more angry and vindictive. We do not know when it will slither into our bed and bite us."

Rani Chennamma said, "That's what I also know at heart. That's the reason why I have been very alert. I know our Kittur fort is a very formidable one, but our army is nothing before the large army of the Company sarkar. Our weapons cannot be a match to their superior weapons and war techniques. Just four days ago we sent an urgent message to the Raja of Kolhapur for military help. I have been waiting for his answer."

"You have done the very right thing, Daughter," said His Holiness, "you have to do all that you can to save the honour of Kittur."

The Rani continued, "Besides, we have taken prisoners about forty Company persons including two important civil officers, i.e., Stevenson and Walker Elliot."

His Holiness listened to her words very carefully, "You have done your best, daughter. But, I am afraid, this is not the final victory. You'll have to be more alert in future. We have already wounded the demon and we do not know when he will pounce upon us."

It was already late in the night. Rani Chennamma and her sardars shuffled out of the monastery and returned to their respective abodes.

* * *

The next morning all the Sardars attended the meeting in the Durbar Hall of the palace presided over by Rani Chennamma. The Durbar Hall was strictly guarded by the sentries.

As the Rani beckoned, Sardar Gurusiddhappa stood up and said, "Gentlemen, Rani Sarkar has called this meeting to discuss what course of action we have to follow next. We shall all come to a consensus after discussion," and sat down.

There was a murmur in the hall of mutual consultation and exchange of views and opinions.

After a few minutes went by, Sardar Gurusiddhappa said, "Gentlemen, you could express your views one by one."

Avaradi Virappa stood up and said, "We must treat all the Company prisoners as hostages until the Company sarkar agrees to our terms and conditions."

Himmat Singh stood up and said, "Sardar Virappa's suggestion is a good one. But we should not take any hasty decision. We must use the prisoners as messengers of good will to their government. That is the first stage. If we cannot succeed in it, then we can move on to the second stage."

Then Sardar Gurusiddhappa stood up and said, "Rani Sarkar, in case the British Officers do not agree to our terms, we shall treat these prisoners as hostages. We'll have to take revenge upon these fellows in a proper manner."

His eyes appeared fiery as usual. He looked at the members of the meeting and sat down.

"What is your opinion, Sardar Virappa?" asked Rani Chennamma.

Sardar Virappa stood up and said, "Rani Sarkar, in my opinion we should resort to all these methods suggested by the members here, very discreetly. We should also try for amity with the Company sarkar and plead for the restoration of autonomy to our kingdom. Meanwhile we should also muster up our military strength to fight for the motherland. We should be willing to spill our blood for the honour of our land."

Rani Chennamma listened to the opinions of all the sardars, who happened to be her well-wishers. She said in her serene, but firm patriotic voice, "Gentlemen, there is no disagreeing with your views at all. We shall act accordingly but in a gradual manner. We shall treat Stevenson and Elliot amicably and ask them to plead for our causes and wait for the result We have already sought the help of the Raja of Kolhapur and many other kings of the Deccan. If all of our native kings join together we can fight the Company sarkar very easily. Sardar Gurusiddhappa, tomorrow you meet Elliot and Stevenson and ask them to do as I suggested."

* * *

The next day, Sardar Gurusiddhappa, Avaradi Virappa and Sardar Himmat Singh went to the prison. The native guards stood up to attention and saluted the authorities ceremonially. As they walked to the dungeon rooms, they saw Stevenson and Elliot were reclining against the walls of their respective rooms behind the bars. The two important prisoners were blinking at the officers of Kittur helplessly. Sardar Gurusiddhappa beckoned to them. Then Stevenson and Elliot shuffled towards them and stood askance behind the bars.

Avaradi Virappa said to them in Kannada, which was translated into English by the *dubhasi,* "Gentlemen, you need not worry about your stay and security here. No harm will be done to you. You'll not be troubled in any way. On the contrary you'll be treated well as our guests."

Stevenson and Elliot muttered, "Thank you."

Sardar Gurusiddhappa said, "Gentlemen, we have sent an appeal to the Governor, Elphinstone at Bombay to restore autonomy to our kingdom. We have also written to him how we have been ill-treated by Thackeray. We will not give you any trouble until we hear from the Governor of Bombay. Our Rani has even permitted you to correspond with your authorities and keep them informed about the state of affairs at Kittur. You should not misinterpret our humanitarian gesture as our weakness. We, the people of Kittur, love freedom more than our life. In case the Company tries to overrun Kittur by military strength, we will kill both of you first and then kill our own women including Rani Chennamma and fight for freedom on the battlefield until we breathe our last."

Then Sardar Himmat Singh said in a gruff voice, "Gentlemen be careful. If you indulge in any mischief we'll twist your necks within no time. If at all you are still alive, it is only because of our Rani's extraordinary kindness."

Stevenson and Elliot were really touched by Rani Chennamma's humanitarianism. But at the same time a tremor passed through their spines when they remembered the threats also. Then Sardar Gurusiddhappa, Avaradi Virappa and Himmat Singh walked out of the prison building in a jubilant mood.

* * *

The Company prisoners were awakened by the twitter of birds on trees and the sound of *shahnai* wafting from the palace yard. Stevenson and Elliot completed their morning ablutions. The sentries offered them their breakfast of *chapatis* and brinjal curry and chutney. The prisoners completed their breakfast with their fingers because they were not offered forks and knives. Then they asked for some paper, pen and ink. The sentries gave them some rough paper and a small bottle of black ink and a sharpened stick. Stevenson dipped the slender stick in the ink bottle and began to scribble on the rough paper and addressed it to the Commissioner in the Deccan. The stick made a creaking sound as he scribbled the letter on:

> From:
> J.A.R.Stevenson Esq.   24th October, 1824
> To
> W.Chaplin
> Commissioner in Deccan.

Sir,

It is my melancholic duty to inform you of the death of Mr. Thackeray. He was shot yesterday when on his way to the gateway of Kittur fort. The Sardars of Kittur had for some day shown great dissatisfaction and at last refused to attend to my directions and having shut the gates refused admittance to any person. For the safety of the treasure Mr. Thackeray had found it requisite to place a guard of *sepoys* and a few guns in the front and upon access being refused to Captain Black of the Madras Artillery to relieve the guard, Mr. Thackeray warned the Sardars that the gate would be blown open if not opened in a *gharee*.

As the gate was opened, and as no person appeared with any answer Captain Black, Captain. Sewell and Lieutenant Deighton, with two guns proceeded to blow the gate open. I must shorten my melancholic story. The peons from the Fort made a sally and took the guns and put every person to the sword that came in their way. Just at this time, poor Thackeray unfortunately appeared and was shot. The three Artillery Officers, I fear, have also fallen. Mr. Elliot and myself escaped but were soon taken. Our own lives were with difficulty saved and we are now prisoners. They refuse to relieve us until they hear from Bombay but we do not consider our lives safe as the peons are under no command when once their blood is warmed. Nor do we consider the word of the Sardars in the least to be depended on, if the answer from Bombay to their letter is unfavorable to their wishes. The Sardars say that if they are attacked, they intend first killing the women and then themselves.

Excuse this hurried scrawl. I write with a stick.

Kittur

I have
Sd/-
J.A.R. Stevenson.

After completing the letter, Mr. Stevenson read it once again. He dotted the 'i's and crossed the 't's. He put commas and full stops wherever necessary. Then he folded the letter neatly and put it inside a cover and handed it over to the jail officer.

Then the sentry took the ink bottle, the stick and the paper to the next room and gave them to Mr. Elliot. Mr. Elliot took the writing materials, sat in the attentive position and began to scribble the letter as follows:

Besides Mr. Stevenson and Mr. Elliot, one of the Sirastedars Srinivasarao and a European Artillery-man with 30 to 40 *sepoys* and native Horse Artillery are prisoners. The leader in the present disturbance is Sardar Gurusiddhappa, who acts entirely in the name of the Dowager Desai Chennavva, the widow of Desai Mallasarja. The letter sustains her right to the succession in the preference to the widow of the late Desai. His party having now gone so far, talks of resisting to the last if Government does not agree to their proposition. Mr. Stevenson and myself are to be detained till the answer to their communication arrives hoping that our safety will induce government to consider their claims more favorably, should decisive measures be adopted, I have no doubt, they will resist to the last and probably wreak their vengeance on us. Gurusiddhappa is a weak character but most obstinate. He is collecting his s*etsunadis* from every side and the fort probably now contains upward of 5,000 men.

Sd/-
Elliot.

Elliot scribbled his signature read the letter and corrected the mistakes. He then folded the same, put it into an envelope and handed it over to the jail officer of Kittur. The jail officer took the two letters of Stevenson and Elliot to his chamber near the entrance of the building. He asked the *dubhasi* to seal the letters. Accordingly he folded the letters, put them into two separate covers, sealed them properly and handed them to the native messengers.

* * *

On the 24 of October 1824, Diwan Gurusiddhappa bowed himself into Rani Chennamma's Durbar Hall and sat in his chair.

"How are things going, Sardar Gurusiddhappa?" asked Rani Chennamma. "Rani Sarkar," said Sardar Gurusiddhappa "yesterday we met Stevenson and Elliot and conveyed your orders. We have also asked them to write to their authorities and sent the letters through the Sirastedar Srinivasarao under strict warning to return to Kittur immediately. Srinivasarao is accompanied by our soldier."

"Sardar Sir," said Rani Chennamma sitting upright on her cushioned seat, "you have done the right thing. Today you send a small unit of our army to guard the ferry on the Malaprabha River near Mugutkhan-Hubballi and prevent the Company army from crossing it and hold them back as long as possible. Ask them to sink all the boats on the riverside. In the meanwhile, you please send another small platoon to patrol the road between Mugutkhan - Hubballi and Kittur."

"Rani Sarkar," said Sardar Gurusiddhappa, "I shall do so instantly."

He bowed to the Rani and went out of the Durbar Hall.

He rode his horse straight to the military officer and ordered two units of the army to proceed. Within half an hour all the soldiers of the two units sheathed their swords, sat on their horses and marched towards Mugutkhan-Hubballi on the rugged path.

The horses broke into a canter raising cloudlets of dust behind them. The soldiers whistled occasionally. The horses whinnied as if in response to the riders' whistles and cheers. When they reached the midway between Kittur and Mugutkhan-Hubballi, one platoon halted there to patrol along the road.

The second platoon went ahead. The deer and wild cats were scared away by the sound of horses' hooves. The monkeys grimaced at the soldiers from the trees and ran away from there. The peacocks folded their tails and scampered away across the road. At last the soldiers reached the sandy banks of the River Malaprabha, where the water was flowing with a gentle murmur. The *koels* cooed occasionally punctuating the silence there. The *dalavai* of the platoon called the ferrymen, who were crouching on the sand under the umbrageous shelter of banyan trees there. The sand was dotted with innumerable tiny, red Banyan fruits all over there. The ferrymen got up, adjusted their dhotis and rushed towards the *dalavai* and joined their palms reverentially.

"Gentlemen," said the *dalavai*, "our Rani has ordered that all the boats on the river should be sunk immediately and prevent the Company army from crossing over here. Our soldiers will help you to sink them. You please show them all the boats at various spots."

The ferrymen understood the gravity of the situation and said, "As you wish sir."

Then four soldiers walked into the river to the nearest boat and pushed it ahead for about twenty feet where the water was neck-deep. Then they tilted it gently into the water until water filled it up and down went the boat to the bottom of the river creating circles of big waves and air bubbles. Then the soldiers waded through the water to the bank. Their garments were all wet up to their necks. Water dripped from their bodies continuously. Then they rushed to the other parts of the river and sank several others. The *dalavai* followed the ferrymen and soldiers and supervised the work. After confirming that all the boats on the river were sunk, he ordered his soldiers to stand at regular distances and patrol.

* * *

Meanwhile Rani Chennamma called a confidential meeting at her Durbar. All the courtiers and Sardars gave their opinion in the meeting. After mutual consultation they arrived at a common consensus. At last Sardar Gurusiddhappa stood up and said, "As per the direction of Rani Sarkar, we have to depute our *vakil* Srinivasarao to go to Dharwad and try for negotiation and peaceful settlement of the matter. Do you have any objection or other suggestions?"

"No objection at all. We fully support Rani Sarkar's decision," said a senior Sardar.

Then Sardar Gurusiddhappa consulted Rani Chennamma in a confidential tone. He then called the *vakil* Srinivasarao and briefed him about the terms and conditions of the negotiation. Srinivasarao noted down the important points on a piece of paper. Then he saluted the Rani ceremonially and walked out of the Durbar Hall. He went straight to the place where his horse was tethered. He untethered it and quickly mounted it and began to spur it in the flanks. The horse carried him towards Dharwad along the winding roads of undulating land.

* * *

Chaplin, the Commissioner of the Deccan, at Pune was shocked out of his wits when he heard the news of Thackeray's death at Kittur insurrection.

"I still cannot believe," said he to his assistant, "that Mr. Thackeray with all his shrewdness and competence could be killed by the fellows of Kittur. His death has been an unforgettable stigma on our Company prestige.

"What I guess Sir," said his assistant, "is that things must have happened in an unexpected manner. Otherwise Mr. Thackeray would not have succumbed to such a small kingdom as Kittur."

"Now, we cannot keep quiet," said Chaplin in an impassioned tone, "it is a great insult to our imperial power. I must do all I can for wiping out the kingdom of Kittur." His assistant approved it with his silence.

Two days later, when Chaplin was busy attending to the routine matters of the office, a messenger came from Dharwad and delivered a confidential letter and explained orally how the Rani of Kittur had sent her lawyer for peaceful negotiations. Chaplin ripped open the letter and pored over it curiously. Then he folded it up and kept it back in the cover. He leant his face against his palms, closed his eyes for a few moments and deliberated the matter.

Then he opened his eyes and said to his assistant, "The only way to defeat the Rani is to take her by surprise. We require some time to mobilize our forces at different headquarters. Until then we shall pretend to carry on negotiations with the Rani."

"Yes, that's a very good idea, Sir," said the assistant.

Chaplin then said, "We shall appoint Mr. R. Eden as the Acting Political Agent with headquarters at Belgaum and Mr. Munro the Junior as the Acting Collector at Dharwad. You please send an order to Mr. Eden authorizing him to carry on negotiations with the Rani of Kittur until further instruction."

The assistant called his scribe and dictated the orders and corrected the drafts with his quill. Then Chaplin scribbled his signature below the matter at the right-hand corner. The assistant folded the letters and kept them in two separate covers and handed them to the messengers. When the messengers left for Belgaum and Dharwad, Chaplin began to send instructions to all the military headquarters to be ready to proceed.

* * *

Colonel Pearce, Commander of the Headquarters Field Force Doab at Belgaum, had been sending detailed information about the forces that he had sent to Kittur. As he received directions from Chaplin at Pune, he instructed Lieutenant Colonel McLeod to proceed towards Kittur. Accordingly Lieutenant Colonel McLeod led his 4th Regiment Light Cavalry from Belgaum. The brown coloured horses whinnied and ran ahead raising cloudlets of dust behind them. As they gathered speed after leaving the outskirts of Belgaum, the rhythm of their hooves scared the wayside birds and wild animals. They marched ahead for a few miles.

*   *   *

Colonel F. Pearce heaved a sigh of relief after dispatching Lieutenant Colonel. McLeod towards Kittur. He sat with Mr. I.I.O.Donoghue, Assistant Quartermaster General of the Army and began to chat with him. A butler came and served some whiskey-*pani* and two egg omelettes. Both of them helped themselves. They silently sipped the whiskey from the decanters and swallowed the pieces of omelettes in between. Then the butler brought a box of *cheroots* and kept it on the tray. Colonel F. Pearce and I.I.O Donoghue picked up the *cheroots*, lit them and began to puff at them leisurely. The curls of smoke rose up in the air in the form of gyres.

They were about to leave for their residential quarters when a messenger from Dharwad came and saluted them.

Colonel Pearce said, "Welcome gentleman. What's the matter?"

The messenger said in his usual Company accent, "I have been sent by the Army Officer at Dharwad. We have planned to attack Dharwad. Hence our officer has requested you to send some army to Dharwad immediately."

On hearing this message Colonel Pearce lost his temper and burst out, "Oh my God! Just a couple of hours ago we sent Mr. McLeod's Light Cavalry to Kittur. I do not know how much that Rani of Kittur wants to trouble us. Yet I must admire her tact and courage."

He stood up and walked a few paces up and down in his office. Thus having made up his mind, he instructed I.I.O Donoghue, "Gentleman, please send a messenger posthaste to Lieutenant Colonel McLeod asking him to proceed towards Dharwad instead of Kittur." Donoghue then ordered his scribe to write an urgent letter, which read as follows:

> Assistant Quartermaster General's
> Office, Camp: Belgaum.
> Date: October 1824
> To
> Lieutenant Colonel McLeod
> Commanding 4th Regiment Light Cavalry
>
> Sir,
>   The calamitous event that occurred on the 23rd instant at Kittur, and caused the death of Mr. Thackeray, also the destruction as well, of the Horse Brigade, as of a company of the 5th Regiment Native Infantry and the confinement

in that of Messers Elliot and Stevenson, has given rise to a general insurrection throughout the country, which is said to be strongly patrolled between the Malaprabha River and Kittur, besides the boats on that river being sunk.

Added to these circumstances, information has been received of it being the intention of the Kittur Insurgents to attack Dharwad, where is the Principal Collector's Treasury, besides a considerable number of convicts; and that fortress has consequently become exposed to a great danger from its vicinity to the place of rebellion.

It is, therefore, necessary to interpose an adequate force between Kittur and Dharwad, to cover the latter place from any meditated attack of the Insurgents.

With this view, the Ordnance, and several Detachments of Corps, detailed in the margin are to compose such force, which is placed under your immediate command.

You will accordingly move it tomorrow morning upon Mugutkhan-Hubballi on the Malaprabha River, when the Ordnance arrives, you will cross that river and proceed to occupy a position nearly midway between Kittur and Dharwad, but rather more towards the latter than the former place so as to cover it.

You will be pleased to consider the Detachment under your command as one of observation to gain information regarding the movement of the rebels, rather than aggression; and to that end you will detach strong camp patrols, and make occasional reconnaissance with both Cavalry and Infantry, towards Kittur of the result of which, with information you may judge necessary, you will keep District Headquarters constantly advised.

Ignorance of who is the late Mr. Thackeray's successor in the Civil Department, prevents Colonel Pearce from giving any instructions relative to your communication with that Gentleman; but, should any one address you as such, you will accordingly communicate with them regarding the existing state of affairs; nor however attempting any attack upon the Fort of Kittur without Colonel Pearce's previous sanction to the measure.

You are to communicate with reserve with the officer commanding at Dharwad.

Sd/-

I.I.O Donoghue

Asst. Quartermaster General

He ran his eyes quickly upon the letter and put his signature. The clerk collected the letter, folded it and inserted it into a cover. The attendant called the courier, who sat in the room outside, and handed over the letter to him for dispatch.

Colonel Pearce called Assistant Quartermaster General and enquired about the action taken by the latter.

Donoghue replied, "Just now I dispatched a message to Colonel McLeod, Sir."

"That is very good," said Colonel Pearce, "Now we have to inform the Quartermaster-General at Pune about the steps we have taken. Otherwise he'll be restless."

"Yes sir, we must," said Donoghue. Then the scribe was called in. The scribe came in with his paraphernalia of quill, ink bottle, white paper and blotting paper and sat at his table ready to take down. Colonel Pearce cleared his throat and dictated the letter.

Colonel Pearce

Commander of the Headquarters Field Force.
Belgaum
25, Oct. 1824

...I have in consequence directed the movement under Lieutenant Colonel McLeod 4th Cavalry of as great a portion of that regiment as can be mounted with the exception of one of squadrons and sick horses, of as many squadrons, as there are bullocks to draw them, of a Company of His Majesty's 46th Foot, of the two flank Companies of the 49th Regiment and of a Company of Pioneers.

I have also ordered the immediate march of the 23rd Light Infantry from Solapur upon Belgaum carriage being supplied for their knapsacks.

I have further solicited from the Officer Commanding in the ceded Districts an immediate aid in troops as follows: Company of European Foot Artillery; two complete Companies of His

Majesty's 46th Foot, a Regiment of Native Infantry which troops or any force that can be afforded, I have requested may march upon Dharwad.

I apprehend, however, additional troops may become requisite.

Sd/-
Colonel Pearce

Then Colonel Pearce dictated another letter to the Officer Commanding at Bellary, requesting him to send a Company of European Foot Artillery, two Complete Companies of H.M.46th Foot and Regiment of Native Infantry. After the two letters were drafted, he glanced through them and underlined a few important words and scribbled his signature on them. The scribe collected them from Colonel Pearce and stamped the official seal below the signatures. He folded and kept them in two separate covers and secured them properly with gum. He then handed them to two couriers. Colonel Pearce heaved a sigh of relief and pressed the button of the call-bell, which produced a metallic ring. The butler in the white uniform rushed in and waited obediently.

"Get some tea and *cheroots*," Colonel Pearce ordered.

Within a few minutes he returned with a tray containing the teakettle and cups and a box of *cheroots*. Colonel Pearce and Donoghue helped themselves and began to sip the tea in a relaxed manner. They lit the *cheroots* and puffed them leisurely and watched the spirals of smoke rising in the air.

* * *

A few sardars, including Gurusiddhappa and others, walked up to the prison, where Stevenson and Elliot had been kept in separate rooms. They were accompanied by the court *dubhasi*. The prisoners, who were relaxing on the stone-beds, got up and shuffled up to the bars and stood askance. The sardars, who were accompanied by the soldiers, started addressing them.

"Gentlemen," said Sardar Gurusiddhappa, "you write to your authorities how the tragedy happened all because of Thackeray's rashness. We had appealed to Mr. Chaplin and even to the Governor Elphinstone, but they did not care to understand our problems or even to reply to our appeals."

"Yes, yes," said Stevenson, "I shall inform everything to our authorities. I shall appeal to them to view your problems sympathetically."

"Gentleman," said another sardar, "If your government refuses to restore our freedom back to us, we are going to kill you mercilessly. Beware of that." He gesticulated menacingly.

A tremour of fear went down the spine of Stevenson. Then the sardars and the patriots repeated the threats.

Elliot also promised, "Yes, I have already written to my superiors. I shall write once again."

"Otherwise," said a sardar, "your head will be severed with a swish of the sword within no time." He gesticulated threateningly.

Elliot felt a sudden blackout of consciousness for a moment. After shouting a few more threats, they stalked out of the prison yard.

Stevenson and Elliot slumped on their respective beds. Stevenson felt that he would perhaps not be able to see his wife or children or his hometown or motherland. The whole of his past life began to unroll itself before his mind's eye. Tears trickled in his eyes. Elliot, who leant against the wall, also grew nostalgic.

"Would I be ever able to see the faces of my people?" thought he inwardly.

He remembered the countryside of England and pined for it. Both of them fell into a siesta. In his dream Stevenson hugged his child and then waltzed with his wife happily in the hall of his house in England.

When the servant brought the lunch of *rotis*, curd and brinjal curry in brass pots and pans, he stood silently for a couple of minutes and watched the Company prisoners. First he peeped into Stevenson's room. He was surprised to see that Stevenson was smiling in his sleep. Then he gently walked to the other room where he saw Elliot dozing against the wall. Droplets of saliva trickled out of his mouth. The turban-clad servant then struck the bars of the prison cell with his cane, which produced a sudden metallic ring. The prisoners were jolted back into the world of reality. Stevenson was so sad to know that he was reduced to the level of a prisoner in the kingdom of Kittur.

Elliot also was awakened by the sound and wiped the saliva from the sides of his mouth with the back of his palm. The soldier opened the small window. The servant handed over the pans and bowls containing *rotis*, rice, curd and curry and locked the window again. Then he opened the window of Elliot's room, and handed over the pans and bowls to Elliot. The soldier locked the window. The servants went to other jail buildings to dole out the daily share of lunch to other Company prisoners. Stevenson, Elliot and other prisoners found it rather difficult to handle the regional food with their fingers. They missed the forks and spoons very miserably. But yet they seemed to enjoy the native food because of their monstrous hunger. After finishing their lunch, they reclined on the hard bed of stones rather uncomfortably. As they were used to comfortable cushions in their houses, here they felt a strange pain in their limbs. But alas, they had no choice at all. For a moment, Elliot felt rather angry with Thackeray for making them suffer so much unnecessarily on account of his over-ambition and rashness.

The rigor of the afternoon sun had lessened when Stevenson woke up. He washed his face with water and quaffed half a bowl of water. He was feeling a little fresh now and thought well about the Rani of Kittur. In his heart of hearts he knew that he and the other Company prisoners had never been treated badly, though the courtiers were threatening them time and again. He beckoned to the sentry to bring some paper and quill. The sentry went to the prison officer and came back after a few moments with a few sheets of paper, inkpot and a fine reed, and handed them over carefully through the iron bars to Mr. Stevenson, who collected them and sat to write a letter to Mr. Chaplin.

From:
J.A.R.Stevenson, Esq. 25th Oct.1824

To
W.Chaplin Esqr.
Commissioner in the Deccan.

Sir,

I wrote to you yesterday a hurried letter
mentioning the proceedings of the unfortunate
23rd. I shall endeavour to give you a more
detailed account of the events, which led to the
catastrophe. I believe the last letter you received
from Mr. Thackeray was dated about the 18th and
mentioned his proposed arrangements in the event
of Government coinciding in his opinion as to
there being no lawful heir to the Samanth; he at
the same time sent a map of the country and some
trees of the family. Mr. Thackeray conceiving that
under any circumstance he would be called upon
to take temporary charge of the country during
the minority of the widow, appointed Amaldars to
examine the accounts of the several villages and
to get them into some kind of order to facilitate
future arrangements. The treasure and jewels had
been sealed up, but as it afterwards appeared that
there were great numbers of notorious thieves
among the peons and that they were all under the
command of Horakeri Virappa, who was supposed
to share in their booty. Mr. Thackeray did not
conceive the treasure safe under such a guard,

he, therefore, on the 21st determined to place a guard of *sepoys* on each gateway, a measure that he had avoided hitherto as he knew it would give disgust. He also required that the leading men should enter into a penalty bond rendering themselves answerable for the security of the treasure. This they refused to do until they had gone for orders of the former Desaini Channavva. They also refused without her order to tell their guard at the gateways to abstain from any disputes with the *sepoy* guards. However, we ourselves proceeded to the gateways and cautioned the peons against any violence, reminding them of the reclamation formerly issued making the Company the permanent authority for a time. This was late in the evening. Mr. Thackeray then proposed to call on the ladies of the family and to tell them his reasons for having acted as he had, and to inform them of what he had heard from Government and what he expected to hear, but they declined receiving his visit stating that indisposition prevented them, but that they would see him the following day. Mr. Thackeray consequently postponed his departure to Dharwad which had been fixed for that night, but the next day when he went to the *kacheri* in the fort with the intention of paying the proposed visit, no person of the family nor any of the Sardars would come to him when called to accompany him to the Desai's house where they were all assembled. He had occasion to call for them several times but they as often refused to come as it was reported that the *shetsunadis* and peons were assembling from the villages. Mr. Thackeray requested Captain Black to bring into the fort two guns in order to intimidate the leaders. A gun was placed at each gateway. This was on the evening of the 22nd. On the morning of the 23rd when the Artillery Officer proceeded to the fort to change the guard, he found the outer gate locked and was refused admittance. Several messages were sent by Mr. Thackeray, but none of them were attended to. Captain Black then brought down the remaining two guns (the only forces we had left outside the fort) and Mr. Thackeray requested that he would give them a *ghurree* (24 minutes) to consider about opening the gate before he proceeded to blow the gate open. The end of the unfortunate day I reported yesterday. Gurusiddhappa, one of the Head Sardars and Chennavva the former Desai's widow, exasperated at some supposed neglect of Mr. Thackeray has worked up the minds of the rest. They now find that matters proceeded much farther then they intended and they seem to depend upon the hostage they hold in their power as their only hopes of consideration. We have been informed by Gurusiddhappa, who still treats us with respect, that we shall be detained until answers to their letters arrive from Government, that if they are favourable we shall be released, but if otherwise, he says, that they have determined to destroy the women and the prisoners and to fall in the defence of the palace; he is induced to hold this language from fear of the consequence of what has happened and not, I think, with any idea of forcing a compliance to the continuation of the Samsthan. The force from Belgaum has, we hear, moved as far as the river, but I almost doubt its being strong enough to take the palace, which now contains, I hear, 10,000 men. Under these circumstances and in the absence of any orders or directions from Government or of any officer with sufficient authority to treat, have written to the commanding officer recommending a halt until directions have been received and informing him that we shall fall victims to the fury of the mob immediately if fire is opened on the palace; of this I have no doubt. Indeed we have been so informed by some of the Sardars and the sample of their ungovernable spirit and fury, which we have unfortunately witnessed on the 23rd, can leave doubt. The Sirastedar Srinivasarao, who is a fellow prisoner, has been allowed to carry our letter to the camp on condition of his again returning to him Gurusiddhappa has expressed himself in the same terms as he has to us. I do not think that the present unfortunate business or alternative arrangements can be settled without your personal presence. I think I have now told you as many particulars as I can by letter; should I ever again have the pleasure of seeing you I can enter more particularly into events. I may, however, add that I believe from the accounts, there is no doubt of their being able to raise 10,000 men; that there are now in the fort 12 or 14 large guns; besides these, 4 taken from the artillery; and that the Sirastedar informed me that both the leaders and men appeared desperate.

Kittur   Sd/
25th Oct., 1824   J.A.R.Stevenson

Having completed the letter, Mr. Stevenson read it once gain and made corrections here and there. He then handed it over to the prison officer who took it to his office room, where he censored it and gave it to his clerk to seal it properly and offer it to the messenger.

* * *

On the 27th of October, 1824, there was great jubilation in the city of Kittur. The precincts of the palace were decorated with festoons of mango leaves, dandelions, chrysanthemums and roses. The pennants were fluttering from the nooks and corners of the palace. The *shahnai* players, drummers and cymbal-players were playing happy tunes of *Malakaunsa Raga.* All the arrangements for the coronation of Sawai Mallasarja II were made in the Chowkimath Monastery on the outskirts of the city. All the men, women and children dressed in their best dhotis, saris and upper garments walked towards the monastery in a jubilant mood. None of them bothered to cook their lunch at home as they were going to be fed the coronation-feast by the royal family.

*   *   *

A couple of days after the coronation of Sawai Mallasarja II, Sardar Gurusiddhappa called a meeting of all the military officers and Sardars in the meeting Hall. After much discussion, they unanimously decided to attack the Company Treasury at Dharwad. Sardar Gurusiddhappa therefore, ordered a detachment of his army to proceed to Dharwad and wait there for an opportune time. Accordingly about three hundred soldiers were kept ready to move towards Dharwad. The soldiers discussed among themselves how the other native chiefs were rebelling against the Company government.

*   *   *

Colonel Pearce was informed by his spies that many of the native chiefs and kings were organizing their troops and rising against the Company government. Hence, he, like other officers, had become more alert and was trying his best to suppress the local insurgents as far as possible. The intelligence he gathered from his spies was passed on by him to his higher officers as well as to his subordinates. He felt that the rebellious mood of Kittur people was very contagious and spreading to the surrounding principalities. While he sat in his office brooding about these activities, a spy came to him ceremoniously.

"Well, gentlemen, what's the latest news? Is there anything serious?" asked Colonel Pearce.

"Yes Sir, according to the latest information I have received, the Kittur people are now planning to attack the Treasury at Dharwad."

Colonel Pearce cocked his ears and sat upright and said," What did you say? Are they planning to attack Dharwad office? Are you sure of your information?"

"Yes Sir, I am very sure about my information. I have collected the news from very reliable sources," said the spy.

"Then, thank you very much. We shall act accordingly," said Colonel Pearce and struck the call bell. The servant appeared with a bow.

"Call the scribe," he said.

Within a few minutes the scribe entered with a quill, inkbottle and paper.

"Please take down," said Colonel Pearce and began to dictate the letter. The scribe settled down in his chair and began to write the letter to:

Quartermaster-General
Belgaum

Sir,

I have the honour of further reporting for the information of His Excellency the Commander in Chief, that according to under mentioned alterations, the Force mentioned in my earlier letter of the 25th instant, to which are added the troop of the 4th Cavalry and two Companies of 49th Regiment which moved during the night of the 23rd, but could not cross the Malaprabha, marching yesterday morning from Belgaum under the command of Lieutenant Colonel McLeod, 4th Regiment Light Cavalry.

3 squadrons of the 4th Light Cavalry
2 brass 12 lbs. field guns
The Company of His Majesty's 46th Foot
Augmented to 100 Rank and File.

In consequence of intelligence that the Kittur insurgents meditate an attack upon Dharwad, where is the Principal Collector's Treasury, and a considerable number of convicts, who rose upon the guards over them on the last day of the late Mohurram Festival when sixteen were killed, I altered the movement of Lieutenant Colonel McLeod's Detachment to a position between Kittur and Dharwad, instead of upon the former place. And I do myself the honour to endorse a copy of the letter of instructions given to Lieutenant Colonel McLeod for his guidance.

A squadron of the 4th Cavalry has been detained at Belgaum in consequence of a report of the appearance in the neighbourhood of Horsemen. Besides the squadron, the recruits, sick horses and families remain at Belgaum.

I have applied to the Officer Commanding at Chitradurga for an immediate aid in any portion of the force there that he may be able to spare for the purpose of temporarily reinforcing the Garrison of Dharwad.

And I have recommended to the Commissioner that a Bombay Regiment of Native Infantry, or at least a wing of one, be sent to Sholapur to place the 23rd Infantry at that station.

Sd/-
Colonel Pearce

Colonel Pearce signed the letter and dictated another letter to the Officer Commanding at Chitradurga asking him to send a contingent of fighting forces to Kittur. Colonel Pearce felt restless all through the day. He consulted his subordinate officers again and again for the details of how to corner the patriots of Kittur. He smoked his pipe continuously like a steam engine and gulped down innumerable pegs of whiskey almost every half an hour.

* * *

Mr. Eden, who had been appointed as Acting Political Agent after the demise of Thackeray, proceeded from Belgaum to Dharwad. After the tedious journey in the horse-carriage along the undulating land, he reached Dharwad. He was received very warmly by his officers at the Dharwad Headquarters situated on the hillock, which commanded a very beautiful view of the surrounding landscape. He went to the residence, where he had his breakfast of omelette, toast and aromatic hot tea after completing his morning ablutions. He put on his cleanly washed and ironed uniform, hat upon his head and walked to the office just a few yards away from there. He sat at his table and reported himself to duty by signing the joining report. He then called a meeting of all the subordinate officers and gathered a good deal of information about his predecessor Thackeray's activities and sacrifice. With the help of the detailed report by the officers Mr. Eden could now visualize the whole picture of what must have happened in the Company encounter with Kittur.

The guard bowed himself in and announced, "Mr. Srinivasarao, *vakil* from Kittur wants to see you, Sir."

Eden became alert all of a sudden and looked at the other officers meaningfully and asked them, "Who's this man?

"He is a lawyer from Kittur, Sir. He brings message from Rani Chennamma to our office," said one of the officers.

Then Eden thought inwardly that there was no harm in meeting the lawyer.

"All right, please send him in," he said.

Then the guard went out and after a couple of minutes ushered the *vakil* in. Srinivasarao, who was clad in a white immaculate dhoti and black coat with a scarf slung on his shoulders walked in briskly and bowed to Eden by joining his palms. He was accompanied by two native guards of Kittur. Eden beckoned to him to be seated in the chair meant for the guests. The two native guards stood at a safe distance.

"Yes, Mr. Srinivasarao, what's the matter?"

Srinivasarao adjusted his scarf delicately on his chest, cleared his throat and said, "See Sir, our Rani Sarkar has sent me here to clarify a few things with you."

Eden with greenish eyes was staring at the lawyer attentively and said, "All right. Please go on."

"You see Sir," continued Srinivasarao, "we have heard that your army is likely to cross the Malaprabha River near Mugutkhan-Hubballi. This news has caused further irritation and tension to our Rani and sardars. I have been sent here to warn you not to allow the army to cross the river near Mugutkhan-Hubballi in the interest of peace for both the parties. If by any chance your army is seen crossing the river there, then our people of Kittur are sure to give a tough fight and treat the prisoners mercilessly. Now the choice is yours."

Eden felt rather embarrassed to hear the warning from the Rani but tried to hide it. His throat was parched. He quaffed half a glass of water and wiped his mouth with his handkerchief. He knew that the situation was very delicate now. He had also been warned by the higher authorities to play safe for some time until further plans were defined.

"All right, Mr. Srinivasarao. I have noted the contents of your message and communicate the same to my superiors."

Srinivasarao noticed that Eden's face had grown pale. He stood up and walked out of the chamber briskly followed by the native guards. Eden was staring at the back of Srinivasarao until he disappeared from the door. He was thinking about what steps to take after consulting the higher authorities.

For two days, i.e., 26 and 27 October 1824, he stayed at Dharwad and familiarized himself with all the details of the activities that were going on in and around Kittur and Dharwad. He was informed about how the patriots of

Kittur were bent on fighting with the Company and only too willing to lay down their lives for their Rani as well as kingdom. On 27 October 1824, evening, he started his journey back to Belgaum in the horse-carriage. As the horses began to move ahead, the carriage began to jig up and down the uneven path across the countryside. As twilight set in, stars began to twinkle in the sky. The cold breeze whipped him in the face through the window. He took out his pipe and began to puff at it. The spirals of smoke wafted in the air. Occasionally he took a swig from his whiskey bottle. As the carriage-gathered speed he fell asleep on the cushion.

When the carriage reached Belgaum and stopped with a jerk, Eden was awakened. The horses were neighing. The driver opened the door of the carriage and helped Eden to get off the vehicle. He then carried the boxes and bundles and followed Eden to his residence. Eden took off his hat and boots, changed his uniform and slipped into the nightgown. The driver went back to the carriage to unyoke the horses. Eden, who was feeling cold all over, jumped into the bed and lay there hugging the warm body of his wife.

* * *

The next morning Eden went to his office at Belgaum and sat at his table attending to the routine work. He checked the muster roll to see whether the subordinate officers had signed in it or not in his absence for two days. His mind was filled with the information about the Rani of Kittur, who was a very tough one, in his opinion. He admired her courage in spite of her being the enemy of the Company government.

He was jerked back into the awareness of the mundane official work only when the butler came with a tray of kettle and cups and kept them on the table.

Eden poured some tea in the china-cup and sipped it slowly. Then he began to puff at his pipe. The spirals of smoke wafted slowly in the room. When his mind was relaxing like this, the subordinate officer brought the mail and placed it on the table. Eden ripped a cover open and lo, it was a letter from Stevenson who had been imprisoned in Kittur. He read it with great attention. As he completed the reading, he could imagine the miserable plight of the two officers, i.e., Stevenson and Elliot under the custody of the inimical Rani. He could visualize the entire picture of what might happen to them. They might be stabbed to death with other prisoners, if the Rani's expectations were not fulfilled at least for a temporary while.

As he imagined the situation, tears gathered in his eyes, which he wiped on his handkerchief quickly, lest he should be seen crying by his subordinates. Now he realized the enormity of his responsibility. He immediately sent for his scribe and dictated an urgent message to Colonel Pearce:

From:
R. Eden Esqr,

To
Colonel Pearce
Commanding Field Force, Doab.   28th October 1824

Sir,

With reference to your letter to the Officer Commanding the field detachment under date of this day and which has been shown to me by Major Donoghue, I would submit to your consideration that the movement of my force across the river before I can give an assurance to the Kittur Chiefs that it is not our intention to attack their fort or their country till definitive directions shall have been received from Bombay will probably cause so great an alarm as to put the lives of Messers Stevenson and Elliot in danger. I expect the Kittur *vakil* immediately, after which I shall be able to judge what effect such a movement is likely to produce and will inform you of it; but I would beg to recommend that the order be suspended till I have sufficient time to inform the Kittur Chiefs our intention is not to attack them till directions arrive from Bombay.

I shall be glad to be favoured with your reply.

Belgaum	Sd/-
28th Oct.,1824	R.Eden.

He put his signature after carefully going through it. Then he asked the scribe to pass it on to the dispatching clerk. Accordingly the scribe sealed the envelope after placing the folded letter into it and handed it over to the dispatching clerk. Then the messenger was ordered to take the letter to Colonel Pearce.

* * *

As soon as Colonel Pearce ripped the letter open and scanned the lines, he realized the urgency of the message. He struck the bell hurriedly. His subordinate officer entered his chamber with a formal salute. He discussed the matter with him and asked him to send the message to Lieutenant Colonel McLeod. The subordinate officer rushed to his room and began to carry out the task assigned to him. Within an hour the message was dispatched to Lieutenant Colonel McLeod with the swiftest possible rider. Pearce felt a sense of relief when he learnt about the dispatch of the message. He started smoking his pipe in a leisurely manner. The spirals of bluish smoke began to waft in the air.

* * *

Rachappa, the *vakil* of Kittur was briefed by Sardar Gurusiddhappa on behalf of the Rani about the terms to be discussed. He had noted the important points not only mentally about also on a piece of paper.

He left Kittur in the early morning when the stars were still twinkling in the sky. He wore a thick woolen shawl around his shoulders and whipped his horse gently now and then. He was accompanied by half a dozen soldiers.

The sun had already risen in the eastern sky by the time he reached Belgaum. He went straight to the Kittur Guest House, where he completed his morning ablutions. The triple mark of *vibhuti* looked prominent on his forehead. He, then, had his breakfast of *roti,* brinjal curry and curd served by the native servants. He put on his black coat and wound a yellow turban around his head. He mounted his horse and rode towards the Company offices. He was accompanied by his followers.

As he entered the compound, they jumped off their horses and walked to the main entrance. Rachappa said to the Company attendant there, "Please tell Eden Saheb that I have been sent by the Rani of Kittur to discuss a few things with him."

He waited patiently in the big cane chair. Within a few minutes, the attendant came out and said, "Please come in."

He then ushered them into the office chamber of Mr. Eden. Rachappa joined his palms in greeting to Eden, who reciprocated it with his raised right palm and beckoned him to be seated. Rachappa sat in the chair while his assistant stood at a reverential distance.

"What's the matter, Mr. Rachappa?" asked Eden in a rather dry tone.

"Sir," said Rachappa, "we have been informed that your soldiers are likely to cross the river near Mugutkhan-Hubballi. If that is done, the soldiers of Kittur will not sit quiet. They will have to face it very heroically."

Eden listened to his words quite patiently and said, "Our intention is not to attack Kittur. Our army is only to cross the river at some spot. And Mugutkhan-Hubballi happens to be that spot for crossing. That's all. Why do you take it so seriously?"

"We cannot but take it seriously," replied Rachappa, "what else can we do? Our Rani is very serious about it. Our soldiers are very tense. There is bound to be a clash if your army crosses the river at Mugutkhan-Hubballi."

Eden heard his words patiently but he could not afford to shout at him, as he remembered the confidential advice of his superiors who had instructed him to play safe for the time being.

"Where do you think should our army cross the river, if not at Mugutkhan-Hubballi?" he asked in a controlled manner. Rachappa said, "You may as well cross the river at Yenagi, instead of at Mugutkhan-Hubballi. That will not upset our Rani so much."

Eden closed his eyes and remained silent for a few seconds. He clasped his fingers and then unclasped them. Finally he said, "All right, Mr. Rachappa, let your Rani rest assured about it. I shall see that our army crosses the river at Yenagi instead of at Mugutkhan-Hubballi."

Rachappa felt satisfied by Eden's answer. He thanked Eden and walked out of his chamber, followed by his assistant.

* * *

Eden could not lose any time. He, therefore, discussed the matter with his assistants. Then he dispatched an urgent note to Colonel Pearce regarding the outcome of his discussion with lawyer Rachappa from Kittur.

> From:
> R.Eden Esqr.
>
> To
> Colonel Pearce
> Commanding Field Force, Doab.   28th, 1824

Sir,

Since my last of this date I have had an interview with the Kittur *vakil* Rachappa and have succeeded in convincing him that our intention is not to attack Kittur till directions have been received from Bombay.

He agrees that should the force cross the river at Yenagi, which is in our own country and not take up a position nearer Kittur than Narendra that his master will have implicit confidence in an assurance from me to that effect and only request time to be allowed him to communicate our determination before the force is moved from Mugutkhan-Hubballi; as this request appears reasonable I think the period till tomorrow afternoon may be given him to communicate my assurance to Kittur when they will be appraised for our intention as regards a movement of Yenagi towards Dharwad; the *vakil* requests a pass from you to the messenger who conveys my assurance to Kittur that he may not meet interruptions before any of our forces. I beg leave to be favored with your reply with as little delay as possible.

Belgaum   Sd/-
28th Oct, 1824   R.Eden

The letter was immediately dispatched to Colonel Pearce. The messenger took the letter to the Headquarters of Field Force at Doab. When the letter was finally handed over to Colonel Pearce in his office, he pored his eyes over the words and grasped the contents. He understood the gravity of the situation and discussed it with his subordinate officer. He called his clerk and dictated the following letter:

From:
Colonel Pearce,
Commanding Field Force, Doab.

To
The Acting Political Agent
Southern Maratha Country.   28th Oct., 1824

Sir,

I have the honour to acknowledge the receipt of Mr. Eden's two letters of this date.

As the movement of the force under Lieutenant Colonel McLeod's command from its present position to Yenagi will occupy two days and afford ample time for any communication from you to reach the Kittur Chief, I will so far meet your wishes as to direct that detachment shall not cross the Malaprabha but only be held in readiness to do so on receiving orders to that effect.

This deviation from the instructions to Lieutenant Colonel McLeod to cross the river at Mugutkhan-Hubballi is the utmost that a sense of duty will allow me to concede to your wishes and I request it may be clearly understood that under all circumstance the force will be directed to cross the day after that on which it reaches Yenagi.

The Kittur *vakil's* messenger shall be furnished with a pass early tomorrow morning.

Headquarters   Sd/-
Field Force, Doab   F.Pearce
28th Oct., 1824

He signed the letter and dispatched it to the Acting Political Agent through the messenger. The messenger collected the letter and mounted his horse and rode towards Dharwad

Then Colonel Pearce instructed his subordinates to move the force towards Yenagi instead of Mugutkhan-Hubballi. Accordingly the soldiers had their sumptuous breakfast. They put on their uniforms, collected their guns and swords. The servants strapped the horses with saddles. The horses were whinnying occasionally. Then the soldiers mounted their respective horses and held their reins. As the Commander blew his shrill whistle and shouted 'March,' they began to goad the horses, which strutted ahead slowly. After a few minutes the horses' pace fell into a regular rhythm of hooves thereby raising clouds of dust behind them.

*   *   *

Rachappa reached Kittur and rested at his residence for a couple of hours. After refreshing himself with breakfast consisting of *chapatis,* curd and curry, he walked to Sardar Gurusiddhappa's residence and narrated all that had transpired between Eden and himself. Among other details he explained how the Company were willing to oblige the Rani's requests to cross the Malaprabha River not at Mugutkhan-Hubballi but at Yenagi and how they had requested the Rani for unconditional release of the Company prisoners. Sardar Gurusiddhappa listened to the *vakil* attentively and noted all the important points. After the *vakil* took his leave, Sardar Gurusiddhappa rode to the palace, and conveyed to the Rani the information received from Rachappa. The Rani thought for a moment that the release of the prisoners might soften the hard hearts of the Company authorities though she was not very sure about that. Sardar Gurusiddhappa expressed his own doubt about the policies and approaches of the Company.

"Any way we shall keep our army ready for the battle and be prepared for the worst," said Rani Chennamma.

"All our soldiers are ready for the battle any time. Rani Sarkar, we have also sent messages to the Maharaja of Kolhapur and others and been waiting for their help," said Sardar Gurusiddhappa.

"We shall consolidate our forces and unite all our friends in the Deccan to fight the Company. There is simply no alternative to it," said Rani Chennamma.

"Yes, Rani Sarkar, we cannot rest at all until the last drop of blood remains in our last soldier," said Sardar Gurusiddhappa. Then he bowed to the Rani and walked out of the palace.

* * *

Elphinstone, the Governor of Bombay learnt that all the Company officers were worried about the plight of the prisoners like Stevenson and Elliot at the mercy of the Rani of Kittur. In turn he also grew anxious about the prisoners. As a political authority he considered it as a matter of prestige. That a great Company government should suffer such humiliation at the hands of a native Rani was indeed embarrassing for them. Nor had he any willingness to give any assurance to the people of Kittur about its future independence.

Things had come to a stand still. Governor Elphinstone realized the gravity of the situation and could not sit idle any longer. He wanted to discuss the matter personally with Chaplin. He, therefore, proceeded from Bombay to Pune with his official retinue and sent for Chaplin and discussed all the details.

Chaplin explained to His Excellency all the measures he had taken to suppress and control the insurgents of Kittur. He also informed His Excellency how the Rani of Kittur wanted to be independent and now did not want to release the prisoners until she received an assurance from the Company government about the independence of Kittur kingdom. Although His Excellency Elphinstone came to know the contention of both the parties, he had to take a pro-Company decision because of his deep-seated imperialism. After a thorough examination of the facts collected from all possible sources available to him, His Excellency instructed Chaplin and other subordinates to publish a proclamation that the State of Kittur lapsed to the Company consequent upon the extinction of the Desai's family. The clerk recorded the minutes prepared by His Excellency Elphinstone on 31ˢᵗ October 1824 as follows:

Having come to this place to have an opportunity of consulting with His Excellency the Governor-in-Chief and the Commissioner the following may be considered as their sentiments as well as my own.

The principal circumstance which has come to my knowledge since my last minute and the only one that occasion any doubt of the expediency of proceeding as there suggested, in the fact that Mr. Stevenson and Mr. Elliot with several *sepoys* and others are prisoners in the hands of the insurgents, and are threatened with death unless certain terms said to have been proposed to me are complied with. No proposals have been received subsequent to the breaking out of the insurrection. But it seems nearly certain that the restoration of the Samsthan to its former footing is among the demands alluded to.

The situation of the prisoners is extremely distressing, that of Mr. Stevenson and Mr. Elliot is particularly alarming and an anxiety for their fate is executed by the firmness, which they show amidst their dangers.

But however willing we may be to make concessions to purchase the safety of these gentlemen, a regard to the public interests and the security of every European in India renders it necessary that we should not encourage the idea that any desperate adventurer may obtain a compliance with his demands or even secure impunity for his offence by possessing himself of an European hostage. On the other hand I cannot believe that any submission to the demands of the insurgents is necessary to attain the object so much desired. If the whole garrison of Kittur or even all the principal Chiefs were reduced to despair of their own safety they might be impelled to wreak their vengeance, but if all could be promised pardon and safety, I cannot conceive that they would reject the offer because they were refused the restoration of the Samsthan or the impunity of their leader when they must be certain that no effort or sacrifice of theirs could have power to extort these concessions.

It only remains, therefore, to ascertain to what extent we can promise impunity and the general advantages we can hold out to those who return to their duty without creating an impression of our weakness or encouraging the commission of similar outrages in future. The revolt of the people of Kittur, however, culpable, appears to have been entirely free from every suspicion of treachery. As far as we can discover, it was produced by the too great eagerness of the gentleman whose death is the greatest part of the disorder to enforce an anxious measure with means entirely inadequate to the purpose. It may have been promoted by the influence of Chennavva, but it could only have been brought into execution by the orders and the example of Gurusiddhappa, that Sardar appears to have assumed the direction of the whole enterprise and to have made use of it to gratify his revenge against his personal enemies. It is he also who still appears to act as the avowed head of the insurgents, although he makes use of the name of Chennamma, the stepmother of the late Desai. It is on Gurusiddhappa, therefore, that the responsibility of the whole transaction should fall. Even if Chennamma were equally guilty (of which there is no proof) the punishment of a woman of her rank would be highly unpopular in consistence with the usual practice of our Government. No notice should, therefore, be taken of the suspicions which exist against her. All the other insurgents should be offered a free pardon and should be allowed the same advantages that they would have enjoyed had the insurrection never taken place with the exception of the guilty chiefs who should be treated with less indulgence than was designed.

In pursuance of this plan I would recommend that a proclamation should be published without delay stating that the Desai of Kittur having died without children or relations and his principal servants having been found to have set up a false adoption after his death have forged his name and to have got possession of his treasure by fraudulent means became necessary for Mr. Thackeray to take charge of his lands and effects that it was the intention of Government, if any Desai of the founder of the Samsthan could be found to have made out a new grant in his favour, if no descendant was found, it was intended to resume the lands but to make an ample provision for the widow and the principal servants and to have continued all *shetsundees* as has been done in the rest of the Company's country. The private property, treasure etc., of the Desai, would either case have been left to his widow. During the investigation, however, Gurusiddhappa instigated the people of Kittur to shut their gate on Mr. Thackeray and on endeavoring to force them, he was shot, the *sepoys* and *golandazs*, who were with him to the number of 150 were overpowered and the guns taken.

Considering that the people of Kittur, who had been placed under the immediate Government of his own Desai and taught to regard Kittur as a separate Samsthan may not have been fully aware of the extent of their allegiance to the Company Government, that they were misled by the principal officer of the late Desai, and that their resistance to the troops of the Government was free from premeditation and treachery, the Governor-in-Council is pleased to grant a full and free pardon to the whole of these misguided men provided they return to obedience to the Government. Gurusiddhappa alone is exempted from this pardon and even he shall be exempted from capital punishment provided he immediately submits and surrenders himself.

As many of the insurgents as submit before the 20th of November next, shall retain their *Inams* and *Wattans* and all the *shetsundees* shall be maintained on the usual footing. The claims of such of the principal servants as shall not have taken prominent part in the rebellion to some provision for their support shall be taken into no consideration. A suitable allowance shall be made for the widow of the late Desai and such provision as the Government on enquiry may judge proper shall be granted to the other females of the family.

The treasure and private property of the late Desai will still be considered as belonging to his widow and if any part of it has escaped plunder it will be restored to her.

The whole of the Sardar and Sepoys in Kittur shall be held responsible for the safety of the two gentlemen and the other prisoners; should any injury be offered to them the Sardars and all the guilty persons shall be punished with such severity as shall be a terror to future offenders.

Colonel Pearce should be instructed to articulate the proclamation and act on the principles of it. A letter should be addressed by the Commissioner to the principal Jagirdars and the Raja of Kolhapur acquainting them with what has been passed and warning them to prevent their dependents from joining the insurgents. A similar communication should be made through Mr. Dunlop to Wadi (Waree). A Maratta (Maratha) copy of the Commissioner's letter should be sent to that gentleman for his adoption.

All communications with the insurgents and all arrangements regarding the Kittur country should be left to Colonel Pearce till Mr. Chaplin's arrival until which time he should avoid running any risks.

Mr. Chaplin will probably be at Belgaum by the 15th or 20th and the troops will be assembled by the end of the month, should no submission have been made before that time. Colonel Pearce should be directed to use every exertion to prevent the escape of the garrison from Kittur and especially to prevent them making their way to the jungles. It would be better that he should suspend his attack until his whole force is collected even if it should occasion a fortnight's delay than commence with a force sufficient to make the place but not sufficient to intercept the fugitives.

The military arrangements, which I concur with the Commander-in-Chief in thinking necessary for the occasion, are shown in the following table with the probable dates of their accompaniment.

Corps	From	To	Date of arrival
6th N.I.	Satara	Belgaum	24th November
Horse Artillery	Poona	Belgaum	24th November
7th M.Lieutenant Cavalry	Sholapur	Belgaum	11th November
23rd M.N.I.			
50 Artillery Men			
1st European regiment 3 N.I.	Bombay	Vengorla	--
1 Company or Artillery			
2 Companies H.N. 46th Regt.			
1st Regiment N.I.	Bellary	Belgaum	--

If it should appear by the returns at Bombay that there is a deficiency of ordinance and store at Belgaum, they should be supplied from the presidency.

From the uncertainty regarding the period required to collect carriages no dates can be fixed for the arrival of the troops from Bellary to Bombay, but the former supplied for by Colonel Pearce on the 25th instant, and as the others will move light it is probable both will be at Belgaum before the end of November.

As time is already of the greatest consequence, I have requested the Commissioner to adopt the measures above-described and the

Commander-in-Chief has issued the requisite orders for the execution of the military arrangements concerned.

Colonel Kennedy has also been directed to concentrate two of his regiments in a camp somewhere in the south of his district where he can be prepared in case the insurgents shall attempt to take refuse in the Wadi (Ware) country or any of the other jungle tracts in the neighborhood.

The absence of the two kings' regiments required by the supreme Government, the dispatch of the three native regiments to Assergur and the circumstance of the Madras Government being unable to replace the two regiments taken from the Southern Maratha Country for Solapur, have created considerable distress for want of troops in the part of the country.

It will probably be necessary to move the battalion left at Solapur to Satara without delay. That place when it can be avoided should never be left with less than two battalions.

If the terms offered should not induce the insurgents to submit, a native regiment should be sent from Bombay to the Deccan and in its place, supplied by calling out the Portuguese militia.

Notice should be sent to the Madras Government of the death of Mr. Thackeray, with an expression of deep concern with which the Governor in Council communicates the fate of the gentleman whose distinguished talents and eminent public zeal render his loss of a severe misfortune, both to the presidency to which he belonged and to that which had so long profited by his most valuable services.

His Excellency signed the minute and then returned from Pune to Bombay with all his retinue. He had realized how the native Rani of Kittur had been a very tough lady and how in spite of his admiration for her mettle, he had to vanquish her in the interest of the Company rule in India.

After half a day's rest he began to send messages to different military heads of South India hectically. He issued instructions to the Commander-in-Chief, Sir Alexander Campbell to send whatever army Colonel Pearce might require and further to send messages to Bellary, Gooty, Bangalore and Arcot regarding the regiments and contingents of the army units to be sent to Kittur. His subordinates were working very hard in the office.

The Governor sipped his wine and puffed at his pipe leisurely for about ten minutes. Then he remembered other details, by looking into the military files. He sent a message to the Chief Secretary to ask Cole, the Company resident in Mysore, to send about 1,000 *siledar* horses of the Mysore army to move towards Kittur. Then he instructed the Company resident in Hyderabad to send a contingent to Kittur in the first week of November. He dictated letters to Lieutenant Colonel Wagh (at Madras) commanding at Malabar and Canara, to send a contingent of army to Honavar and Sadasivagad, with a view to rushing this army from the western area to Kittur.

All these arrangements were made through Mr. T. Babington, Principal Collector, Mangalore. His Excellency Elphinstone heaved a sigh of relief only after sending out the instructions to the various military officers. He started smoking his pipe incessantly, raising curls of smoke in the air. As he stood on the balcony of his office he saw the waves of the sea rushing in continuously upon the shore.

* * *

Rani Chennamma waited eagerly for a positive answer from the Company government. Sardar Gurusiddhappa and other courtiers kept her informed about the latest communications received from the Company officers.

"They seem to be so reluctant to concede to our terms," said Sardar Gurusiddhappa.

"In that case, let us also stick to our principles," said another courtier.

"We shall not release the prisoners without having some assurance from the highest authorities," said Sardar Gurusiddhappa.

Rani Chennamma said to the courtiers, "Now that we have received Governor Elphinstone's reply, we shall depute our *vakil* Govinda Srinivasa to Munro, Acting Collector of Dharwad, to explain all the details personally."

All the courtiers assented to the Rani's suggestion.

"In that case, shall I dictate a letter, Rani Sarkar?" asked Sardar Gurusiddhappa. Soon the scribe was sent for. Within a few minutes the scribe walked in with the paraphernalia of quill, inkbottle and paper and squatted before his small desk.

Sardar Gurusiddhappa dictated the letter, which the scribe scribbled with a crackling sound. "First complete the formal compliments."

"Yes Sir, the compliments are over now," said the scribe.

"Now start the letter," said Sardar Gurusiddhappa:

> The letter sent by you has been received. Its contents are understood. You wish to desire that the person, who had gone to wait upon the gentlemen at Belgaum, should be dispatched to Dharwad. This person is indisposed; we have therefore sent to you Gavinda Srinivasa, who will explain matters personally. We have mentioned how very averse the Samsthan is to warfare but to the letter communicating this no answer has been received. Your armies are collecting from the four quarters. Let the protection of the Samsthan be a constant consideration with you. What more need we write?

After the completion of the letter the scribe read it out once again and stamped the royal seal below it and took the signature of Sardar Gurusiddhappa on behalf of Rani Chennamma. The letter then was handed over to the courier, who mounted his horse and rode towards Dharwad to reach it to Munro. The Durbar for the day was over.

The next day Sardar Gurusiddhappa met the Rani at her residence in the palace. The Rani had just returned from her *puja* room. The *vibhuti* marks looked very bright on her forehead.

After the exchange of amicabilities, Rani Chennamma asked him, "Sardar Gurusiddhappa, how are our prisoners, I mean, the Company men, women and children?"

Sardar Gurusiddhappa replied, "They are all right, Rani Sarkar. In fact we have been giving them special attention. I don't think they feel that they are prisoners. They don't lack anything."

The Rani remained silent for a moment. Then she said, "Yet, my heart cries for them. I can understand how much they must be missing their husbands and fathers." She heaved a sigh.

"What to do Rani Sarkar?" said Sardar Gurusiddhappa. "This is all inevitable in the political fight. We have to harden our hearts to all these things."

Two tears seemed to trickle down from the Rani's big and bright eyes. She appeared to think something inwardly. Then she came out with an answer, "Sardar Gurusiddhappa, I think we can release all the forty Company prisoners except Stevenson and Elliot. Why to detain these innocent women and children? Let them join their kith and kin. You know I am a woman. Only a woman can understand another woman. Besides, the release of these women and children may soften the hearts of the Company authorities towards our Samsthan. What do you think of this proposal?"

Sardar Gurusiddhappa could easily follow the line of the Rani's thinking. He also knew her maternal heart and humanitarian concern even for the enemies.

"We shall do as you wish, Rani Sarkar," said Gurusiddhappa.

She said, "You consult the other sardars also. And let me know in the evening." He took his leave of the Rani after bowing to her with joined palms.

* * *

The next morning, all the Sardars of Kittur gathered in the Durbar Hall and exchanged their views about the idea of releasing the ordinary prisoners consisting of women and children.

One of the sardars opined, "Releasing these prisoners may change the hearts of the Company authorities in our favor."

Another sardar said. "These women prisoners may carry a very good impression about our Rani Sarkar."

Yet another one interrogated, "Why not detain the prisoners until the Company government yields to our request for freedom?"

Thus they had a prolonged discussion about the pros and cons of releasing the prisoners and expressed all sorts of contradictory opinions. Finally they agreed to assent to whatever the Rani had proposed.

By that time Rani Chennamma's arrival was announced by the servants. The Sardars, therefore, grew attentively silent. After a few minutes, the Rani entered the hall gracefully. Even the rustle of her silk sari could be heard in the pin drop silence of the Durbar Hall. She walked towards the throne and sat on it.

She then asked the audience in her melodious voice, "Gentlemen, what's your opinion about the release of our prisoners?"

Again the sardars began to whisper and murmur among themselves. The Rani sat expecting their answer.

Finally Sardar Gurusiddhappa stood up and said, "Rani Sarkar, all our Sardars have exchanged their views amongst themselves so far. Now they have decided to approve of whatever decision you take."

The Rani remained silent for a moment.

"Gentlemen," she said, "we have to brave the danger no matter whether we release or detain the prisoners. After all, what have the innocent women and children done to us? Let us err on the humanitarian side and release them today. What's your opinion?"

Again there was whispering and murmuring in the audience, for a few seconds.

Finally, one of the sardars stood up and said, "Whatever the Rani Sarkar has decided is okay by all of us."

The Rani was happy to know that the sardars had understood the spirit of her words. Her face beamed with a serene smile. She, then said, "I am happy to have the support of my Sardars for my decision. Sardar Gurusiddhappa, kindly arrange for the release of the forty prisoners today."

Sardar Gurusiddhappa said, "It shall be done, Rani Sarkar."

* * *

The next morning the European prisoners were attending to the morning ablutions. The birds were chirping on the nearby trees. Some of the male prisoners, who heard the birds singing, wished they too were birds. They remembered their wives and children and longed to see and hug them. Similarly the female prisoners had grown nostalgic. They felt so eager to get back to their husbands and children. Of course, they lacked nothing in the prison. The Rani of Kittur had arranged for excellent treatment for them. Their only problem was that they were away from their kith and kin. Their nostalgia was cut off when the prison staff went around distributing their breakfast of *chapatis*, curds and curry. Both the women prisoners and the men prisoners savoured the native items of breakfast in their respective cells. They inwardly thanked the Rani for treating them so well. Then they relaxed against the stonewalls of prison-buildings.

About half an hour must have gone by, when a pleasant surprise was a waiting them. The turban-clad native officers and soldiers went around in the prison corridors. The officers were instructing something in Kannada to their subordinates which the European prisoners could not understand at all. Then the guards came to the prison doors and clicked the locks open. The jail officers beckoned to the prisoners to walk out. The prisoners were so happy that they cried and shouted for joy. They walked out of their prisons with lightened hearts and breathed the fresh air around them. All the men prisoners released from the prison walked towards a big Banyan tree and waited there with grins and smiles on their faces. Then the women and children including Thackeray's two children, who were released from the other prison buildings, walked with shrieks and tears of joy. The children jumped and scampered. All of them joined the men under the tree. There was a lot of hugging, kissing and hand shaking among the newly released prisoners. Then they were all led in horse carriages towards Dharwad where Lieutenant Colonel McLeod's detachment was stationed.

Though the Company soldiers were happy about the release of the forty prisoners from Kittur, they were not totally satisfied. They still worried about the two men-prisoners, Stevenson and Elliot. Munro, who sat in his office at Dharwad worried about the safety of the two important officers in the Kittur prisons. What if they were tortured or even murdered by the Rani's reckless soldiers? He thought any hasty action against the Rani would endanger the precious lives of the two officers. He, therefore, wrote a detailed letter to Chaplin on 7 November 1824 apprising him of the plight of Stevenson and Elliot and requested him to be discreet in the matter until the opportune time.

On the same day Munro sent a reply to Rani Chennamma with the intention of convincing her about the release of the two officers:

> Your letter has been received and its purport understood. You have mentioned that you do not wish for discord; the guilt of having imprisoned two gentlemen in your fort becomes greater every day. I can discover no benefit which is likely to accrue to you from their continued confinement; that occurrence, however, tends to dishonour the Sarkar. Those gentlemen are intimately acquainted with the nature of the late affair at

Kittur; through them when released it may be as well known to the Sarkar; they may plead your cause; their release, therefore, seems to be the only road by which you can hope to receive the leniency of Government.

I request, therefore, that the gentlemen may be sent here and that your *karbharis* may wait upon me to state the Kittur affairs and your wishes for the information of Government. The business is of the first importance and cannot be settled through persons who have little or no authority. Send three or four of your *karbharis* from whom I may enquire the state of affairs. Should matters not be adjusted by their intervention there shall be no impediment to their return; they shall be sent back in safety to Jagir; you are well aware however of this. What more need I say?

Collector Munro scanned the letter carefully and scribbled his signature below it. He rang the bell and handed over the letter to his subordinate officer who arranged for its immediate dispatch. The courier collected the letter, put it safely in the bag and started riding his horse towards Kittur. He whistled a western tune occasionally or shoed away the menacing monkeys on the way.

* * *

When the letter was handed over to the inward section of the administrative office of the Kittur kingdom, the courier felt a sigh of relief for the day. Rani Chennamma and Rani Viravva had grown restless for the last few months. They felt that their kingdom had fallen into unprecedented difficulty.

Rani Chennamma, who relaxed on the silk bed in her chamber, was awakened by the maidservant, who announced that Sardar Gurusiddhappa was waiting in the Durbar Hall on an urgent mission. Rani Chennamma donned a silk sari, placed the hem over her head and walked to the Durbar Hall when all the courtiers had gathered. They stood up for a few seconds as a mark of respect for her and sat down after she sat down.

Then the Rani looked enquiringly at Sardar Gurusiddhappa, who said, "Rani Sarkar, we have received a letter from Collector Munro. Shall I have it read and translated?"

The Rani gave her consent by the nod of her head. Then Sardar Gurusiddhappa waved his right palm at the official *dubhasi,* who unfolded the letter and began to read the letter loudly, clearly and slowly. Everybody listened to the words very carefully.

When the reading was over, the faces of everyone had grown grim with seriousness.

Rani Chennamma broke the silence by saying, "Gentlemen, you have heard the opinion of Collector Munro. The Company fellows seem to be so adamant about their views. Let's think for a couple of days as to what to be done next. Later, let's pool our opinions and arrive at a consensus."

Then the courtiers stood up and made way for the Rani to walk out of the Durbar Hall.

A couple of days went by in cogitation and mutual consultation. Rani Chennamma discussed the matter confidentially with her own daughter-in-law, Viravva. The courtiers also thought about the matter and discussed it with one another whenever and wherever it was possible. Even the laymen and men folk of Kittur took the problem seriously and discussed it among themselves and also felt that the solution to it was not so easy. They somehow felt that the kingdom was inflicted with the adverse influence of Rahu and heaved sighs of helplessness.

The Rani called the council meeting on 12 November 1824. Sardar Gurusiddhappa, Sardar Mallappa, Sangolli Rayanna and many other sardars and military officers gathered in the Durbar Hall. The whole building was strictly guarded by the soldiers. The commoners of Kittur were not allowed to come anywhere near the fort at least for that day. The Rani with the bright white marks of *vibhuti* upon her forehead sat on the throne with dignity.

"Gentlemen, what have you thought about the problem?" she asked.

The sardars stood up one by one and expressed their considered opinion. Finally all of them agreed upon the point that the Governor be urged to allow the kingdom of Kittur to retain its original independence. Sardar Gurusiddhappa mentally codified the consensus of the council, which was approved by the Rani. He dictated the final form of the letter as follows. The scribe wrote it down carefully:

> The letter sent by you reached us; its purport has been understood. You wrote that you could not see the advantage that could accrue to us by the detention of the two gentlemen as prisoners,

that the circumstance had only the effect of casting reflection upon the Sarkar. To this, we reply that the imprisonment of the two gentlemen is of use to the Samsthan; by their means and their representation to Government we wish that arrangements should be made for the continuation of the Samsthan according to ancient usage. In this hope they are retained; all the circumstances of the case are known to these kind gentlemen; they were appointed by Mr. Thackeray as his agents with authority to conduct the affairs of the Samsthan.

Regarding what you say respecting the dishonor, which attaches to the Government by the imprisonment of the gentlemen, we have to reply that such has never been our wish; or we should not thus long have maintained a friendship with the Company Government. For the purpose of conciliation we have hitherto behaved in exact conformity to the wishes of the Saheb (Mr. Thackeray). Notwithstanding this, however, he has brought this state of affairs upon us. What remedy do we have?

In reply to your request that the *karbharis* should have an interview with you to arrange matters and report the same to the Government, we have to state, you are the person by whom matters should be settled. We have, by letter, made you acquainted with all the circumstances of the case; we have no apprehensions for the safety of the *karbharis,* should they be sent to you;

and when a letter should be received from you intimating that the Samsthan shall be continued to us as formerly, then the *karbharis* shall wait upon you, let the ancient good feeling towards the Samsthan be continued in you. What more need we write? You have engaged in this affair. That you will represent to the Government whatever may benefit the Samsthan is our hope. Upon this score we are not apprehensive. Govinda Srinivasa will relate other particulars in person.

The scribe completed all the epistolary formalities. He cleared his throat and began to read the letter loudly so that the Rani and the Sardars might listen to it carefully. When he received their silent approval, he got it signed by Sardar Gurusiddhappa and put the royal seal below it. He folded the letter, put it in a big cover and pasted it properly. He then, handed it over to the courier to be delivered to the Collector of Dharwad, i.e., Munro.

The courier collected the letter and mounted his horse and whipped it gently. The horse trotted until it reached the outskirts of Kittur. Then the courier whipped it again which gave a smart of pain to the horse. It, therefore, broke into the usual speed by raising its tail in a flourish.

He reached Dharwad and rode straight to the Collector's office. He sought permission and entered Munro's chamber and handed over the letter. Munro stared at the courier for a moment and beckoned to the clerk who received the letter from the courier. The courier then excused himself and walked out of the chamber. The clerk opened the packet with a pair of scissors and handed over the letter to Munro who read it very meticulously. As the matter in the letter was rather delicate, he could not take any independent decision. He thought about it for two full days but finally he forwarded the letter to Chaplin with his own remarks in the covering letter:

> From:
> I.C.Munro Esqr.
> Acting Collector of Dharwad
>
> To
> W. Chaplin Esqr.
> Poona
> Sir,   14th November, 1824

I have the honour to enclose answer to my letter to Kittur, a copy of which was transmitted in my letter of the 6th instant, to your address.

It is with regret that I observe the disposition displayed in the letter. I shall, however, feel sanguine that the high tone assumed by the Managers will abate as the troops approach Kittur; the enclosure speaks the sentiments of the ringleaders in the late unfortunate affair. And it is not from them we can look for a ready compliance, aware as they must be that the Government will not pass over in oblivion an act which has deprived it of the services of four valuable officers. I had no conversation with the *karkun,* who stated that the letter contained every information which he could impart nor have I answered the letter of which he was the bearer; which proves the futility of negotiation till we have the means of inducing a more compliant disposition on the part of the Managers.

Sd/-

I.C. Munro

The Acting Collector, Munro, signed the covering letter and enclosed Rani Chennamma's letter with it and asked his subordinate to dispatch it to Chaplin. The subordinate officer kept the two letters in a bigger cover, sealed it with wax and the signet and sent the mail through the courier to Poona.

* * *

Chaplin was really irritated to read Rani Chennamma's letter and Munro's remarks about it. The matter was so serious that he could not settle it only through correspondence. He thought over it for a couple of days but could not take any decision independently. He could not act humanitarianly towards Kittur as the Company government had its own plans and policies. He could not take any decision regarding Kittur without the prior permission from H.E. the Governor of Bombay, Elphinstone.

Chaplin, therefore, went on an official tour to Bombay. He was accompanied by three of his subordinates with all the relevant files and papers. He took rest in the office Guest House for the night. Next morning, he went with his office staff to His Excellency Elphinstone's bungalow and sent word through the servants. The servant returned within a couple of minutes and beckoned to Chaplin to go into His Excellency's chamber.

Chaplin took off his hat and said, "Good morning, Your Excellency," with a bow of his head.

"Good morning, Mr. Chaplin. Please be seated," said His Excellency in a dignified tone.

Meanwhile a Company servant brought a tray with biscuits and teacups. He placed the cups and plates containing biscuits before them gently and went away.

"Please help yourself," said His Excellency.

Chaplin took up a few biscuits and crunched them and then sipped the aromatic tea leisurely. His Excellency also sipped his tea in a royally slow manner. Then the servant came into the chamber and took out the tray with cups and saucers.

His Excellency cleared his throat and said, "Now, tell me, what's the urgency?"

Chaplin sat upright and explained the problems, "Your Excellency, the Rani of Kittur is a lady with great self-respect and adamant too. We have already lost Mr. Thackeray and a number of other military officers and soldiers. Presently Mr. Elliot and Mr. Stevenson are under the Rani's custody. She has written clearly that she will not release the two officers until we promise them that they will have their Samsthan for themselves."

His Excellency was listening to every detail very carefully without even winking. "What are the military arrangements you have made to control them?" he asked in a serious tone.

"Our detachments have been installed around Kittur within a radius of about 30 to 40 miles. Before proceeding further, we would like to know our Excellency's answer to Rani Chennamma's request for retaining their Samsthan," said Chaplin.

His Excellency closed his eyes for a few moments, shook his head, smacked his lips and said in a firm voice, "No, that cannot be. The Rani's request cannot be granted. The Samsthan has got to be annexed to the Company government. There is simply no alternative."

Chaplin had expected such an answer from the Governor, as he knew the policy of the East India Company. But he wanted to bring the other details to the Governor's notice.

"But, Your Excellency there is a small problem to be tackled before we proceed further," said Mr. Chaplin.

H.E. Elphinstone looked askance at him.

Chaplin explained, "Your Excellency, our two precious officers, Mr. Elliot and Mr. Stevenson have been kept in prison by the Rani. She has already retained only these two officers in the hope that we may concede to her request. Mr. Elliot and Mr. Stevenson have also written to us that although they have been kept in prison they have been treated very courteously by the Rani. In case we attack the fort of Kittur, we are sure to lose the lives of our two important officers."

The Governor understood the gravity of the situation and the dilemma involved in it. He thought about it for a few minutes and examined the file of correspondence tensely.

Then he said, "Mr. Chaplin, I know the situation is very tricky. We have to use a little tact now. You please go over to the spot and study the situation. I shall empower you to take any decision in line with our policy and annex the Samsthan to the Company. Is that okay?"

"That's what I wanted to know, Your Excellency. I wanted permission to take decision on the spot. We have very little time at our disposal now. I'll have to return tonight."

He stood up with a bow to the Governor and stalked out briskly. The Governor heaved a sigh of relief, lit a *cheroot* and began to puff at it in a leisurely manner.

Chaplin left Bombay for Belgaum on 17 November 1824, along with the troops available at Bombay and collected the troops at Pune. Word was sent by Chaplin to the Raja of Kolhapur, who was requested by the Rani of Kittur to help her vanquish the Company. The Raja of Kolhapur was always pretending to be friendly with the Company, although he hated them secretly and was biding his time to defeat them at an opportune time. He, therefore, sent word to Chaplin who was camping near Kolhapur on his way to Belgaum, that he was unable to see him on account of ill health. Instead he sent his officers to meet the Collector and pretend to please him. Then Chaplin left Kolhapur with his troop further south. The Raja of Kolhapur got news about the departure of Chaplin. He thought it right time to start the march of his own army. Accordingly he started with 5000 foot, 100 horse and 7 guns and marched slowly across the undulating land and camped near Yamakanamaradi, amidst sylvan surroundings.

In order not to arouse Chaplin's suspicion about his loyalty, the Raja of Kolhapur sent word to Chaplin that he was coming to meet the latter. But Chaplin, shrewd as he was, had gathered sufficient intelligence about the Raja of Kolhapur's ambivalent plans. He was, therefore, very angry with the Raja of Kolhapur and sent a message to him that he had no time to meet the latter and that the latter need not meet him.

The Raja of Kolhapur took the insult as part of the political game. Notwithstanding Chaplin's negative instruction, he proceeded further with his army and camped near the Malaprabha valley of Munavalli edged with beautiful hillocks.

Chaplin was also sending letters to all the *jagirdars,* who were loyal to the Company, to lend their troops in fighting against the rebellious Rani of Kittur. Most of the Deccan Chiefs sent their military units to join the Company army with pleasure. The Patwardhan of Sangli, Gopal Rao, Chief of Jamakhandi and the Chief of Mudhol were very happy to please the Company Government by lending their military forces.

When Chaplin reached Belgaum, he learnt that all the military detachments were coming towards Kittur as per his instructions. The Company troops under Lieutenant Colonel McLeod advanced from Dharwad to Tadakod village about six miles east of Kittur and camped there. Colonel Fred Pearce had come to know that the Kittur Fort was very strong and therefore could not be broken by ordinary cannons. He, therefore, sent an official order to Colonel Seely of Madras Regiment, who was in charge of the battering train, to arrange to send the train to Kittur.

Meanwhile Colonel Pearce fell seriously ill and was hospitalized. The doctors examined him and recommended long rest for him. It was reported to the higher authorities and a request for substitute arrangement was made. Accordingly Colonel Pearce was replaced by Colonel Deacon, who was stationed at Solapur.

Colonel Seely rushed to Belgaum on 24 November 1824 and studied the geographical details of the area. He realized that the area was full of rugged hills and hillocks, and therefore, the battering train could not be moved so easily towards Kittur. He, therefore, arranged for adequate number of bullocks and servants, and led them with him on the same day to Vengurla. The next day, the battering train trundled along the footpath across the hillocks and declivities. It was quite a task for the servants to reach it to Kittur. The bullocks heaved, bellowed and panted to drag the heavy weapon in the hot sun. The servants had to struggle a lot in taking the heavy train across the Western Ghats. They heaved a sigh of relief when they reached Kittur and parked it in front of the Main Gate of Kittur Fort.

By 25 November 1824, all the preparations seemed to be complete. As per the master plan, all the Company troops had arrived and camped at the strategic spots around Kittur. Lieutenant Colonel Walker of the Madras Regiment was posted at Khanapur, a town in possession of the Company, to command the detachment there. Major Trewson was posted to command the unit stationed at Belgaum. The military plan of the Company was to attack Kittur from three sides: from north from Belgaum, from southeast from Dharwad via Tadakod and from west from Khanapur. The forces were to move simultaneously towards Kittur and attack from all the three sides.

Within a couple of days detachments from Mysore, Chitradurga, Madras, Arcot, Solapur, Satara, Bombay, Pune and Vengurla had been posted within a radius of about one and a half miles from Kittur.

* * *

Rani Chennamma had called a secret meeting of all her officers and well-wishers. Sardar Gurusiddhappa, who was apprised of the whole situation by his spies, was disturbed a bit. The meeting was heavily guarded by the soldiers.

When the meeting began, Rani Chennamma sat upright on her throne. The bright white horizontal marks of *vibhuti* shone on her broad forehead. The sobriety of her appearance was enough to shame the courtiers who seemed to be disturbed inwardly.

Sardar Gurusiddhappa stood up and said, "My dear countrymen, you all know what an emergency has arisen in our kingdom. As per the report of our spies, the Company army surrounding our Kittur totals about 25,000. It is, obviously a very big number compared to our military capacity. The Raja of Kolhapur promised to help us. Every one of you knows the situation.

There were whispers and murmurs among the members of the audience.

Finally Rani Chennamma said in her sturdy but melodious voice, "My dear brothers and elders, whatever is happening to Kittur is known to you. We had only angered the cobra last time. The cobra has been contemplating vengeance all these days. Now it is ready to pounce on us and devour us. Let us not fear anything. We shall fight until the last drop of blood remains in our body. We shall never tolerate the sight of the fall of Kittur. We shall be ready to lay down our lives for our beloved kingdom. My dear brothers, the Kittur kingdom is yours and you are the kingdom. All of you get ready to bring victory to Kittur or die a heroic death on the battlefield. Is there anything more honorable than a heroic death on the battlefield?"

The whole audience appeared to be electrified by the Rani's hortative speech. Their hairs stood on end.

Sardar Gurusiddhappa and others shouted the slogans: "Victory to Kittur kingdom! Victory to Rani Chennamma!" The whole auditorium echoed the spirited words.

Then with a heroic determination the courtiers and the officers stalked out of the Durbar Hall.

* * *

Chaplin was known as a shrewd politician. He came down to Kittur to supervise and monitor all the military activities to be carried out in the next few days. His intention was to see that Kittur was cut off from the outside world. He wanted that there should be no communication whatever between Kittur and other villages or Samsthans. According to the intelligence he had gathered, the Raja of Kolhapur might side with the Rani of Kittur. He had firmly decided to abort the plan of the Raja of Kolhapur. He, therefore, began to dictate the letter to Captain Crew of the Mysore Horse Artillery on the 11 December 1824. The scribe began to scribble the letter as dictated by Mr. Chaplin:

As the fort of Kittur had already begun to insist by firing all-day and as I have some reason to apprehend that the Raja of Kolhapur may come down to assist the rebels, I have to request that you will be so good as to push on another party of horse accompanied by 500 infantry of his neighborhood. If the cavalry party consists of the Closepet horse and guns it would be highly useful in keeping in check any enemy that might approach to interrupt our operations here.

This urgent letter was sent to Captain Crew with a messenger at the earliest possible time.

* * *

Sivabasappa, the Chief Security Officer of the Kittur Fort, met Chaplin stealthily in his camp and sought an audience with him. He introduced himself and confided in him,

"Saheb, I shall secretly help you to capture the Kittur fort if you promise to reward me properly, i.e., by giving me the Samsthan as a gift afterwards."

Chaplin stared at Sivabasappa, who giggled rather sheepishly. He understood the conspiratorial tone of Sivabasappa. He wanted to exploit him for his own purpose.

He, therefore, said with a malicious smile, "All right, Mr. Sivabasappa, you help us secretly to defeat your Rani. Then we shall definitely give the right kind of reward."

Sivabasappa felt elated by the promise of a reward. He thanked Chaplin profusely and returned home dreaming about his own grand future and turn of luck.

*   *   *

The natives of Kittur were ready for any eventuality. The soldiers had occupied their places at all the strategic points of Kittur fort and city. Sardar Gurusiddhappa was eagerly trying to communicate with the Raja of Kolhapur who had camped at Munavalli. He and his other leaders knew that the Company troops had camped all around Kittur. They had not realized the fact that they could neither send nor receive any message from other villages or cities. They felt stranded. Yet as per Rani Chennamma's instructions, Sardar Gurusiddhappa sent a few messages to Munavalli.

He asked them, "You go by the north-east gate of the fort and try to reach Munavalli and convey Rani Sarkar's message to the Raja of Kolhapur and ask him to bring his army at the earliest to our rescue."

Accordingly the five messengers clad in civil dress mounted their horses and rode towards the northeastern gate of the fort. The soldiers who stood on the towers of the fort were watching the exit of their messengers. As the messengers sneaked out of the northeastern gate and went a few yards, they were prevented by the Company soldiers. The messengers drew their swords and began to fight with the Company soldiers.

The Kittur soldiers, who were watching from the towers of the fort, were terribly angered by the intervention by the Company soldiers. They, therefore, shot their bullets on the Company soldiers. In this scuffle two Company soldiers were killed and tumbled down from their horses and fell dead in the pool of blood. Along with them, their horses also were killed and sagged to the earth.

As the news circulated among the Company circles, they were terribly angered and therefore opened fire at the fort. The heroic soldiers of Kittur fort also answered it properly by firing back at them. Sardar Gurusiddhappa was informed about this scuffle.

By that time the messengers themselves returned and explained to him what had happened to them. Sardar Gurusiddhappa grew a little grim and rushed to the Rani's chamber to inform her about what had been happening.

* * *

Rani Chennamma's *vakil* was desperately trying to negotiate with Mr. Chaplin.

He went to Chaplin's office and requested, "You have promised to consider our case more favorably. Until and unless we get an assurance from you about our freedom, our Rani is not willing to release the prisoners."

But Chaplin seemed to be angered by the recent firing from the Kittur fort upon the Company soldiers causing the death of two. His face grew red with anger and his eyes were blood shot.

"You see, Mr. Srinivasarao, we have waited very patiently up till now. You have been provoking our soldiers unnecessarily. I cannot concede to any of your requests until and unless you release the prisoners. If you did not surrender before the midnight of 1 December, I shall have to order my army to attack the fort from all the sides and breach it."

The *vakil* was disconcerted by a point-blank answer from Chaplin. He felt humiliated and went pale in the face and walked back with his guards to Diwan Gurusiddhappa.

Meanwhile Chaplin, who was very angry and tense at the same time, sent a detailed report to Mr. Newnan about the latest developments and outlined the steps he would take if the Company prisoners were not released and the Kittur leaders did not lay down their arms. The letter was dispatched to Mr. Newnan post-haste.

Diwan Gurusiddhappa was also shocked by the arrogant answers sent by Mr. Chaplin through the *vakils*. He went along with other Sardars to the Rani's chamber and consulted her. They were dispirited by the discourteous answers of Chaplin. They realized the serious determination of the Company government to cow them down.

Diwan Gurusiddhappa expressed his opinion about the situation to Rani Chennamma, "Rani Sarkar, I feel these fellows are hell-bent on destroying us. Let's gain a little more time and stop all firing at least temporarily to earn their goodwill. We can think of an amicable settlement after releasing the prisoners."

Rani Chennamma listened to him carefully and deliberated with the other sardars. "Let us try for the last time. They may concede to our request if we release the prisoners who also may plead for our cause. It may soften their hearts," said the Rani calmly.

All the Sardars also felt that it might work.

The next morning, Chaplin sent a message through his messenger to Rani Chennamma that if the two Company officers were not returned by 10.00 a.m. the entire Kittur army would be massacred. As the Rani had already deliberated with her sardars the previous night, she instructed Diwan Gurusiddhappa to brief the *vakils*. Accordingly the *vakils* were briefed properly and sent to Chaplin.

They pleaded, "Chaplin saheb, our Rani Sarkar wants to know whether you agree that there would be no war if the two prisoners are safely returned."

Chaplin was really fed up with the adamancy of the Rani and did not want to protract the idle game, especially when all the preparations for the war were made meticulously. He wanted to end the dilly-dallying by telling a lie.

"All right, Mr. Srinivasarao, you may tell your Rani. I shall give my word of honour that we will stop all the hostilities and continue our negotiations if our two officers are safely returned to us."

Chaplin smiled a wan but hypocritical smile. Srinivasarao was a little surprised by the unexpectedly positive and conciliatory answer coming from Chaplin.

"Thank you very much, Chaplin Saheb. I shall convey this message to our Rani Sarkar who will be very happy to hear it."

The *vakil* rode back to the fort along with the guards and communicated all the details of Chaplin's answer.

All through the day, Rani Chennamma deliberated with her Sardars about the pros and cons of releasing Elliot and Stevenson. In the evening, Sardar Gurusiddhappa and others went to the prisoner, Elliot. Elliot who was brooding about his Company, home, wife and children was awakened out of it when he heard the sound of steps and human voices. The grill door was unlocked by the guards. Sardar Gurusiddhappa followed by other Sardars walked to him and stood in a circle around him.

Elliot saw them and felt a bit nervous and faltered, "What's the matter?" His question was accompanied by an interrogative gesture of his right hand.

Sardar Gurusiddhappa, who adjusted his turban around his head said, "See, Elliot Saheb, our Rani Sarkar has decided to release you."

Elliot could not believe his ears. He felt so ecstatic inwardly that his heart began to flutter. A broad smile settled on his lips.

Sardar Gurusiddhappa continued, "But on one condition."

"What's that?" asked Elliot in a weak voice.

"On condition that you swear by your God that you will tell your authorities how well we have treated you and that you should plead for the freedom of Kittur," said Sardar Gurusiddhappa.

"I shall definitely do that," replied Elliot.

"No, you must swear by your God to that effect," said another sardar.

Then Elliot crossed himself religiously and said, "I swear by Lord Jesus Christ that I shall report about how well you have treated me and that I shall request my superiors to restore your independence to you."

The leaders were satisfied by this answer and walked out of the building. Then the guards closed the grill door and locked it safely.

They then went to the next building where Stevenson was imprisoned. The guards opened the grill door at the Diwan's gesture. Sardar Gurusiddhappa and others stood around Stevenson, who felt uneasy and looked askance at them.

Sardar Gurusiddhappa announced, "Stevenson saheb, our Rani Sarkar has decided to release you."

No sooner had Stevenson heard these words than his heart began to beat fast. They told him the condition on which he would be released. Stevenson instantly dreamt of a reunion with his colleagues and the members of his family. He readily agreed to oblige them and swore by the name of Jesus Christ. Then all the Sardars walked out of his building.

Though the guards locked the grill door after the departure of the leaders, Stevenson felt an unprecedented lightness of heart consequent upon the removal of a big burden. Both Elliot and Stevenson were enjoying inwardly the prospects of their release and saw a peculiar beauty in Nature, especially the rosy tint of sunset, through their respective windows.

Three hours after sunset, on 1 December 1824, Sardar Gurusiddhappa and a few other leaders went to the buildings where Elliot and Stevenson were imprisoned. They were accompanied by the native soldiers. The guards opened the grill doors and let out the prisoners who saw each other after so many weeks and smiled the smiles of mutual recognition. Sardar Gurusiddhappa ordered them,

"You must speak to your authorities as you have sworn by your God."

Both Elliot and Stevenson nodded their assent and said "Yes, yes."

The soldiers went all around them. They walked in the light of torches carried by the servants. As they came to the main gate of the fort, a small door was opened and all of them passed through it carefully. Then the door was closed immediately by the guards.

As they had sent a message to Chaplin in the camp beforehand, they knew the Company officers would be very happy to receive their countrymen released after such a long drawn negotiation. They walked to Chaplin's tent and shook hands with him. Chaplin was very happy to see Mr. Elliot and Mr. Stevenson and welcomed them with a warm smile.

Sardar Gurusiddhappa said, "See, Chaplin Saheb, our Rani Sarkar has released these prisoners because of the promise you made of stopping the war immediately and restoring our freedom."

Chaplin felt a bit embarrassed and could not respond whole-heatedly. He just said, "Ahem", "Yes", and "Let's see", in a rather cold fashion.

Sardar Gurusiddhappa adjusted his turban and twirled his moustaches instinctively and ordered Elliot and Stevenson, "Elliot and Stevenson Sahebs, you tell your authorities in our presence whatever you have sworn to."

First Elliot cleared his throat and said, "See sir, I would like to bring to your kind notice the fact that the Rani has treated us very well. I never lacked anything there. I cannot ever forget her humanitarian approach."

Then Stevenson also added, "In fact, that was my experience also. The Rani never treated me as an enemy, but on the contrary extended all the hospitality as if I was their guest."

Chaplin sat listening to their words in a nonchalant manner. He did not have the heart to appreciate Rani Chennamma's humanitarian approach. Sardar Gurusiddhappa beckoned again to Elliot and Stevenson.

Elliot continued, "Sir, since the Rani has treated us so well, we feel that she should be allowed to manage her kingdom all by herself."

Then Stevenson added, "By restoring their freedom, we can earn her goodwill and have her support in our future ventures."

Chaplin listened to their words rather impatiently. Sardar Gurusiddhappa and his companions were eager to have a positive answer from Chaplin.

He asked him, "Chaplin Saheb, as per your wish and promise, our Rani Sarkar has released the prisoners. Now please tell us your answer, which we have to convey to our Rani."

The *vakil* pleaded, "As per your promise, you have to continue the autonomy of the Kittur Samsthan by abrogating the provision in the proclamation declaring Kittur Samsthan as a Company Territory."

Chaplin was rather reluctant to articulate anything clearly. He wanted to be conveniently ambiguous in his tone.

He said, "Mr. Gurusiddhappa, I'll have to have some time to think and answer your Rani. We shall talk about it tomorrow."

Sardar Gurusiddhappa did not want to be too harsh. He wanted to allow them some time at least to consolidate their ideas.

He, therefore, said, "All right, we shall wait until tomorrow morning for your answer."

So they returned to the palace through the small door of the Main-Gate. Even when they were trying for amicable settlement, they used to hear the fighting going on from both the sides in an offence-and-defence fashion.

*   *   *

After the leaders had returned to the fort, there was a great excitement in the Company military camps. All the officers in other tents rushed to Chaplin's tent. Chaplin was so happy that he sent for his scribe and dictated the letter reporting everything to Newnham. The letter ran as follows:

> I have much pleasure in stating that the two gentlemen were brought into camp at 9 o'clock this evening and I think that this particular act of submission may be an earnest intention of the insurgent Chiefs to conform to the remaining part of my stipulation; at present however, the *vakils* plead vehemently that the Samsthan may be continued and an act of oblivion passed urging that the *katak* soldiery, who appear to be under little control of their leaders are bent upon resistance unless more favorable terms than those offered in the proclamation are concerned. I have finally informed them that I cannot make any substantive

alteration in the conditions of the proclamation but that in consideration of their having well treated Messers Stevenson and Elliot and of their having at last released those gentlemen, I will put them most liberal construction upon every part of the condition, provided the fort be given up and the garrison surrendered by 10 o'clock tomorrow morning.

While the *vakil* and others deputed to accompany Messers Stevenson and Elliot were yet in my tent, many guns were fired from the fort and a party of Horse and Foot approaching one of our piquets, they were driven back by a discharge of grape from one of our six pounders, and it has been argued that hostilities shall be sustained on either side each keeping within his own limits till the hour tomorrow above specified. I am sorry to say that I have no confidence that this engagement will be fulfilled on the enemy's part, as their people are evidently under no sort of discipline.

There is no reason to fear that in spite of every endeavour to give publicity to our proclamation we have been but partially successful, the villagers out station being cut off from communication with the fort and no paper being allowed to reach the inside without first passing through the hands of the leader Gurusiddhappa, who has, of course, suppressed all the copies that have come into his possession, he being the only person excepted from the general amnesty.

I had it read over to all the people who accompanied Messers. Stevenson and Elliot to camp this morning and as it consisted of many people, the contents must have now become very clear to all who are interested.

Before the above-mentioned gentlemen were allowed to quit the fort they were sworn to intercede on behalf of the Samsthan and they have accordingly said everything that they could do with justice as to their own good treatment by Gurusiddhappa and as to his forbearance from committing devastations, as he might have done since the chief authority has been in his hands.

Colonel Deacon with the Battering Train arrived within four miles of camp this morning, some difficulty in passing a swamp having delayed the progress of the guns longer than was expected.

The letter was completed with the usual epistolary formalities added to it and dispatched to Mr. Newnham with a courier. Then Mr. Chaplin sent another letter to Rani Chennamma asking her to surrender her army to the Company authorities.

Then Chaplin said, "Let's celebrate the safe arrival of our colleagues tonight."

He ordered his steward to arrange a party. The steward and other servants kept small wooden tables in the midst and brought a number of whiskey bottles, glasses, onions, potato chips and vegetable slices. All the

Company officers poured the whiskey into their glasses and raised them in their hands and said, "Cheers".

Chaplin and others said in a chorus, "Let's drink to the health of Mr. Elliot and Mr. Stevenson."

Then they sipped their whiskey with occasional belches. Many an air bubble ascended to the top of their glasses. In between the sips, they ate the onion pieces and potato chips. Then a few guitar players and drummers came into the tent and began to play a few Western songs, which created a smoothing effect upon their minds.

As the effect of the whiskey began to work upon them, they slowly got up and walked to the adjoining tents and began to waltz with their ladies until they were terribly hungry. After waltzing to their hearts' content, they rushed to the kitchen tent and fell upon chicken and mutton dishes. After happily gourmandizing, they doddered back to their respective tents, slumped on their beds and slept like logs.

* * *

The letter dictated by Chaplin about midnight of 2 December 1824 was sent to Rani Chennamma through Narsing Rao. When Sardar Gurusiddhappa received it in the court hall in the presence of the Rani, he handed it over to the *dubhasi* to read. As the translator went on reading out the lines, the faces of the courtiers grew grim and serious. They had hoped that Chaplin would keep his word of restoring the autonomy of Kittur after their release of prisoners, Elliot and Stevenson. But contrary to their expectations, Chaplin had asked the people of Kittur to surrender themselves to the Company rule according to the proclamation. Otherwise their lives would not be spared –so had Chaplin threatened.

Rani Chennamma's face grew red with anger and she shouted, "Chaplin seems to be a treacherous fellow. Yesterday only he had promised that all hostility would be stopped if we released the prisoners. We all took him on his word. But this morning he has gone back on them. This is sheer treachery and shamelessness."

She looked ferocious like an exasperated lioness. Even the sardars of Kittur felt nervous at the sight of her angry gestures. They knew that she normally never lost her temper. But this time her anger knew no bounds. For a moment there was pin drop silence in the hall.

Finally Sardar Gurusiddhappa cleared his throat and said, "Rani Sarkar, kindly tell us what we should do now. There is hardly any time at our disposal. We have to be quick in our decisions and actions now."

Everybody sat silent interrogatively looking at the Rani. She closed her eyes for a moment and deliberated about what had to be done next. The bright marks of *vibhuti* seemed to add to the ferocity of her anger.

Then she opened her eyes and ordered the Diwan and Commander, "Sardar Gurusiddhappa, please send our last letter to Chaplin showing the contradiction between his promise and his action. Meanwhile, send orders to our army to be ready for any eventuality."

After further consultations with the Rani and other sardars, the Diwan dictated the following letter on behalf of Rani Chennamma and Rani Viravva to Chaplin:

Your letter of yesterday's date has been received and the communication conveyed through Narsing Rao Maunder understood by us; in neither can we perceive any symptoms of benefit towards the Samsthan. You desire in your letter that all the people should come forth from the fort loyally disposed towards the Government, and that, failing to do so, their lives would not be saved.

Mr. Thackeray, by his severity, brought this present state of affairs on us. We were extremely desirous that through your coming everything should be continued to us upon the ancient footing, but you have felt differently disposed towards us have written as we have mentioned. You wrote that if we released the gentlemen there would be no war; upon this promise we released the gentlemen; your horse began to advance and your battery was prepared to open upon us. Our horses were then sent out as a picket and four cannon shots were fired at them. We then fired two guns; we committed no aggression until we had been attacked by you in the first instance.

You wish the fort to be evacuated. To this we reply that we consider you as our superior and could not have believed that we should have been brought to this condition. You wrote that if we did not surrender and declare ourselves loyal subjects of the Government by 10 o'clock today, you would commence an attack upon us. We were before told by you that there would be no war and were satisfied that an investigation would be made respecting Mr. Thackeray's proceedings and that the Samsthan would be confirmed to us. We can perceive, in your last letter, no demonstration of such a result. You desire us today to declare our allegiance to the Company Government. We accompanied and assisted General Wellesley with our arms. We acted as allies to Major General Sir Thomas Munro, Governor of Belgaum, when he, feeling satisfied with the assistance that we had afforded, gave us a *Sannad* for the continuation of our Samsthan from generation to generation, which Sannad by your kindness had been in force up to this day. What can we now write in reply to your communication, that putting aside investigation you will attack us? You are superior. Let it be your part to acquire to yourself renown by supporting us and the 1,000 dependents, who are with us; we were wholly averse to war. You, disregarding this feeling, show a disposition to be hostile. When the period given us shall have expired, what remedy do we have? It is according to your pleasure.

Let your favorable disposition towards the Samsthan be continued undiminished.

After adding the usual epistolary formalities, the *dubhasi* took the signature of the Diwan on it. Then it was sent with a messenger to Mr. Chaplin. Two hours had already elapsed after sunrise. Meanwhile orders were sent by Rani Chennamma to different commanders of her army at different vantage points to take charge of their respective units and be ready for action.

Sardar Gurusiddhappa gently said, "Rani Sarkar, I really do not know what has happened to the Raja of Kolhapur. He had promised to help us with his army. I know he hates the Company people to the core. I do not know why he is still camping at Munavalli."

"It is possible that the Company officers are holding him up. Otherwise he would not have tarried like this," said Rayanna of Sangolli.

"If God wills it," said Rani Chennamma, "the Raja of Kolhapur will definitely come to our help. Let's wait and see."

* * *

When Chaplin received the letter of Rani Chennamma and Rani Viravva, he ignored it as callously as a butcher hearing the bleating of a lamb he was going to cut into pieces. Now that his two officers Elliot and Stevenson were released and safely returned by the Rani, he was in no way obliged to her – so he thought. Now that the Battering Train had come to Kittur and the entire army of 25,000 was ready for action, he did not want to hear any appeal from any native ruler. He thought it was his duty to help the Company government to extend its territory and prove the imperial authority of the Company Rule. He, therefore, did not bother to consider the Rani's request for freedom. He was eagerly waiting for the response from the fort up to 10 o'clock.

He was getting more and more impatient as he waited for some response, no matter whether it was positive or negative. Another half an hour went by. Then came the messengers from the fort and conveyed the message that the Rani was not willing to accept the conditions laid down by him. The Rani had clearly refused to surrender her army or fort to the Company authority.

Though Chaplin's blood was up for a moment at the knowledge of the Rani's adamancy, still he admired her courage in his heart of hearts. But there was no time for him to indulge in these humanitarian feelings, as he had to discharge his formidable responsibility. He remembered that he had been empowered by the Governor Elphinstone to declare martial law in the Maratha country to paralyze the rebellious activities of the insurgents. He therefore called his assistant and asked him to notify the declaration of Martial Law in the country. Accordingly the assistant officer sent a copy of the declaration. The same was pasted at different places and read out to the natives of Kittur and surrounding villages. But it, instead of cowing them down, aggravated their anger further.

When it was brought to the notice of Rani Chennamma and her Sardars, they fumed with anger at the treachery of Chaplin. Rani Chennamma roared like a lioness, "My countrymen, there is no way out for any of us now. Our choice is only between freedom and heroic death on the battlefield. There is no time for us to tarry." All the Sardars and leaders went to their respective military units and took charge of them. Whereas Rani Chennamma waited in the fort with her soldiers, Sardar Gurusiddhappa led the army stationed at the Gadadamaradi and was assisted by other leaders like Avaradi Virappa, Golandaz Himmat Singh, Narsing Rao, Guruputrappa, Appana Desagaon,

Sangolli Rayanna, Bichagatti Chennabasappa and Gajavira. Vengeance against the Company was writ large upon their faces. The naked swords held by the soldiers flashed in the sunlight. The clip-clop of horses' hooves and neighing were heard every now and then. The whole army of Kittur was excited with patriotism.

* * *

Meanwhile a contingent of the Company army had advanced towards the Western side of Kemmanamaradi, which was strongly guarded by Rani Chennamma's patriotic soldiers. The large Company army of more than 25,000 strong spread itself around Kemmanamaradi by moving some of the regiments to the north by the side of Ranagatti tank and another regiment to the south towards Tumbikeri. Colonel Deacon supervised the arrangement of the army by riding his horse from one end to the other. The Company soldiers in their uniforms held their guns erect in their hands. After Colonel Deacon satisfied himself about the platoons, he rode back to his central elevated palace. The soldiers, who had held up their right hands to their foreheads in the gesture of salute, brought them down. Then Colonel Walker stood in attention position and ordered at the top of his voice, "Platoon No1. Attention!" The soldiers, who were in a resting position by leaning their guns away from them, brought their heels together with a click and held their guns vertically erect. As they stamped the earth with their right feet, clouds of dust wafted up in the air. Their guns glistened and glinted in the morning sun and were recently greased with the fat of cows.

*   *   *

The native soldiers of Kittur, who stood at Kammanamaradi, were led by Avaradi Virappa. They were clad in tight pajamas and half-shirts secured with lace on their chest. They wore helmets on their heads. They were ready to lay down their lives for their Rani and for their beloved kingdom. There was a light of patriotism shining in their eyes. While they held the handles of swords in sheaths with their right hands, they twirled their moustaches impatiently. As Avaradi Virappa stood on his massive Persian horse, he looked very impressive. The bright marks of *vibhuti* on his forehead added nobility to his gravity. He took a round from his horse and supervised the arrangement of platoons in the desired order. The soldiers stood in a saluting position as he rode past them.

Then he returned to the centre and shouted in an exhorting voice, "Victory to Rani Chennamma! Victory to the patriots of Kittur!"

The patriotic slogan seemed to electrify the soldiers in an unprecedented fashion and their hearts began to dance as it were with patriotic zeal.

*   *   *

Colonel Walker stood to attention with a click of his heels. He, then, shouted at the top of his voice, "Platoon No. 1, Attention!"

Suddenly the platoon in the front stood to attention with a click of heels and a chorus of thumps upon the earth thereby raising the tiny clouds of dust. The birds in the surrounding Benjamin trees were scared away by the sudden thump upon the earth. Colonel Walker blew his shrill whistle, which created a grim silence in the atmosphere and every soldier became tense and ready for action.

Then he ordered at the top of this voice, "March forward and attack!" The Company soldiers held their guns in ready position with bayonets pointed towards the Kittur enemies and marched ahead in a rhythmic and stylized fashion.

Likewise Colonel Deacon rode his horse to the regiments stationed near Ranagatti tank and Tumbikeri and ordered Lieutenant Colonel. McLeod, Lieutenant Colonel Munro and Lieutenant Trewson to march forward and attack. Immediately Lieutenant Colonel McLeod and Lieutenant Colonel Munro blew their whistles consecutively to their respective platoons and shouted orders. Thus within a few minutes the Company soldiers started their attack from three directions simultaneously.

*   *   *

Avaradi Virappa, who sat on his stallion expectantly and waited for the Company enemies, was unusually alert. Within a few minutes he saw the Company army stirring and slowly creeping towards Kemmanamaradi. Suddenly Avaradi Virappa, Golandaz Himmat Singh and other leaders shouted orders to their respective platoons. There was a big commotion among the soldiers of Kittur who cheered themselves, "Victory to Rani Chennamma, Victory to Kittur kingdom." They drew out their sparkling swords and held them high in the air and rushed forward towards the Company enemies.

* * *

As both the armies rushed at each other, there was a riot of roaring, yelling and clank of the clash of arms. The soldiers of Kittur swayed their swords dexterously, while the Company soldiers tried to pierce the soldiers of Kittur with their bayonets. There was a big din of roaring and shouting. The soldiers of Kittur remembered Rani Chennamma's words and felt enthused to fight with the enemies with firm determination. They cleverly avoided the sharp points of bayonets darted at them by the Company soldiers and managed to pierce their swords into the chests or abdomens or arms of the enemies. As the swords cut deep into the enemies' flesh, blood spurted out and many of the enemies were mortally wounded.

The sight of the fellow soldiers being wounded exasperated the other soldiers of the Company army and they began to fight with greater vehemence. When the soldiers of Kittur darted their swords into the enemies' flesh, the enemies sagged with a yell into the pools of their own blood. The soldiers of Kittur shouted the cry of victory.

Similarly when the Company soldiers shot their bullets at the soldiers of Kittur, the latter fell to the ground instantly with piercing shrieks. Within a few hours the dead bodies of both the armies were lying on the battlefield in picturesque disarray. The sight of the death of many Company soldiers angered the living soldiers to a great extent. So they began to take revenge upon the soldiers of Kittur with a renewed zest. They pierced the soldiers of Kittur with their bayonets and fire their guns at them thereby causing a number of deaths and wounds. The shots of the gun produced clouds of gunpowder smoke, which wafted in the air and restricted the vision for a few moments. As the fighting continued more and more soldiers of both the armies fell and the battlefield was strewn with countless dead bodies. By about the mid-noon, the first batches of both the armies were reduced to dead bodies and carrions, and eagles began to circle in the sky for their unprecedented feast.

As the afternoon advanced, the soldiers of Kittur were overwhelmed by the new batches of Company soldiers rushing in upon them. As hours elapsed, many soldiers of Kittur fell in pools of blood and attained heroic death on the battlefield. Even on their dead faces could be seen the sense of satisfaction writ large as they had sacrificed themselves for their Rani and their kingdom. Almost an equal number of Company soldiers were also killed before they were replaced by the new batches of soldiers rushing into the battlefield. The only strength of the soldiers of Kittur was their patriotism and their old-fashioned swords.

But the Company soldiers were at an advantage in that they had superior weapons like guns with bayonets greased with the fat of cows and pigs. Besides, their number was much larger than that of Kittur soldiers. By the evening, a large majority of the soldiers of Kittur were killed on the battlefield and the remaining few realizing the futility of further fight after sunset returned to their homes a bit disappointed. Throughout the day, shelling continued between the Kittur Fort and the Company army. As the soldiers of Kittur died in large numbers on the Kemmanamaradi battlefield, the Company soldiers felt triumphant and cheerful. When they returned to their tents there was a great jubilation among them. They caroused, sang and danced until they felt sleepy. Colonel Walker and Colonel Deacon, Colonel Trewson etc., were so happy that they quaffed as much whiskey *pani* as they liked and smoked to their hearts' content.

*   *   *

Girimalla, a soldier of Kittur, who had witnessed his companions dying at the hands of Company soldiers, felt a bit nervous that he too might follow suit. He thought of his young wife and children and felt concerned about them so much that he wanted not to participate in the next day's war.

It was about midnight. The stars in the dark sky were shining serenely and the whole atmosphere was quiet. All the other soldiers had started snoring. Girimalla slowly got up and sneaked out of the military camp. He walked towards his home in the city of Kittur like a thief. Lest people should wake up and recognize him, he went to the back door of his house and tapped it gently. There was silence. Then he tapped a little louder. Then there was some response.

"Who's that?" Girimalla heard the voice of his wife from inside the house.

"It's me," said Girimalla. The backdoor was opened and his wife Mahadevi looked askance at him.

"Why, what happened? Why have you come at this odd hour of the night?" asked Mahadevi.

"Oh hush!" said Girimalla, "don't talk so loudly."

He pushed her aside, sneaked into the house and sat on a bag of jowar and said, "My dear, I have sneaked away from the battlefield for your sake."

On hearing these words Mahadevi was annoyed beyond measure. Her blood was up. She blurted out, "What? You have escaped from the battlefield like a coward? What should the Rani do if every soldier behaves like you?"

Girimalla was surprised by his wife's answer. He had expected her to welcome him with open arms.

"Talk less loudly, my dear, lest the neighbours should wake up and overhear us," said Girimalla trying to silence his wife.

But Mahadevi raised her voice further and shouted, "I don't care. Let them hear. I am really ashamed of having a cowardly husband like you, who returns from the battle field like a thief and without fighting heroically for the motherland."

She instantly removed her sacramental *tali,* hurled against his cheek so forcefully that his cheek began to smart with pain. He rubbed it gently to ease the pain. But his mental humiliation was even more painful than the physical one. He felt deeply annoyed to be insulted by his own beloved wife. He had mistaken her to be a maudlin wife, but now he realized what mettle she had.

He thought that his wife also had been inspired by Rani Chennamma's heroic spirit. Now he thought that earning the admiration from his wife was as good as earning the admiration from Rani Chennamma herself. He felt deeply nettled and did not know how to talk with his wife or show his face to her. He had a hurried meal and rested for about four hours there. He felt deeply insulted by her action. He had determined to go back to the battlefield.

He said to Mahadevi, "My dear, I had mistaken you for a docile wife interested only in the domestic security and happiness. It's only now that I realize what mettle you are made of. I'll go back to the battlefield and fight until my last breath. Goodbye."

He caressed her cheeks and went away after closing the back door behind him. Mahadevi opened the backdoor and saw his figure disappear in the dark. She felt proud of herself and her husband only now. She slept a carefree sleep that night.

* * *

On the 4th morning, the soldiers of Kittur were ready on the battlefield at Gadadamaradi. They were commanded by Sardar Avaradi Virappa. The few soldiers who survived in the previous day's battle on Kemmanamaradi also joined those on the Gadadamaradi. Girimalla, who was insulted by his own wife, was determined to fight until he breathed his last.

As the sun rose in the eastern sky, shelling started between the Kittur fort and the Company camp. Within an hour a battle proper started. The whistles and bugles were heard on both the sides. Colonel Deacon ordered his army to attack. Sardar Virappa also shouted his orders to the patriotic soldiers. The enemies rushed at each other with a vengeance.

The Kittur soldiers fought with an unprecedented bravery and hacked many Company soldiers to death.

Soldier Girimalla killed three to four enemies valiantly. The words of his wife were still ringing in his ears. He no longer cared for his life, as he had consecrated it to his motherland. Sardar Virappa was actively directing his soldiers and trying to energize them.

As the day advanced, many soldiers on both sides were killed and their dead bodies lay helter-skelter on the battlefield. But soon fresh batches of Company soldiers swooped on the Kittur soldiers. As the former outnumbered the latter, there was simply no balance between the two either in statistics or in the quality of weapons. Many of the Kittur soldiers lay dead on the battlefield. They had paid their last homage to their Rani and attained heroic Heaven. Soldier Girimalla was also finally killed by the bullets of Company soldiers.

As the sun descended in the western horizon, most of the Kittur soldiers had lost their lives. Sardar Virappa felt disheartened for a while. The few soldiers, who survived, retreated into the Fort, which was their last hope.

That night Colonel Deacon was extremely happy. There was great excitement in the Company military camp. The soldiers drank their whiskey, danced and sang to their hearts' content.

* * *

That night when the dead body of Girimalla was brought home by the surviving soldiers, Mahadevi felt proud of her husband, though she had been widowed.

She told the other womenfolk, who had gathered there, "My husband has laid down his life as the last sacrifice to the Rani of Kittur."

The tears, which trickled in her eyes, were both of sorrow and joy. She, who had removed her sacramental *tali,* now searched for it in the niche of the family deity, took it and put it around her neck. While she sat beside the cadaver of her husband, the men folk decorated it with *vibhuti* marks, flowers and propped the body in a lotus-posture. They put the sword across its laps. When the hearse was taken out, Mahadevi silently shed tears of sorrow and appreciation for her husband's patriotic fight.

* * *

On the 5th morning Colonel Deacon was happy to see the soldiers of Kittur stationed at Gadadamaradi being vanquished. The vast stretch of the hillock was dotted with pools of blood and helmets of dead soldiers. He ordered his soldiers to move towards the fort along with the battering train. The Company soldiers, who were in a jovial mood, moved enthusiastically towards the fort. The battering train was hitched to half a dozen hefty bullocks, which were whipped by sturdy servants. As the bullocks pulled the heavy weapon, it trundled along the undulating path. It moved very slowly. Finally when they reached the fort, the servants steered the bullocks in such a way that the battering train was stationed with its nozzle facing the main gate of the Kittur fort.

* * *

Sardar Gurusiddhappa, Sangolli Rayanna and other courtiers of Kittur met Rani Chennamma in the court-hall and discussed the matter seriously.

Sardar Gurusiddhappa told Rani Chennamma, "Rani Sarkar, we have lost countless soldiers. The Company also has lost a number of their soldiers. But their army is many times bigger than ours. And then their weapons are also superior to ours."

The Rani sat upright on her throne, and said, "Sardar Gurusiddhappa, you did not allow me to fight yesterday. I would have died fighting with the enemy. Death is far better than this humiliation."

"Rani Sarkar," said Sardar Gurusiddhappa, "you need not come out of the palace as long as we are alive. We shall fight until the last drop of blood remains in our body."

Rani Chennamma looked rather helpless. Her daughter-in-law Rani Viravva also sat behind her and looked pale.

Sardar Gurusiddhappa said, "Rani Sarkar, the Chhatrapati of Kolhapur did not offer us the help he had promised. We have no means of contacting him."

Rani Chennamma said, "Sardar, now it is too late to take care of ourselves."

Sangolli Rayanna said, "Now that the Company enemies have surrounded the fort, our cannons should be operated continuously from the ramparts."

"Yes," said Sardar Gurusiddhappa, "I have given instructions to our soldiers to that effect."

After the confidential consolation, Sardar Gurusiddhappa and other courtiers dispersed and went back to their respective positions to direct the military operations. The shelling was started by the Company army. It was answered by the Kittur cannons. Deep rumbles were heard and clouds of black stinking smoke wafted in the air. The dialogue of firing continued all through the morning. The soldiers had secured the gates of Kittur fort and were firing their cannons at the Company army waiting outside.

The big boom and rumble of shelling could be heard all through the day. However, in the late afternoon, the cannons of Kittur were silenced. Sardar Gurusiddhappa ran his soldiers there to inspect what had happened to the cannons. The soldiers went to the ramparts of the fort and inspected the gunpowder magazine and alas, found that it had been rendered ineffective by some treacherous people of their own kingdom. The soldiers, who saw the dismal scene, felt discouraged. They rushed back and reported everything to Sardar Gurusiddhappa.

One of the soldiers reported, "Sir, we saw the gunpowder magazine with our own eyes. The gunpowder has been adulterated with cow dung and grains of millet. Therefore, the gunpowder is not catching fire."

Sardar Gurusiddhappa was shocked out of his wits. He leaned his forehead upon his two palms and exclaimed, "O God! What treachery! And that too at such a critical time! I can never believe it."

He heaved a deep sigh. "You fellow, go quick and find out who are the fellows, who have betrayed us like this."

The soldiers saluted and went back. Sardar Gurusiddhappa was really shaken to the roots. He could not contain his deep sorrow at the inhuman treachery. His helplessness was almost proportionate to his anger.

He rode his horse to the palace and rushed into the Rani's chamber and reported, "Rani Sarkar, we are ruined by the treachery of our own people."

Rani Chennamma contorted her face and asked him, "What is that? Sardar Gurusiddhappa, tell me clearly."

Sardar Gurusiddhappa's face grew grim and he said, "How shall I tell you, Rani Sarkar? Our own people have mixed cow dung and grains of millet in the gunpowder. Out cannons have, therefore, been silenced forever. I do not know what to do."

Tears trickled down his eyes in spite of his deliberate effort to keep his composure. For a moment Rani Chennamma was disconcerted to such an extent that she did not know what to say. Never in her life was she so speechless as today.

However she quickly recovered her sense of shock, cleared her throat and said, "Sardar Gurusiddhappa, you find out the traitors and punish them appropriately. Meanwhile, let the fort be guarded strictly on all sides. Let the cannons be abandoned for the time being."

Sardar Gurusiddhappa instinctively bowed to the Rani and rushed out of the chamber to supervise the military activities.

When he went back to the ramparts of the fort, two soldiers came and reported after a ceremonial salute, "As per the intelligence collected by our people, it is Kannur Virasangappa and Hurakadli Mallappa, who are said to have tampered with the gunpowder. Now they are absconding somewhere."

Sardar Gurusiddhappa's blood began to boil with uncontrollable anger and his moustaches twitched. He shouted, "Havaldar, go and trace out the two traitors in the fort and bring them to me at the earliest."

The Havaldar saluted and rushed out to carry out the Commander's order. His soldiers began to examine every nook and corner of the fort. The whole atmosphere was tense inside the fort of Kittur. Alas! The soldiers of Kittur had given up the use of cannons at the most crucial time in the history of Kittur kingdom.

At last the soldiers brought the traitors, Kannur Virasangappa and Hurakadli Mallappa with their hands bound behind them and stood them before Commander Gurusiddhappa. The traitors did not have the courage to look into the eyes of the Commander.

Gurusiddhappa's blood began to boil at the very sight of the traitors. He gnashed his teeth in anger and roared at them, "So you are the dogs, who have done this shit-eating business? What had the Rani done to you to deserve this treachery? You ungrateful wretches! You have shamelessly betrayed the gem of a ruler whose salt you have eaten for generations."

His anger burst into action. His palms were itching irritably. He stretched his right palm and slapped them with such force that his palms began to ache. Likewise the cheeks of the traitors also began to smart with sharp pain. He shouted at them once again, "You whoresons, you have cut the very hands which offered you food. I am sure you will rot in hell for eternity. Even hell will be ashamed of accommodating you there. I am ashamed to see your faces. *Thoo*! You, scoundrels."

He spat on their faces. Then he turned to the soldiers and ordered them, "You take away these scoundrels and have them trampled by the elephants."

The soldiers dragged the traitors away from there to the nearby plain. Then the Commander's order was conveyed to the *mahout*. They led a well-trained elephant from an elevated shed and brought it to the plain. As the *mahout* sitting on the large back of the elephant pierced it with his trident, the animal lifted its trunk with a flourish and trumpeted hoarsely. As the *mahout* goaded it, it increased its pace and reached the plain. The other soldiers had bound the hands and feet of the two traitors and laid them on the earth. Soon a large crowd of citizens collected to witness the scene.

The traitors realized their folly and repented inwardly that they should not have tampered with the gunpowder. They also realized that the bribe they had taken from the Company officers was not accompanying them to hell with their departing spirits. They remembered their wives and children who would be widowed and forlorn in addition to suffering the stigma of belonging to the treacherous family. But alas, this realization came too late. They also remembered how well the Rani had treated them all through their life. Their hearts were fluttering ceaselessly.

As the solider blew his whistle, the *mahout* dismounted from the elephant and led it to the traitors laid across its patch. The *mahout* pointed the backs of the traitors, but the elephant hesitated for moment and shied away. It trumpeted hoarsely. But the *mahout* goaded it once again by piercing its flanks with his sharp trident. The elephant then seemed to be angered, lifted its fore legs and placed them on the backs of the two traitors who cried in a shrill and heart-rending voice. Their bodies were squeezed to the ground. The *mahout* pierced the elephant further. So the animal stepped upon the back of the traitors. And lo, the bodies of the traitors smashed and the entrails came out with the blood spurting and oozing out. The dead bodies of the traitors lay inert there. The onlookers, who stood at a safe distance, covered their eyes with their palms out of pity and fear and left the place. Even the *mahout* and the other soldiers had tears in their eyes. Then the elephant was led back to its shed. As soon as the soldiers left the bodies of the traitors there, kites and eagles swooped down upon them to make a grand feast of them.

* * *

The whole day the cannons of Kittur remained unused because the gunpowder could not be replenished in such a hurry. Everybody including the Rani and her leaders were helpless because of the treacherous enemies inside the kingdom. But, however, they wanted to do their best to protect the fort and their honour as long as they could. Most of the soldiers, who were handling the cannons, took up the handguns and began to fire at the enemies from the nooks of the parapets, from all the sides. Commander Gurusiddhappa and others were directing the soldiers.

Outside the fort, Colonel Deacon stood with his army in front of the main gate. Colonel Walker was assisting him. Others like Lieutenant Colonel McLeod, Captain Crew of Mysore Horse Artillery, Colonel Trewson etc., surrounded the Kittur fort and began to fire at the gates continuously. They had realized by now what they had heard about the impregnable fort of Kittur. It was built with hard-red granite stones, which could not be broken very easily. The gates were also made of strong wood and steel and could not be broken easily.

Inside the fort Rani Chennamma and daughter-in-law, Rani Viravva waited in their chamber along with a few soldiers and bodyguards. The Rani had realized that the Kittur kingdom was coming to an end now. Death was the only way out from a life of struggle and humiliation. Though a woman, she was made of very hard mettle. She goaded the young Rani Viravva and was ready for any eventuality. She knew that the soldiers of Kittur were loyal and patriotic and many of them had already laid down their lives for the sake of their beloved kingdom. She knew that the Kittur Fort was surrounded by the large army of the Company. She instinctively knew the result, but she seemed to be only waiting patiently for the declaration of it.

She remembered His Holiness's words about the ephemerality of mortal life and the futility of the entire struggle. The only solution suggested by His Holiness was to bear all the sorrow of life patiently and retain the equanimity of mind. Though she had suffered a lot in her life after the death of her husband Mallasarja and acquired a philosophical resignation in her outlook, now the words of His Holiness rushed into her memory with a special significance. She was jerked into reality from the philosophical speculation when she heard the loud stutter from outside the fort.

"What is that new type of sound?" Rani Chennamma asked her bodyguards.

They listened to it carefully and said, "The enemies seem to have started the battering train to breach our Main- Gate."

Rani Chennamma felt that the end of Kittur was fast approaching.

As per Colonel Deacon's order, the battering train stationed in front of the main gate was operated along with other cannons. The Company soldiers seemed to be in a very confident mood and operated the machines very enthusiastically. The shells whizzed and whistled before hitting the fort walls or gate. Clouds of smoke wafted in the air emitting a sharp smell of gunpowder all around. The bullets were hit by the soldiers of Kittur also on the Company soldiers. There was a regular dialogue of firings. But the continuous stutter of the battering train was deafening and irritating especially to the soldiers of Kittur waiting within the fort. All the birds and animals were scared away from the Kittur fort by the deafening blasts and boom of shells.

As the sun went down in the western horizon, darkness descended everywhere. The torches were lit in the Kittur fort and were fixed in all the important corners. The tiny halos of yellow light shone at regular intervals but yet the darkness surrounding them seemed to be overwhelming. It seemed that the sun was setting eternally on the Kittur kingdom.

The Company soldiers outside the fort lit their torches and candles in their camps. But the battering train was operated continuously. The stone walls of the fort remained impregnable. Hence Colonel Deacon asked the operator of the battering train to concentrate on the front gate made of wood and steel bars. The operator turned the nozzle of his weapon to the gate and continued to fire. The shells cut deep holes in the wooden panels and split them sufficiently. The Kittur soldiers stood ready inside the front gate of the fort to fight the final battle with the Company soldiers and save the precious life of their Rani and their beloved kingdom. Commander Gurusiddhappa was directing his soldiers.

The Battering Train was shelling the Main-Gate of Kittur Fort ceaselessly and bored countless holes in it. Colonel Deacon had made it a question of prestige and wanted to see that the gate was broken. He, therefore, shifted the operators but kept the deadly machine in operation continuously. Now that darkness had descended everywhere, the Company officers and their soldiers could see only the silhouette of the fort in the starlight of the night and pale yellowish tint of the torches from behind the parapets of the fort. The shelling continued for about three to four hours after sunset.

Alas! The Main-Gate of the Fort was broken and the Company soldiers raised a jubilant cheer. The soldiers of Kittur were alarmed at the sight of the breach of the main gate, which they could control no longer. But they stood ready for the final battle.

When the front gate of the fort was broken and splintered into pieces, the Company soldiers shouted for joy and began to barge their way into it. As they rushed into the fort, the soldiers of Kittur put up a brave fight with them and hacked the Company soldiers to death. In that scuffle many soldiers on both the sides lost their lives and sagged down to the earth. But yet the soldiers of Kittur fought bravely before laying down their lives. Many Company soldiers died and some of them were mortally wounded and maimed.

Munro, who entered the gate with a deep vindictive feeling, was stabbed in the chest and flanks by two soldiers of Kittur and sagged to the earth. He lost the power of movement of limbs and the power of speech. After a couple of hours of fight, most of the soldiers of Kittur had lost their lives and offered their blood sacrifice to their beloved Rani. The other soldiers of Kittur, who realized the futility of fighting with the Company soldiers countless in number, began to run for their lives in the dark. Although many Company soldiers had died, they were replaced by fresh batches of vindictive soldiers who shot the native soldiers mercilessly. The Sardars like Avaradi Virappa, Kinkeri Venkanna, Kumma Imam and others thought that it was useless to fight with the large Company army. They thought of their own personal safety and escaped from the fort into the jungles and rushed towards the Western Ghats near Shumsherghurh separately. They whipped their horses desperately through the wood in the darkness, scaring away birds and beasts.

Commander Gurusiddhappa and other leaders, who understood the gravity of the situation, grew helpless and desperate and thought not of the kingdom but only of the safety of Rani Chennamma and Rani Viravva, who were in the inner chambers of the Fort.

So they rushed there and implored Rani Chennamma with joined palms, "Rani Sarkar, the story of Kittur is finished. There is no point in being here. We request you to escape from here and that quickly too."

But Rani Chennamma said in a firm voice, "Sardar Gurusiddhappa, do you think my life is more precious than yours and those of all our loyal and heroic soldiers?"

Commander Gurusiddhappa implored her further, "In a way, it is so, Rani Sarkar. We'll be here to face the enemies. We're here to fight for you so that you may live safely. I shall send a few escorts with you. Please escape from here."

But Rani Chennamma did not agree with him. She stood up in a heroic posture and said, "Sardar Gurusiddhappa, don't worry about my or Viravva's safety. Please remember that I am not a coward, though born as a woman. I am the wife of Raja Mallasarja. I shall be with all of you here. Whatever happens to you will happen to me."

On hearing the heroic words of the Rani, Commander Gurusiddhappa did not know how to persuade her and just stood before her with other leaders to protect her from the enemies who were likely to rush into the chamber very soon. But he joined his palms to Rani Chennamma and requested, "Rani Sarkar, this is not the time to think like this. Our loyal soldiers will take you out of the palace through the northeastern gate. You may escape towards Sangolli."

Sangolli Rayanna also implored her, "Mother, please hurry up and all the three of you mount your horses."

Rani Chennamma seemed to be affected by the implorations of her well wishes. But she said, "No, no. Let us not run away from here like cowards. I shall stay here along with you and brave the danger. My life is not more important than yours."

The Sardars felt helpless to know that the Rani never thought of her safety. Rani Chennamma, her daughter-in-law Rani Viravva and Janakibai sat in their chamber of the palace.

*   *   *

As a majority of Kittur soldiers lay in the pools of blood, the Company soldiers began to advance slowly towards the central palace of the Rani. As they shot their bullets at the palace, the bullets hit the wall or columns in the dark. Whenever the bullets hit the soldiers, they fell to the earth with a piteous shriek. Similarly when the guns were shot from the palace windows and nooks, some of the Company soldiers shrieked and slumped dead. But the other Company soldiers ignored the dead soldiers and marched ahead. As many guns were shot at the palace gate, the native soldiers guarding it fell dead.

There was relatively greater silence now on the palace campus. The Company soldiers entered the hall and shot at the Kittur guards mercilessly. The entire palace seemed to be in a sepulchral silence. As the Company soldiers marched ahead in the hall and were searching for the native soldiers and shooting them, the heavy sound of their boots and the clatter of their guns could be heard in the clear silence.

At last when they entered the inner chamber, they were so happy to see Rani Chennamma and her daughter-in-law Rani Viravva sitting there. Sardar Gurusiddhappa, Himmat Singh, Sangolli Rayanna and other leaders were also there in the palace, standing helplessly and looking at the Company soldiers.

Colonel Deacon ordered his soldiers, "Arrest all the leaders."

Suddenly the Company soldiers surrounded the leaders and arrested them in their own palace by keeping a strict watch over them. The other sardars and soldiers had deserted the palace. The sardars and leaders inwardly felt that it was no use resisting at this juncture, when they were at the mercy of the enemies. They also thought of the future and safety of their wives and children and other dependents.

Colonel Deacon addressed them, "Gentlemen, you are no longer the loyal servants of your Rani. You are under our control now. I order you to surrender yourselves and your arms. If you try to rebel against the Company government, all of you will have to be hanged."

The heartless words of the inimical authorities sent a tremour through the spines of the sardars and leaders, who visualized for a moment the picture of their being hanged. The dreadful fear awakened a practical wisdom in them. They looked at one another.

Finally one of the sardars spoke for all of them, "Saheb, we shall surrender ourselves with our arms if you promise to spare our lives."

All the other sardars nodded their assent. Colonel Deacon was inwardly happy to notice that the insurgents were sufficiently cowed down and thought it proper to pardon them.

He said loudly, "We'll definitely spare your lives if you lay down your arms and surrender yourselves."

"Yes Saheb, we'll do so," said the leading sardar. "That's good," said Colonel Deacon with a sense of satisfaction and ordered his soldiers, "You collect their arms and keep a watch over them till morning."

Accordingly the Company soldiers walked up to the Sardars and unbuckled their swords along with sheaths and collected them. Then they threw them in a nearby room and locked it. The sardars began to doze on the carpets on which they sat, while the Company soldiers watched over them diligently. A mourning silence reigned in the palace. Kites and eagles were feasting on the dead bodies lying everywhere inside the fort walls.

There was simply no limit to the joy of Colonel Deacon and other military officers. They were extremely happy to have vanquished the rebellious Rani of Kittur, who had given them such a tough fight. They sat in their tents and drank whiskey, smoked their pipes and caroused until they fell asleep. They were all overwhelmed with a sense of unprecedented satisfaction.

On the 5th morning, the Company soldiers surrounded the soldiers of Kittur, who had remained in the fort without trying to escape. They were disheartened to know that their Sardars had surrendered themselves the previous night itself. Besides, they had a fear that they may be tortured by the Company authorities, who had seized the fort now. When the military officers repeated Colonel Deacon's orders, the native soldiers surrendered themselves and helplessly handed over their swords and guns to the Company soldiers.

Before 8 o'clock on the morning of 5th December 1824, the Company troops occupied the upper and the lower forts and took charge of everything. Then all of them gathered in the open space before the lower fort.

Colonel Deacon, Lieutenant Colonel McLeod, Captain Spiller and Captain Jameson and others stood in front of their troops. A band stood by the side of the soldiers. A Company soldier clambered up to the top of the fort and pulled down the *Nandi Dwaja* of Kittur, crumpled it in his palm and threw it down on the roof. Then he hitched the Union Jack to the string and unfurled it. It began to flutter in the morning sun. Simultaneously Colonel Deacon unfurled the Union Jack from the flagpole erected on the ground before the Fort. The band played the British national anthem, while the Company soldiers stood in a saluting position. As the saxophone, bugle and the big drums sounded in a chorus, the Company soldiers beamed with smiles on their faces.

Apart from the army of the East India Company, the subsidiary forces maintained on behalf of the Indian Princely States also was utilized. The army so mobilized was from Gulart, central India and deployment of troops from Burma War. So it encompassed the entire Indian peninsula and was larger than that mobilized for the war against Tipu Sultan.

Chaplin was very ecstatic about his victory over the Rani of Kittur. He was so jubilant over the whole achievement that he sent a detailed letter to Newnham the same day about the happenings during the past few days:

> Adverting to my dispatch of yesterday evening communicating the surrender of Kittur, I have the honour to acquaint for the information of the Honorable Governor in Council that the actual occupation of the fort was last night resisted by

the garrison notwithstanding all Colonel Deacon's personal endeavour to persuade them to submit, but in the course of the night the principal of the insurgent Chiefs surrendered themselves on condition of their lives being spared and the remainder of the soldiery that had not previously escaped being quite disheartened by the energetic measures pursued against them agreed this morning to lay down their arms; both upper and lower forts were in consequence occupied by the Company troops at about 8 a.m. this morning.

The names of the Chiefs, who had given themselves up, are specified in the margin.

A small body is supposed to have escaped at the head, which is Avaradi Virappa, who had throughout the affairs been a ringleader of the soldiery and apprehensive of being called to account for former acts of atrocity has been prominent in his opposition to Government. He is supposed to have gone off towards Shumshergarh accompanied by Kinkery Venkanna, who is chief of a party of Munsches, and three Gumasthas named Govindayya, Narayana and Yashavanta.

Kumma Imam of Deogaon, chief of a gang of desperadoes, is said also to have fled in the same direction. I have offered rewards for the apprehension of each of these persons.

It is supposed, if hard pressed, that the fugitive will endeavour to escape down the Ghats into the Goa territory. I do not imagine they will attempt to hold Shumshergarh, to occupy which fort I have requested Colonel Deacon to send a military detachment.

Colonel Deacon has already at my suggestion made very practicable arrangement for the protection of the females of the family of the late Desai for whom it is my intention to recommend a suitable maintenance.

A committee has been appointed by that officer to make an inventory of the treasure and property taken which I presume is considerable, as I am informed that only a small portion of which was sealed up by Mr. Thackeray has been abstracted by rebels.

I propose for the present to confine the most prominent of the Kittur insurgents in the fort of Belgaum until I am furnished with the orders of the Government for my guidance by the conditions on which they surrendered, their lives must be spared but they are liable to such other punishment as Honorable Governor in Council may deem appropriate to the overt act of rebellion of which they have been infatuated enough to be guilty notwithstanding the uncommonly lenient and liberal terms that we held out to them provided they returned to their allegiance without further resistance.

I have great pleasure in stating that I feel much indebted to Colonel Walker of the 8th Madras for the promptitude with which he cooperated with me, before Colonel Deacon's arrival and my acknowledgements are no less due to Colonel

Deacon for his cordial assistance whilst my negotiations were pending. The able and judicious arrangements which the latter distinguished officer has been enable in so short a space of time to reduce the strong fort of Kittur, defended as they were by garrison of an unusually determined character for its spirit and energy, are far above my praise but will, I am sure, be fully appreciated by the Hon'ble Governor in Council.

The gallantry of the troops led on by Colonel McLeod of the 4th Madras Cavalry to the assault of the enemy's entrenched post of Kemmanamaradi which I had myself the satisfaction of witnessing from an adjoining height will, I doubt not, be brought to the notice of Government by the proper authority.

I cannot close the dispatch without expressing also my appreciation of the zeal and activity of Captain Spiller and James of my escort.

As soon as Chaplin scribbled his signature below the contents of the letter, the clerk put it in a cover and sealed it with wax and dispatched it to Newnham, Secretary to the Governor Elphinstone at Bombay.

*   *   *

Colonel Deacon, who was in an ecstatic mood, visited the Kittur Fort in the afternoon of 5 December 1824 and saw the helpless womenfolk of the Desai's family and made arrangement for their protection by appointing guards at all the doors of their chambers. The womenfolk, who had lost their beloved Rani forever, shed incessant tears and did not know what to do or where to go. They observed a sort of mourning period by abstaining from food and water for a couple of days. They knew they were imprisoned for the entire span of their life.

The natives of Kittur, who knew the latest developments about the kingdom and especially about their beloved Rani, whom they considered as their godmother, abstained from food, drink and sleep and brooded over the tragedy that had befallen to her, her family and kingdom. Now Rani Chennamma had become a prisoner in her own palace. Could there be anything more tragic than that? they wondered.

The next day Colonel Deacon came to the chamber and said to them, "Rani Chennamma, you are all under arrest. You just follow us."

The Company soldiers had seized the bodyguards of the Rani and taken away their swords from them. The bodyguards stood helplessly blinking at them. Rani Chennamma, Rani Viravva and the young Rani Janakibai looked at one another helplessly.

The leader of the Company army shouted his orders once again, "Come on, just follow us."

Rani Chennamma knew that it was no use resisting the enemies now, after losing all the wealth and glory of Kittur kingdom. Nor did she care for her life, which was after all so ephemeral. She beckoned to her young female companions who followed the cordon of the Company soldiers.

* * *

Chaplin was ecstatic about the victory over Kittur. He ordered his assistants to take into custody the prominent rebels like Sardar Gurusiddhappa, Sangolli Rayanna and others, and kept them under strict watch. Then he familiarized himself with the details of Kittur wealth and property with the help of Stevenson, Elliot and other officers, who knew certain things about Kittur. Chaplin was happy to learn that Kittur kingdom had fabulous wealth and income for its size. He, therefore, ordered his confidant officers to take stock of all the Kittur property.

The officers looked diligently into the registers of Kittur and found that the Kittur kingdom had 286 villages and 72 hamlets and that the annual income from them was about Rs. 4, 00,000. The officers were really very much impressed by the figures. The next day they ransacked all the treasuries of the kingdom and were flabbergasted to find that the total cash amounted to Rs. 16, 00,000. They heaped all the jewellery, silver and gold ornaments on a carpet in a room. The multi-coloured gems and stones dazzled their eyes. They had never seen such exotically beautiful ornaments in their lives. They inwardly felt that their arrival into the Oriental country was justified as it could compensate for their separation from their motherland by its rich wealth of jewels and gold.

The goldsmith officially appointed weighed each and every ornament and tested them against the test stone and calculated the total worth, which amounted to nearly Rs. 4, 00,000. The officers were ecstatic when they heard the figure. All the cash and jewellery were classified and placed into separate boxes sealed properly, kept in a big hall and locked. It was guarded by the soldiers twenty-four hours a day.

The next day the Company officers went around the military sheds of Kittur and counted the horses, camels and elephants. They were again impressed by the large stock of these animals. The whole day was occupied in counting them. When they enquired of the servants in charge of them, they replied, "Our Rani had bought them from Arabian and Persian agents."

The camels, though gaunt, were really very tall and could be used for carrying big loads. Likewise the elephants were also very large in size and agile in their limbs and bore marks of *vibhuti* all around them. In the evening the clerks totalled up the figures and could see the total graph, which showed that the Rani owned 3,000 horses, 2,000 camels and about a hundred elephants.

Colonel Deacon was so happy that he exclaimed, "That's why the Rani was so confident of herself. The military strength is really very large for the size of the kingdom."

He puffed at his hookah very contentedly. Then he told his assistants, "Tomorrow you finish the stock verification of the arms. Then we shall pack them off to the East India Company at Bombay."

The assistant said, "Yes Sir," and went away.

The next day the Company officers went about the fort precincts and inspected all the cannons and guns and other weapons to be found at different places and had them counted and classified. When they went to the top of the fortification, they found a number of brass and iron cannons installed at various strategic places. Similarly they found a large number of miscellaneous arms like swords, bows, arrows, spears etc. When they went to the gunpowder store, they found a large stock of gunpowder. The Company officers felt profusely impressed as if they were dissecting the anatomy of a lioness after killing her with great efforts.

Finally the clerk gave a graph of the total figures. The Rani, according to the figures, had 36 cannons and 56 guns and countless miscellaneous weapons. Colonel Deacon was again very much impressed by the figures. He could not help admiring the Rani and the military strength of her kingdom. Now that the stock verification was over, the Company officers began to think of the next procedures.

As the authorities of the East India Company were apprehensive that the patriots of Kittur kingdom might seek the help of the Portuguese rulers of Goa, they had stationed their army along the Western Ghats to prevent any possible transaction between Kittur and Goa.

* * *

Rani Chennamma wondered about the strange course of her Destiny. She felt that the wheel of Time had turned conspicuously. She thought what was once at the height had come down to the lowest point. The philosophical speculation about the changing directions of Destiny seemed to give her a new strength of stoic resignation.

When she noticed that the womenfolk, who were her kith and kin, were crying and sobbing, she tried to console them, "My dear sisters, don't cry or lose heart. We must all endure whatever suffering comes our way. Crying will not in any way prevent it, if we are destined to go through it."

The women, who wiped their tears with the ends of their saris, were momentarily silenced and pacified, although they were not able to understand the deeper significance of the Rani's words. But on the whole, they felt as if they were suspended in an abysmal darkness. A kind of mourning atmosphere continued for the Rani's family at Kittur.

* * *

Now that all the stock verification was done meticulously, Chaplin wanted the annexation of the Kittur kingdom to the East India Company government to be legally completed. He therefore got a document drafted on the government paper in which the Rani of Kittur had to surrender the kingdom of Kittur with all its property to the Company government. The document was carefully read and scrutinized by the assistant officers of Chaplin. Then he himself took the document to the Kittur fort.

He sent word to Rani Chennamma to meet him in the hall. The Rani walked under heavy military protection to the hall where Chaplin waited with his assistants. The Rani's lawyers and translators were also summoned there. The Rani sat in the cushioned chair and looked at the Company officers interrogatively.

Chaplin cleared his throat and said, "Rani Saheba, the Company government wants that you sign this document here."

He held up the neatly drafted document in black indelible ink. The lawyer explained the matter and the *dubhasi* translated it for the Rani, who looked rather puzzled.

"Why is it necessary?" she asked.

"It is very necessary for official purposes," explained Chaplin. Rani Chennamma hesitated for a moment. She could not consult any Sardar now, as none of them were present around her. Her helplessness was total. Yet she wanted to know the contents of the document. The lawyer read out the documents. Her heart grew heavy with sorrow. Rani Viravva and Rani Janakibai were staring at her helplessly. Rani Chennamma knew the futility of refusing to sign the document now. She said 'all right' with a sigh. Immediately a Company officer dipped a quill in the black indelible ink and kept it on the table for her. The right hand of Rani Chennamma, which had wielded the sword and fought the Company enemies, could not lift the little featherweight of the quill now. Her fingers grew powerless and were unable to hold the quill properly. But yet she managed to pick up the quill with her tremulous fingers and scribbled her signature upon the document.

Chaplin said to Rani Chennamma, "Rani Saheba, though we have fought against you, we have great respect for you. You have done your duty as a true patriot. Besides you have treated all the British officers, their wives and children with great affection and courtesy when they were imprisoned in your fort. The Company, therefore, grants a minimum of eleven villages for your livelihood and the necessary staff of servants to look after you."

Rani Chennamma looked at Chaplin and exclaimed helplessly, "Whoever can avert the course of Destiny?"

Chaplin felt satisfied, took up the document and walked away jubilantly. Rani Chennamma leant against the back of the chair and closed her eyes for a few seconds. Tears gushed out of her eyes in spite of her lioness-like spirit. Rani Viravva and Rani Janakibai sobbed in muffled voices. The assistants of Chaplin explained to the Rani how the Company Government had assigned sixty five servants for Rani Chennamma, eighty five servants for Rani Viravva and forty five servants for Janakibai for around the clock service. Rani Chennamma and her two companions did not feel any reduction in the comforts of life although they were all mentally depressed by the loss of the kingdom to the East India Company. As they sat in a morose mood, the Company guards watched them with silent indifference.

* * *

Now that the legal formalities of annexation were completed and all the rebellious sardars of Kittur were captured and kept under control, Chaplin was beaming with pleasure. He consulted his assistants and other officers for a couple of days about all the details of his next plans. The news of Rani Chennamma signing the document of surrender to the Company Government under duress spread in the city of Kittur like wildfire and made the citizens very melancholic.

The next day, Chaplin sent an order to Colonel Deacon to arrange for the transportation of the Rani and her two companions to the jail of Bailahongala. Colonel Deacon arranged for a *sarot* near the entrance of the fort.

Rani Chennamma, Rani Viravva and Rani Janakibai completed their morning ablutions and had their breakfast. The Company officers had never touched the jewels and gold ornaments on their persons. They relaxed on their divans.

Suddenly a scuffle of boots was heard. Gradually the sound grew louder. The Rani and her two companions cocked their ears and listened to the sound carefully. Within a few seconds a Company officer entered the palace along with soldiers.

The Chief Officer said, "Rani Saheba, you get ready with your companions. We have orders to take you to Dharwad."

Rani Chennamma felt as if her soul was crushed to death. But yet she bore the humiliation heroically. She stood up boldly and looked at her two companions. She followed the chief officer. Rani Viravva and Rani Janakibai followed her silently. All the three of them walked out of the fort. Near the front door stood the *sarot* with four horses harnessed to it. The driver sat ready at his seat. Rani Chennamma, Rani Viravva and Janakibai shuffled to the chariot and sat in the covered carriage. As the Chief Officer beckoned, the driver whipped the horses of the carriage, which trotted ahead gently. The wheels of the carriage creaked and rattled. The Company soldiers followed it on their horses.

As the *sorot* moved along the main road of Kittur, the natives stood at their doors, windows and on their roofs sobbing and crying at the sight of their beloved Rani being taken to jail.

"We do not know what all evils we have to see in the *Kali Yuga!*" exclaimed an old woman and cried. They stood and saw them until the *sarot* rattled along the distant road and finally disappeared from their sight. Whereas the men folk sobbed silently, the women-folk wailed loudly by beating their chests.

"The red-faced monsters are taking away our mother, Chennamma. May their wives become widows!" wailed an old woman and cried in a loud voice.

"The red-faced monkeys are taking away our food-giver, Rani Chennamma so mercilessly. May their corpses be burnt to ashes!" wailed another old woman and yelled piteously.

"The mean-minded brutes have arrested the tigress called Rani Chennamma so heartlessly. May they be roasted in hell!" wailed another young lady.

They snapped the knuckles of their palms and cursed the Company officers and soldiers. They felt as if they had lost their beloved Rani for good and mourned her metaphorical death. They were so sad and morose that they did not kindle their ovens or have their bath and *puja* or their routine work for three days consecutively.

* * *

The womenfolk, who were all distant relatives of Rani Chennamma, felt as if the whole sky had fallen on their heads. With the departure of their beloved Rani, who was more than a mother to them felt a big void in their life. They sobbed and cried until exhausted. They did not touch either food or water or care for the daily chores.

They mourned the exodus of the Rani. The entire fort appeared like a ferocious hell.

* * *

After the Fort of Kittur was captured, Sivabasappa felt jubilant and hoped to fulfil his grand dream. He, therefore, rushed to Chaplin and saluted him with joined palms. He heroically described how he had adulterated the gunpowder in the powder magazine of Kittur with cow dung and millet and rendered it dysfunctional and how it had rendered the Kittur forces helpless.

He then requested Chaplin, "Saheb, I have rendered extraordinary help to you. As you have promised, I have to get my reward."

Chaplin listened to him quite patiently and said rather seriously, "Dear Mr. Sivabasappa, you must get the right reward according to our secret agreement. You have betrayed your own dynamic Rani, whose salt you have eaten. Though your Rani happens to be our enemy, she has done her duty in fighting for her kingdom. When she is ready to die for her kingdom, do you have any right to live? Treacherous fellows like you deserve nothing but death as the reward."

Sivabasappa began to quake with fear. He bowed down to Chaplin's feet and requested him, "Saheb, it is all right even if you don't give me the Samsthan as a gift. But please spare my life."

But Chaplin did not concede to his request. As per Chaplin's order, Sivabasappa was taken by the Company soldiers. He was tied to the nozzle of a cannon inside the compound of the Kittur fort and shot dead. As the cannon fire exploded, the body of Sivabasappa splintered into pieces and fell in diverse directions.

* * *

Rani Chennamma and her two daughters-in-law were detained in the Collector's bungalow at Dharwad for one day and then they were taken to Bailahongala.

When the *sarot* reached the fort at Bailahongala, the ladies were asked to dismount. Rani Chennamma, Rani Viravva and Rani Janakibai got off from the carriage. The horses neighed occasionally. The chief officer beckoned to the three royal females to follow him. They followed the officers languorously. They ascended the stone-steps of the fort, which was built with brown stone. They entered the fort and were led through the semi-dark corridors to the grilled room, which was very dark. All the three of them were kept in three separate rooms. The soldiers locked them in and stood guard outside. The chief officer walked out of the fort and went back to Dharwad. The dungeon was musty and dusty. There was no sufficient light, nor was there proper ventilation. Rani Chennamma felt almost stifled in the encircling darkness. They were so tired that they slumped on the cotton blankets on hard beds.

* * *

As per Chaplin's orders, Captain Elliot, Captain Stevenson and other Company officers busied themselves in arranging the cash, jewels, pearls, silver and gold ornaments etc., to be packed and sealed in big wooden boxes. The servants went on piling them in the boxes by turns, securing them properly with sturdy iron locks. In the other part of the Kittur fort the other soldiers were busy packing the arms like swords, axes, spears and guns in bigger boxes. Nearly two days were spent in packing all the wealth belonging to Rani Chennamma.

On 13th and 14th December 1824, the auction of the prize property was carried out. The Captain purchased a very handsome but curious short spear (Javelin) and a large Talwar (Demascus's Blade) of excellent quality. Of these latter there were a great number, with different pattern hilt, all containing silver, and crimson velvet sheaths. Of the jerreeds there were but two; the shaft was richly worked with a scale loop about the centre, to protect the hand when grasping it accompanied with a red velvet sheath, mounted with silver. They had probably belonged to the Raja's own family. There was an abundance of most valuable Cashmere shawls which sold at high prices, though far under their real worth. The prize agents had been appointed by votes of corps.

The prize money with interest amounted in May 1829 to Rs. 12,60,107, one eighth of which (upwards of a lakh and a half) fell to the Commander Lieutenant Colonel deacon, who must have considered himself pretty handsomely remunerated for his services, seeing, he joined the force only three days before the place fell, snug in his palanquin from Jaulnah. The rest of the prize money was shared by European officers, Warrant Officers, Non-Commissioned Officers, Rank and File, and Natives.

On the third day, the cash boxes and arms were kept in horse carriages and transported to Bombay under the military protection. Then several camels were loaded with two boxes each of jewellery, and pearls and other silver and golden ornaments, and followed by Company soldiers on horses and led through short routes across the fields to Bombay. The camels sauntered gawkily and lethargically with their upturned faces. Because of the heavy load upon their backs, they walked rather slowly. The citizens of Kittur, who witnessed the shameless plundering of Rani Chennamma's wealth by the Company rulers, shed tears and cursed them from the bottom of their hearts. They felt as though they were robbed of their own private wealth. The loaded camels and horsemen following them walked across the fields without caring for crops or creepers. Most of the crop was crushed under the feet of these animals. As the sun was very hot in the afternoon, one of the camels, which were walking across the jowar field, seemed to have felt tired and slept there leisurely in the cool shade of a mango tree. The gentle breeze blowing occasionally lulled it into sweet sleep. The camel closed its eyes and slept peacefully. All the other camels went ahead excepting this one, which was covered by the tall jowar crop.

Sangappa, a farmer from Pattihal, went to his field in the evening as usual with his sickle in hand. He saw that the camels had trodden through his field and destroyed much of the jowar crop.

He cursed the Company rulers, "These monkey-faced *firangis* have been playing havoc with our life."

He spat into their imaginary faces and inspected the crop here and there at random. As he came near the mango tree, he was pleasantly surprised to see a camel dozing in the cool shade of the mango tree! His heart seemed to dance when he went close to it and said to himself, "This must be some precious wealth which the Company fellows are transporting to their headquarters."

A clever idea flashed across his mind, "Why not save them for me?"

He lost no time in dilly-dallying. He went near the dozing camel and cut the ropes and leather straps binding the wooden boxes to its back. As the leather straps were rent, the heavy boxes slid on both sides of the animal to the earth. The camel seemed to be relieved of a big burden and looked around with pleasure. It appeared to thank the farmer for the relief. Sangappa uprooted two jowar stalks and struck the camel on its haunches. The camel which was feeling fresh now after a couple of hours' sleep and relieved of the heavy burden on its back, stood up on its long legs and walked ahead gawkily. As it waded through the jowar crop, the stalks were broken and crushed under its heavy feet.

Sangappa looked around the field and was very happy to know that nobody was watching the camel. He felt the two boxes with his fingers and tried to imagine what it might be containing. "Who knows how and when my luck turns!" he said to himself.

He sat near the boxes until darkness descended upon the earth and rushed home then.

Sangappa called his son to the inner room in his house and whispered into his ears what he had seen in his field. Then he called his wife and confided the secret to her. The son hitched two hefty bullocks to the cart and tied a lamp below the axle of the cart. He sat in his cart with a couple of strong ropes and a big carpet beneath him. The young son smacked his lips and produced a stimulating sound to goad the bullocks. Occasionally he whipped them gently.

The cart trundled along the gravelly path. The villagers were already making ready to go to sleep. Dim lamps flickered in the houses. Nobody knew why Sangappa was taking his cart out at the odd time of night and where. Soon the cart went out of the village and followed the cart track in-between the fields. The wheels of the cart were producing a gentle sound of crunching as they ran along the sandy path. The nocturnal silence in the fields was punctuated by the shrill chorus of crickets. The dim light of the lamp threw up the enlarged shadow of the spokes of wheels and legs of bullocks all around the bordering banks. Many times Sangappa and his son had to duck their heads in order to avoid being scraped by the thorns of the overhanging Hawthorne trees. Finally when they reached their field and parked the cart near the mango tree, Sangappa took his son and showed him the two big boxes.

The son said, "Father, these boxes are far bigger than I had imagined."

He was really thrilled at the sight of the treasure. Then both of them laboured hard, lifted the boxes and pushed them into the cart one after the other. They covered them with the big carpet and secured them with ropes. Then they drove the cart back to their home. There was total silence in the village.

That night they were too tired to open the sealed boxes. Most of their energy was spent in hiding the boxes in their inner room. Sangappa's wife was impressed by the very size of the boxes. All of them had a hurried meal and slept dreaming of prosperous days ahead.

The next morning they woke up and immersed themselves in the usual domestic chores. They did not reveal the secret to any of their neighbours. They waited eagerly for the night. When night descended on the earth, the noises of the village faded out slowly. Sangappa went about in the lane just to confirm that the neighbors had gone to sleep. Then he returned home and locked his door firmly.

He, his wife and son entered the inner room in the dim light of oil-lamps. The wife held the lamps according to the needs of her husband and son. The young son yanked the locks of the boxes with an iron rod. When they opened the boxes, lo, they were all dazzled by the sight of invaluable gold and silver ornaments, jewels, pearls, ambers, topazes etc. For a moment they could not believe their own eyes. They did not know whether they were seeing reality or dreaming. They were almost on the verge of fainting out of immeasurable ecstasy. Sangappa's wife was simply overwhelmed at the sight of the precious ornaments and stones.

She burst out, "God has granted all my secret desires." and joined her palms in salutation. "Welcome to you, Goddess Lakshmi. Never ever leave my house," she said imploringly.

They took out the precious wealth and classified them in different cloth bags and hid them in their cellar. They took the two big boxes to the backyard and burnt them lest they should be punished by the *firangi* soldiers.

The next night, Sangappa and his young son kept the bags containing all the jewellery and ornaments on the shelves near the ceiling and covered them with wooden planks nailed into the sides. When the shelves were thus covered with planks, they looked like beams and nobody could suspect any wealth being hidden inside them. Sangappa and his son heaved a sigh of relief after completing the task successfully. Now they could live free from inquisitive eyes of neighbors or *firangi* soldiers, who were likely to visit them any time.

* * *

The Chief Commander of the Kittur army, Sardar Gurusiddhappa and other prominent rebels were kept in jail at Belgaum in separate cells. The Company officers continued to watch the behaviour of these prisoners very carefully. As days went by, the Company officers made enquiries about each prisoner and were able to have a mental picture about their behaviour. Chaplin wrote to the Political Agent at Dharwad recommending the release of some prisoners of Kittur, who were men of no consequence. After receiving the letter from Chaplin, the Political Agent at Dharwad sent his assistant to the prison at Belgaum to fetch the five prisoners, namely, Timmappa Daftary, Balappa Kotya, Narsing Rao Mummadar, Kaone Kogonavar and Sheikh Junglee Jamadar. After a few minutes the jail attendants brought these prisoners handcuffed. They stood askance before the officer who asked them, "See fellows, we will release you on condition that you will behave properly and keep away from all rebellious activities."

The five prisoners, who were longing to see their wives and children, thought that they should not miss the unexpected opportunity. Almost all of them agreed to the condition. Then the jail clerks took their thumb impressions on the papers and released them from the jail. The prisoners felt as if they had a second birth in the mortal world and rushed back to their homes with an unprecedented joy.

* * *

But a few other rebels were detained in the jails as they were suspected to be very dangerous to the Company government. Mr. Chaplin had collected sufficient intelligence about the prisoners and sent it up to Bombay and was waiting for His Excellency's order. The leading rebels like Baba Naik, Basalingappa, Rudranaik, Kulbasappa, Yelnaik, Appanna, Bhima, Ranoji, Koneri, Kenchappa, Nemanna, and Appaji were all kept in jail at Belgaum and guarded very strictly by the Company soldiers.

After a few days Chaplin received a direction from Mr. I. P. Willoughby on behalf of the Governor in Council. He sent the same to Nisbet ordering him to comply with the Governor's order. Nisbet, therefore, arranged for the transportation of the prisoners listed by Willoughby, like Rudranaik, Yelnaik, Appanna, Ranoji, Koneri and Nemanna to the port of Bombay.

The next day they were all carried in the covered horse-carriages to the port from where they had to be taken in a ship to the Company isles. The prisoners, on coming to know about the punishment meted out to them, felt very sad about their wives, children and other kith and kin. They shed tears silently, but they had the satisfaction of having fought for Rani Chennamma. When their beloved Rani herself had been wasting away her precious life in the musty cell of the prison, what about the nonentities like them? So they thought and consoled themselves. After reaching Bombay, they were pushed into the cabins of a large ship. But they did not know which country they were being taken to.

* * *

When the parents, wives and children of these prisoners came to know that their men folk were taken out of the Hindustan territory to *vilayat* country for good, they felt a sudden void in their hearts. They beat their chests, sobbed piteously and cursed the red-monkey race of the Company authorities. They felt that their men folk had died a metaphorical death. They spent the rest of their lives in trying to guess and visualize where their men folk must be living and what they might be doing. Their children went on crying for their fathers and brothers until they were reconciled to their absence with the march of time.

* * *

Commander Gurusiddhappa, Sangolli Rayanna, Balnaik Basalingappa, Kalabasappa, Bhima, Kenchappa and Appaji were all kept behind bars at Belgaum as they were supposed to be the ringleaders of rebellion at Kittur. The Company officers had marked them as most dangerous fellows who could fan the fire of rebellion at Kittur at the slightest possible provocation. Mr. Nisbet, the Jail Officer, had warned his guards to watch over them carefully and not to allow them to have any communication with the natives of Kittur. These prisoners were counting their days and hours for the possible release or escape. Their minds were busy thinking of various possibilities of regaining the Kittur kingdom for Rani Chennamma and her descendants. They grew nostalgic about the past glory of Kittur and the happy days of their youth and began to recreate them mentally.

Commander Gurusiddhappa gnashed his teeth in anger at the very memory of the treacherous behaviour of the Company officers. He imagined himself ripping open the body of each one of the Company officers and drinking their blood to his heart's content. But alas, he could not do anything of that sort. He would lean against the bars of the prison and think in vain of recovering the lost kingdom. He would shed tears imagining what might Rani Chennamma be doing or feeling in the dark dungeon of Bailahongala.

* * *

The Political Agent of Dharwad sought permission from Chaplin and announced a prize of Rs. 30,000 for those, who could help the Company government to capture Avaradi Virappa and his companions. Accordingly a few village criers were sent out to the surrounding villages of Kittur to announce the same. The criers went to the villages on horsebacks with their drums and sticks. They went to the central squares of the villages and sounded their drums. The villagers cocked their ears and listened more carefully. They walked in the direction from which the sound came and stood around the crier. The crier raised the pitch of his voice and announce, "Listen to me, gentlemen, listen to me. The Company government would offer a prize of Rs. 30,000 to anyone, who would capture Avaradi Virappa and his companions and surrender them to the Collector of Dharwad. *Dhum, Dhum*." The villagers dispersed after listening to the crier and turn a deaf ear to his words. Then the crier went to another part of the village and repeated the Government announcement. He then rode to the next village and announced the order. Within a week's time the news circulated in all the neighbouring villages. The natives of the villages around Kittur grew more and more alert about the fugitives and indifferent to the *firangis'* orders.

* * *

The prominent prisoners were all detained in the prison at Bailahongala. The Company officers conducted a trial and cross-questioned each one of them. They had collected intelligence about these leading rebels through the other natives of Kittur, who had turned treacherous for the paltry sum of money they had received from the Company officers.

After conducting detailed enquiry, the Company officers found that the forty rebels led by Sardar Gurusiddhappa were very tough and firm patriots, who refused to surrender themselves. All the oral and documentary evidences confirmed that they had taken an active part in the patriotic fight.

They found that Sangolli Rayanna could not be punished, as there was no documentary evidence against him. He was, therefore, taken back to Kittur and released there. But the other forty prominent prisoners like Sardar Gurusiddhappa. Avaradi Virappa, Babasaheb Jamadar, Toragi Ramanagowda, etc., were all led to the fort of Belgaum. Then they were led to the plain on which stood a few Banyan trees from which hung several inviting nooses.

They stood there nonchalantly in the face of death. They were all guarded by the Company soldiers with guns in their hands. Then the Jail Officer raised his voice and asked the leader Sardar Gurusiddhappa, "Gentlemen, you are all condemned by the Government Order to be hanged to death. But before that we shall have to fulfil your last wish in your life. Tell me what your wish is."

He stared into Sardar Gurusiddhappa's eyes and waited for his answer. Sardar Gurusiddhappa looked at the Jail Officer and replied, "I have no wish whatever."

The Jail Officer was nonplussed by the unexpected answer. He then asked the other captives in the line. They also repeated Sardar Gurusiddhappa's answer. Though apparently stunned by the arrogant answer of the prisoners, he admired them inwardly. But he was bound by duty to have them hanged at the scheduled time.

He shouted his orders to his assistants who beckoned to their soldiers. The soldiers blindfolded the eyes of the prisoners with black cloth and tied their hands behind their backs. The prisoners lost their vision and felt an overwhelming darkness around them. The Officer sounded his whistle. The Company soldiers led them by hand to the huge Banyan trees and made them mount the wooden stools. Then they slipped the nooses around the prisoners' necks carefully. When the next whistle sounded, the soldiers pulled away the stools from beneath the prisoners quickly. Lo, all the forty prisoners were suspended in the air and felt a stifling suffocation and gradual blackout of consciousness. The spectators who watched the scene felt a tremour through their spines and began to cry and wail instinctively. Within a few minutes the limbs of the prisoners grew numb and their dead bodies began to dangle from the trees.

The Jail Officers and their soldiers took off their hats for a second and put them on and returned to their barracks. The leading rebels, who had eaten the salt of Rani Chennamma and enjoyed the pomp and glory of Kittur kingdom, had laid down their lives as a token of their love and respect for their beloved Rani. The cadavers of Sardar Gurusiddhappa and other rebels were not buried properly, but thrown on the open ground for kites and birds to feed on them.

* * *

Lord Amhert was instructed by his masters at the time of his nomination to the Governor-Generalship of India 'to proceed against the Indian press.' He, therefore, tried his best to curtail its liberty as much as possible. Those were the darkest days of the Indian history, when the press censorship was at its peak. Therefore all that happened at Kittur and in India between May and December 1824 remained eclipsed forever from the historical records.

* * *

There was an uneasy calm in the Kittur territory for some time. The patriots of Kittur dreamed of regaining the kingdom. The impressive fortress and the beautiful towers of the palace, which were the visible embodiments of the past glory of Kittur, kept the hopes green in the minds of the patriots. Chaplin thought that the imposing fortress, which kept alive the memory of Rani Chennamma in the minds of the people, should be razed to the ground so that they should no longer act as constant reminders of its former glory. He, therefore, ordered his soldiers to demolish the main portion of the beautiful fortress.

Accordingly the Company soldiers brought ramrods, sledge hammers, pickaxes and other tools. They climbed the roof of the palace and began to break the beautiful parapets, turrets and walls strenuously. As the walls of the palace were built with hard and strong rocks, the soldiers had to struggle a lot to demolish it. As the sounds of thuds and strokes were heard by the people of Kittur city, they flocked to the spot possibly to prevent the demolition. But they were easily frightened by the Company soldiers, who stood in a circle around the palace with their guns at the ready position. They became totally helpless and shed tears incessantly. As the demolition continued for a few days, there were clouds of dust wafting in the air. After the completion of the demolition, the whole site was filled with big heaps of debris.

Then the Company soldiers announced publicly that people could buy the debris at the rate of Rs. 5 per cartload. Soon the news circulated fast not only in the city of Kittur, but also in the surrounding villages and cities.

Consequently both rich and poor people began to flock to the spot. They bought the cartloads of debris, which included rocks, wooden pillars, doorframes, window frames of teak, wooden grills etc., and transported them to their places in order to recycle them for the construction of their own houses, temples and monasteries. Some of the wooden doors were taken to Dharwad and fitted to the walls of the Collector's Bungalow. Some tall wooden pillars were taken to Hubballi, where they were used for the construction of the front portion of the Monastery called Murusavira Math. A few pillars were taken to Dharwad and used for the construction of the Rayara Math and Vitthal Mandir. Similarly wooden pillars and doorframes were taken and used for the construction of Ganapati temple at Belgaum, Shankara Math at Rabakavi and some *wadas* at Savadatti. In a way the glory and grandeur of the palace entered the homes, temples and monasteries in an altered shape.

* * *

When Sangolli Rayanna was left free at Kittur, the Company officer returned to Bailahongala on horseback. Now Rayanna had to walk the entire distance from Kittur to his native village, Sangolli. As he started walking, he instinctively halted in front of the fort of Kittur. As he cast his eyes upon it, he was shocked by the sight of the broken fort with yawning gaps in the walls, which looked so grotesque. He was deeply annoyed by the callous disfiguration of the beautiful fort of Kittur, which was a source of inspiration to the citizens. The columns were broken. The half columns, gaping holes in the walls, and the broken turrets were looking deserted. Kites, monkeys and donkeys had already had their shelter there. As he keenly observed the dilapidation of the fort, he felt deeply annoyed. He tried to visualize the glory of Rani Chennamma when she had lived there along with Raja Mallasarja. He felt the contrast between the past and the present to be very conspicuous. Tears trickled down his cheeks without his knowing. He tried to imagine how much agony Rani Chennamma would feel if she could see the fort in its present state of dilapidation. He wiped the tears from his eyes, but more tears gushed out from his eyes. What right had the red-faced Company monkeys to come to our country and rob us of our wealth and property? We must not allow this to happen, he thought. He made up his mind. He bent down, took a fistful of earth and swore, "My respected mother Rani Chennamma, I consecrate my life for restoring the lost kingdom and fight to the last drop of blood in my body." Then he rubbed a dot of the earth on his forehead. He felt a kind of satisfaction after making up his mind to fight for the Rani. Then he walked briskly towards his village, Sangolli.

*   *   **

Rani Chennamma, who stayed in the jail of Bailahongala, had grown conspicuously old after the kingdom of Kittur was annexed to the Company government. More than half of her hair had grown grey and wrinkles had appeared on her beautiful face. The agony of having lost the prestigious kingdom could not be forgotten so easily. Of course, she lacked nothing in the jail. She was attended to by her close relatives and she did not feel any change or reduction in the style of her living. The Company authorities had allowed her full freedom within the fort, which was encircled by a moat guarded by the Company soldiers from outside. But she worried deeply about Rani Viravva, who had matured only after coming to stay in the fort of Bailahongala as a prisoner. She felt sad about the meaninglessness of Rani Viravva's marital life. It was very unfortunate that the young Rani Viravva had matured only after becoming a widow and that too in the jail. She, therefore, treated the young widow with great affection and concern.

Rani Chennamma wanted to forget the agony of her soul mainly by engaging herself in religious austerities. She used to spend her mornings and evenings in the worship of *istalinga* and the treatment of *jangamas*. The Company authorities had no objection to the free entry or exit of the *jangamas*. But whenever Rani Chennamma had her spare time, she would grow nostalgic and dream of the past glory of Kittur during the days of her husband Mallasarja. She would remember all the leaders and soldiers who had laid down their lives for the sake of Kittur kingdom and thank them inwardly. Likewise she would sympathize with all the women, who had been widowed or lost their fathers or brothers or sons in the battle. She prayed for their safety. Tears would trickle down her cheeks automatically. Then she would live in a wishful fantasy of recovering the lost kingdom.

As days rolled by, she began to forget her sorrow by engaging herself in the worship of *istalinga,* reading of Virasaiva scriptures and treatment of *jangamas.* All the female relatives, who stayed with her in separate cells, would try their best to keep her in good humour.

* * *

When Rani Chennamma and Rani Viravva and other members of the royal family were imprisoned in the fort of Bailahongala, the Rani had been granted permission by the Company government to receive the holy *jangamas* from the Kallumath Monastery and participate in the daily *puja*. So the holy *jangamas* were easily allowed entry into the fort.

But as days went by the authorities of the Company government suspected that the free entry of the *jangamas* into the prison might encourage a secret conspiracy among the patriots of Kittur kingdom against the Company government, they prohibited the visit of the *jangamas* to the Rani in the fort. Rani Chennamma, who was very religious by nature, would not feel happy unless she participated in the daily *puja* by the *jangamas*. She felt deeply hurt and depressed by the prohibition of the *jangamas* for the holy worship. She, therefore, stopped having her food.

On hearing this decision of Rani Chennamma, Captain Harris grew apprehensive about the difficulties that he would have to face in future in case the Rani died of starvation in the fort. He grew alert and rushed to the fort and saw Rani Chennamma in her cell.

He greeted politely and requested her, "Rani Sahiba, it is not right on your part to go without food like this."

"Does your Sarkar think like that?" asked Rani Chennamma ironically. "Don't think like that, Rani Sahiba. This is my request to you," said Captain Harris.

"See, Captain Sir, I have become a prisoner in my own kingdom. Having lost my kingdom, which was my life-breath itself, what is the use of continuing to live? Hence I have decided to fast unto death," she said in a sad tone.

"See, Rani Sahiba, please don't talk about dying. Please tell me about the obstacles for your not taking your food. I shall try to remove those obstacles. Otherwise you will cause serious trouble for an innocent officer like me," he said thereby acquainting the Rani about his own difficulty as a Company officer.

"Captain Sir, I am not so callous as to cause trouble to innocent people. But is it possible for you to restart our daily *puja* by the *jangamas* and solve our problem?" asked the Rani.

"Rani Sahiba, I shall honestly try to solve your problem. Who is the person, who can conduct your daily *puja* and the rituals? Please tell me," assured Captain Harris.

"If you see His Holiness Siddheswara Swamiji and convey our request, he will arrange to send some of the *jangamas* of his monastery to conduct our daily *puja* here," said Rani Chennamma.

"All right, Rani Sahiba, I shall try sincerely to oblige you and help you have your food," said Captain Harris and saluted her with joined palms.

"Captain Harris, you are really a good man with sincere feelings. When I see you, I wonder if there can be such good people even among the British," she said appreciatively.

"Rani Sahiba, you are a great lady. That is why you speak so nobly with such dignity and self-respect. I am very thankful to you for that. I shall forthwith arrange for your *puja*. I request you to start having your food after the Swamiji comes here and performs the *puja*," said Captain Harris.

"All right, Captain Harris, I shall start having my food after His Holiness comes and performs the *puja*," promised Rani Chennamma.

Captain Harris was relieved of great tension. He went out of the prison cell and the fort, and ordered that His Holiness be invited to the fort to perform the *puja* for the Rani. Accordingly His Holiness Siddheswara Swami from the monastery was brought to the fort and admitted into the prison cell of Rani Chennamma. The maidservants arranged all the *puja* items and kept everything ready.

His Holiness sat on the wooden seat in front of Rani Chennamma and began to perform the *puja*. After completing the *puja*, he asked Rani Chennamma, "Mother, how did you restart this *puja*, which was stopped by the Company officers?"

"Your Holiness, this a blessing of Lord Gurusiddha. Captain Harris, who is in charge of this fort, is really a thorough gentleman. He is known for his humanitarian attitude. It seems he came to know of my fasting unto death and grew worried. He, therefore, permitted us to resume our regular *puja* now. Tell me Your Holiness, what is the use of being alive when I have lost my kingdom?"

"Mother, don't be disappointed so soon. Our patriotic Rayanna has been recruiting the soldiers for his private army with an intention of regaining the kingdom of Kittur."

"What? Did the Company sarkar not arrest and imprison him?"

"No, Mother. Rayanna, Channabasappa, Gangadhara and their followers have not been arrested by the Company sarkar now. All these people have been camping in the thick forest near Sangolli. They have been planning to loot the treasury of the Company sarkar."

"Are you speaking the truth, Your Holiness?"

"I am telling the truth, Mother. Shortly Rayanna wants to attack the fort of Bailahongala, release you all and recover the Kittur kingdom. He has been organizing his army systematically."

Rani Chennamma shed tears of joy on hearing the news of Rayanna's patriotic activities. She exclaimed," I am really happy to know that there are still such patriots left in the Kittur kingdom. I have received a secret message sent by Rayanna about his plans. I am alive only because of such hope that Rayanna would fight for the kingdom and possibly recover it soon."

"Until something good happens, please be calm and patient, Mother. Please do not lose heart or worry about anything," said His Holiness and took his leave.

*   *   *

When Rayanna came to know that the regular *puja* was resumed at the chamber of Rani Chennamma in the fort, he wrote a letter to His Holiness Siddheswara Swami and sought his permission to impersonate as a junior *jangama* and visit the Rani in the prison. His Holiness sent positive reply to Rayanna to encourage him in his patriotic mission.

After a few days His Holiness sent a letter to Captain Harris inviting him to the monastery. Suspecting that there might be some other problem Captain Harris visited the Swami in the monastery and asked him the reason for his invitation. His Holiness received Captain Harris politely and expressed his views, "Harris Saheb, I have not been feeling well for the last three or four days. Hence it might not be possible for me to visit the Rani for the *puja*. I just wanted to bring this to your notice."

Captain Harris was worried about the Rani's health. He said with anxiety, "If Your Holiness stop performing the *puja*, the Rani will stop having her food also. Then what is the solution for this?"

"You need not worry about it, Harris Saheb. Our disciple will continue our *puja* according to the tradition of the monastery. This is known to the Rani Sarkar also. I shall send my disciple to perform the *puja* if you approve of it," said the Swami.

Captain Harris was relieved of his professional tension and permitted His Holiness Siddheswara Swami to send his disciple for the *puja* in the fort. He went back to his office and instructed his subordinates to allow the junior *jangama* to enter the fort and perform the *puja* for the Rani.

* * *

Rayanna went to the monastery and met His Holiness, who permitted him to wear the guise of a holy man. Accordingly he doffed his civil dress and donned the saffron robes. He had shaved his beard and moustaches clean the previous day. He smeared the *vibhuti* marks on his forehead, belly and forearms and looked exactly like a holy man from the monastery. He held a staff in his hand.

When the junior *jangama* went to the fort at Bailahongala, the guards admitted him easily without any objection, as Captain Harris had ordered them to that effect. As he entered the chamber of Rani Chennamma, he was shocked to notice that the Rani had already lost her youthful vigour and gloss and looked rather emaciated. Her eyes had sunk deep into the sockets. Grey hair peeped out of the hem of her sari worn around her head. He felt deeply agonized to see her plight. But still he did not betray his true feelings.

He sat on the wooden seat in front of the Rani and performed the *puja*. The Rani observed the performance with a sort of calmness and satisfaction.

After the *puja* was over, he said,   "Mother, I cannot come here for the *puja* from tomorrow onwards."

"Why? Is the senior swami so unwell as to dissuade you from coming here?" asked Rani Chennamma with anxiety.

"Nothing of that sort has happened, Mother," said the *jangama* with a smile on his face.

"Then? If His Holiness is all right, why did you come here? Who are you?" asked Rani Chennamma with a sense of surprise.

"I am your loyal servant Rayanna. Mother I deem myself lucky to have your *darsan*," he said and prostrated at the feet of the Rani.

"Are you my beloved son Rayanna? What a pleasant surprise! I could not identify you at all because you have removed your mustache and beard. How did you manage to come here in spite of the heavy security at the gate of the fort?"

"That is the hitch, Mother. It's because of the strict security that I resorted to this trick and this guise of a holy man," he said in a low pitch.

"I am so very happy to see you, my dear Rayanna, that too after such a long time."

"Mother, I am also so happy to see you. But at the same time I am so sad to see you in this poor condition of health and depressed mood. I feel like crying at your sight, Mother," he said wiping the tears gushing from his eyes.

"How can I be happy, my dear Rayanna? For whom should I live? For what ideals should I live? Tell me, my dear son?"

"Kindly stop worrying about the kingdom, and take care of your health. Mother, now the time is coming for the recovery of our kingdom. I am building my private army under the guidance of Virappa Nayaka. Many leaders like Bichagatti Channabasu, Gangadhara, Gajavira, Bhimya Jiddimani, Waddar Yallana, Bommanna and other leaders have joined me along with their armies. We are planning to attack the Company army all of a sudden and regain our Kingdom" said the *jangama* and explained other details of his organization.

"My dear son, your intention is very noble. But you require a big army, a number of weapons and a lot of money for the maintenance of it all. How will you manage that?" she asked with concern.

"Mother, what you say is true. My little army is not enough to fight the Company sarkar. Tomorrow I am going to Surpur to seek the military help from the Rajasaheb. We have other plans too. At any cost we want to hoist our Nandi Dwaja on the fort of Kittur on the coming Vijayadasami day. That is our great dream," he said with great enthusiasm.

Every word of Rayanna soothed the heart of Rani Chennamma. Overwhelmed with gratitude, she became speechless for a few moments. She immediately took out the bundle of her gold ornaments like gem-studded girdle, bracelets, necklace of pearls and other precious ornaments and handed them over to Rayanna and blessed him, "May the Great Mother Rajarajeswari bless you with victory. May your efforts bear fruit soon! You take this gold and meet the expenses of your army and to help you in your patriotic adventure. This is my last wish. May God bless you, my son Rayanna," said Rani Chennamma with her eyes filled with tears.

"Mother, kindly be free from anxiety. I have dedicated my life to solve your problem and make you happy. That is exactly the reason why I have come here in this guise to seek your guidance and blessings," he said and prostrated at her feet.

He put the bundle of ornaments in his saffron sling bag and slowly walked out of her chamber and the fort.

The guards did not suspect anything about the *jangama* and let him out freely.

Rayanna went to the outskirts of Bailahongala, where one of his assistants was waiting for him with a horse tethered to a tree. He removed his saffron robes and put on his civil dress and became Rayanna once again. He jumped on the horseback and rode towards Sangolli.

Rayanna returned to his native village and conveyed all the news to his bosom friends, Channabasappa and Virappa Nayaka. They felt a great pity for Rani Chennamma's condition. Virappa Nayaka and Gangadhara decided to see the Rani in the prison somehow or the other and console her.

After the departure of the *jangama* from the fort the security guards received intelligence that the *jangama* was none other than Rayanna himself. The Company authorities felt ashamed of themselves for their inability to detect the fake *jangama*, who had visited the Rani. They suspected that Rayanna and his companions might rekindle the conspiracy against the Company sarkar and therefore, they tightened the security further. Moreover, they kept Rani Chennamma and Rani Viravva in separate chambers thereby preventing any mutual consultation and contact between the two. Consequently Rani Chennamma began to feel terribly lonely and depressed.

* * *

Sangolli Rayanna busied himself in organizing a band of rebels and began to attack all the Company officers around Belgaum area. In order to pay the salary for his companions he began to loot the shops belonging to rich men. He became a legendary figure for the patriots of Kittur but an object of terror and inconvenience to the Company officers.

* * *

Rani Janakibai had lost her husband quite early in life, but she had been able to bear it only because of the dynamic support of her mother-in-law Rani Chennamma. The personal loss of husband and the general loss of the kingdom of Kittur had made her rather withdrawn. She felt a general alienation from worldly matters. She used to sit alone in her cell for long hours.

Whenever she went to the corridor of the prison, she would stare in the direction of Kittur nostalgically and remember all the past glory of life and brood over the irony of her life. As days went by, she lost her weight and grew emaciated like a cane and light as a bird. None of her relatives could console her. She took less and less food and slept less and less. Finally one day she reclined on her bed and breathed her last.

The prison officers came to her and tried to awaken her. They felt her pulse and tested her respiration. They were sure that she was dead and conveyed the same news to the Company authorities in Belgaum Headquarters.

Rani Chennamma rushed to her and fell upon her and cried piteously. "Did you leave me for good, my dear Janaki?" she mourned. There was nobody to console Rani Chennamma. Likewise Rani Viravva also cried piteously over the dead body of Janakibai. Soon the news circulated in Bailahongala and other neighbouring villages. People flocked and stood at the gate of the Fort at Bailahongala, to pay their last homage to the late Janakibai.

Her dead body was propped against the wall and decorated with flowers and garlands by a Virasaiva priest. After the ritual *puja* was rendered to the dead body, the hearse was taken out in a procession towards the Kallumath Monastery to the accompaniment of *bhajan*-chorus. The people showed their respect to her by tossing puffed rice and burning crackers.

One of the womenfolk burst out, "What a dark age has come to our land now! We have to see the death of the young ones before that of old ones!"

Rani Chennamma felt a sense of emptiness of life and spent her days mechanically.

*   *   *

After the death of Janakibai, the Company authorities felt relieved as they thought they had fewer problems now about the Kittur kingdom, which had come into their hands. But alas! Their expectations were nullified by the patriots of Kittur. The natives of Kittur kingdom had not forgotten the glory of their Rani. They were trying to organize a fresh rebellion against the Company Raj. Songolli Rayanna was the chief among the rebels. He wanted to keep the promise he had made to Rani Chennamma. Now Rani Viravva, the young girl, stayed in the prison of Bailahongala along with Rani Chennamma. Rani Viravva's life was utterly meaningless. She had been married to Prince Sivalingarudrasarja when she was only a minor girl of eleven years. But she matured only after becoming a widow and began to languish in the Fort of Bailahongala as a prisoner. She had no children. Nor did she have brothers or sisters. Thus her life was full of depression, frustration and disillusionment.

The Collector of Dharwad used to send a pension of Rs. 2500 per month to Rani Chennamma and Rani Viravva through the clerk, Govinda Srinivasa Itagi. He used to send some fruits and sweets also along with pension and diplomatically ask her to be happy. Although Rani Viravva was only eighteen years or so old, she was a very spirited girl like Rani Chennamma. She was happy to note that the well-wishers of the kingdom were organizing a fresh rebellion against the Company government. She, therefore, sent gold and money secretly to Sardars asking them to continue the fight. She dreamt of restoring the kingdom to Sawai Mallasarja II, the adopted son of Raja Sivalingarudrasarja.

But the Company officers, who collected some intelligence from the Kittur area, learnt that Rani Viravva was secretly encouraging the rebellious activities of the patriots, and decided to shift her from the fort of Bailahongala to that of Kusugal. The news circulated in the villages with the speed of wind.

Soon the patriots gathered in front of the fort at Bailahongala and began to shout slogans, "Victory to Rani Viravva!" "Rani Viravva should not be removed from here."

There was a big hullabaloo. The Company officers were surprised at the patriotic zeal of the people of Kittur kingdom. They suspected that the presence of Rani Viravva at the fort of Bailahongala would only aggravate the problem. They, therefore, busied themselves with making military arrangements and sent telegraphic messages to the nearest headquarters. Within a couple of hours an army of about a thousand soldiers gathered around Bailahongala fort, where Rani Chennamma and Rani Viravva were imprisoned. The Company soldiers with their weapons naturally prevented the patriots of Kittur from pursuing their demands. The unarmed patriots grew helpless and were dispersed by the Company soldiers. Finally Rani Viravva was ordered to leave the fort of Bailahongala and proceed to the fort of Kusugal.

Rani Viravva hugged Rani Chennamma and burst out, "Dear mother, this is our last meeting. I am not sure I shall be able to see you again in my lifetime. If I die, let's meet in Heaven."

Both of them cried over each other's shoulders. The Company soldiers stood there silently watching the touching scene. Then Rani Viravva disengaged herself from Rani Chennamma's arms and walked out of the fort and followed the Company soldiers with a heavy heart. She sat in the chariot under military protection. The horses began to jog trot as the driver whipped them gently. Clouds of dust were raised behind them. The chariot was followed by armed soldiers on horseback. The native men and women followed the soldiers shedding tears for Rani Viravva and cursing the Company government from the bottom of their hearts.

They reached the fort at Kusugal and asked Rani Viravva to get off the chariot. She walked into the fort and stayed there. It was surrounded by vast fields of crop. But she had no heart at all to observe the beauty of the greenery there. She felt terribly lonely and nostalgic about her past life. She decreased the intake of food and grew weaker and weaker day by day. The prison officer reported the matter to the authorities who grew apprehensive about her health. The Collector of Dharwad ordered that she should be kept under the care of her relatives at Dharwad. The soldiers, therefore, arranged for her transport in the chariot from Kusugal Fort to Dharwad.

For some days she was kept in the Ulavi Chennabasaveswara Temple at Dharwad. She was said to be suffering from some severe bellyache. But she never allowed herself to be treated by the Company doctor appointed by the Collector of Dharwad.

After a fortnight or so, Rani Viravva recovered her health to some extent. Then her nostalgia returned to her. She remembered the glorious past of the Kittur kingdom and wanted to have a glance at the fort of Kittur. But the Company authorities did not allow her to go to Kittur lest her presence should galvanize the rebellious activities of the patriots once again. Instead, they asked her to climb the roof of the temple and have a glance at the fort of Kittur from a distance. She therefore climbed the roof of the Chennabasaveswara Temple situated on a hillock of Dharwad and stared in the direction of Kittur. She saw the broken palace towers of Kittur in the hazy horizon. She heaved a deep sigh and shed tears remembering all the glory of the past. After staring at the tower of Kittur palace for a long time, she slowly climbed down from the roof of the temple with the help of a ladder propped there by the Company soldiers. Then she walked to the *sanctum sanctorum* of the temple and had a *darsan* of the deity,

Lord Chennabasaveswara, and offered her salutations to it.

She was taken in a chariot to Happalisetti's residence in the Raviwarpet Lane. Happalisetti happened to be a distant relative of Rani Viravva. He was asked by the Collector of Dharwad to take care of Rani Viravva. He did not have the courage to refuse to oblige the Collector of Dharwad. Rani Viravva felt slightly better in the company of her distant relatives in Happalisetti's house. But she was not cheerful inwardly as she had taken to heart everything that had happened to the members of the royal family of Kittur. She spent her days in daily *puja* and grew more and more withdrawn. She did not have any hope of a worthwhile future. She was not allowed to meet any native of the Kittur kingdom. She was heavily guarded by the Company soldiers, who stood around Happalisetti's house.

In spite of the imprisonment of Rani Viravva, the Company authorities were worried about her. They apprehended that her presence was a legal threat to their government. Baber, the Collector of Dharwad, therefore, sent for Happalisetti and asked him to see him at his residence. Happalisetti walked up the distance from Raviwarpet Lane to the Collector's residence on the hillock at dusk.

The Collector welcomed him with a smile and asked him to be seated. Then a servant came and gave both of them some tea and biscuits. There was nobody in the room except the two. The Collector asked Happalisetti, "Mr. Setti, how is Rani Viravva? Is she all right? How is her health?"

Happalisetti cleared his throat and replied, "She is all right, Saheb. But she does not show any interest in life. She sits brooding over the lost kingdom and glory."

"Is that so?" said the Collector nonchalantly. He lowered his voice and said, "Mr. Shetti, I sent for you for some confidential work. Hope you will oblige me."

"Tell me Saheb, what is it? Is there anything that I can do for you?" he said.

"See, Mr. Setti, Rani Viravva's presence is a constant source of threat for our government. The rebels may resume their activities against us any time. You must help us to put an end to it."

"How can I help you in this, Saheb?" asked Happalisetti.

The Collector stared at him meaningfully and said, "You have to finish her somehow or other."

"What?" exclaimed Happalisetti with a sense of shock. "What will people say if I do this heinous act?" he said.

"Don't be shocked, Mr. Setti. I shall arrange to give you some huge amount and also a prestigious award from our Government if you oblige us. Think over it coolly."

"If I cannot oblige you, Saheb?" asked Happalisetti.

"Mr. Setti, the consequences will be dire for you if you don't oblige us. We know how to dislodge you from the city of Dharwad and send you away to some far off place. Please think of the consequences before you dare refuse our request."

Happalisetti broke into sweat when he thought of the consequences of antagonizing the powerful authorities of the Company government. He instantly thought of what would happen to his family if he earned their wrath. He thought for a few moments.

Finally he promised the Collector, "All right, Saheb, I shall do it."

The Collector shook hands with him with a smile on his face.

The Setti went home. Within a couple of days, he consulted a private *hakim* and bought a poisonous herb. He asked his wife secretly to grind the herbal root and mix it with gravy every day and serve it to Rani Viravva. His wife who was greedy by nature and who dreamt of having a big sum of money from the Company officers began to manage it very systematically. Even while offering the poisoned gravy with rice to Rani Viravva, she would talk sweetly and humour her.

Within a few days Rani Viravva began to suffer from dysentery. She grew more and more enervated as days went by. There was no well-wisher in the family who could detect the treachery of the Setti couple. Everybody pretended to be worried about her health, though inwardly they were happy to know the progress of the effect of slow poisoning on her.

After a fortnight's time Rani Viravva breathed her last. They arranged for the funeral of the late Rani Viravva and buried her in their own backyard.

The very next day, Happalisetti rushed to the Collector's residence and happily reported the matter. The Collector was very happy to learn the news of the death of Rani Viravva. He heaved a deep sigh of relief.

He shook hands with the Setti and said, "Now the problem of Kittur is clinched forever."

Then he went into his inner chamber and brought out a big purse containing gold coins and handed it over to Happalisetti. Setti bowed to the Collector gratefully and walked back to his house. He saw to it that none of his neighbours came to know the death of Rani Viravva or her burial in their backyard. There was great but muffled excitement in his household.

In spite of the extraordinary care taken by the members of Happalisetti's family to maintain the secrecy of Rani Viravva's death, the news had somehow percolated to the villages of Kittur kingdom. Both men and women offered their homage of tears to the departed young Rani.

Rani Chennamma was spending her last days in the prison of Bailahongala. Now and then she used to hear the reports of rebellious activities of Rayanna and other patriots and feel happy about their attachment to the lost kingdom.

One day the news of the unexpected death of Rani Viravva reached Rani Chennamma. She was shocked beyond measure by the sad news. She suspected that there must be treachery behind the unnatural death of Rani Viravva, but she had no means of verifying the facts. She shed tears incessantly and abstained from food and water for many days. As days went by, she grew more and more emaciated and decrepit. Her face had developed deeper wrinkles and her head was full of grey hair. Nearly five years had elapsed since she was brought to the Fort of Bailahongala.

On the 2nd of February 1829, she sat on her bed staring at the broken tower of Kittur palace through the round window of the prison and breathed her last. Her dead body sagged on the bed. When the maidservants discovered that their beloved Rani was no more, they began to cry and shriek piteously. Soon they bathed her body and propped it against the wall. They decorated it with flowers and offered *puja* to it in the traditional Virasaiva manner. There was an unusual serenity upon Rani Chennamma's face. Her forehead was decked with the marks of holy *vibhuti* and her neck with pearls and diamonds. The distant relatives, who heard the news, rushed to the jail and began to mourn in a heart-rending manner.

"How could you forget the glorious kingdom and leave us deserted here?" cried one of them.

"Did you say goodbye to the *firangis* in order to join your lord Mallasarja in Heaven?" cried another woman.

The other women narrated the whole history of Kittur in their singsong tones of mourning. As the news of her death circulated in the surrounding villages, all the leading patriots rushed to the fort at Bailahongala to pay their last homage to their beloved Rani. The *bhajan*-chorus narrated the glory of Rani Chennamma, Raja Mallasarja and the Kittur kingdom in glowing terms to the accompaniment of drums and pipes. Then the decorated body of Rani Chennamma was kept in the flower-decked hearse, mounted on a chariot and taken out in a procession. It was finally taken to the Chowkimath Monastery.

The Company soldiers fired a few guns and cannons in honour of the late queen, who had given such a tough fight to the Company government. They offered her military salute to the accompaniment of band music. Finally, the Virasaiva priest conducted the last *puja* to the dead body of the Rani, lowered it into the pit of the grave and buried her according to the Virasaiva rituals. The people returned to their homes offering their last salute to the beloved Rani. A great void was created in the hearts of the natives of Kittur and the surrounding villages of the kingdom.

*   *   *

Although the Kittur kingdom was lost physically to the Company government, it remained evergreen in the memory of the people who tried to immortalize it in their songs and poems, plays, myths and legends. Magundi Basava, one of the court-poets of Kittur, wrote a narrative *lavani* about the beloved Rani Chennamma and Raja Mallasarja. Several other poets and folk-singers composed their own songs and sang them in the lanes of villages that once belonged to Kittur kingdom, and inspired the people to continue their life heroically facing all the contingencies of their life.

After a couple of years, a folk-singer stood on an elevated place near a cross-roads at Kittur and sang the *lavani* composed by Magundi Basava to the accompaniment of his flat little drum:

> Let me pray to the Lord
> Of the Universe and
> Narrate the story of Kittur
> And its war. Listen to me
> Carefully, gentlemen:

> When Thackeray came to Kittur
> Claiming it to be his,

The citizens of Kittur
Had coroneted a prince
And lived happily.
Thackeray grew angry
And questioned the Queen:
Who permitted you to coronate the prince
When the kingdom belongs to us?

The Queen grew ferocious
With anger and roared
Like a veritable lioness
And gave a clarion call for war.

The death of Thackeray in the war
Came as a bolt from the blue
To the servants of the Company,
Who collected their armies
From directions different.

The Queen ordered her soldiers
To be ready to fight and fall
For their kingdom beloved.

Both the armies encountered
Each other and fought vehemently.
John Mandel was pierced
With a spear by the Kittur soldier

The next day Chaplin arrived
With countless cannons
And wrecked the fort.

Then the Queen handed over
The kingdom to the Company,
Went to Bailahongala
To die in the prison.

Magundi Basava is my name,
I sing the song soulfully,
Listen to me carefully,
Gentlemen, listen to me.

* * *

Glossary

Aksata: Consecrated rice mixed with turmeric or vermillion powder sprinkled on the couple during the wedding ceremony

Amaldar: Revenue Collector

Arati: Holy wick-lamp wavered circularly in front of a person or deity by married women

Basadi: Jaina monastery or temple

Basava Purana: *Legend of Basava* written by Bhimakavi

Bhajan: A philosophical or devotional song

Bhairava Kankana: A band of yellow silk string tied around the right wrist of a man, who has to act as the bodyguard of the king and be ready to sacrifice his life for his kingdom

Bhavi: A non-Virasaiva or an agnostic or non-believer

Biriyani: A dish of spiced rice cooked with meat

Chowbari: Watchman, who watches the people or enemies in all the four directions.

Dalapati: Leader or chief of the army

Dalavai: General or Commander of the army

Diwankhana: Meeting Hall, or auditorium

Dubhasi: A bilingual scholar or translator

Dundume: A particular kind of folk-song popularized in Kittur kingdom

Ekdari: Mono-stringed musical instrument

Firangi: Foreign or White (people)

Gamaka: A stylized mode of Karnataki singing

Ghata Sthapana: Establishing the deities for worship during the Navaratri festival

Golandaz: Cannon operator

Gowda: A village-chief or town-chief

Gumastha: Clerk

Hakim: Physician, doctor

Holige: A sweet pancake made of wheat flour and lentils and eaten with ghee

Howdah: A decorated seat upon an elephant's back

Inamdar: Holder of a land-grant

Ingrezi: English, or British

Jagirdar: Landlord

Jangama: A Virasaiva itinerant preacher

Kacheri: Office

Kali: Dark Goddess of Death

Karbhari: Secretary

Karkun: Clerk

Karadi Majalu: Playing the large drum

Karni: Scribe, a type of drum

Kevada: Screw pine known for its sweet and sharp fragrance

Killedar: A security officer of the fort

Kinkaff: Silk cloth interwoven with silver or gold thread, brocade

Koel: Cuckoo, or nightingale

Lavani: Ballad

Linga: Lord Supreme, The Absolute

Madarangi: Henna

Mamool: Usual fee, tribute, bribe or gift

Mangalarati: Holy wick-lamp, benedictory song

Mantapa: Porch or canopy

Mantra: Spell, or incantation

Mridanga: A horizontal double-headed drum

Muttaide: A married lady wearing five symbols of marriage, like, nose-ring or stud, bangles, toe-ring and sacramental *tali* around the neck and a vermillion dot on the forehead.

Nazrana: Tax or tribute to be paid to a king or feudal chieftains by people.

Pancaksari Mantra: A spell containing five letters like *Om Namah Sivaya*

Paradi Payasa: Sweet porridge with granules

Peeshish: Tribute

Prasada: Consecrated food

Pagdi: A royal turban decorated with pearls and tassels

Puja: Holy service rendered to a deity

Punya: Virtuous deed in the past or present life

Rahut: Horse rider, cavalryman

Ranahalige: Military drum

Roti: Light flat bread made of jowar or wheat

Rudraksi: Beads of a rosary

Sarangi: A stringed musical instrument

Saranjam: Paraphernalia

Sardar: Courtier

Sarja: Tiger

Sarot: A horse carriage

Shahnai: A wind instrument known for its sweet sound

Shetsanadi: Owner of a land-grant, who has to help the king during the time of war or emergency

Sirastedar: Revenue officer

Siledar: A sergeant or military officer under a dalavai

Sobhana: First night after marriage

Subhedar: Administrator of a small division

Sumangale: A married woman, believed to be auspicious

Talavara: Watchman

Tali: Sacramental necklace of black beads tied around the neck of a married woman

Tambula: A roll of areca nut and leaves, and lime paste with other condiments like cloves and cardamoms.

Tirtha: Holy water

Vadyana: Girdle

Vilayat: Foreign

Vibhuti: Holy ash made of burnt cow dung smeared on the forehead and other upper limbs of the body.

Wada: A big house or mansion with a high compound usually inhabited by Desais and Deshpandes

Walikar: Messenger, letter carrier

Wattandar: Landlord

* * *

Printed in the United States
By Bookmasters